THE BODLEY HEAD
SCOTT FITZGERALD
VOLUME 6

THE BODLEY HEAD

SCOTT FITZGERALD

VOLUME 6

SHORT STORIES

SELECTED AND INTRODUCED BY

MALCOLM COWLEY

THE BODLEY HEAD

LONDON SYDNEY
TORONTO

SBN 370 00566 x

All rights reserved
This selection © The Bodley Head Ltd 1963

Revised version of the story
A Patriotic Short © 1962
by Charles Scribner's Sons

Printed and bound in Great Britain for
The Bodley Head Ltd
9 Bow Street, London WC2
by William Clowes & Sons Ltd, Beccles
Set in Plantin
First published 1963
Reprinted 1968

CONTENTS

III
RETROSPECTIVE: BASIL AND JOSEPHINE

EDITOR'S NOTE

WHEN I said in the preceding volume that Fitzgerald's stories, taken together, formed a sort of autobiography, I did not mean to suggest that they could be followed as a guide to the events of his life. They changed or disguised the events, as stories always do, but the best of them served as a faithful record of his emotions. 'Rewrite from mood,' he kept adjuring himself. In the end it was his life, as lived, that became the most impressive of his fictional creations. If we acquire some knowledge of the life, it gives a new dimension to the stories, and these in turn help us to understand the life by telling us how Fitzgerald felt in each new situation.

That is the rule, but the Basil stories are an exception. They tell us nothing about Fitzgerald's emotions at the time of writing, which was 1928, except that he was unhappy about the present and in a mood for retrospection. He relived his boyhood in the stories and made little effort to disguise the fact that he was writing autobiography. Almost every incident happened in life, and almost every character can be identified. Basil Duke Lee was of course Fitzgerald himself; his friends Riply Buckner, Bill Kampf, and Hubert Blair were, in life and respectively, Cecil Reid, Paul Ballion, and Reuben Warner. The Scandal Detectives of the first story really existed, and their Book of Scandal has been preserved in the shape of a 'Thoughtbook' that Fitzgerald kept when he was fourteen; most of his thoughts were about girls. St Regis School, where Basil was 'The Freshest Boy,' was of course the Newman School; during his first year at Newman, Fitzgerald was quite as miserable as his hero. 'The Captured Shadow' was the name of a play that he wrote and directed for the Elizabethan Club in St Paul before his sixteenth birthday. It was a success, as in the story.

There were nine Basil stories in all; one has never been published, and the other eight appeared in the *Saturday Evening Post*. Maxwell Perkins of Scribner's wanted to bring them out as a book, but Fitzgerald hesitated, partly because he feared they were too much like the Penrod stories that Booth Tarkington, an older Princeton author, had written as he emerged from a period of heavy drinking. Actually the children of the Penrod stories were of another generation and they were observed, not felt from within, but that didn't reassure Fitzgerald. He said in his notebook: 'Tarkington. I have a horror of going into a personal debauch and coming out of it de-vitalized with no interest except an acute observation of the behaviour of coloured people, children and dogs.' At last Perkins convinced him that he should revise five of his stories for republication in *Taps at Reveille*.

I have included four of the revised stories in the present group and have added Perkins's favourite, 'A Night at the Fair.' Together these stories carry Basil from his first affair of the heart, at fourteen, to his foretaste of fame and his discovery of something he wanted to do more than anything else in the world; at this point the sequence can properly end. The remaining Basil stories, not in-cluded, are those which carry him through St Regis and into his freshman year at Yale. They are more contrived and not on the same level of direct personal feeling.

The Josephine stories—five of them originally, pub-lished in 1930 and 1931—were also retrospective, but in a different fashion, since Fitzgerald was trying to think his way back into the mind of a Chicago girl with whom he was desperately in love during his years at Princeton. Besides suggesting Josephine she was also Isabelle, in *This Side of Paradise,* and Judy Jones, the heroine of 'Winter Dreams'; her real name, no longer a secret, was Ginevra King. Long afterwards she said in a letter to Arthur Mizener, 'I was too thoughtless in those days and too much in love with love to think of consequences. These things he has emphasized—and overemphasized in the Josephine stories but it is only fair to say that I asked for some of them.' When she paid a short visit to Hollywood in 1937, Fitzgerald had lunch with her and was almost ready to fall in love all over again. He once considered making a book out of the stories, to be called *My Girl Josephine,* but most of them were too loosely constructed to be his best work. Three were revised for *Taps at Reveille.* Of these I have chosen two: 'First Blood' for its picture of Chicago society in the tea-dancing era—Fitzgerald was always good on Chicago —and for the havoc wrought by a believable witch of sixteen; 'A Woman with a Past' for her dreams, her substantial values, and what she felt about her first big dance in New Haven.

BASIL

THE SCANDAL DETECTIVES

[1928]

IT WAS a hot afternoon in May and Mrs Buckner thought that a pitcher of fruit lemonade might prevent the boys from filling up on ice cream at the drug store. She belonged to that generation, since retired, upon which the great revolution in American family life was to be visited; but at that time she believed that her children's relation to her was much as hers had been to her parents, for this was more than twenty years ago.

Some generations are close to those that succeed them; between others the gap is infinite and unbridgeable. Mrs Buckner—a woman of character, a member of Society in a large Middle-Western city—carrying a pitcher of fruit lemonade through her own spacious back yard, was progressing across a hundred years. Her own thoughts would have been comprehensible to her great-grandmother; what was happening in a room above the stable would have been entirely unintelligible to them both. In what had once served as the coachman's sleeping apartment, her son and a friend were not behaving in a normal manner, but were, so to speak, experimenting in a void. They were making the first tentative combinations of the ideas and materials they found ready at their hand— ideas destined to become, in future years, first articulate, then startling and finally commonplace. At the moment when she called up to them they were sitting with disarming quiet upon the still unhatched eggs of the mid-twentieth century.

Riply Buckner descended the ladder and took the lemonade. Basil Duke Lee looked abstractedly down at the transaction and said, 'Thank you very much, Mrs Buckner.'

'Are you sure it isn't too hot up there?'

'No, Mrs Buckner. It's fine.'

It was stifling; but they were scarcely conscious of the heat, and they drank two tall glasses each of the lemonade without knowing that they were thirsty. Concealed beneath a sawed-out trapdoor from which they presently took it was a composition book bound in imitation red leather which currently absorbed much of their attention. On its first page was inscribed, if you penetrated the secret of the lemon-juice ink: 'THE BOOK OF SCANDAL, written by Riply Buckner, Jr., and Basil D. Lee, Scandal Detectives.'

In this book they had set down such deviations from rectitude on the part of their fellow citizens as had reached their ears. Some of these false steps were those of grizzled men, stories that had become traditions in the city and were embalmed in the composition book by virtue of indiscreet exhumations at family dinner tables. Others were the more exciting sins, confirmed or merely rumoured, of boys and girls their own age. Some of the entries would have been read by adults with bewilderment, others might have inspired wrath, and there were three or four contemporary reports that would have prostrated the parents of the involved children with horror and despair.

One of the mildest items, a matter they had hesitated about setting down, though it had shocked them only last year, was: 'Elwood Leaming has been to the Burlesque Show three or four times at the Star.'

Another, and perhaps their favourite, because of its uniqueness, set forth that 'H. P. Cramner committed some theft in the East he could be imprisoned for and had to come here'—H. P. Cramner being now one of the oldest and 'most substantial' citizens of the city.

The single defect in the book was that it could only be enjoyed with the aid of the imagination, for the invisible ink must keep its secrets until that day when, the pages being held close to the fire, the items would appear. Close inspection was necessary to determine which pages had been used—already a rather grave charge against a certain couple had been superimposed upon the dismal facts that Mrs R. B. Cary had consumption and that her son, Walter Cary, had been expelled from Pawling School. The purpose of the work as a whole was not blackmail. It was treasured against the time when its protagonists should 'do something' to Basil and Riply. Its possession gave them a sense of power. Basil, for instance, had never seen Mr H. P. Cramner make a single threatening gesture in Basil's direction, but let him even hint that he was going to do something to Basil and there preserved against him was the record of his past.

It is only fair to say that at this point the book passes entirely out of this story. Years later a janitor discovered it beneath the trapdoor, and finding it apparently blank, gave it to his little girl; so the misdeeds of Elwood Leaming and H. P. Cramner were definitely entombed at last beneath a fair copy of Lincoln's Gettysburg Address.

The book was Basil's idea. He was more the imaginative and in most ways the stronger of the two. He was a shining-eyed, brown-haired boy of fourteen, rather small as yet, and bright and lazy at school. His favourite character in fiction was Arsène Lupin, the gentleman burglar, a romantic phenomenon lately imported from Europe and much admired in the first bored decades of the century.

Riply Buckner, also in short pants, contributed to the partnership a breathless practicality. His mind waited upon Basil's imagination like a hair trigger and no scheme was too fantastic for his immediate 'Let's do it!' Since the school's third baseball team, on which they had been pitcher and catcher, decomposed after an unfortunate April season, they had spent their afternoons struggling to evolve a way of life which should measure up to the mysterious energies fermenting inside them. In the cache beneath the trapdoor were some 'slouch' hats and bandanna handkerchiefs, some loaded dice, half a pair of handcuffs, a rope ladder of a tenuous crochet persuasion for rear-window escapes into the alley, and a make-up box containing two old theatrical wigs and crêpe hair of various colours—all to be used when they decided what illegal enterprises to undertake.

Their lemonades finished, they lit Home Runs and held a desultory conversation which touched on crime, professional baseball, sex and the local stock company. This broke off at the sound of footsteps and familiar voices in the adjoining alley.

From the window, they investigated. The voices belonged to Margaret Torrence, Imogene Bissel and Connie Davies, who were cutting through the alley from Imogene's back yard to Connie's at the end of the block. The young ladies were thirteen, twelve and thirteen years old respectively, and they considered themselves alone, for in time to their march they were rendering a mildly daring parody in a sort of whispering giggle and coming out strongly on the finale: 'Oh, my dar-ling Clemen-tine.'

Basil and Riply leaned together from the window, then remembering their undershirts sank down behind the sill.

'We heard you!' they cried together.

The girls stopped and laughed. Margaret Torrence chewed exaggeratedly to indicate gum, and gum with a purpose. Basil immediately understood.

'Whereabouts?' he demanded.

'Over at Imogene's house.'

They had been at Mrs Bissel's cigarettes. The implied recklessness of their mood interested and excited the two boys and they prolonged the conversation. Connie Davies had been Riply's girl during dancing-school term; Margaret Torrence had played a part in Basil's recent past; Imogene Bissel was just back from a year in Europe. During the last month neither Basil nor Riply had thought about girls, and, thus refreshed, they became

conscious that the centre of the world had shifted suddenly from the secret room to the little group outside.

'Come on up,' they suggested.

'Come on out. Come on down to the Wharton's yard.'

'All right.'

Barely remembering to put away the Scandal Book
and the box of disguises, the two boys hurried out,
mounted their bicycles and rode up the alley.

The Whartons' own children had long grown up, but
their yard was still one of those predestined places where
young people gather in the afternoon. It had many advantages. It was large, open to other yards on both sides,
and it could be entered upon skates or bicycles from the
street. It contained an old seesaw, a swing and a pair
of flying rings; but it had been a rendezvous before these
were put up, for it had a child's quality—the thing that
makes young people huddle inextricably on uncomfortable steps and desert the houses of their friends to herd
on the obscure premises of 'people nobody knows.' The
Whartons' yard had long been a happy compromise; there
were deep shadows there all day long and ever something
vague in bloom, and patient dogs around, and brown
spots worn bare by countless circling wheels and dragging
feet. In sordid poverty, below the bluff two hundred feet
away, lived the 'micks'—they had merely inherited the
name, for they were now largely of Scandinavian descent
—and when other amusements palled, a few cries were
enough to bring a gang of them swarming up the hill,
to be faced if numbers promised well, to be fled from
into convenient houses if things went the other way.

It was five o'clock and there was a small crowd gathered
there for that soft and romantic time before supper—a
time surpassed only by the interim of summer dusk
thereafter. Basil and Riply rode their bicycles around
abstractedly, in and out of trees, resting now and then
with a hand on someone's shoulder, shading their eyes
from the glow of the late sun that, like youth itself,

is too strong to face directly, but must be kept down to
an undertone until it dies away.

Basil rode over to Imogene Bissel and balanced idly
on his wheel before her. Something in his face then must
have attracted her, for she looked up at him, looked at
him really, and slowly smiled. She was to be a beauty
and belle of many proms in a few years. Now her large
brown eyes and large beautifully shaped mouth and the
high flush over her thin cheek bones made her face
gnome-like and offended those who wanted a child to
look like a child. For a moment Basil was granted an
insight into the future; the spell of her vitality crept
over him suddenly. For the first time in his life he realized
a girl completely as something opposite and comple-
mentary to him, and he was subject to a warm chill of
mingled pleasure and pain. It was a definite experience
and he was immediately conscious of it. The summer
afternoon became lost in her suddenly—the soft air, the
shadowy hedges and banks of flowers, the orange sunlight, the laughter and voices, the tinkle of a piano over
the way—the odour left all these things and went into
Imogene's face as she sat there looking up at him with
a smile.

For a moment it was too much for him. He let it go,
incapable of exploiting it until he had digested it alone.
He rode around fast in a circle on his bicycle, passing
near Imogene without looking at her. When he came
back after a while and asked if he could walk home
with her, she had forgotten the moment, if it had ever
existed for her, and was almost surprised. With Basil
wheeling his bicycle beside her, they started down the
street.

'Can you come out tonight?' he asked eagerly. 'There'll
probably be a bunch in the Whartons' yard.'

'I'll ask mother.'

'I'll telephone you. I don't want to go unless you'll
be there.'

'Why?' She smiled at him again, encouraging him.

'Because I don't want to.'

'But why don't you want to?'

'Listen,' he said quickly. 'What boys do you like better than me?'

'Nobody. I like you and Hubert Blair best.'

Basil felt no jealousy at the coupling of this name with his. There was nothing to do about Hubert Blair but accept him philosophically, as other boys did when dissecting the hearts of other girls.

'I like you better than anybody,' he said deliriously.

The weight of the pink dappled sky above him was not endurable. He was plunging along through air of ineffable loveliness while warm freshets sprang up in his blood and he turned them, and with them his whole life, like a stream towards this girl.

They reached the carriage door at the side of her house.

'Can't you come in, Basil?'

'No.' He saw immediately that that was a mistake, but it was said now. The intangible present had eluded him. Still he lingered. 'Do you want my school ring?'

'Yes, if you want to give it to me.'

'I'll give it to you tonight.' His voice shook slightly as he added,

'That is, I'll trade.'

'What for?'

'Something.'

'What?' Her colour spread; she knew.

'You know. Will you trade?'

Imogene looked around uneasily. In the honey-sweet silence that had gathered around the porch, Basil held his breath.

'You're awful,' she whispered. 'Maybe. . . . Good-bye.'

II

It was the best hour of the day now and Basil was terribly happy. This summer he and his mother and sister were going to the lakes and next fall he was starting away to school. Then he would go to Yale and be a great athlete, and after that—if his two dreams had fitted onto each other chronologically instead of existing independently side by side—he was due to become a gentleman burglar. Everything was fine. He had so many alluring things to think about that it was hard to fall asleep at night.

That he was now crazy about Imogene Bissel was not a distraction, but another good thing. It had as yet no poignancy, only a brilliant and dynamic excitement that was bearing him along towards the Wharton yard through the May twilight.

He wore his favourite clothes—white duck knickerbockers, pepper-and-salt Norfolk jacket, a Belmont collar and a grey knitted tie. With his brown hair wet and shining, he made a handsome little figure as he turned in upon the familiar but not reënchanted lawn and joined the voices in the gathering darkness. Three or four girls who lived in neighbouring houses were present, and almost twice as many boys; and a slightly older group adorning the side veranda made a warm, remote nucleus against the lamps of the house and contributed occasional mysterious ripples of laughter to the already overburdened night.

Moving from shadowy group to group, Basil ascertained that Imogene was not yet here. Finding Margaret Torrence, he spoke to her aside, lightly.

'Have you still got that old ring of mine?'

Margaret had been his girl all year at dancing school, signified by the fact that he had taken her to the cotillion which closed the season. The affair had languished towards the end; none the less, his question was undiplomatic.

'I've got it somewhere,' Margaret replied carelessly. 'Why? Do you want it back?'

'Sort of.'

'All right. I never did want it. It was you that made me take it, Basil. I'll give it back to you tomorrow.'

'You couldn't give it to me tonight, could you?' His heart leaped as he saw a small figure come in at the rear gate. 'I sort of want to get it tonight.'

'Oh, all right, Basil.'

She ran across the street to her house and Basil followed. Mr and Mrs Torrence were on the porch, and while Margaret went upstairs for the ring he overcame his excitement and impatience and answered those questions as to the health of his parents which are so meaningless to the young. Then a sudden stiffening came over him, his voice faded off and his glazed eyes fixed upon a scene that was materializing over the way.

From the shadows far up the street, a swift, almost flying figure emerged and floated into the patch of lamplight in front of the Whartons' house. The figure wove here and there in a series of geometric patterns, now off with a flash of sparks at the impact of skates and pavement, now gliding miraculously backwards, describing a fantastic curve, with one foot lifted gracefully in the air, until the young people moved forward in groups out of the darkness and crowded to the pavement to watch. Basil gave a quiet little groan as he realized that of all possible nights, Hubert Blair had chosen this one to arrive.

'You say you're going to the lakes this summer, Basil. Have you taken a cottage?'

Basil became aware after a moment that Mr Torrence was making this remark for the third time.

'Oh, yes, sir,' he answered—'I mean, no. We're staying at the club.'

'Won't that be lovely?' said Mrs Torrence.

Across the street, he saw Imogene standing under the lamp-post and in front of her Hubert Blair, his jaunty cap on the side of his head, manoeuvring in a small circle. Basil winced as he heard his chuckling laugh. He did not perceive Margaret until she was beside him, pressing his ring into his hand like a bad penny. He muttered a strained hollow good-bye to her parents, and, weak with apprehension, followed her back across the street.

Hanging back in a shadow, he fixed his eyes not on Imogene but on Hubert Blair. There was undoubtedly something rare about Hubert. In the eyes of children less than fifteen, the shape of the nose is the distinguishing mark of beauty. Parents may call attention to lovely eyes, shining hair or gorgeous colouring, but the nose and its juxtaposition on the face is what the adolescent sees. Upon the lithe, stylish, athletic torso of Hubert Blair was set a conventional chubby face, and upon this face was chiselled the piquant, retroussé nose of a Harrison Fisher girl.

He was confident; he had personality, uninhibited by doubts or moods. He did not go to dancing school—his parents had moved to the city only a year ago—but already he was a legend. Though most of the boys disliked him, they did homage to his virtuosic athletic ability, and for the girls his every movement, his pleasantries, his very indifference, had a simply immeasurable fascination. Upon several previous occasions Basil had discovered this; now the discouraging comedy began to unfold once more.

Hubert took off his skates, rolled one down his arm and caught it by the strap before it reached the pavement; he snatched the ribbon from Imogene's hair and made off with it, dodging from under her arms as she pursued him, laughing and fascinated, around the yard. He cocked one foot behind the other and pretended to lean an elbow against a tree, missed the tree on purpose and gracefully saved himself from falling. The boys watched him noncommittally at first. Then they, too, broke out into activity, doing stunts and tricks as fast as they could think of them until those on the porch craned their necks at the sudden surge of activity in the garden. But Hubert coolly turned his back on his own success. He took Imogene's hat and began setting it in various quaint ways upon his head. Imogene and the other girls were filled with delight.

Unable any longer to endure the nauseous spectacle, Basil went up to the group and said, 'Why, hello, Hube,' in as negligent a tone as he could command.

Hubert answered: 'Why, hello, old—old Basil the Boozle,' and set the hat a different way on his head, until Basil himself couldn't resist an unwilling chortle of laughter.

'Basil the Boozle! Hello, Basil the Boozle!' The cry circled the garden. Reproachfully he distinguished Riply's voice among the others.

'Hube the Boob!' Basil countered quickly; but his ill humour detracted from the effect though several boys repeated it appreciatively.

Gloom settled upon Basil, and through the heavy dusk the figure of Imogene began to take on a new, unattainable charm. He was a romantic boy and already he had endowed her heavily from his fancy. Now he hated her for her indifference, but he must perversely linger near in the vain hope of recovering the penny of ecstasy so wantonly expended this afternoon.

He tried to talk to Margaret with decoy animation, but Margaret was not responsive. Already a voice had gone up in the darkness calling in a child. Panic seized upon him; the blessed hour of summer evening was almost over. At a spreading of the group to let pedestrians through, he manoeuvred Imogene unwillingly aside.

'I've got it,' he whispered. 'Here it is. Can I take you home?'

She looked at him distractedly. Her hand closed automatically on the ring.

'What? Oh, I promised Hubert he could take me home.' At the sight of his face she pulled herself from her trance and forced a note of indignation. 'I saw you going off with Margaret Torrence just as soon as I came into the yard.'

'I didn't. I just went to get the ring.'

'Yes, you did! I saw you!'

Her eyes moved back to Hubert Blair. He had replaced

his roller skates and was making little rhythmic jumps and
twirls on his toes, like a witch doctor throwing a slow
hypnosis over an African tribe. Basil's voice, explaining
and arguing, went on, but Imogene moved away. Helplessly he followed. There were other voices calling in the
darkness now and unwilling responses on all sides.

'All right, mother!'

'I'll be there in a second, mother.'

'Mother, can't I please stay out five minutes more?'

'I've got to go,' Imogene cried. 'It's almost nine.'

Waving her hand and smiling absently at Basil, she
started off down the street. Hubert pranced and stunted
at her side, circled around her and made entrancing little
figures ahead.

Only after a minute did Basil realize that another young
lady was addressing him.

'What?' he demanded absently.

'Hubert Blair is the nicest boy in town and you're the
most conceited,' repeated Margaret Torrence with deep
conviction.

He stared at her in pained surprise. Margaret wrinkled
her nose at him and yielded up her person to the now-
insistent demands coming from across the street. As Basil
gazed stupidly after her and then watched the forms of
Imogene and Hubert disappear around the corner, there
was a low mutter of thunder along the sultry sky and a
moment later a solitary drop plunged through the lamplit
leaves overhead and splattered on the sidewalk at his feet
The day was to close in rain.

III

It came quickly and he was drenched and running before
he reached his house eight blocks away. But the change
of weather had swept over his heart and he leaped up
every few steps, swallowing the rain and crying 'Yo-o-o!'
aloud, as if he himself were a part of the fresh violent
disturbance of the night. Imogene was gone, washed out

like the day's dust on the sidewalk. Her beauty would come back into his mind in brighter weather, but here in the storm he was alone with himself. A sense of extraordinary power welled up in him, until to leave the ground permanently with one of his wild leaps would not have surprised him. He was a lone wolf, secret and untamed; a night prowler, demoniac and free. Only when he reached his own house did his emotion begin to turn, speculatively and almost without passion, against Hubert Blair.

He changed his clothes, and putting on pyjamas and dressing-gown descended to the kitchen, where he happened upon a new chocolate cake. He ate a fourth of it and drank most of a bottle of milk. His elation somewhat diminished, he called up Riply Buckner on the phone.

'I've got a scheme,' he said.

'What about?'

'How to do something to H. B. with the S. D.'

Riply understood immediately what he meant. Hubert had been so indiscreet as to fascinate other girls besides Miss Bissel that evening.

'We'll have to take in Bill Kampf,' Basil said.

'All right.'

'See you at recess tomorrow. . . . Good night!'

IV

Four days later, when Mr and Mrs George P. Blair were finishing dinner, Hubert was called to the telephone. Mrs Blair took advantage of his absence to speak to her husband of what had been on her mind all day.

'George, those boys, or whatever they are, came again last night.'

He frowned.

'Did you see them?'

'Hilda did. She almost caught one of them. You see, I told her about the note they left last Tuesday, the one that said, "First warning, S.D.," so she was ready for them. They rang the back-door bell this time and she answered it straight from the dishes. If her hands hadn't been soapy she could have caught one, because she grabbed him when he handed her a note, but her hands were soapy so he slipped away.'

'What did he look like?'

'She said he might have been a very little man, but she thought he was a boy in a false face. He dodged like a boy, she said, and she thought he had short pants on. The note was like the other. It said "Second warning, S.D." '

'If you've got it, I'd like to see it after dinner.'

Hubert came back from the phone. 'It was Imogene Bissel,' he said. 'She wants me to come over to her house. A bunch are going over there tonight.'

'Hubert,' asked his father, 'do you know any boy with the initials S.D.?'

'No, sir.'

'Have you thought?'

'Yeah, I thought. I knew a boy named Sam Davis, but I haven't seen him for a year.'

'Who was he?'

'Oh, a sort of tough. He was at Number 44 School when I went there.'

'Did he have it in for you?'

'I don't think so.'

'Who do you think could be doing this? Has anybody got it in for you that you know about?

'I don't know, papa; I don't think so.'

'I don't like the looks of this thing,' said Mr Blair thoughtfully. 'Of course it may be only some boys, but it may be—'

He was silent. Later, he studied the note. It was in red ink and there was a skull and crossbones in the corner, but being printed, it told him nothing at all.

Meanwhile Hubert kissed his mother, set his cap jauntily on the side of his head, and passing through the kitchen stepped out on the back stoop, intending to take the usual short cut along the alley. It was a bright moonlight night and he paused for a moment on the stoop to tie his shoe. If he had but known that the telephone call just received had been a decoy, that it had not come from Imogene Bissel's house, had not indeed been a girl's voice at all, and that shadowy and grotesque forms were skulking in the alley just outside the gate, he would not have sprung so gracefully and lithely down the steps with his hands in his pockets or whistled the first bar of the Grizzly Bear into the apparently friendly night.

His whistle aroused varying emotions in the alley. Basil had given his daring and successful falsetto imitation over the telephone a little too soon, and though the Scandal Detectives had hurried, their preparations were not quite in order. They had become separated. Basil, got up like a Southern planter of the old persuasion, just outside the Blairs' gate; Bill Kampf, with a long Balkan moustache attached by a wire to the lower cartilage of his nose, was approaching in the shadow of the fence; but Riply Buckner, in a full rabbinical beard, was impeded by a length of rope he was trying to coil and was still a hundred feet away. The rope was an essential part of their plan; for, after much cogitation, they had decided what they were going to do to Hubert Blair. They were going to tie him up, gag him and put him in his own garbage can.

The idea at first horrified them—it would ruin his suit, it was awfully dirty and he might smother. In fact the garbage can, symbol of all that was repulsive, won the day only because it made every other idea seem tame. They disposed of the objections—his suit could be cleaned, it was where he ought to be anyhow, and if they left the lid off he couldn't smother. To be sure of this they had paid a visit of inspection to the Buckners' garbage can and stared into it, fascinated, envisaging Hubert among the rinds and eggshells. Then two of them, at least, resolutely put that part out of their minds and concentrated upon the luring of him into the alley and the overwhelming of him there.

Hubert's cheerful whistle caught them off guard and each of the three stood stock-still, unable to communicate with the others. It flashed through Basil's mind that if he grabbed Hubert without Riply at hand to apply the gag as had been arranged, Hubert's cries might alarm that gigantic cook in the kitchen who had almost taken him the night before. The thought threw him into a state of indecision. At that precise moment Hubert opened the gate and came out into the alley.

The two stood five feet apart, staring at each other, and all at once Basil made a startling discovery. He discovered he liked Hubert Blair—liked him as well as any boy he knew. He had absolutely no wish to lay hands on Hubert Blair and stuff him into a garbage can, jaunty cap and all. He would have fought to prevent that contingency. As his mind, unstrung by his situation, gave pasture to this inconvenient thought, he turned and rushed out of the alley and up the street.

For a moment the apparition had startled Hubert, but when it turned and made off he was heartened and gave chase. Out-distanced, he decided after fifty yards to let well enough alone; and returning to the alley, started rather precipitously down towards the other end—and came face to face with another small and hairy stranger.

Bill Kampf, being more simply organized than Basil, had no scruples of any kind. It had been decided to put Hubert into a garbage can, and though he had nothing at all against Hubert, the idea had made a pattern on his brain which he intended to follow. He was a natural man—that is to say, a hunter—and once a creature took on the aspect of a quarry, he would pursue it without qualms until it stopped struggling.

But he had been witness to Basil's inexplicable flight, and supposing that Hubert's father had appeared and was now directly behind him, he, too, faced about and made off down the alley. Presently he met Riply Buckner, who, without waiting to inquire the cause of his flight, enthusiastically joined him. Again Hubert was surprised

into pursuing a little way. Then, deciding once and for
all to let well enough alone, he returned on a dead run
to his house.

Meanwhile Basil had discovered that he was not pursued, and keeping in the shadows, made his way back
to the alley. He was not frightened—he had simply been
incapable of action. The alley was empty; neither Bill
nor Riply was in sight. He saw Mr Blair come to the
back gate, open it, look up and down and go back into
the house. He came closer. There was a great chatter in
the kitchen—Hubert's voice, loud and boastful, and Mrs
Blair's frightened, and the two Swedish domestics contributing bursts of hilarious laughter. Then through an open
window he heard Mr Blair's voice at the telephone:

'I want to speak to the chief of police. . . . Chief, this
is George P. Blair. . . . Chief, there's a gang of toughs
around here who—'

Basil was off like a flash, tearing at his Confederate
whiskers as he ran.

V

Imogene Bissel, having just turned thirteen, was not accustomed to having callers at night. She was spending a bored
and solitary evening inspecting the month's bills which
were scattered over her mother's desk, when she heard
Hubert Blair and his father admitted into the front hall.

'I just thought I'd bring him over myself,' Mr Blair
was saying to her mother. 'There seems to be a gang
of toughs hanging around our alley tonight.'

Mrs Bissel had not called upon Mrs Blair and she was
considerably taken aback by this unexpected visit. She
even entertained the uncharitable thought that this was
a crude overture, undertaken by Mr Blair on behalf of
his wife.

'Really!' she exclaimed. 'Imogene will be delighted
to see Hubert, I'm sure. . . . Imogene!'

'These toughs were evidently lying in wait for Hubert,'

continued Mr Blair. 'But he's a pretty spunky boy and he managed to drive them away. However, I didn't want him to come down here alone.'

'Of course not,' she agreed. But she was unable to imagine why Hubert should have come at all. He was a nice enough boy, but surely Imogene had seen enough of him the last three afternoons. In fact, Mrs Bissel was annoyed, and there was a minimum of warmth in her voice when she asked Mr Blair to come in.

They were still in the hall, and Mr Blair was just beginning to perceive that all was not as it should be, when there was another ring at the bell. Upon the door being opened, Basil Lee, red-faced and breathless, stood on the threshold.

'How do you do, Mrs Bissel? Hello, Imogene!' he cried in an unnecessarily hearty voice. 'Where's the party?'

The salutation might have sounded to a dispassionate observer somewhat harsh and unnatural, but it fell upon the ears of an already disconcerted group.

'There isn't any party,' said Imogene wonderingly.

'What?' Basil's mouth dropped open in exaggerated horror, his voice trembled slightly. 'You mean to say you didn't call me up and tell me to come over here to a party?'

'Why, of course not, Basil!'

Imogene was excited by Hubert's unexpected arrival and it occurred to her that Basil had invented this excuse to spoil it. Alone of those present, she was close to the truth; but she underestimated the urgency of Basil's motive, which was not jealousy but mortal fear.

'You called *me* up, didn't you, Imogene?' demanded Hubert confidently.

'Why, no, Hubert! I didn't call up anybody.'

Amid a chorus of bewildered protestations, there was another ring at the doorbell and the pregnant night yielded up Riply Buckner, Jr., and William S. Kampf. Like Basil, they were somewhat rumpled and breathless, and they no less rudely and peremptorily demanded the whereabouts of the party, insisting with curious vehemence that Imogene had just now invited them over the phone.

Hubert laughed, the others began to laugh and the tensity relaxed. Imogene, because she believed Hubert, now began to believe them all. Unable to restrain himself any longer in the presence of this unhoped-for audience, Hubert burst out with his amazing adventure.

'I guess there's a gang laying for us all!' he exclaimed. 'There were some guys laying for me in our alley when I went out. There was a big fellow with grey whiskers, but when he saw me he ran away. Then I went along the alley and there was a bunch more, sort of foreigners or something, and I started after'm and they ran. I tried to catch'm, but I guess they were good and scared, because they ran too fast for *me*.'

So interested were Hubert and his father in the story that they failed to perceive that three of his listeners were growing purple in the face or to mark the uproarious laughter that greeted Mrs Bissel's polite proposal that they have a party, after all.

'Tell about the warnings, Hubert,' prompted Mr Blair. 'You see, Hubert had received these warnings. Did you boys get any warnings?'

'I did,' said Basil suddenly. 'I got a sort of warning on a piece of paper about a week ago.'

For a moment, as Mr Blair's worried eye fell upon Basil, a strong sense not precisely of suspicion but rather of obscure misgiving passed over him. Possibly that odd aspect of Basil's eyebrows, where wisps of crêpe hair still lingered, connected itself in his subconscious mind with what was bizarre in the events of the evening. He shook his head somewhat puzzled. Then his thoughts glided back restfully to Hubert's courage and presence of mind.

Hubert, meanwhile, having exhausted his facts, was making tentative leaps into the realms of imagination.

'I said, "So, you're the guy that's been sending these warnings," and he swung his left at me, and I dodged and swung my right back at him. I guess I must have landed, because he gave a yell and ran. Gosh, he could run! You ought to of seen him, Bill,—he could run as fast as you.'

'Was he big?' asked Basil, blowing his nose noisily.

'Sure! About as big as father.'

'Were the other ones big too?'

'Sure! They were pretty big. I didn't wait to see. I just yelled, "You get out of here, you bunch of toughs, or I'll show you!" They started to sort of fight, but I swung my right at one of them and they didn't wait for any more.'

'Hubert says he thinks they were Italians,' interrupted Mr Blair. 'Didn't you, Hubert?'

'They were sort of funny-looking,' Hubert said. 'One fellow looked like an Italian.'

Mrs Bissel led the way to the dining-room, where she had caused a cake and grape juice supper to be spread. Imogene took a chair by Hubert's side.

'Now tell me all about it, Hubert,' she said, attentively folding her hands.

Hubert ran over the adventure once more. A knife now made its appearance in the belt of one conspirator; Hubert's parleys with them lengthened and grew in volume and virulence. He had told them just what they might expect if they fooled with him. They had started to draw knives, but had thought better of it and taken to flight.

In the middle of this recital there was a curious snorting sound from across the table, but when Imogene looked over, Basil was spreading jelly on a piece of coffee cake and his eyes were brightly innocent. A minute later, however, the sound was repeated, and this time she intercepted a specifically malicious expression upon his face.

'I wonder what you'd done, Basil,' she said cuttingly. 'I'll bet you'd be running yet!'

Basil put the piece of coffee cake in his mouth and immediately choked on it—an accident which Bill Kampf and Riply Buckner found hilariously amusing. Their amusement at various casual incidents at table seemed to increase as Hubert's story continued. The alley now swarmed with malefactors, and as Hubert struggled on against overwhelming odds, Imogene found herself growing restless—without in the least realizing that the tale was boring her. On the contrary, each time Hubert recollected new incidents and began again, she looked spitefully over at Basil, and her dislike for him grew.

When they moved into the library, Imogene went to the piano, where she sat alone while the boys gathered around Hubert on the couch. To her chagrin, they seemed quite content to listen indefinitely. Odd little noises squeaked out of them from time to time, but whenever the narrative slackened they would beg for more.

'Go on, Hubert. Which one did you say could run as fast as Bill Kampf?'

She was glad when, after half an hour, they all got up to go.

'It's a strange affair from beginning to end,' Mr Blair was saying. 'I don't like it. I'm going to have a detective look into the matter tomorrow. What did they want of Hubert? What were they going to do to him?'

No one offered a suggestion. Even Hubert was silent, contemplating his possible fate with certain respectful awe. During breaks in his narration the talk had turned to such collateral matters as murders and ghosts, and all the boys had talked themselves into a state of considerable panic. In fact each had come to believe, in varying degrees, that a band of kidnappers infested the vicinity.

'I don't like it,' repeated Mr Blair. 'I fact I'm going to see all of you boys to your own homes.'

Basil greeted this offer with relief. The evening had been a mad success, but furies once aroused sometimes get out of hand. He did not feel like walking the streets alone tonight.

In the hall, Imogene, taking advantage of her mother's somewhat fatigued farewell to Mr Blair, beckoned Hubert back into the library. Instantly attuned to adversity, Basil listened. There was a whisper and a short scuffle, followed by an indiscreet but unmistakable sound. With the corners of his mouth falling, Basil went out the door. He had stacked the cards dexterously, but Life had played a trump from its sleeve at the last.

A moment later they all started off, clinging together in a group, turning corners with cautious glances behind and ahead. What Basil and Riply and Bill expected to see as they peered warily into the sinister mouths of alleys and around great dark trees and behind concealing fences they did not know—in all probability the same hairy and grotesque desperadoes who had lain in wait for Hubert Blair that night.

VI

A week later Basil and Riply heard that Hubert and his mother had gone to the seashore for the summer. Basil was sorry. He had wanted to learn from Hubert some of the graceful mannerisms that his contemporaries found so dazzling and that might come in so handy next fall when he went away to school. In tribute to Hubert's passing, he practised leaning against a tree and missing it and rolling a skate down his arm, and he wore his cap in Hubert's manner, set jauntily on the side of his head.

This was only for a while. He perceived eventually that though boys and girls would always listen to him while he talked, their mouths literally moving in response to his, they would never look at him as they had looked at Hubert. So he abandoned the loud chuckle that so annoyed his mother and set his cap straight upon his head once more.

But the change in him went deeper than that. He was no longer sure that he wanted to be a gentleman burglar, though he still read of their exploits with breathless admiration. Outside of Hubert's gate, he had for a moment felt morally alone; and he realized that whatever combinations he might make of the materials of life would have to be safely within the law. And after another week he found that he no longer grieved over losing Imogene. Meeting her, he saw only the familiar little girl he had always known. The ecstatic moment of that afternoon had been a premature birth, an emotion left over from an already fleeting spring.

He did not know that he had frightened Mrs Blair out of town and that because of him a special policeman walked a placid beat for many a night. All he knew was the vague and restless yearnings of three long spring months were somehow satisfied. They reached combustion in that last week—flared up, exploded and burned out. His face was turned without regret towards the boundless possibilities of summer.

BASIL
A NIGHT AT THE FAIR
[1928]

THE two cities were separated only by a thin well-bridged river; their tails curling over the banks met and mingled, and at the juncture, under the jealous eye of each, lay, every fall, the State Fair. Because of this advantageous position, and because of the agricultural eminence of the state, the fair was one of the most magnificent in America. There were immense exhibits of grain, livestock and farming machinery; there were horse races and automobile races and, lately, aeroplanes that really left the ground; there was a tumultuous Midway with Coney Island thrillers to whirl you through space, and a whining, tinkling hoochie-coochie show. As a compromise between the serious and the trivial, a grand exhibition of fireworks, culminating in a representation of the Battle of Gettysburg, took place in the Grand Concourse every night.

At the late afternoon of a hot September day two boys of fifteen, somewhat replete with food and pop, and fatigued by eight hours of constant motion, issued from the Penny Arcade. The one with dark, handsome, eager eyes was, according to the cosmic inscription in his last year's Ancient History, 'Basil Duke Lee, Holly Avenue, St Paul, Minnesota, United States, North America, Western Hemisphere, the World, the Universe.' Though slightly shorter than his companion, he appeared taller, for he projected, so to speak, from short trousers, while Riply Buckner, Jr, had graduated into long ones the week before. This event, so simple and natural, was having a disrupting influence on the intimate friendship between them that had endured for several years.

During that time Basil, the imaginative member of the

firm, had been the dominating partner, and the displace-
ment effected by two feet of blue serge filled him with
puzzled dismay—in fact, Riply Buckner had become
noticeably indifferent to the pleasure of Basil's company
in public. His own assumption of long trousers had seemed
to promise a liberation from the restraints and inferiorities
of boyhood, and the companionship of one who was, in
token of his short pants, still a boy was an unwelcome
reminder of how recent was his own metamorphosis. He
scarcely admitted this to himself, but a certain shortness
of temper with Basil, a certain tendency to belittle him
with superior laughter, had been in evidence all afternoon.
Basil felt the new difference keenly. In August a family
conference had decided that even though he was going
East to school, he was too small for long trousers. He
had countered by growing an inch and a half in a fortnight, which added to his reputation for unreliability,
but led him to hope that his mother might be persuaded,
after all.

Coming out of the stuffy tent into the glow of sunset,
the two boys hesitated, glancing up and down the crowded
highway with expressions compounded of a certain ennui
and a certain inarticulate yearning. They were unwilling
to go home before it became necessary, yet they knew
they had temporarily glutted their appetite for sights;
they wanted a change in the tone, the motif, of the day.
Near them was the parking space, as yet a modest yard;
and as they lingered indecisively, their eyes were caught
and held by a small car, red in colour and slung at that
proximity to the ground which indicated both speed of
motion and speed of life. It was a Blatz Wildcat, and
for the next five years it represented the ambition of
several million American boys. Occupying it, in the posture
of aloof exhaustion exacted by the sloping seat, was a
blonde, gay, baby-faced girl.

The two boys stared. She bent upon them a single
cool glance and then returned to her avocation of reclining
in a Blatz Wildcat and looking haughtily at the sky. The

two boys exchanged a glance, but made no move to go. They watched the girl—when they felt that their stares were noticeable they dropped their eyes and gazed at the car.

After several minutes a young man with a very pink face and pink hair, wearing a yellow suit and hat and drawing on yellow gloves, appeared and got into the car. There was a series of frightful explosions; then, with a measured tup-tup-tup from the open cut-out, insolent, percussive and thrilling as a drum, the car and the girl and the young man, whom they had recognized as Speed Paxton, slid smoothly away.

Basil and Riply turned and strolled back thoughtfully towards the Midway. They knew that Speed Paxton was dimly terrible—the wild and pampered son of a local brewer—but they envied him—to ride off into the sunset in such a chariot, into the very hush and mystery of night, beside him the mystery of that baby-faced girl. It was probably this envy that made them begin to shout when they perceived a tall youth of their own age issuing from a shooting gallery.

'Oh, El! Hey, El! Wait a minute!'

Elwood Leaming turned around and waited. He was the dissipated one among the nice boys of the town— he had drunk beer, he had learned from chauffeurs, he was already thin from too many cigarettes. As they greeted him eagerly, the hard, wise expression of a man of the world met them in his half-closed eyes.

'Hello, Rip. Put it there, Rip. Hello, Basil, old boy. Put it there.'

'What you doing, El?' Riply asked.

'Nothing. What are you doing?'

'Nothing.'

Elwood Leaming narrowed his eyes still further, seemed to give thought, and then made a decisive clicking sound with his teeth.

'Well, what do you say we pick something up?' he

suggested. 'I saw some pretty good stuff around here this afternoon.'

Riply and Basil drew tense, secret breaths. A year before they had been shocked because Elwood went to the burlesque shows at the Star—now here he was holding the door open to his own speedy life.

The responsibility of his new maturity impelled Riply to appear most eager. 'All right with me,' he said heartily.

He looked at Basil.

'All right with me,' mumbled Basil.

Riply laughed, more from nervousness than from derision. 'Maybe you better grow up first, Basil.' He looked at Elwood, seeking approval. 'You better stick around till you get to be a man.'

'Oh, dry up!' retorted Basil. 'How long have you had yours? Just a week!'

But he realized that there was a gap separating him from these two, and it was with a sense of tagging them that he walked along beside.

Glancing from right to left with the expression of a keen and experienced frontiersman, Elwood Leaming led the way. Several pairs of strolling girls met his mature glance and smiled encouragingly, but he found them unsatisfactory—too fat, too plain or too hard. All at once their eyes fell upon two who sauntered along a little ahead of them, and they increased their pace, Elwood with confidence, Riply with its nervous counterfeit and Basil suddenly in the grip of wild excitement.

They were abreast of them. Basil's heart was in his throat. He looked away as he heard Elwood's voice.

'Hello, girls! How are you this evening?'

Would they call for the police? Would his mother and Riply's suddenly turn the corner?

'Hello, yourself, kiddo!'

'Where you going, girls?'

'Nowhere.'

'Well, let's all go together.'

Then all of them were standing in a group and Basil

was relieved to find that they were only girls his own age, after all. They were pretty, with clear skins and red lips and maturely piled up hair. One he immediately liked better than the other—her voice was quieter and she was shy. Basil was glad when Elwood walked on with the bolder one, leaving him and Riply to follow with the other, behind.

The first lights of the evening were springing into pale existence; the afternoon crowd had thinned a little, and the lanes, empty of people, were heavy with the rich various smells of popcorn and peanuts, molasses and dust and cooking Wienerwurst and a not-unpleasant over-tone of animals and hay. The Ferris wheel, pricked out now in lights, revolved leisurely through the dusk; a few empty cars of the roller coaster rattled overhead. The heat had blown off and there was the crisp stimulating excitement of Northern autumn in the air.

They walked. Basil felt that there was some way of talking to this girl, but he could manage nothing in the key of Elwood Leaming's intense and confidential manner to the girl ahead—as if he had inadvertently discovered a kinship of tastes and of hearts. So to save the progression from absolute silence—for Riply's contribution amounted only to an occasional burst of silly laughter— Basil pretended an interest in the sights they passed and kept up a sort of comment thereon.

'There's the six-legged calf. Have you seen it?'

'No, I haven't.'

'There's where the man rides the motorcycle around. Did you go there?'

'No, I didn't.'

'Look! They're beginning to fill the balloon. I wonder what time they start the fireworks.'

'Have you been to the fireworks?'

'No, I'm going tomorrow night. Have you?'

'Yes, I been every night. My brother works there. He's one of them that helps set them off.'

'Oh!'

He wondered if her brother cared that she had been picked up by strangers. He wondered even more if she felt as silly as he. It must be getting late, and he had promised to be home by half-past seven on pain of not being allowed out tomorrow night. He walked up beside Elwood.

'Hey, El,' he asked, 'where we going?'

Elwood turned to him and winked. 'We're going around the Old Mill.'

'Oh!'

Basil dropped back again—became aware that in his temporary absence Riply and the girl had linked arms. A twinge of jealousy went through him and he inspected the girl again and with more appreciation, finding her prettier than he had thought. Her eyes, dark and intimate, seemed to have wakened at the growing brilliance of the illumination overhead; there was the promise of excitement in them now, like the promise of the cooling night.

He considered taking her other arm, but it was too late; she and Riply were laughing together at something —rather, at nothing. She had asked him what he laughed at all the time and he had laughed again for an answer. Then they both laughed hilariously and sporadically together.

Basil looked disgustedly at Riply. 'I never heard such a silly laugh in my life,' he said indignantly.

'Didn't you?' chuckled Riply Buckner. 'Didn't you, little boy?'

He bent double with laughter and the girl joined in. The words 'little boy' had fallen on Basil like a jet of cold water. In his excitement he had forgotten something, as a cripple might forget his limp only to discover it when he began to run.

'You think you're so big!' he exclaimed. 'Where'd you get the pants? Where'd you get the pants?' He tried to work this up with gusto and was about to add: 'They're your father's pants,' when he remembered that Riply's father, like his own, was dead.

2*

The couple ahead reached the entrance to the Old Mill and waited for them. It was an off hour, and half a dozen scows bumped in the wooden offing, swayed by the mild tide of the artificial river. Elwood and his girl got into the front seat and he promptly put his arm around her. Basil helped the other girl into the rear seat, but, dispirited, he offered no resistance when Riply wedged in and sat down between.

They floated off, immediately entering upon a long echoing darkness. Somewhere far ahead a group in another boat were singing, their voices now remote and romantic, now nearer and yet more mysterious, as the canal doubled back and the boats passed close to each other with an invisible veil between.

The three boys yelled and called, Basil attempting by his vociferousness and variety to outdo Riply in the girl's eyes, but after a few moments there was no sound except his own voice and the continual bump-bump of the boat against the wooden sides, and he knew without looking that Riply had put his arm about the girl's shoulder.

They slid into a red glow—a stage set of hell, with grinning demons and lurid paper fires—he made out that Elwood and his girl sat cheek to cheek—then again into the darkness, with the gently lapping water and the passing of the singing boat now near, now far away. For a while Basil pretended that he was interested in this other boat, calling to them, commenting on their proximity. Then he discovered that the scow could be rocked and took to this poor amusement until Elwood Leaming turned around indignantly and cried:

'Hey! What are you trying to do?'

They came out finally to the entrance and the two couples broke apart. Basil jumped miserably ashore.

'Give us some more tickets,' Riply cried. 'We want to go around again.'

'Not me,' said Basil with elaborate indifference. 'I have to go home.'

Riply began to laugh in derision and triumph. The girl laughed too.

'Well, so long, little boy,' Riply cried hilariously.

'Oh, shut up! So long, Elwood.'

'So long, Basil.'

The boat was already starting off; arms settled again about the girls' shoulders.

'So long, little boy!'

'So long, you big cow!' Basil cried. 'Where'd you get the pants? Where'd you get the pants?'

But the boat had already disappeared into the dark mouth of the tunnel, leaving the echo of Riply's taunting laughter behind.

It is an ancient tradition that all boys are obsessed with the idea of being grown. This is because they occasionally give voice to their impatience with the restraints of youth, while those great stretches of time when they are more than content to be boys find expression in action and not in words. Sometimes Basil wanted to be a little bit older, but no more. The question of long pants had not seemed vital to him—he wanted them, but as a costume they had no such romantic significance as, for example, a football suit or an officer's uniform, or even the silk hat and opera cape in which gentlemen burglars were wont to prowl the streets of New York by night.

But when he awoke next morning they were the most important necessity in his life. Without them he was cut off from his contemporaries, laughed at by a boy whom he had hitherto led. The actual fact that last night some chickens had preferred Riply to himself was of no importance in itself, but he was fiercely competitive and he resented being required to fight with one hand tied behind his back. He felt that parallel situations would occur at school, and that was unbearable. He approached his mother at breakfast in a state of wild excitement.

'Why, Basil,' she protested in surprise, 'I thought when we talked it over you didn't especially care.'

'I've got to have them,' he declared. 'I'd rather be dead than go away to school without them.'

'Well, there's no need of being silly.'

'It's true—I'd rather be dead. If I can't have long trousers I don't see any use in my going away to school.'

His emotion was such that the vision of his demise began actually to disturb his mother.

'Now stop that silly talk and come and eat your breakfast. You can go down and buy some at Barton Leigh's this morning.'

Mollified, but still torn by the urgency of his desire, Basil strode up and down the room.

'A boy is simply helpless without them,' he declared vehemently. The phrase pleased him and he amplified it. 'A boy is simply and utterly helpless without them. I'd rather be dead than go away to school—'

'Basil, stop talking like that. Somebody has been teasing you about it.'

'Nobody's been teasing me,' he denied indignantly— 'nobody at all.'

After breakfast, the maid called him to the phone.

'This is Riply,' said a tentative voice. Basil acknowledged the fact coldly. 'You're not sore about last night, are you?' Riply asked.

'Me? No. Who said I was sore?'

'Nobody. Well, listen, you know about us going to the fireworks together tonight.'

'Yes.' Basil's voice was still cold.

'Well, one of those girls—the one Elwood had—has got a sister that's even nicer than she is, and she can come out tonight and you could have her. And we thought we could meet about eight, because the fireworks don't start till nine.'

'What do?'

'Well, we could go on the Old Mill again. We went around three times more last night.'

There was a moment's silence. Basil looked to see if his mother's door was closed.

'Did you kiss yours?' he demanded into the transmitter.

'Sure I did!' Over the wire came the ghost of a silly laugh. 'Listen, El thinks he can get his auto. We could call for you at seven.'

'All right,' agreed Basil gruffly, and he added, 'I'm going down and get some long pants this morning.'

'Are you?' Again Basil detected ghostly laughter. 'Well, you be ready at seven tonight.'

Basil's uncle met him at Barton Leigh's clothing store at ten, and Basil felt a touch of guilt at having put his family to all this trouble and expense. On his uncle's advice, he decided finally on two suits—a heavy chocolate brown for every day and a dark blue for formal wear. There were certain alterations to be made but it was agreed that one of the suits was to be delivered without fail that afternoon.

His momentary contriteness at having been so expensive made him save car-fare by walking home from downtown. Passing along Crest Avenue, he paused speculatively to vault the high hydrant in front of the Van Schellinger house, wondering if one did such things in long trousers and if he would ever do it again. He was impelled to leap it two or three times as a sort of ceremonial farewell, and was so engaged when the Van Schellinger limousine turned into the drive and stopped at the front door.

'Oh, Basil,' a voice called.

A fresh delicate face, half buried under a mass of almost white curls, was turned toward him from the granite portico of the city's second largest mansion.

'Hello, Gladys.'

'Come here a minute, Basil.'

He obeyed. Gladys Van Schellinger was a year younger than Basil—a tranquil, carefully nurtured girl who, so local tradition had it, was being brought up to marry in the East. She had a governess and always played with a certain few girls at her house or theirs, and was not allowed the casual freedom of children in a Midwestern city. She was never present at such rendezvous as the

Whartons' yard, where the others played games in the afternoons.

'Basil, I wanted to ask you something—are you going to the State Fair tonight?'

'Why, yes, I am.'

'Well, wouldn't you like to come and sit in our box and watch the fireworks?'

Momentarily he considered the matter. He wanted to accept, but he was mysteriously impelled to refuse—to forgo a pleasure in order to pursue a quest that in cold logic did not interest him at all.

'I can't. I'm awfully sorry.'

A shadow of discontent crossed Gladys's face. 'Oh? Well, come and see me sometime soon, Basil. In a few weeks I'm going East to school.'

He walked on up the street in a state of dissatisfaction. Gladys Van Schellinger had never been his girl, nor indeed anyone's girl, but the fact that they were starting away to school at the same time gave him a feeling of kinship for her—as if they had been selected for the glamorous adventure of the East, chosen together for a high destiny that transcended the fact that she was rich and he was only comfortable. He was sorry that he could not sit with her in her box tonight.

By three o'clock, Basil, reading the *Crimson Sweater* up in his room, began giving attentive ear to every ring at the bell. He would go to the head of the stairs, lean over and call, 'Hilda, was that a package for me?' And at four, dissatisfied with her indifference, her lack of feeling for important things, her slowness in going to and returning from the door, he moved downstairs and began attending to it himself. But nothing came. He phoned Barton Leigh's and was told by a busy clerk: 'You'll get that suit. I'll guarantee that you'll get that suit.' But he did not believe in the clerk's honour and he moved out on the porch and watched for Barton Leigh's delivery wagon.

His mother came home at five. 'There were probably

more alterations than they thought,' she suggested help-fully. 'You'll probably get it tomorrow morning.'

'Tomorrow morning!' he exclaimed incredulously. 'I've got to have that suit tonight.'

'Well, I wouldn't be too disappointed if I were you, Basil. The stores all close at half-past five.'

Basil took one agitated look up and down Holly Avenue. Then he got his cap and started on a run for the street car at the corner. A moment later a cautious afterthought caused him to retrace his steps with equal rapidity.

'If they get here, keep them for me,' he instructed his mother—a man who thought of everything.

'All right,' she promised dryly, 'I will.'

It was later than he thought. He had to wait for a trolley, and when he reached Barton Leigh's he saw with horror that the doors were locked and the blinds drawn. He intercepted a last clerk coming out and explained vehemently that he had to have his suit tonight. The clerk knew nothing about the matter . . . Was Basil Mr Schwartze?

No, Basil was not Mr Schwartze. After a vague argument wherein he tried to convince the clerk that whoever promised him the suit should be fired, Basil went dispiritedly home.

He would not go to the fair without his suit—he would not go at all. He would sit at home and luckier boys would go adventuring along its Great White Way. Mysterious girls, young and reckless, would glide with them through the enchanted darkness of the Old Mill, but because of the stupidity, selfishness and dishonesty of a clerk in a clothing store he would not be there. In a day or so the fair would be over—forever—those girls, of all living girls the most intangible, the most desirable, that sister, said to be nicest of all—would be lost out of his life. They would ride off in Blatz Wildcats into the moonlight without Basil having kissed them. No, all his life—though he would lose the clerk his position: 'You see now

what your act did to me'—he would look back with infinite regret upon that irretrievable hour. Like most of
us, he was unable to perceive that he would have any
desires in the future equivalent to those that possessed
him now.

He reached home; the package had not arrived. He
moped dismally about the house, consenting at half-past
six to sit silently at dinner with his mother, his elbows on
the table.

'Haven't you any appetite, Basil?'

'No, thanks,' he said absently, under the impression he
had been offered something.

'You're not going away to school for two more weeks.
Why should it matter—'

'Oh, that isn't the reason I can't eat. I had a sort of
headache all afternoon.'

Towards the end of the meal his eye focused abstractedly on some slices of angel cake; with the air of a som-
nambulist, he ate three.

At seven he heard the sounds that should have ushered
in a night of romantic excitement.

The Leaming car stopped outside, and a moment later
Riply Buckner rang the bell. Basil rose gloomily.

'I'll go,' he said to Hilda. And then to his mother, with
vague impersonal reproach, 'Excuse me a minute. I just
want to tell them I can't go to the fair tonight.'

'But of course you can go, Basil. Don't be silly. Just
because—'

He scarcely heard her. Opening the door, he faced
Riply on the steps. Beyond was the Leaming limousine, an
old high car, quivering in silhouette against the harvest
moon.

Clop-clop-clop! Up the street came the Barton Leigh
delivery wagon. Clop-clop! A man jumped out, dumped
an iron anchor to the pavement, hurried along the street,
turned away, turned back again, came towards them with
a long square box in his hand.

'You'll have to wait a minute,' Basil was calling wildly.

'It can't make any difference. I'll dress in the library. Look here, if you're a friend of mine, you'll wait a minute.' He stepped out on the porch. 'Hey, El, I've just got my —got to change my clothes. You can wait a minute, can't you?'

The spark of a cigarette flushed in the darkness as El spoke to the chauffeur; the quivering car came to rest with a sigh and the skies filled suddenly with stars.

Once again the fair—but differing from the fair of the afternoon as a girl in the daytime differs from her radiant presentation of herself at night. The substance of the cardboard booths and plaster palaces was gone, the forms remained. Outlined in lights, these forms suggested things more mysterious and entrancing than themselves, and the people strolling along the network of little Broadways shared this quality, as their pale faces singly and in clusters broke the half darkness.

The boys hurried to their rendezvous, finding the girls in the deep shadow of the Temple of Wheat. Their forms had scarcely merged into a group when Basil became aware that something was wrong. In growing apprehension, he glanced from face to face and, as the introductions were made, he realized the appalling truth—the younger sister was, in point of fact, a fright, squat and dingy, with a bad complexion brooding behind a mask of cheap pink powder and a shapeless mouth that tried ceaselessly to torture itself into the mould of charm.

In a daze he heard Riply's girl say, 'I don't know whether I ought to go with you. I had a sort of date with another fellow I met this afternoon.'

Fidgeting, she looked up and down the street, while Riply, in astonishment and dismay, tried to take her arm. 'Come on,' he urged. 'Didn't I have a date with you first.'

'But I didn't know whether you'd come or not,' she said perversely.

Elwood and the two sisters added their entreaties.

'Maybe I could go on the Ferris wheel,' she said grudgingly, 'but not the Old Mill. This fellow would be sore.'

Riply's confidence reeled with the blow; his mouth fell ajar, his hand desperately pawed her arm. Basil stood glancing now with agonized politeness at his own girl, now at the others, with an expression of infinite reproach. Elwood alone was successful and content.

'Let's go on the Ferris wheel,' he said impatiently. 'We can't stand here all night.'

At the ticket booth the recalcitrant Olive hesitated once more, frowning and glancing about as if she still hoped Riply's rival would appear.

But when the swooping cars came to rest she let herself be persuaded in, and the three couples, with their troubles, were hoisted slowly into the air.

As the car rose, following the imagined curve of the sky, it occurred to Basil how much he would have enjoyed it in other company, or even alone, the fair twinkling beneath him with new variety, the velvet quality of the darkness that is on the edge of light and is barely permeated by its last attenuations. But he was unable to hurt anyone whom he thought of as an inferior. After a minute he turned to the girl beside him.

'Do you live in St Paul or Minneapolis?' he inquired formally.

'St Paul. I go to Number 7 School.' Suddenly she moved closer. 'I bet you're not so slow,' she encouraged him.

He put his arm around her shoulder and found it warm. Again they reached the top of the wheel and the sky stretched out overhead, again they lapsed down through gusts of music from remote calliopes. Keeping his eyes turned carefully away, Basil pressed her to him, and as they rose again into darkness, leaned and kissed her cheek.

The significance of the contact stirred him, but out of the corner of his eye he saw her face—he was thankful when a gong struck below and the machine settled slowly to rest.

The three couples were scarcely reunited outside when Olive uttered a yelp of excitement.

'There he is!' she cried. 'That Bill Jones I met this afternoon—that I had the date with.'

A youth of their own age was approaching, stepping like a circus pony and twirling, with the deftness of a drum major, a small rattan cane. Under the cautious alias, the three boys recognized a friend and contemporary—none other than the fascinating Hubert Blair.

He came nearer. He greeted them all with a friendly chuckle. He took off his cap, spun it, dropped it, caught it, set it jauntily on the side of his head.

'You're a nice one,' he said to Olive. 'I waited here fifteen minutes this evening.'

He pretended to belabour her with the cane; she giggled with delight. Hubert Blair possessed the exact tone that all girls of fourteen, and a somewhat cruder type of grown women, find irresistible. He was a gymnastic virtuoso and his figure was in constant graceful motion; he had a jaunty piquant nose, a disarming laugh and a shrewd talent for flattery. When he took a piece of toffee from his pocket, placed it on his forehead, shook it off and caught it in his mouth, it was obvious to any disinterested observer that Riply was destined to see no more of Olive that night.

So fascinated were the group that they failed to see Basil's eyes brighten with a ray of hope, his feet take four quick steps backwards with all the guile of a gentleman burglar, his torso writhe through the parting of a tent wall into the deserted premises of the Harvester and Tractor Show. Once safe, Basil's tensity relaxed, and as he considered Riply's unconsciousness of the responsibilities presently to devolve upon him, he bent double with hilarious laughter in the darkness.

Ten minutes later, in a remote part of the fair-grounds, a youth made his way briskly and cautiously towards the

fireworks exhibit, swinging as he walked a recently purchased rattan cane. Several girls eyed him with interest,
but he passed them haughtily; he was weary of people
for a brief moment—a moment which he had almost mis-
laid in the bustle of life—he was enjoying his long pants.

He bought a bleacher seat and followed the crowd
around the race track, seeking his section. A few Union
troops were moving cannon about in preparation for the
Battle of Gettysburg, and, stopping to watch them, he
was hailed by Gladys Van Schellinger from the box
behind.

'Oh, Basil, don't you want to come and sit with us?'

He turned about and was absorbed. Basil exchanged
courtesies with Mr and Mrs Van Schellinger and he was
affably introduced to several other people as 'Alice Riley's
boy,' and a chair was placed for him beside Gladys in
front.

'Oh, Basil,' she whispered, glowing at him, 'isn't this
fun?'

Distinctly, it was. He felt a vast wave of virtue surge
through him. How anyone could have preferred the society
of those common girls was at this moment incomprehensible.

'Basil, won't it be fun to go East? Maybe we'll be on
the same train.'

'I can hardly wait,' he agreed gravely. 'I've got on long
pants. I had to have them to go away to school.'

One of the ladies in the box leaned towards him. 'I
know your mother very well,' she said. 'And I know
another friend of yours. I'm Riply Buckner's aunt.'

'Oh, yes!'

'Riply's such a nice boy,' beamed Mrs Van Schellinger.

And then, as if the mention of his name had evoked
him, Riply Buckner came suddenly into sight. Along the
now empty and brightly illuminated race track came a
short but monstrous procession, a sort of Lilliputian burlesque of the wild gay life. At its head marched Hubert
Blair and Olive, Hubert prancing and twirling his cane like

a drum major to the accompaniment of her appreciative screams of laughter. Next followed Elwood Leaming and his young lady, leaning so close together that they walked with difficulty, apparently wrapped in each other's arms. And bringing up the rear without glory were Riply Buckner and Basil's late companion, rivalling Olive in exhibitionist sound.

Fascinated, Basil stared at Riply, the expression of whose face was curiously mixed. At moments he would join in the general tone of the parade with silly guffaw, at others a pained expression would flit across his face, as if he doubted that, after all, the evening was a success.

The procession was attracting considerable notice—so much that not even Riply was aware of the particular attention focused upon him from this box, though he passed by it four feet away. He was out of hearing when a curious rustling sigh passed over its inhabitants and a series of discreet whispers began.

'What funny girls!' Gladys said. 'Was that first boy Hubert Blair?'

'Yes.' Basil was listening to a fragment of conversation behind:

'His mother will certainly hear of this in the morning.'

As long as Riply had been in sight, Basil had been in an agony of shame for him, but now a new wave of virtue, even stronger than the first, swept over him. His memory of the incident would have reached actual happiness, save for the fact that Riply's mother might not let him go away to school. And a few minutes later, even that seemed endurable. Yet Basil was not a mean boy. The natural cruelty of his species towards the doomed was not yet disguised by hypocrisy—that was all.

In a burst of glory, to the alternate strains of Dixie and The Star-Spangled Banner, the Battle of Gettysburg ended. Outside by the waiting cars, Basil, on a sudden impulse, went up to Riply's aunt.

'I think it would be sort of a—a mistake to tell Riply's mother. He didn't do any harm. He—'

Annoyed by the events of the evening, she turned on him cool, patronizing eyes.

'I shall do as I think best,' she said briefly.

He frowned. Then he turned and got into the Van Schellinger limousine.

Sitting beside Gladys in the little seats, he loved her suddenly. His hand swung gently against hers from time to time and he felt the warm bond that they were both going away to school tightened around them and pulling them together.

'Can't you come and see me tomorrow?' she urged him. 'Mother's going to be away and she says I can have anybody I like.'

'All right.'

As the car slowed up for Basil's house, she leaned towards him swiftly. 'Basil—'

He waited. Her breath was warm on his cheek. He wanted her to hurry, or, when the engine stopped, her parents, dozing in back, might hear what she said. She seemed beautiful to him then; that vague unexciting quality about her was more than compensated for by her exquisite delicacy, the fine luxury of her life.

'Basil—Basil, when you come tomorrow, will you bring that Hubert Blair?'

The chauffeur opened the door and Mr and Mrs Van Schellinger woke up with a start. When the car had driven off, Basil stood looking after it thoughtfully until it turned the corner of the street.

BASIL

THE FRESHEST BOY

[1928]

IT WAS a hidden Broadway restaurant in the dead of the night, and a brilliant and mysterious group of society people, diplomats and members of the underworld were there. A few minutes ago the sparkling wine had been flowing and a girl had been dancing gaily upon a table, but now the whole crowd were hushed and breathless. All eyes were fixed upon the masked but well-groomed man in the dress suit and opera hat who stood nonchalantly in the door.

'Don't move, please,' he said, in a well-bred, cultivated voice that had, nevertheless, a ring of steel in it. 'This thing in my hand might—go off.'

His glance roved from table to table—fell upon the malignant man higher up with his pale saturnine face, upon Heatherly, the suave secret agent from a foreign power, then rested a little longer, a little more softly perhaps, upon the table where the girl with dark hair and dark tragic eyes sat alone.

'Now that my purpose is accomplished, it might interest you to know who I am.' There was a gleam of expectation in every eye. The breast of the dark-eyed girl heaved faintly and a tiny burst of subtle French perfume rose into the air. 'I am none other than that elusive gentleman, Basil Lee, better known as the Shadow.'

Taking off his well-fitting opera hat, he bowed ironically from the waist. Then, like a flash, he turned and was gone into the night.

'You get up to New York only once a month,' Lewis Crum was saying, 'and then you have to take a master along.'

Slowly, Basil Lee's glazed eyes returned from the barns and billboards of the Indiana countryside to the interior of the Broadway Limited. The hypnosis of the swift telegraph poles faded and Lewis Crum's stolid face took shape against the white slip-cover of the opposite bench.

'I'd just duck the master when I got to New York,' said Basil.

'Yes, you would!'

'I bet I would.'

'You try it and you'll see.'

'What do you mean saying I'll see, all the time, Lewis? What'll I see?'

His very bright dark-blue eyes were at this moment fixed upon his companion with boredom and impatience. The two had nothing in common except their age, which was fifteen, and the lifelong friendship of their fathers— which is less than nothing. Also they were bound from the same Middle-Western city for Basil's first and Lewis's second year at the same Eastern school.

But, contrary to all the best traditions, Lewis the veteran was miserable and Basil the neophyte was happy. Lewis hated school. He had grown entirely dependent on the stimulus of a hearty vital mother, and as he felt her slipping farther and farther away from him, he plunged deeper into misery and homesickness. Basil, on the other hand, had lived with such intensity on so many stories of boarding-school life that, far from being homesick, he had a glad feeling of recognition and familiarity. Indeed, it was with some sense of doing the appropriate thing, having the traditional rough-house, that he had thrown Lewis's comb off the train at Milwaukee last night for no reason at all.

To Lewis, Basil's ignorant enthusiasm was distasteful —his instinctive attempt to dampen it had contributed to the mutual irritation.

'I'll tell you what you'll see,' he said ominously. 'They'll catch you smoking and put you on bounds.'

'No, they won't, because I won't be smoking. I'll be in training for football.'

'Football! Yeah! Football!'

'Honestly, Lewis, You don't like anything, do you?'

'I don't like football. I don't like to go out and get a crack in the eye.' Lewis spoke aggressively, for his mother had canonized all his timidities as common sense. Basil's answer, made with what he considered kindly intent, was the sort of remark that creates lifelong enmities.

'You'd probably be a lot more popular in school if you played football,' he suggested patronizingly.

Lewis did not consider himself unpopular. He did not think of it in that way at all. He was astounded.

'You wait!' he cried furiously. 'They'll take all that freshness out of you.'

'Clam yourself,' said Basil, coolly plucking at the creases of his first long trousers. 'Just clam yourself.'

'I guess everybody knows you were the freshest boy at the Country Day!'

'Clam yourself,' repeated Basil, but with less assurance. 'Kindly clam yourself.'

'I guess I know what they had in the school paper about you—'

Basil's own coolness was no longer perceptible.

'If you don't clam yourself,' he said darkly, 'I'm going to throw your brushes off the train too.'

The enormity of this threat was effective. Lewis sank back in his seat, snorting and muttering, but undoubtedly calmer. His reference had been to one of the most shameful passages in his companion's life. In a periodical issued by the boys of Basil's late school there had appeared, under the heading Personals:

'If someone will please poison young Basil, or find some other means to stop his mouth, the school at large and myself will be much obliged.'

The two boys sat there fuming wordlessly at each other. Then, resolutely, Basil tried to re-inter this unfortunate souvenir of the past. All that was behind him now. Perhaps he had been a little fresh, but he was making a new start. After a moment, the memory passed and with it the train and Lewis's dismal presence—the breath of the East came sweeping over him again with a vast nostalgia. A voice called him out of the fabled world; a man stood beside him with a hand on his sweater-clad shoulder.

'Lee!'

'Yes, sir.'

'It all depends on you now. Understand?'

'Yes, sir.'

'All right,' the coach said, 'go in and win.'

Basil tore the sweater from his stripling form and dashed out on the field. There were two minutes to play and the score was 3 to 0 for the enemy, but at the sight of young Lee, kept out of the game all year by a malicious plan of Dan Haskins, the school bully, and Weasel Weems, his toady, a thrill of hope went over the St Regis stand.

'33-12-16-22!' barked Midget Brown, the diminutive little quarterback.

It was his signal——

'Oh, gosh!' Basil spoke aloud, forgetting the late unpleasantness. 'I wish we'd get there before tomorrow.'

II

ST REGIS SCHOOL, EASTCHESTER,
November 18, 19——

'DEAR MOTHER: There is not much to say today, but I thought I would write you about my allowance. All the boys have a bigger allowance than me, because there are a lot of little things I have to get, such as shoe laces, etc. School is still very nice and am having a fine time, but football is over and there is not much to do. I am going to New York this week to see a show. I do not know yet what it will be, but probably the Quacker Girl or little boy Blue as they are both very good. Dr Bacon is very nice and there's a good phycission in the village. No more now as I have to study Algebra.

'Your Affectionate Son,
'BASIL D. LEE.'

As he put the letter in its envelope, a wizened little boy came into the deserted study hall where he sat and stood staring at him.

'Hello,' said Basil, frowning.

'I been looking for you,' said the little boy, slowly and judicially. 'I looked all over—up in your room and out in the gym, and they said you probably might of sneaked off in here.'

'What do you want?' Basil demanded.

'Hold your horses, Bossy.'

Basil jumped to his feet. The little boy retreated a step.

'Go on, hit me!' he chirped nervously. 'Go on, hit me, cause I'm just half your size—Bossy.'

Basil winced. 'You call me that again and I'll spank you.'

'No, you won't spank me. Brick Wales said if you ever touched any of us—'

'But I never did touch any of you.'

'Didn't you chase a lot of us one day and didn't Brick Wales—'

'Oh, what do you want?' Basil cried in desperation.

'Doctor Bacon wants you. They sent me after you and somebody said maybe you sneaked in here.'

Basil dropped his letter in his pocket and walked out —the little boy and his invective following him through the door. He traversed a long corridor, muggy with that odour best described as the smell of stale caramels that is so peculiar to boys' schools, ascended a stairs and knocked at an unexceptional but formidable door.

Doctor Bacon was at his desk. He was a handsome, redheaded Episcopal clergyman of fifty whose original real interest in boys was now tempered by the flustered cynicism which is the fate of all headmasters and settles on them like green mould. There were certain preliminaries before Basil was asked to sit down—gold-rimmed glasses had to be hoisted up from nowhere by a black cord and fixed on Basil to be sure that he was not an impostor; great masses of paper on the desk had to be shuffled through, not in search of anything but as a man nervously shuffles a pack of cards.

'I had a letter from your mother this morning—ah—Basil.' The use of his first name had come to startle Basil. No one else in school had yet called him anything but Bossy or Lee. 'She feels that your marks have been poor. I believe you have been sent here at a certain amount of—ah—sacrifice and she expects—'

Basil's spirit writhed with shame, not at his poor marks but that his financial inadequacy should be so bluntly stated. He knew that he was one of the poorest boys in a rich boys' school.

Perhaps some dormant sensibility in Doctor Bacon became aware of his discomfort; he shuffled through the papers once more and began on a new note.

'However, that was not what I sent for you about this afternoon. You applied last week for permission to go to New York on Saturday, to a matinée. Mr Davis tells me that for almost the first time since school opened you will be off bounds tomorrow.'

'Yes, sir.'

'That is not a good record. However, I would allow you to go to New York if it could be arranged. Unfortunately, no masters are available this Saturday.'

Basil's mouth dropped ajar. 'Why, I—why, Doctor Bacon, I know two parties that are going. Couldn't I go with one of them?'

Doctor Bacon ran through all his papers very quickly. 'Unfortunately, one is composed of slightly older boys and the other group made arrangements some weeks ago.'

'How about the party that's going to the *Quaker Girl* with Mr Dunn?'

'It's that party I speak of. They feel that the arrangements are complete and they have purchased seats together.'

Suddenly Basil understood. At the look in his eye Doctor Bacon went on hurriedly:

'There's perhaps one thing I can do. Of course there must be several boys in the party so that the expenses of the master can be divided up among all. If you can find two other boys who would like to make up a party, and let me have their names by five o'clock, I'll send Mr Rooney with you.'

'Thank you,' Basil said.

Doctor Bacon hesitated. Beneath the cynical incrustations of many years an instinct stirred to look into the unusual case of this boy and find out what made him the most detested boy in school. Among boys and masters there seemed to exist an extraordinary hostility towards him, and though Doctor Bacon had dealt with many sorts of schoolboy crimes, he had neither by himself nor with the aid of trusted sixth-formers been able to lay his hands on its underlying cause. It was probably no single thing, but a combination of things; it was most probably one of those intangible questions of personality. Yet he remembered that when he first saw Basil he had considered him unusually prepossessing.

He sighed. Sometimes these things worked themselves out. He wasn't one to rush in clumsily. 'Let us have a better report to send home next month, Basil.'

'Yes, sir.'

Basil ran quickly downstairs to the recreation room. It was Wednesday and most of the boys had already gone into the village of Eastchester, whither Basil, who was still on bounds, was forbidden to follow. When he looked at those still scattered about the pool tables and piano, he saw that it was going to be difficult to get anyone to go with him at all. For Basil was quite conscious that he was the most unpopular boy at school.

It had begun almost immediately. One day, less than a fortnight after he came, a crowd of the smaller boys, perhaps urged on to it, gathered suddenly around him and began calling him Bossy. Within the next week he had two fights, and both times the crowd was vehemently and eloquently with the other boy. Soon after, when he was merely shoving indiscriminately, like everyone else, to get into the dining-room, Carver, the captain of the football team, turned about and, seizing him by the back of the neck, held him and dressed him down savagely. He joined a group innocently at the piano and was told, 'Go on away. We don't want you around.'

After a month he began to realize the full extent of his unpopularity. It shocked him. One day after a particularly bitter humiliation he went up to his room and cried. He tried to keep out of the way for a while, but it didn't help. He was accused of sneaking off here and there, as if bent on a series of nefarious errands. Puzzled and wretched, he looked at his face in the glass, trying to discover there the secret of their dislike—in the expression of his eyes, his smile.

He saw now that in certain ways he had erred at the outset—he had boasted, he had been considered yellow at football, he had pointed out people's mistakes to them, he had showed off his rather extraordinary fund of general information in class. But he had tried to do better and couldn't understand his failure to atone. It must be too late. He was queered forever.

He had, indeed, become the scapegoat, the immediate villain, the sponge which absorbed all malice and irritability abroad—just as the most frightened person in a party seems to absorb all the others' fear, seems to be afraid for them all. His situation was not helped by the fact, obvious to all, that the supreme self-confidence with which he had come to St Regis in September was thoroughly broken. Boys taunted him with impunity who would not have dared raise their voices to him several months before.

This trip to New York had come to mean everything to him—surcease from the misery of his daily life as well as a glimpse into the long-waited heaven of romance. Its postponement for week after week due to his sins—he was constantly caught reading after lights, for example, driven by his wretchedness into such vicarious escapes from reality—had deepened his longing until it was a burning hunger. It was unbearable that he should not go, and he told over the short list of those whom he might get to accompany him. The possibilities were Fat Gaspar, Treadway, and Bugs Brown. A quick journey to their rooms showed that they had all availed them-selves of the Wednesday permission to go into Eastchester for the afternoon.

Basil did not hesitate. He had until five o'clock and his only chance was to go after them. It was not the first time he had broken bounds, though the last attempt had ended in disaster and an extension of his confinement. In his room, he put on a heavy sweater—an overcoat was a betrayal of intent—replaced his jacket over it and hid a cap in his back pocket. Then he went downstairs and with an elaborately careless whistle struck out across the lawn for the gymnasium. Once there, he stood for a while as if looking in the windows, first the one close to the walk, then one near the corner of the building. From here he moved quickly, but not too quickly, into a grove of lilacs. Then he dashed around the corner, down a long stretch of lawn that was blind from all windows and, parting the strands of a wire fence, crawled through and stood upon the grounds of a neighbouring estate. For the moment he was free. He put on his cap against the chilly November wind, and set out along the half-mile road to town.

Eastchester was a suburban farming community, with a small shoe factory. The institutions which pandered to the factory workers were the ones patronized by the boys

—a movie house, a quick-lunch wagon on wheels known as the Dog and the Bostonian Candy Kitchen. Basil tried the Dog first and happened immediately upon a prospect.

This was Bugs Brown, a hysterical boy, subject to fits and strenuously avoided. Years later he became a brilliant lawyer, but at that time he was considered by the boys of St Regis to be a typical lunatic because of his peculiar series of sounds with which he assuaged his nervousness all day long.

He consorted with boys younger than himself, who were without the prejudices of their elders, and was in the company of several when Basil came in.

'Who-ee!' he cried. 'Ee-ee-ee!' He put his hand over his mouth and bounced it quickly, making a wah-wah-wah sound. 'It's Bossy Lee! It's Bossy Lee! It's Boss-Boss-Boss-Boss-Bossy Lee!'

'Wait a minute, Bugs,' said Basil anxiously, half afraid that Bugs would go finally crazy before he could persuade him to come to town. 'Say, Bugs, listen. Don't, Bugs—wait a minute. Can you come up to New York Saturday afternoon?'

'Whe-ee-ee!' cried Bugs to Basil's distress. 'Whee-ee-ee!'

'Honestly, Bugs, tell me, can you? We could go up together if you could go.'

'I've got to see a doctor,' said Bugs, suddenly calm. 'He wants to see how crazy I am.'

'Can't you have him see about it some other day?' said Basil without humour.

'Whee-ee-ee!' cried Bugs.

'All right then,' said Basil hastily. 'Have you seen Fat Gaspar in town?'

Bugs was lost in shrill noise, but someone had seen Fat: Basil was directed to the Bostonian Candy Kitchen.

This was a gaudy paradise of cheap sugar. Its odour, heavy and sickly and calculated to bring out a sticky sweat upon an adult's palms, hung suffocatingly over the whole vicinity and met one like a strong moral dissuasion at the door. Inside, beneath a pattern of flies, material as black point lace, a line of boys sat eating heavy dinners of banana splits, maple nut, and chocolate marshmallow nut sundaes. Basil found Fat Gaspar at a table on the side.

Fat Gaspar was at once Basil's most unlikely and most ambitious quest. He was considered a nice fellow—in fact he was so pleasant that he had been courteous to Basil and had spoken to him politely all fall. Basil realized that he was like that to everyone, yet it was just possible that Fat liked him, as people used to in the past, and he was driven desperately to take a chance. But it was undoubtedly a presumption, and as he approached the table and saw the stiffened faces which the other two boys turned towards him, Basil's hope diminished.

'Say, Fat—' he said, and hesitated. Then he burst forth suddenly. 'I'm on bounds, but I ran off because I had to see you. Doctor Bacon told me I could go to New York Saturday if I could get two other boys to go. I asked Bugs Brown and he couldn't go, and I thought I'd ask you.'

He broke off, furiously embarrassed, and waited. Suddenly the two boys with Fat burst into a shout of laughter.

'Bugs wasn't crazy enough!'

Fat Gaspar hesitated. He couldn't go to New York Saturday and ordinarily he would have refused without offending. He had nothing against Basil; nor, indeed, against anybody; but boys have only a certain resistance to public opinion and he was influenced by the contemptuous laughter of the others.

'I don't want to go,' he said indifferently. 'Why do you want to ask *me*?'

Then, half in shame, he gave a deprecatory little laugh and bent over his ice cream.

'I just thought I'd ask you,' said Basil.

Turning quickly away, he went to the counter and in a hollow and unfamiliar voice ordered a strawberry

3+s.f.6

sundae. He ate it mechanically, hearing occasional whispers and snickers from the table behind. Still in a daze, he started to walk out without paying his check, but the clerk called him back and he was conscious of more derisive laughter.

For a moment he hesitated whether to go back to the table and hit one of those boys in the face, but he saw nothing to be gained. They would say the truth—that he had done it because he couldn't get anybody to go to New York. Clenching his fists with impotent rage, he walked from the store.

He came immediately upon his third prospect, Treadway. Treadway had entered St Regis late in the year and had been put in to room with Basil the week before. The fact that Treadway hadn't witnessed his humiliations of the autumn encouraged Basil to behave naturally towards him, and their relations had been, if not intimate, at least tranquil.

'Hey, Treadway,' he called, still excited from the affair in the Bostonian, 'can you come up to New York to a show Saturday afternoon?'

He stopped, realizing that Treadway was in the company of Brick Wales, a boy he had had a fight with and one of his bitterest enemies. Looking from one to the other. Basil saw a look of impatience in Treadway's face and a faraway expression in Brick Wales's, and he realized what must have been happening. Treadway, making his way into the life of the school, had just been enlightened as to the status of his roommate. Like Fat Gaspar, rather than acknowledge himself eligible to such an intimate request, he preferred to cut their friendly relations short.

'Not on your life,' he said briefly. 'So long.' The two walked past him into the Candy Kitchen.

Had these slights, so much the bitterer for their lack of passion, been visited upon Basil in September, they would have been unbearable. But since then he had developed a shell of hardness which, while it did not add to his attractiveness, spared him certain delicacies of torture.

In misery enough, and despair and self-pity, he went the other way along the street for a little distance until he could control the violent contortions of his face. Then, taking a roundabout route, he started back to school.

He reached the adjoining estate, intending to go back the way he had come. Half-way through a hedge, he heard footsteps approaching along the sidewalk and stood motionless, fearing the proximity of masters. Their voices grew nearer and louder; before he knew it he was listening with horrified fascination:

'—so, after he tried Bugs Brown, the poor nut asked Fat Gaspar to go with him and Fat said, "What do you ask me for?" It serves him right if he couldn't get anybody at all.'

It was the dismal but triumphant voice of Lewis Crum.

III

Up in his room, Basil found a package lying on his bed. He knew its contents and for a long time he had been eagerly expecting it, but such was his depression that he opened it listlessly. It was a series of eight colour reproductions of Harrison Fisher girls 'on glossy paper, without printing or advertising matter and suitable for framing.'

The pictures were named Dora, Marguerite, Babette, Lucille, Gretchen, Rose, Katherine, and Mina. Two of them—Marguerite and Rose—Basil looked at, slowly tore up, and dropped in the waste-basket, as one who disposes of the inferior pups from a litter. The other six he pinned at intervals around the room. Then he lay down on his bed and regarded them.

Dora, Lucille, and Katherine were blonde; Gretchen was medium; Babette and Mina were dark. After a few minutes, he found that he was looking oftenest at Dora and Babette and, to a lesser extent, at Gretchen, though the latter's Dutch cap seemed unromantic and precluded the element of mystery. Babette, a dark little violet-eyed beauty in a tight-fitting hat, attracted him most; his eyes came to rest on her at last.

'Babette,' he whispered to himself—'beautiful Babette.'

The sound of the word, so melancholy and suggestive, like 'Vilia' or 'I'm happy at Maxim's' on the phonograph, softened him and, turning over on his face, he sobbed into the pillow. He took hold of the bed rails over his head and, sobbing and straining, began to talk to himself brokenly—how he hated them and whom he hated—he listed a dozen—and what he would do to them when he was great and powerful. In previous moments like these he had always rewarded Fat Gaspar for his kindness, but now he was like the rest. Basil set upon him, pummelling him unmercifully, or laughed sneeringly when he passed him blind and begging on the street.

He controlled himself as he heard Treadway come in, but did not move or speak. He listened as the other moved about the room, and after a while became conscious that there was an unusual opening of closets and bureau drawers. Basil turned over, his arm concealing his tear-stained face. Treadway had an armful of shirts in his hand.

'What are you doing?' Basil demanded.

His room-mate looked at him stonily. 'I'm moving in with Wales,' he said.

'Oh!'

Treadway went on with his packing. He carried out a suitcase full, then another, took down some pennants and dragged his trunk into the hall. Basil watched him bundle his toilet things into a towel and take one last survey about the room's new barrenness to see if there was anything forgotten.

'Good-bye,' he said to Basil, without a ripple of expression on his face.

'Good-bye.'

Treadway went out. Basil turned over once more and choked into the pillow.

'Oh, poor Babette!' he cried huskily. 'Poor little Babette! Poor little Babette!'

Babette, svelte and piquante, looked down at him coquettishly from the wall.

IV

Doctor Bacon, sensing Basil's predicament and perhaps the extremity of his misery, arranged it that he should go into New York, after all. He went in the company of Mr Rooney, the football coach and history teacher. At twenty Mr Rooney had hesitated for some time between joining the police force and having his way paid through a small New England college; in fact he was a hard specimen and Doctor Bacon was planning to get rid of him at Christmas. Mr Rooney's contempt for Basil was founded on the latter's ambiguous and unreliable conduct on the football field during the past season—he had consented to take him to New York for reasons of his own.

Basil sat meekly beside him on the train, glancing past Mr Rooney's bulky body at the Sound and the fallow fields of Westchester County. Mr Rooney finished his newspaper, folded it up and sank into a moody silence. He had eaten a large breakfast and the exigencies of time had not allowed him to work it off with exercise. He remembered that Basil was a fresh boy, and it was time he did something fresh and could be called to account. This reproachless silence annoyed him.

'Lee,' he said suddenly, with a thinly assumed air of friendly interest, 'why don't you get wise to yourself?'

'What, sir?' Basil was startled from his excited trance of this morning.

'I said why don't you get wise to yourself?' said Mr Rooney in a somewhat violent tone. 'Do you want to be the butt of the school all your time here?'

'No, I don't,' Basil was chilled. Couldn't all this be left behind for just one day?

'You oughtn't to get so fresh all the time. A couple of times in history class I could just about have broken your neck.' Basil could think of no appropriate answer. 'Then out playing football,' continued Mr Rooney, '—you didn't have any nerve. You could play better than a lot of 'em when you wanted, like that day against the Pomfret seconds, but you lost your nerve.'

'I shouldn't have tried for the second team,' said Basil. 'I was too light. I should have stayed on the third.'

'You were yellow, that was all the trouble. You ought to get wise to yourself. In class, you're always thinking of something else. If you don't study, you'll never get to college.'

'I'm the youngest boy in the fifth form,' Basil said rashly.

'You think you're pretty bright, don't you?' He eyed Basil ferociously. Then something seemed to occur to him that changed his attitude and they rode for a while in silence. When the train began to run through the thickly clustered communities near New York, he spoke again in a milder voice and with an air of having considered the matter for a long time:

'Lee, I'm going to trust you.'

'Yes, sir.'

'You go and get some lunch and then go on to your show. I've got some business of my own I got to attend to, and when I've finished I'll try to get to the show. If I can't, I'll anyhow meet you outside.' Basil's heart leaped up. 'Yes, sir.'

'I don't want you to open your mouth about this at school—I mean, about me doing some business of my own.'

'No, sir.'

'We'll see if you can keep your mouth shut for once,' he said, making it fun. Then he added, on a note of moral sternness, 'And no drinks, you understand that?'

'Oh, no, sir!' The idea shocked Basil. He had never tasted a drink, nor even contemplated the possibility, save the intangible and non-alcoholic champagne of his café dreams.

On the advice of Mr Rooney he went for luncheon to the Manhattan Hotel, near the station, where he ordered a club sandwich, French fried potatoes, and a chocolate parfait. Out of the corner of his eye he watched the non-chalant, debonair, blasé New Yorkers at neighbouring tables, investing them with a romance by which these possible fellow citizens of his from the Middle West lost nothing. School had fallen from him like a burden; it was no more than an unheeded clamour, faint and far away. He even delayed opening the letter from the morning's mail which he found in his pocket, because it was addressed to him at school.

He wanted another chocolate parfait, but being reluctant to bother the busy waiter any more, he opened the letter and spread it before him instead. It was from his mother:

'DEAR BASIL: This is written in great haste, as I didn't want to frighten you by telegraphing. Grandfather is going abroad to take the waters and he wants you and me to come too. The idea is that you'll go to school at Grenoble or Montreux for the rest of the year and learn the languages and we'll be close by. That is, if you want to. I know how you like St Regis and playing football and baseball, and of course there would be none of that; but on the other hand, it would be a nice change, even if it postponed your entering Yale by an extra year. So, as usual, I want you to do just as you like. We will be leaving home almost as soon as you get this and will come to the Waldorf in New York, where you can come in and see us for a few days, even if you decide to stay. Think it over, dear.

'With love to my dearest boy,
'MOTHER.'

Basil got up from his chair with a dim idea of walking over to the Waldorf and having himself locked up safely until his mother came. Then, impelled to some gesture, he raised his voice and in one of his first basso notes called boomingly and without reticence for the waiter. No more St Regis! No more St Regis! He was almost strangling with happiness.

'Oh, gosh!' he cried to himself. 'Oh, golly! Oh, gosh! Oh, gosh!' No more Doctor Bacon and Mr Rooney and Brick Wales and Fat Gaspar. No more Bugs Brown and on bounds and being called Bossy. He need no longer hate them, for they were impotent shadows in the stationary world that he was sliding away from, sliding past, waving his hand. 'Good-bye!' he pitied them. 'Good-bye!'

It required the din of Forty-second Street to sober his maudlin joy. With his hand on his purse to guard against the omnipresent pickpocket, he moved cautiously toward Broadway. What a day! He would tell Mr Rooney —Why, he needn't ever go back! Or perhaps it would be better to go back and let them know what he was going to do, while they went on and on in the dismal, dreary round of school.

He found the theatre and entered the lobby with its powdery feminine atmosphere of a matinée. As he took out his ticket, his gaze was caught and held by a sculptured profile a few feet away. It was that of a well-built blond young man of about twenty with a strong chin and direct grey eyes. Basil's brain spun wildly for a moment and then came to rest upon a name—more than a name—upon a legend, a sign in the sky. What a day! He had never seen the young man before, but from a thousand pictures he knew beyond the possibility of a doubt that it was Ted Fay, the Yale football captain, who had almost single-handed beaten Harvard and Princeton last fall. Basil felt a sort of exquisite pain. The profile turned away; the crowd revolved; the hero disappeared.

But Basil would know all through the next hours that Ted Fay was here too.

In the rustling, whispering, sweet-smelling darkness of the theatre he read the programme. It was the show of all shows that he wanted to see, and until the curtain actually rose the programme itself had a curious sacredness—a prototype of the thing itself. But when the curtain rose it became waste paper to be dropped carelessly to the floor.

ACT I. *The Village Green of a Small Town near New York*

It was too bright and blinding to comprehend all at once, and it went so fast that from the very first Basil felt he had missed things; he would make his mother take him again when she came—next week—tomorrow.

An hour passed. It was very sad at this point—a sort of gay sadness, but sad. The girl—the man. What kept them apart even now? Oh, those tragic errors and misconceptions. So sad. Couldn't they look into each other's eyes and *see*?

In a blaze of light and sound, of resolution, anticipation and imminent trouble, the act was over.

He went out. He looked for Ted Fay and thought he saw him leaning rather moodily on the plush wall at the rear of the theatre, but he could not be sure. He bought cigarettes and lit one, but fancying at the first puff he heard a blare of music he rushed back inside.

ACT II. *The Foyer of the Hotel Astor*

Yes, she was, indeed, like a song—a Beautiful Rose of the Night. The waltz buoyed her up, brought her with it to a point of aching beauty and then let her slide back to life across its last bars as a leaf slants to earth across the air. The high life of New York! Who could blame her if she was carried away by the glitter of it

3*

all, vanishing into the bright morning of the amber
window borders or into distant and entrancing music as
the door opened and closed that led to the ballroom?
The toast of the shining town.

Half an hour passed. Her true love brought her roses
like herself and she threw them scornfully at his feet.
She laughed and turned to the other, and danced—
danced madly, wildly. Wait! That delicate treble among
the thin horns, the low curving note from the great
strings. There it was again, poignant and aching, sweeping like a great gust of emotion across the stage, catching
her again like a leaf helpless in the wind:

> 'Rose—Rose—Rose of the night,
> When the spring moon is bright you'll be fair—'

A few minutes later, feeling oddly shaken and exalted,
Basil drifted outside with the crowd. The first thing
upon which his eyes fell was the almost forgotten and
now curiously metamorphosed spectre of Mr Rooney.

Mr Rooney had, in fact, gone a little to pieces. He
was, to begin with, wearing a different and much smaller
hat than when he left Basil at noon. Secondly, his face
had lost its somewhat gross aspect and turned a pure and
even delicate white, and he was wearing his necktie and
even portions of his shirt on the outside of his unaccount-
ably wringing-wet overcoat. How, in the short space of
four hours, Mr Rooney had got himself in such shape is
explicable only by the pressure of confinement in a boys'
school upon a fiery outdoor spirit. Mr Rooney was born
to toil under the clear light of heaven and, perhaps half-
consciously, he was headed toward his inevitable destiny.

'Lee,' he said dimly, 'you ought to get wise to y'self.
I'm going to put you wise y'self.'

To avoid the ominous possibility of being put wise to
himself in the lobby, Basil uneasily changed the subject.

'Aren't you coming to the show?' he asked, flattering
Mr Rooney by implying that he was in any condition to
come to the show. 'It's a wonderful show.'

Mr Rooney took off his hat, displaying wringing-wet matted hair. A picture of reality momentarily struggled for development in the back of his brain.

'We got to get back to school,' he said in a sombre and unconvinced voice.

'But there's another act,' protested Basil in horror. 'I've got to stay for the last act.'

Swaying, Mr Rooney looked at Basil, dimly realizing that he had put himself in the hollow of this boy's hand.

'All righ',' he admitted. 'I'm going to get somethin' to eat. I'll wait for you next door.'

He turned abruptly, reeled a dozen steps, and curved dizzily into a bar adjoining the theatre. Considerably shaken, Basil went back inside.

ACT III. *The Roof Garden of Mr Van Astor's House.*
Night

Half an hour passed. Everthing was going to be all right, after all. The comedian was at his best now, with the glad appropriateness of laughter after tears, and there was a promise of felicity in the bright tropical sky. One lovely plaintive duet, and then abruptly the long moment of incomparable beauty was over.

Basil went into the lobby and stood in thought while the crowd passed out. His mother's letter and the show had cleared his mind of bitterness and vindictiveness— he was his old self and he wanted to do the right thing. He wondered if it was the right thing to get Mr Rooney back to school. He walked towards the saloon, slowed up as he came to it and, gingerly opening the swinging door, took a quick peer inside. He saw only that Mr Rooney was not one of those drinking at the bar. He walked down the street a little way, came back and tried again. It was as if he thought the doors were teeth to bite him, for he had the old-fashioned Middle-Western boy's horror of the saloon. The third time he was successful. Mr Rooney was sound asleep at a table in the back of the room.

Outside again Basil walked up and down, considering. He would give Mr Rooney half an hour. If, at the end of that time, he had not come out, he would go back to school. After all, Mr Rooney had laid for him ever since football season—Basil was simply washing his hands of the whole affair, as in a day or so he would wash his hands of school.

He had made several turns up and down, when, glancing up an alley that ran beside the theatre his eye was caught by the sign, Stage Entrance. He could watch the actors come forth.

He waited. Women streamed by him, but those were the days before Glorification and he took these drab people for wardrobe women or something. Then suddenly a girl came out and with her a man, and Basil turned and ran a few steps up the street as if afraid they would recognize him—and ran back, breathing as if with a heart attack—for the girl, a radiant little beauty of nineteen, was Her and the young man by her side was Ted Fay.

Arm in arm, they walked past him, and irresistibly Basil followed. As they walked, she leaned towards Ted Fay in a way that gave them a fascinating air of intimacy. They crossed Broadway and turned into the Knickerbocker Hotel, and twenty feet behind them Basil followed, in time to see them go into a long room set for afternoon tea. They sat at a table for two, spoke vaguely to a waiter, and then, alone at last, bent eagerly towards each other. Basil saw that Ted Fay was holding her gloved hand.

The tea room was separated only by a hedge of potted firs from the main corridor. Basil went along this to a lounge which was almost up against their table and sat down.

Her voice was low and faltering, less certain than it had been in the play, and very sad: 'Of course I do, Ted.' For a long time, as their conversation continued, she repeated 'Of course I do' or 'But I do, Ted.' Ted Fay's remarks were too low for Basil to hear.

'——says next month, and he won't be put off any more. . . . I do in a way, Ted. It's hard to explain, but he's done everything for mother and me. . . . There's no use kidding myself. It was a foolproof part and any girl he gave it to was made right then and there. . . . He's been awfully thoughtful. He's done everything for me.'

Basil's ears were sharpened by the intensity of his emotion; now he could hear Ted Fay's voice too:

'And you say you love me.'

'But don't you see I promised to marry him more than a year ago.'

'Tell him the truth—that you love me. Ask him to let you off.'

'This isn't musical comedy, Ted.'

'That was a mean one,' he said bitterly.

'I'm sorry, dear, Ted darling, but you're driving me crazy going on this way. You're making it so hard for me.'

'I'm going to leave New Haven, anyhow.'

'No, you're not. You're going to stay and play baseball this spring. Why, you're an ideal to all those boys! Why, if you——'

He laughed shortly. 'You're a fine one to talk about ideals.'

'Why not? I'm living up to my responsibility to Beltzman; you've got to make up your mind just like I have —that we can't have each other.'

'Jerry! Think what you're doing! All my life, whenever I hear that waltz——'

Basil got to his feet and hurried down the corridor, through the lobby and out of the hotel. He was in a state of wild emotional confusion. He did not understand all he had heard, but from his clandestine glimpse into the privacy of these two, with all the world that his short experience could conceive of at their feet, he had gathered that life for everybody was a struggle, sometimes magnificent from a distance, but always difficult and surprisingly simple and a little sad.

They would go on. Ted Fay would go back to Yale, put her picture in his bureau drawer and knock out home runs with the bases full this spring—at 8:30 the curtain would go up and She would miss something warm and young out of her life, something she had had this afternoon.

It was dark outside and Broadway was a blazing forest fire as Basil walked slowly along towards the point of brightest light. He looked up at the great intersecting planes of radiance with a vague sense of approval and possession. He would see it a lot now, lay his restless heart upon this greater restlessness of a nation—he would come whenever he could get off from school.

But that was all changed—he was going to Europe. Suddenly Basil realized that he wasn't going to Europe. He could not forgo the moulding of his own destiny just to alleviate a few months of pain. The conquest of the successive worlds of school, college and New York— why, that was his true dream that he had carried from boyhood into adolescence, and because of the jeers of a few boys he had been about to abandon it and run ignominiously up a back alley! He shivered violently, like a dog coming out of the water, and simultaneously he was reminded of Mr Rooney.

A few minutes later he walked into the bar, past the quizzical eyes of the bartender and up to the table where Mr Rooney still sat asleep. Basil shook him gently, then firmly. Mr Rooney stirred and perceived Basil.

'G'wise to yourself,' he muttered drowsily. 'G'wise to yourself an' let me alone.'

'I am wise to myself,' said Basil. 'Honest, I am wise to myself, Mr Rooney. You got to come with me into the washroom and get cleaned up, and then you can sleep on the train again, Mr Rooney. Come on, Mr Rooney, please——'

V

It was a long hard time. Basil got on bounds again in December and wasn't free again until March. An indulgent mother had given him no habits of work and this was almost beyond the power of anything but life itself to remedy, but he made numberless new starts and failed and tried again.

He made friends with a new boy named Maplewood after Christmas, but they had a silly quarrel; and through the winter term, when a boys' school is shut in with itself and only partly assuaged from its natural savagery by indoor sports, Basil was snubbed and slighted a good deal for his real and imaginary sins, and he was much alone. But on the other hand, there was Ted Fay, and Rose of the Night on the phonograph—'All my life whenever I hear that waltz'—and the remembered lights of New York, and the thought of what he was going to do in football next autumn and the glamorous mirage of Yale and the hope of spring in the air.

Fat Gaspar and a few others were nice to him now. Once when he and Fat walked home together by accident from downtown they had a long talk about actresses— a talk that Basil was wise enough not to presume upon afterwards. The smaller boys suddenly decided that they approved of him, and a master who had hitherto disliked him put his hand on his shoulder walking to a class one day. They would all forget eventually—maybe during the summer. There would be new fresh boys in September; he would have a clean start next year.

One afternoon in February, playing basketball, a great thing happened. He and Brick Wales were at forward on the second team and in the fury of the scrimmage the gymnasium echoed with sharp slapping contacts and shrill cries.

'Here yar!'
'Bill! Bill!'

Basil had dribbled the ball down the court and Brick Wales, free, was crying for it.

'Here yar! Lee! Hey! Lee-y!'

Lee-y!

Basil flushed and made a poor pass. He had been called by a nickname. It was a poor makeshift, but it was something more than the stark bareness of his surname or a term of derision. Brick Wales went on playing, unconscious that he had done anything in particular or that he had contributed to the events by which another boy was saved from the army of the bitter, the selfish, the neurasthenic and the unhappy. It isn't given to us to know those rare moments when people are wide open and the lightest touch can wither or heal. A moment too late and we can never reach them any more in this world. They will not be cured by our most efficacious drugs or slain with our sharpest swords.

Lee-y! It could scarcely be pronounced. But Basil took it to bed with him that night, and thinking of it, holding it to him happily to the last, fell easily to sleep.

BASIL
HE THINKS HE'S WONDERFUL
[1928]

AFTER the college-board examinations in June, Basil Duke Lee and five other boys from St Regis School boarded the train for the West. Two got out at Pittsburgh, one slanted south towards St Louis and two stayed in Chicago; from then on Basil was alone. It was the first time in his life that he had ever felt the need of tranquillity, but now he took long breaths of it; for, though things had gone better towards the end, he had had an unhappy year at school.

He wore one of those extremely flat derbies in vogue during the twelfth year of the century, and a blue business suit become a little too short for his constantly lengthening body. Within he was by turns a disembodied spirit, almost unconscious of his person and moving in a mist of impressions and emotions, and a fiercely competitive individual trying desperately to control the rush of events that were the steps in his own evolution from child to man. He believed that everything was a matter of effort —the current principle of American education—and his fantastic ambition was continually leading him to expect too much. He wanted to be a great athlete, popular, brilliant and always happy. During this year at school, where he had been punished for his 'freshness,' for fifteen years of thorough spoiling at home, he had grown uselessly introspective, and this interfered with that observation of others which is the beginning of wisdom. It was apparent that before he obtained much success in dealing with the world he would know that he'd been in a fight.

He spent the afternoon in Chicago, walking the streets and avoiding members of the underworld. He bought a

detective story called 'In the Dead of Night,' and at
five o'clock recovered his suitcase from the station check
room and boarded the Chicago, Milwaukee and St Paul.
Immediately he encountered a contemporary, also bound
home from school.

Margaret Torrence was fourteen; a serious girl, considered beautiful by a sort of tradition, for she had been
beautiful as a little girl. A year and a half before, after
a breathless struggle, Basil had succeeded in kissing her
on the forehead. They met now with extraordinary joy;
for a moment each of them to the other represented home,
the blue skies of the past, the summer afternoons ahead.

He sat with Margaret and her mother in the dining-
car that night. Margaret saw that he was no longer the
ultraconfident boy of a year before; his brightness was
subdued, and the air of consideration in his face—a mark
of his recent discovery that others had wills as strong
as his, and more power—appeared to Margaret as a
charming sadness. The spell of peace after a struggle
was still upon him. Margaret had always liked him—
she was of the grave, conscientious type who sometimes
loved him and whose love he could never return—and
now she could scarcely wait to tell people how attractive
he had grown.

After dinner they went back to the observation car
and sat on the deserted rear platform while the train
pulled them visibly westward between the dark wide
farms. They talked of people they knew, of where they
had gone for Easter vacation, of the plays they had seen
in New York.

'Basil, we're going to get an automobile,' she said,
'and I'm going to learn to drive.'

'That's fine.' He wondered if his grandfather would
let him drive the electric sometimes this summer.

The light from inside the car fell on her young face,
and he spoke impetuously, borne on by the rush of
happiness that he was going home: 'You know something?
You know you're the prettiest girl in the city?'

At the moment when the remark blurred with the thrilling night in Margaret's heart, Mrs Torrence appeared to fetch her to bed.

Basil sat alone on the platform for a while, scarcely realizing that she was gone, at peace with himself for another hour and content that everything should remain patternless and shapeless until tomorrow.

II

Fifteen is of all ages the most difficult to locate—to put one's fingers on and say, 'That's the way I was.' The melancholy Jaques does not select it for mention, and all one can know is that somewhere between thirteen, boyhood's majority, and seventeen, when one is a sort of counterfeit young man, there is a time when youth fluctuates hourly between one world and another—pushed ceaselessly forward into unprecedented experiences and vainly trying to struggle back to the days when nothing had to be paid for. Fortunately none of our contemporaries remember much more than we do of how we behaved in those days; nevertheless the curtain is about to be drawn aside for an inspection of Basil's madness that summer.

To begin with, Margaret Torrence, in one of those moods of idealism which overcome the most matter-of-fact girls, gave it as her rapt opinion that Basil was wonderful. Having practised believing things all year at school, and having nothing much to believe at that moment, her friends accepted the fact. Basil suddenly became a legend. There were outbreaks of giggling when girls encountered him on the street, but he suspected nothing at all.

One night, when he had been home a week, he and Riply Buckner went on to an after-dinner gathering on Imogene Bissel's veranda. As they came up the walk Margaret and two other girls suddenly clung together, whispered convulsively and pursued one another around the yard, uttering strange cries—an inexplicable business that ended only when Gladys Van Schellinger, tenderly and impressively accompanied by her mother's maid, arrived in a limousine.

All of them were a little strange to one another. Those who had been East at school felt a certain superiority, which, however, was more than counterbalanced by the fact that romantic pairings and quarrels and jealousies and adventures, of which they were lamentably ignorant, had gone on while they had been away.

After the ice cream at nine they sat together on the warm stone steps in a quiet confusion that was halfway between childish teasing and adolescent coquetry. Last year the boys would have ridden their bicycles around the yard; now they had all begun to wait for something to happen.

They knew it was going to happen, the plainest girls, the shyest boys; they had begun to associate with others the romantic world of summer night that pressed deeply and sweetly on their senses. Their voices drifted in a sort of broken harmony in to Mrs Bissel, who sat reading beside an open window.

'No, look out. You'll break it. Bay-zil!'

'Rip-lee!'

'Sure I did!'

Laughter.

> '—on Moonlight Bay
> We could hear their voices call——'

'Did you see——'

'Connie don't—don't! You tickle. Look out!'

Laughter.

'Going to the lake tomorrow?'

'Going Friday.'

'Elwood's home.'

'Is Elwood home?'

> '——you have broken my heart——'

'Look out now!'

'Look out!'

Basil sat beside Riply on the balustrade, listening to Joe Gorman singing. It was one of the griefs of his life that he could not sing 'so people could stand it,' and he conceived a sudden admiration for Joe Gorman, reading into his personality the thrilling clearness of those sounds that moved so confidently through the dark air.

They evoked for Basil a more dazzling night than this, and other more remote and enchanted girls. He was sorry when the voice died away, and there was a re-arranging of seats and a businesslike quiet—the ancient game of Truth had begun.

'What's your favourite colour, Bill?'

'Green,' supplies a friend.

'Sh-h-h! Let him alone.'

Bill says, 'Blue.'

'What's your favourite girl's name?'

'Mary,' says Bill.

'Mary Haupt! Bill's got a crush on Mary Haupt!'

She was a cross-eyed girl, a familiar personification of repulsiveness.

'Who would you rather kiss than anybody?'

Across the pause a snicker stabbed the darkness.

'My mother.'

'No, but what girl?'

'Nobody.'

'That's not fair. Forfeit! Come on, Margaret.'

'Tell the truth, Margaret.'

She told the truth and a moment later Basil looked down in surprise from his perch; he had just learned that he was her favourite boy.

'Oh, yes-s!' he exclaimed sceptically. 'Oh, yes-s! How about Hubert Blair?'

He renewed a casual struggle with Riply Buckner and presently they both fell off the balustrade. The game became an inquisition into Gladys Van Schellinger's carefully chaperoned heart.

'What's your favourite sport?'

'Croquet.'

The admission was greeted by a mild titter.

'Favourite boy?'

'Thurston Kohler.'

A murmur of disappointment.

'Who's he?'

'A boy in the East.'

This was manifestly an evasion.

'Who's your favourite boy here?'

Gladys hesitated. 'Basil,' she said at length.

The faces turned up to the balustrade this time were less teasing, less jocular. Basil depreciated the matter with 'Oh, yes-s! Sure! Oh, yes-s!' But he had a pleasant feeling of recognition, a familiar delight.

Imogene Bissel, a dark little beauty and the most popular girl in their crowd, took Gladys's place. The interlocutors were tired of gastronomic preferences—the first question went straight to the point.

'Imogene, have you ever kissed a boy?'

'No.' A cry of wild unbelief. 'I have not!' she declared indignantly.

'Well, have you ever been kissed?'

Pink but tranquil, she nodded, adding, 'I couldn't help it.'

'Who by?'

'I won't tell.'

'Oh-h-h! How about Hubert Blair?'

'What's your favourite book, Imogene?'

'*Beverly of Graustark.*'

'Favourite girl?'

'Passion Johnson.'

'Who's she?'

'Oh, just a girl at school.'

Mrs Bissel had fortunately left the window.

'Who's your favourite boy?'

Imogene answered steadily, 'Basil Lee.'

This time an impressed silence fell. Basil was not

surprised—we are never surprised at our own popularity —but he knew that these were not those ineffable girls, made up out of books and faces momentarily encountered, whose voices he had heard for a moment in Joe Gorman's song. And when, presently, the first telephone rang inside, calling a daughter home, and the girls, chattering like birds, piled all together into Gladys Van Schellinger's limousine, he lingered back in the shadow so as not to seem to be showing off. Then, perhaps because he nourished a vague idea that if he got to know Joe Gorman very well he would get to sing like him, he approached him and asked him to go to Lambert's for a soda.

Joe Gorman was a tall boy with white eyebrows and a stolid face who had only recently become one of their 'crowd.' He did not like Basil, who, he considered, had been 'stuck up' with him last year, but he was acquisitive of useful knowledge and he was momentarily overwhelmed by Basil's success with girls.

It was cheerful in Lambert's, with great moths batting against the screen door and languid couples in white dresses and light suits spread about the little tables. Over their sodas, Joe proposed that Basil come home with him to spend the night; Basil's permission was obtained over the telephone.

Passing from the gleaming store into the darkness, Basil was submerged in an unreality in which he seemed to see himself from the outside, and the pleasant events of the evening began to take on fresh importance.

Disarmed by Joe's hospitality, he began to discuss the matter.

'That was a funny thing that happened tonight,' he said, with a disparaging little laugh.

'What was?'

'Why, all those girls saying I was their favourite boy.' The remark jarred on Joe. 'It's a funny thing,' went on Basil. 'I was sort of unpopular at school for a while, because I was fresh, I guess. But the thing must be that some boys are popular with boys and some are popular with girls.'

He had put himself in Joe's hands, but he was unconscious of it; even Joe was only aware of a certain desire to change the subject.

'When I get my car,' suggested Joe, up in his room, 'we could take Imogene and Margaret and go for rides.'

'All right.'

'You could have Imogene and I'd take Margaret, or anybody I wanted. Of course I know they don't like me as well as they do you.'

'Sure they do. It's just because you haven't been in our crowd very long yet.'

Joe was sensitive on that point and the remark did not please him. But Basil continued: 'You ought to be more polite to the older people if you want to be popular. You didn't say how do you do to Mrs Bissel tonight.'

'I'm hungry,' said Joe quickly. 'Let's go down to the pantry and get something to eat.'

Clad only in their pyjamas, they went downstairs. Principally to dissuade Basil from pursuing the subject, Joe began to sing in a low voice:

> 'Oh, you beautiful doll,
> You great—big——'

But the evening, coming after the month of enforced humility at school, had been too much for Basil. He got a little awful. In the kitchen, under the impression that his advice had been asked, he broke out again:

'For instance, you oughtn't to wear those white ties. Nobody does that that goes East to school.' Joe, a little red, turned around from the ice box and Basil felt a slight misgiving. But he pursued with: 'For instance, you ought to get your family to send you East to school. It'd be a great thing for you. Especially if you want to go East to college, you ought to first go East to school. They take it out of you.'

Feeling that he had nothing special to be taken out

of him, Joe found the implication distasteful. Nor did
Basil appear to him at that moment to have been per-
fected by the process.

'Do you want cold chicken or cold ham?' They drew
up chairs to the kitchen table. 'Have some milk?'

'Thanks.'

Intoxicated by the three full meals he had had since
supper, Basil warmed to his subject. He built up Joe's
life for him little by little, transformed him radiantly
from what was little more than a Mid-western bumpkin
to an Easterner bursting with *savoir-faire* and irresistible
to girls. Going into the pantry to put away the milk,
Joe paused by the open window for a breath of quiet
air; Basil followed. 'The thing is if a boy doesn't get it
taken out of him at school, he gets it taken out of him
at college,' he was saying.

Moved by some desperate instinct, Joe opened the door
and stepped out onto the back porch. Basil followed. The
house abutted on the edge of the bluff occupied by the
residential section, and the two boys stood silent for a
moment, gazing at the scattered lights of the lower city.
Before the mystery of the unknown human life coursing
through the streets below, Basil felt the purport of his
words grow thin and pale.

He wondered suddenly what he had said and why it
had seemed important to him, and when Joe began to
sing again softly, the quiet mood of the early evening,
the side of him that was best, wisest and most enduring,
stole over him once more. The flattery, the vanity, the
fatuousness of the last hour moved off, and when he
spoke it was almost in a whisper:

'Let's walk around the block.'

The sidewalk was warm to their bare feet. It was only
midnight, but the square was deserted save for their
whitish figures, inconspicuous against the starry darkness.
They snorted with glee at their daring. Once a shadow,
with loud human shoes, crossed the street far ahead,

but the sound served only to increase their own un-
substantiality. Slipping quickly through the clearings
made by gas lamps among the trees, they rounded the
block, hurrying when they neared the Gorman house
as though they had been really lost in a mid-summer
night's dream.

Up in Joe's room, they lay awake in the darkness.

'I talked too much,' Basil thought. 'I probably sounded
pretty bossy and maybe I made him sort of mad. But
probably when we walked around the block he forgot
everything I said.'

Alas, Joe had forgotten nothing—except the advice by
which Basil had intended him to profit.

'I never saw anybody as stuck up,' he said to himself
wrathfully. 'He thinks he's wonderful. He thinks he's
so darn popular with girls.'

III

An element of vast importance had made its appearance
with the summer; suddenly the great thing in Basil's
crowd was to own an automobile. Fun no longer seemed
available save at great distances, at suburban lakes or
remote country clubs. Walking downtown ceased to be
a legitimate pastime. On the contrary, a single block
from one youth's house to another's must be navigated
in a car. Dependent groups formed around owners and
they began to wield what was, to Basil at least, a dis-
concerting power.

On the morning of a dance at the lake he called up
Riply Buckner.

'Hey, Rip, how you going out to Connie's tonight?'

'With Elwood Leaming.'

'Has he got a lot of room?'

Riply seemed somewhat embarrassed. 'Why, I don't
think he has. You see, he's taking Margaret Torrence
and I'm taking Imogene Bissel.'

'Oh!'

Basil frowned. He should have arranged all this a week ago. After a moment he called up Joe Gorman.

'Going to the Davies's tonight, Joe?'

'Why, yes.'

'Have you got room in your car—I mean, could I go with you?'

'Why, yes, I suppose so.'

There was a perceptible lack of warmth in his voice.

'Sure you got plenty of room?'

'Sure. We'll call for you quarter to eight.'

Basil began preparations at five. For the second time in his life he shaved, completing the operation by cutting a short straight line under his nose. It bled profusely, but on the advice of Hilda, the maid, he finally stanched the flow with little pieces of toilet paper. Quite a number of pieces were necessary; so, in order to facilitate breathing, he trimmed it down with a scissors, and with this somewhat awkward moustache of paper and gore clinging to his upper lip, wandered impatiently around the house.

At six he began working on it again, soaking off the tissue paper and dabbing at the persistently freshening crimson line. It dried at length, but when he rashly hailed his mother it opened once more and the tissue paper was called back into play.

At quarter to eight, dressed in blue coat and white flannels, he drew one last bar of powder across the blemish, dusted it carefully with his handkerchief and hurried out to Joe Gorman's car. Joe was driving in person, and in front with him were Lewis Crum and Hubert Blair. Basil got in the big rear seat alone and they drove without stopping out of the city onto the Black Bear Road, keeping their backs to him and talking in low voices together. He thought at first that they were going to pick up other boys; now he was shocked, and for a moment he considered getting out of the car, but this would imply that he was hurt. His spirit, and with it his face, hardened a little and he sat without speaking or being spoken to for the rest of the ride.

After half an hour the Davies's house, a huge rambling bungalow occupying a small peninsula in the lake, floated into sight. Lanterns outlined its shape and wavered in gleaming lines on the gold-and-rose coloured water, and as they came near, the low notes of bass horns and drums were blown towards them from the lawn.

Inside Basil looked about for Imogene. There was a crowd around her seeking dances, but she saw Basil; his heart bounded at her quick intimate smile.

'You can have the fourth, Basil, and the eleventh and the second extra. . . . How did you hurt your lip?'

'Cut it shaving,' he said hurriedly. 'How about supper?'

'Well, I have to have supper with Riply because he brought me.'

'No, you don't,' Basil assured her.

'Yes, she does,' insisted Riply, standing close at hand. 'Why don't you get your own girl for supper?'

—but Basil had no girl, though he was as yet unaware of the fact.

After the fourth dance, Basil led Imogene down to the end of the pier, where they found seats in a motor-boat.

'Now what?' she said.

He did not know. If he had really cared for her he would have known. When her hand rested on his knee for a moment he did not notice it. Instead, he talked. He told her how he had pitched on the second baseball team at school and had once beaten the first in a five-inning game. He told her that the thing was that some boys were popular with boys and some boys were popular with girls—he, for instance, was popular with girls. In short, he unloaded himself.

At length, feeling that he had perhaps dwelt dispro-portionately on himself, he told her suddenly that she was his favourite girl.

Imogene sat there, sighing a little in the moonlight. In another boat, lost in the darkness beyond the pier, sat a party of four. Joe Gorman was singing:

'My little love—
     —in honey man,
He sure has won my——'

'I thought you might want to know,' said Basil to
Imogene. 'I thought maybe you thought I liked somebody else. The truth game didn't get around to me the
other night.'

'What?' asked Imogene vaguely. She had forgotten the
other night, all nights except this, and she was thinking
of the magic in Joe Gorman's voice. She had the next
dance with him; he was going to teach her the words of
a new song. Basil was sort of peculiar, telling her all
this stuff. He was good-looking and attractive and all
that, but—she wanted the dance to be over. She wasn't
having any fun.

The music began inside—'Everybody's Doing It,'
played with many little nervous jerks on the violins.

'Oh, listen!' she cried, sitting up and snapping her
fingers. 'Do you know how to rag?'

'Listen, Imogene'—He half realized that something
had slipped away—'let's sit out this dance—you can tell
Joe you forgot.'

She rose quickly. 'Oh, no, I can't!'

Unwillingly Basil followed her inside. It had not gone
well—he had talked too much again. He waited moodily
for the eleventh dance so that he could behave differently.
He believed now that he was in love with Imogene. His
self-deception created a tightness in his throat, a counterfeit of longing and desire.

Before the eleventh dance he was aware that some party
was being organized from which he was purposely excluded. There were whisperings and arguings among some
of the boys, and unnatural silences when he came near. He
heard Joe Gorman say to Riply Buckner, 'We'll just be
gone three days. If Gladys can't go, why don't you ask
Connie? The chaperons'll—' he changed his sentence as

he saw Basil—'and we'll all go to Smith's for ice-cream soda.'

Later, Basil took Riply Buckner aside but failed to elicit any information: Riply had not forgotten Basil's attempt to rob him of Imogene tonight.

'It wasn't about anything,' he insisted. 'We're going to Smith's, honest. . . . How'd you cut your lip?'

'Cut it shaving.'

When his dance with Imogene came she was even vaguer than before, exchanging mysterious communications with various girls as they moved around the room, locked in the convulsive grip of the Grizzly Bear. He led her out to the boat again, but it was occupied, and they walked up and down the pier while he tried to talk to her and she hummed:

> 'My little lov-in honey man——'

'Imogene, listen. What I wanted to ask you when we were on the boat before was about the night we played Truth. Did you really mean what you said?'

'Oh, what do you want to talk about that silly game for?'

It had reached her ears, not once but several times, that Basil thought he was wonderful—news that was flying about with as much volatility as the rumour of his graces two weeks before. Imogene liked to agree with everyone—and she had agreed with several impassioned boys that Basil was terrible. And it was difficult not to dislike him for her own disloyalty.

But Basil thought that only ill luck ended the intermission before he could accomplish his purpose; though what he had wanted he had not known.

Finally, during the intermission, Margaret Torrence, whom he had neglected, told him the truth.

'Are you going on the touring party up to the St Croix River?' she asked. She knew he was not.

'What party?'

'Joe Gorman got it up. I'm going with Elwood Leaming.'

'No, I'm not going,' he said gruffly. 'I couldn't go.'

'Oh!'

'I don't like Joe Gorman.'

'I guess he doesn't like you much either.'

'Why? What did he say?'

'Oh, nothing.'

'But what? Tell me what he said.'

After a minute she told him, as if reluctantly: 'Well, he and Hubert Blair said you thought—you thought you were wonderful.' Her heart misgave her.

But she remembered he had asked her for only one dance. 'Joe said you told him that all the girls thought you were wonderful.'

'I never said anything like that,' said Basil indignantly, 'never!'

He understood—Joe Gorman had done it all, taken advantage of Basil's talking too much—an affliction which his real friends had always allowed for—in order to ruin him. The world was suddenly compact of villainy. He decided to go home.

In the coat room he was accosted by Bill Kampf: 'Hello, Basil, how did you hurt your lip?'

'Cut it shaving.'

'Say, are you going to this party they're getting up next week?'

'No.'

'Well, look, I've got a cousin from Chicago coming to stay with us and mother said I could have a boy out for the week-end. Her name is Minnie Bibble.'

'Minnie Bibble?' repeated Basil, vaguely revolted.

'I thought maybe you were going to that party, too, but Riply Buckner said to ask you and I thought——'

'I've got to stay home,' said Basil quickly.

'Oh, come on, Basil,' he pursued. 'It's only for two days, and she's a nice girl. You'd like her.'

'I don't know,' Basil considered. 'I'll tell you what

I'll do, Bill. I've got to get the street car home. I'll come out for the week-end if you'll take me over to Wildwood now in your car.'

'Sure I will.'

Basil walked out on the veranda and approached Connie Davies.

'Good-bye,' he said. Try as he might, his voice was stiff and proud. 'I had an awfully good time.'

'I'm sorry you're leaving so early, Basil.' But she said to herself: 'He's too stuck up to have a good time. He thinks he's wonderful.'

From the veranda he could hear Imogene's laughter down at the end of the pier. Silently he went down the steps and along the walk to meet Bill Kampf, giving strollers a wide berth as though he felt the sight of him would diminish their pleasure.

It had been an awful night.

Ten minutes later Bill dropped him beside the waiting trolley. A few last picnickers sauntered aboard and the car bobbed and clanged through the night towards St Paul.

Presently two young girls sitting opposite Basil began looking over at him and nudging each other, but he took no notice—he was thinking how sorry they would all be —Imogene and Margaret, Joe and Hubert and Riply.

'Look at him now!' they would say to themselves sorrowfully. 'President of the United States at twenty-five! Oh, if we only hadn't been so bad to him that night!'

He thought he was wonderful!

IV

Erminie Gilbert Labouisse Bibble was in exile. Her parents had brought her from New Orleans to Southampton in May, hoping that the active outdoor life proper to a girl of fifteen would take her thoughts from love.

But North or South, a storm of sapling arrows flew about her. She was 'engaged' before the first of June.

Let it not be gathered from the foregoing that the somewhat hard outlines of Miss Bibble at twenty had already begun to appear. She was of a radiant freshness; her head had reminded otherwise not illiterate young men of damp blue violets, pierced with blue windows that looked into a bright soul, with today's new roses showing through.

She was in exile. She was going to Glacier National Park to forget. It was written that in passage she would come to Basil as a sort of initiation, turning his eyes out from himself and giving him a first dazzling glimpse into the world of love.

She saw him first as a quiet handsome boy with an air of consideration in his face, which was the mark of his recent re-discovery that others had wills as strong as his, and more power. It appeared to Minnie—as a few months back it had appeared to Margaret Torrence, like a charming sadness. At dinner he was polite to Mrs Kampf in a courteous way that he had from his father, and he listened to Mr Bibble's discussion of the word 'Creole' with such evident interest and appreciation that Mr Bibble thought, 'Now here's a young boy with something *to* him.'

After dinner, Minnie, Basil and Bill rode into Black Bear village to the movies, and the slow diffusion of Minnie's charm and personality presently became the charm and personality of the affair itself.

It was thus that all Minnie's affairs for many years had a family likeness. She looked at Basil, a childish open look; then opened her eyes wider as if she had some sort of comic misgivings, and smiled—she smiled—

For all the candour of this smile, the effect—because of the special contours of Minnie's face and independent of her mood—was sparkling invitation. Whenever it appeared Basil seemed to be suddenly inflated and borne upward, a little farther each time, only to be set down

4+S.F. 6

when the smile had reached a point where it must become a grin, and chose instead to melt away. It was like a drug. In a little while he wanted nothing except to watch it with a vast buoyant delight.

Then he wanted to see how close he could get to it.

There is a certain stage of an affair between young people when the presence of a third party is a stimulant. Before the second day had well begun, before Minnie and Basil had progressed beyond the point of great gross compliments about each other's surpassing beauty and charm, both of them had begun to think about the time when they could get rid of their host, Bill Kampf.

In the late afternoon, when the first cool of the evening had come down and they were fresh and thin-feeling from swimming, they sat in a cushioned swing, piled high with pillows and shaded by the thick veranda vines; Basil put his arm around her and leaned towards her cheek and Minnie managed it that he touched her fresh lips instead. And he had always learned things quickly.

They sat there for an hour, while Bill's voice reached them, now from the pier, now from the hall above, now from the pagoda at the end of the garden, and three saddled horses chafed their bits in the stable and all around them the bees worked faithfully among the flowers. Then Minnie reached up to reality, and they allowed themselves to be found—

'Why, we were looking for you two.'

And Basil, by simply waving his arms and wishing, floated miraculously upstairs to brush his hair for dinner.

'She certainly is a wonderful girl. Oh, gosh, she certainly is a wonderful girl!'

He mustn't lose his head. At dinner and afterwards he listened with unwavering deferential attention while Mr Bibble talked of the boll weevil.

'But I'm boring you. You children want to go off by yourselves.'

'Not at all, Mr Bibble. I was very interested—honestly.'

'Well, you all go on and amuse yourselves. I didn't

realize time was getting on. Nowadays it's so seldom you meet a young man with good manners and good common sense in his head, that an old man like me is likely to go along forever.'

Bill walked down with Basil and Minnie to the end of the pier. 'Hope we'll have a good sailing tomorrow. Say, I've got to drive over to the village and get somebody for my crew. Do you want to come along?'

'I reckon I'll sit here for a while and then go to bed,' said Minnie.

'All right. You want to come, Basil?'

'Why—why, sure, if you want me, Bill.'

'You'll have to sit on a sail I'm taking over to be mended.'

'I don't want to crowd you.'

'You won't crowd me. I'll go get the car.'

When he had gone they looked at each other in despair. But he did not come back for an hour—something happened about the sail or the car that took a long time. There was only the threat, making everything more poignant and breathless, that at any minute he *would* be coming.

By and by they got into the motorboat and sat close together murmuring: 'This fall—' 'When you come to New Orleans—' 'When I go to Yale year after next—' 'When I come North to school—' 'When I get back from Glacier Park—' 'Kiss me once more.'. . . 'You're terrible. Do you know you're terrible?. . . You're absolutely terrible——'

The water lapped against the posts; sometimes the boat bumped gently on the pier; Basil undid one rope and pushed, so that they swung off and away from the pier, and became a little island in the night. . . .

. . . next morning, while he packed his bag, she opened the door of his room and stood beside him. Her face shone with excitement; her dress was starched and white.

'Basil, listen! I have to tell you: Father was talking after breakfast and he told Uncle George that he'd never

met such a nice, quiet, level-headed boy as you, and
Cousin Bill's got to tutor this month, so father asked
Uncle George if he thought your family would let you
go to Glacier Park with us for two weeks so I'd have
some company.' They took hands and danced excitedly
around the room. 'Don't say anything about it, because
I reckon he'll have to write your mother and everything.
Basil, isn't it wonderful?'

So when Basil left at eleven, there was no misery in
their parting. Mr Bibble, going into the village for a
paper, was going to escort Basil to his train, and till
the motor-car moved away the eyes of the two young
people shone and there was a secret in their waving hands.

Basil sank back in the seat, replete with happiness. He
relaxed—to have made a success of the visit was so nice.
He loved her—he loved even her father sitting beside
him, her father who was privileged to be so close to her,
to fuddle himself at that smile.

Mr Bibble lit a cigar. 'Nice weather,' he said. 'Nice
climate up to the end of October.'

'Wonderful,' agreed Basil. 'I miss October now that
I go East to school.'

'Getting ready for college?'

'Yes, sir; getting ready for Yale.' A new pleasurable
thought occurred to him. He hesitated, but he knew that
Mr Bibble, who liked him, would share his joy. 'I took
my preliminaries this spring and I just heard from them
—I passed six out of seven.'

'Good for you!'

Again Basil hesitated, then he continued: 'I got A in
ancient history and B in English history and English A.
And I got C in algebra A and Latin A and B. I failed
French A.'

'Good!' said Mr Bibble.

'I should have passed them all,' went on Basil, 'but
I didn't study hard at first. I was the youngest boy in
my class and I had a sort of swelled head about it.'

It was well that Mr Bibble should know he was taking

no dullard to Glacier National Park. Mr Bibble took a long puff of his cigar.

On second thought, Basil decided that his last remark didn't have the right ring and he amended it a little.

'It wasn't exactly a swelled head, but I never had to study very much, because in English I'd usually read most of the books before, and in history I'd read a lot too.' He broke off and tried again: 'I mean, when you say swelled head you think of a boy just going around with his head swelled, sort of, saying, "Oh, look how much I know!" Well, I wasn't like that. I mean, I didn't think I knew everything, but I was sort of——'

As he searched for the elusive word, Mr Bibble said, 'H'm!' and pointed with his cigar at a spot in the lake.

'There's a boat,' he said.

'Yes,' agreed Basil. 'I don't know much about sailing. I never cared for it. Of course I've been out a little, just tending boards and all that, but most of the time you have to sit with nothing to do. I like football.'

'H'm!' said Mr Bibble. 'When I was your age I was out in the Gulf in a catboat every day.'

'I guess it's fun if you like it,' conceded Basil.

'Happiest days of my life.'

The station was in sight. It occurred to Basil that he should make one final friendly gesture.

'Your daughter certainly is an attractive girl, Mr Bibble,' he said. 'I usually get along with girls all right, but I don't usually like them very much. But I think your daughter is the most attractive girl I ever met.' Then, as the car stopped, a faint misgiving overtook him and he was impelled to add with a disparaging little laugh. 'Good-bye. I hope I didn't talk too much.'

'Not at all,' said Mr Bibble. 'Good luck to you. Goo'-bye.'

A few minutes later, when Basil's train had pulled out, Mr Bibble stood at the news-stand buying a paper and already drying his forehead against the hot July day.

'Yes, sir! That was a lesson not to do anything in a

hurry,' he was saying to himself vehemently. 'Imagine listening to that fresh kid gabbling about himself all through Glacier Park! Thank the good Lord for that little ride!'

On his arrival home, Basil literally sat down and waited. Under no pretext would he leave the house save for short trips to the drug store for refreshments, whence he returned on a full run. The sound of the telephone or the door-bell galvanized him into the rigidity of the electric chair.

That afternoon he composed a wondrous geographical poem, which he mailed to Minnie:

> Of all the fair flowers of Paris,
>   Of all the red roses of Rome,
> Of all the deep tears of Vienna
>   The sadness wherever you roam,
> I think of that night by the lakeside,
>   The beam of the moon and stars,
> And the smell of an aching like perfume,
>   The tune of the Spanish guitars.

But Monday passed and most of Tuesday and no word came. Then, late in the afternoon of the second day, as he moved vaguely from room to room looking out of different windows into a barren lifeless street, Minnie called him on the phone.

'Yes?' His heart was beating wildly.

'Basil, we're going this afternoon.'

'Going!' he repeated blankly.

'Oh, Basil, I'm so sorry. Father changed his mind about taking anybody West with us.'

'Oh!'

'I'm so sorry, Basil.'

'I probably couldn't have gone.'

There was a moment's silence. Feeling her presence over the wire, he could scarcely breathe, much less speak.

'Basil, can you hear me?'

'Yes.'

'We may come back this way. Anyhow, remember we're going to meet this winter in New York.'

'Yes,' he said, and he added suddenly: 'Perhaps we won't ever meet again.'

'Of course we will. They're calling me, Basil. I've got to go. Good-bye.'

He sat down beside the telephone, wild with grief. The maid found him half an hour later bowed over the kitchen table. He knew what had happened as well as if Minnie had told him. He had made the same old error, undone the behaviour of three days in half an hour. It would have been no consolation if it had occurred to him that it was just as well. Somewhere on the trip he would have let go and things might have been worse—though perhaps not so sad. His only thought now was that she was gone.

He lay on his bed, baffled, mistaken, miserable but not beaten. Time after time, the same vitality that had led his spirit to a scourging made him able to shake off the blood like water, not to forget, but to carry his wounds with him to new disasters and new atonements—toward his unknown destiny.

Two days later his mother told him that on condition of his keeping the batteries on charge, and washing it once a week, his grandfather had consented to let him use the electric whenever it was idle in the afternoon. Two hours later he was out in it, gliding along Crest Avenue at the maximum speed permitted by the gears and trying to lean back as if it were a Blatz Bearcat. Imogene Bissel waved at him in front of her house and he came to an uncertain stop.

'You've got a car!'

'It's grandfather's,' he said modestly. 'I thought you were up on that party at the St Croix.'

She shook her head. 'Mother wouldn't let me go—only

a few girls went. There was a big accident over in Minneapolis and mother won't even let me ride in a car unless there's someone over eighteen driving.'

'Listen, Imogene, do you suppose your mother meant electrics?'

'Why, I never thought—I don't know. I could go and see.'

'Tell your mother it won't go over twelve miles an hour,' he called after her.

A minute later she ran joyfully down the walk. 'I can go, Basil,' she cried. 'Mother never heard of any wrecks in an electric. What'll we do?'

'Anything,' he said in a reckless voice. 'I didn't mean that about this bus making only twelve miles an hour—it'll make fifteen. Listen, let's go down to Smith's and have a claret lemonade.'

'Why, Basil Lee!'

BASIL DUKE LEE shut the front door behind him and
turned on the dining-room light. His mother's voice
drifted sleepily downstairs:

'Basil, is that you?'

'No, mother, it's a burglar.'

'It seems to me twelve o'clock is pretty late for a
fifteen-year-old boy.'

'We went to Smith's and had a soda.'

Whenever a new responsibility devolved upon Basil he
was 'a boy almost sixteen,' but when a privilege was in
question, he was 'a fifteen-year-old boy.'

There were footsteps above, and Mrs Lee, in kimono,
descended to the first landing.

'Did you and Riply enjoy the play?'

'Yes, very much.'

'What was it about?'

'Oh, it was just about this man. Just an ordinary play.'

'Didn't it have a name?'

' "Are You a Mason?" '

'Oh.' She hesitated, covetously watching his alert and
eager face, holding him there, 'Aren't you coming to
bed?'

'I'm going to get something to eat.'

'Something more?'

For a moment he didn't answer. He stood in front of
a glassed-in bookcase in the living-room, examining its
contents with an equally glazed eye.

'We're going to get up a play,' he said suddenly. 'I'm
going to write it.'

'Well—that'll be very nice. Please come to bed soon.

4*   105

You were up late last night, too, and you've got dark circles under your eyes.'

From the bookcase Basil presently extracted 'Van Bibber and Others,' from which he read while he ate a large plate of straw softened with a half pint of cream. Back in the living-room he sat for a few minutes at the piano, digesting, and meanwhile staring at the coloured cover of a song from 'The Midnight Sons.' It showed three men in evening clothes and opera hats sauntering jovially along Broadway against the blazing background of Times Square.

Basil would have denied incredulously the suggestion that that was currently his favourite work of art. But it was.

He went upstairs. From a drawer of his desk he took out a composition book and opened it.

BASIL DUKE LEE
St Regis School
Eastchester, Conn.
Fifth Form French

and on the next page, under Irregular Verbs:

PRESENT
je connais   nous con
tu connais
il connaît

He turned over another page.

MR WASHINGTON SQUARE
A Musical Comedy by
Basil Duke Lee
Music by Victor Herbert
ACT I

[*The porch of the Millionaires' Club, near New York. Opening Chorus,* LEILIA *and* DEBUTANTES:

> *We sing not soft, we sing not loud*
> *For no one ever heard an opening chorus,*

We are a very merry crowd
  But no one ever heard an opening chorus.
We're just a crowd of debutantes
  As merry as can be
And nothing that there is could ever bore us
  We're the wittiest ones, the prettiest ones,
    In all society
But no one ever heard an opening chorus.

LEILIA (*stepping forward*): Well, girls, has Mr Washington Square been around here today?

Basil turned over a page. There was no answer to Leilia's question. Instead in capitals was a brand-new heading:

HIC! HIC! HIC!
A Hilarious Farce in One Act
by
Basil Duke Lee

SCENE

[*A fashionable apartment near Broadway, New York City. It is almost midnight. As the curtain goes up there is a knocking at the door and a few minutes later it opens to admit a handsome man in a full evening dress and a companion. He has evidently been imbibing, for his words are thick, his nose is red, and he can hardly stand up. He turns up the light and comes down centre.*

STUYVESANT: Hic! Hic! Hic!

O'HARA (*his companion*): Begorra, you been sayin' nothing else all this evening.

Basil turned over a page and then another, reading hurriedly, but not without interest.

PROFESSOR PUMPKIN: Now, if you are an educated man, as you claim, perhaps you can tell me the Latin word for 'this.'

STUYVESANT: Hic! Hic! Hic!

PROFESSOR PUMPKIN: Correct. Very good indeed. I—

At this point Hic! Hic! Hic! came to an end in mid-sentence. On the following page, in just as determined a hand as if the last two works had not faltered by the way, was the heavily underlined beginning of another:

THE CAPTURED SHADOW
A Melodramatic Farce in Three Acts
by Basil Duke Lee

SCENE

[*All three acts take place in the library of the* VAN BAKERS' *house in New York. It is well furnished with a red lamp on one side and some crossed spears and helmets and so on and a divan and a general air of an oriental den.*

When the curtain rises MISS SAUNDERS, LEILIA VAN BAKER, *and* ESTELLA CARRAGE *are sitting at a table.* MISS SAUNDERS *is an old maid about forty very kittenish.* LEILIA *is pretty with dark hair.* ESTELLA *has light hair. They are a striking combination.*

'The Captured Shadow' filled the rest of the book and ran over into several loose sheets at the end. When it broke off Basil sat for a while in thought. This had been a season of 'crook comedies' in New York, and the feel, the swing, the exact and vivid image of the two he had seen, were in the foreground of his mind. At the time they had been enormously suggestive, opening out into a world much larger and more brilliant than themselves that existed outside their windows and beyond their doors, and it was this suggested world rather than any conscious desire to imitate 'Officer 666' that had inspired the effort before him. Presently he printed ACT II at the head of a new tablet and began to write.

An hour passed. Several times he had recourse to a collection of joke books and to an old Treasury of Wit and Humour which embalmed the faded Victorian cracks of Bishop Wilberforce and Sydney Smith. At the moment when, in his story, a door moved slowly open, he heard a heavy creak upon the stairs. He jumped to his feet, aghast and trembling, but nothing stirred; only a white moth bounced against the screen, a clock struck the half-hour far across the city, a bird whacked its wings in a tree outside.

Voyaging to the bathroom at half-past four, he saw with a shock that morning was already blue at the window. He had stayed up all night. He remembered that people who stayed up all night went crazy and, transfixed in the hall, he tried agonizingly to listen to himself, to feel whether or not he was going crazy. The things around him seemed prenaturally unreal, and rushing frantically back into his bedroom, he began tearing off his clothes, racing after the vanishing night. Undressed, he threw a final regretful glance at his pile of manuscript—he had the whole next scene in his head. As a compromise with incipient madness he got into bed and wrote for an hour more.

Late next morning he was startled awake by one of the ruthless Scandinavian sisters who, in theory, were the Lees' servants. 'Eleven o'clock!' she shouted. 'Five after!'

'Let me alone,' Basil mumbled. 'What do you come and wake me up for?'

'Somebody downstairs.' He opened his eyes. 'You ate all the cream last night,' Hilda continued. 'Your mother didn't have any for her coffee.'

'All the cream!' he cried. 'Why, I saw some more.'

'It was sour.'

'That's terrible,' he exclaimed, sitting up. 'Terrible!'

For a moment she enjoyed his dismay. Then she said, 'Riply Buckner's downstairs,' and went out, closing the door.

'Send him up!' he called after her. 'Hilda, why don't you ever listen for a minute? Did I get any mail?'

There was no answer. A moment later Riply came in.

'My gosh, are you still in bed?'

'I wrote on the play all night. I almost finished Act Two.' He pointed to his desk.

'That's what I want to talk to you about,' said Riply. 'Mother thinks we ought to get Miss Halliburton.'

'What for?'

'Just to sort of be there.'

Though Miss Halliburton was a pleasant person who combined the occupations of French teacher and bridge teacher, unofficial chaperon and children's friend, Basil felt that her superintendence would give the project an unprofessional ring.

'She wouldn't interfere,' went on Riply, obviously quoting his mother. 'I'll be the business manager and you'll direct the play, just like we said, but it would be good to have her there for prompter and to keep order at rehearsals. The girls' mothers'll like it.'

'All right,' Basil agreed reluctantly. 'Now look, let's see who we'll have in the cast. First, there's the leading man —this gentleman burglar that's called The Shadow. Only it turns out at the end that he's really a young man about town doing it on a bet, and not really a burglar at all.'

'That's you.'

'No, that's you.'

'Come on! You're the best actor,' protested Riply.

'No, I'm going to take a smaller part, so I can coach.'

'Well, haven't I got to be business manager?'

Selecting the actresses, presumably all eager, proved to be a difficult matter. They settled finally on Imogene Bissel for leading lady; Margaret Torrence for her friend, and Connie Davies for 'Miss Saunders, an old maid very kittenish.'

On Ripley's suggestion that several other girls wouldn't be pleased at being left out, Basil introduced a maid and a cook, 'who could just sort of look in from the kitchen.' He rejected firmly Riply's further proposal that there should be two or three maids, 'a sort of sewing woman,' and a trained nurse. In a house so clogged with femininity even the most umbrageous of gentleman burglars would have difficulty in moving about.

'I'll tell you two people we won't have,' Basil said meditatively—'that's Joe Gorman and Hubert Blair.'

'I wouldn't be in it if we had Hubert Blair,' asserted Riply.

'Neither would I.'

Hubert Blair's almost miraculous successes with girls had caused Basil and Riply much jealous pain.

They began calling up the prospective cast and immediately the enterprise received its first blow. Imogene Bissel was going to Rochester, Minnesota, to have her appendix removed, and wouldn't be back for three weeks.

They considered.

'How about Margaret Torrence?'

Basil shook his head. He had vision of Leilia Van Baker as someone rarer and more spirited than Margaret Torrence. Not that Leilia had much being, even to Basil —less than the Harrison Fisher girls pinned around his wall at school. But she was not Margaret Torrence. She was no one you could inevitably see by calling up half an hour before on the phone.

He discarded candidate after candidate. Finally a face began to flash before his eyes, as if in another connection, but so insistently that at length he spoke the name.

'Evelyn Beebe.'

'Who?'

Though Evelyn Beebe was only sixteen, her precocious charms had elevated her to an older crowd and to Basil she seemed of the very generation of his heroine, Leilia Van Baker. It was a little like asking Sarah Bernhardt for her services, but once her name had occurred to him, other possibilities seemed pale.

At noon they rang the Beebes' door-bell, stricken by a paralysis of embarrassment when Evelyn opened the door herself and, with politeness that concealed a certain surprise, asked them in.

Suddenly, through the portière of the living-room, Basil saw and recognized a young man in golf knickerbockers.

'I guess we better not come in,' he said quickly.

'We'll come some other time,' Riply added.

Together they started precipitately for the door, but she barred their way.

'Don't be silly,' she insisted. 'It's just Andy Lockheart.'

Just Andy Lockheart—winner of the Western Golf Championship at eighteen, captain of his freshman baseball team, handsome, successful at everything he tried, a living symbol of the splendid, glamorous world of Yale. For a year Basil had walked like him and tried unsuccessfully to play the piano by ear as Andy Lockheart was able to do.

Through sheer ineptitude at escaping, they were edged into the room. Their plan suddenly seemed presumptuous and absurd.

Perceiving their condition Evelyn tried to soothe them with pleasant banter.

'Well, it's about time you came to see me,' she told Basil. 'Here I've been sitting home every night waiting for you—ever since the Davies dance. Why haven't you been here before?'

He stared at her blankly, unable even to smile, and muttered: 'Yes, you have.'

'I have though. Sit down and tell me why you've been neglecting me! I suppose you've both been rushing the beautiful Imogene Bissel.'

'Why, I understand—' said Basil. 'Why, I heard from somewhere that she's gone up to have some kind of an appendicitis—that is—' He ran down to a pitch of inaudibility as Andy Lockheart at the piano began playing a succession of thoughtful chords, which resolved itself into the maxixe, an eccentric step-child of the tango. Kicking back a rug and lifting her skirts a little, Evelyn fluently tapped out a circle with her heels around the floor.

They sat inanimate as cushions on the sofa watching her. She was almost beautiful, with rather large features and bright fresh colour, behind which her heart seemed to be trembling a little with laughter. Her voice and her lithe body were always mimicking, ceaselessly caricaturing every sound and movement nearby, until even those who disliked her admitted that 'Evelyn could always make you laugh.' She finished her dance now with a false stumble and an awed expression, as she clutched at the piano, and Basil and Riply chuckled. Seeing their embarrassment lighten, she came and sat down beside them, and they laughed again when she said: 'Excuse my lack of self-control.'

'Do you want to be the leading lady in a play we're going to give?' demanded Basil with sudden desperation. 'We're going to have it at the Martindale School, for the benefit of the Baby Welfare.'

'Basil, this is so sudden.'

Andy Lockheart turned around from the piano.

'What're you going to give—a minstrel show?'

'No, it's a crook play named "The Captured Shadow." Miss Halliburton is going to coach it.' He suddenly realized the convenience of that name to shelter himself behind.

'Why don't you give something like "The Private Secretary"?' interrupted Andy. 'There's a good play for you. We gave it my last year at school.'

'Oh, no, it's all settled,' said Basil quickly. 'We're going to put on this play that I wrote.'

'You wrote it yourself?' exclaimed Evelyn.

'Yes.'

'My-y gosh!' said Andy. He began to play again.

'Look, Evelyn,' said Basil. 'It's only for three weeks, and you'd be the leading lady.'

She laughed. 'Oh, no. I couldn't. Why don't you get Imogene?'

'She's sick, I tell you. Listen——'

'Or Margaret Torrence?'

'I don't want anybody but you.'

The directness of this appeal touched her and momentarily she hesitated. But the hero of the Western Golf Championship turned around from the piano with a teasing smile and she shook her head.

'I can't do it, Basil. I may have to go East with the family.'

Reluctantly Basil and Riply got up.

'Gosh, I wish you'd be in it, Evelyn.'

'I wish I could.'

Basil lingered, thinking fast, wanting her more than ever; indeed, without her, it scarcely seemed worth while to go on with the play. Suddenly a desperate expedient took shape on his lips:

'You certainly would be wonderful. You see, the leading man is going to be Hubert Blair.'

Breathlessly he watched her, saw her hesitate.

'Good-bye,' he said.

She came with them to the door and then out on the veranda, frowning a little.

'How long did you say the rehearsals would take?' she asked thoughtfully.

II

On an August evening three days later Basil read the play to the cast on Miss Halliburton's porch. He was nervous and at first there were interruptions of 'Louder' and 'Not so fast.' Just as his audience was beginning to be amused by the repartee of the two comic crooks—repartee that had seen service with Weber and Fields—he was interrupted by the late arrival of Hubert Blair.

Hubert was fifteen, a somewhat shallow boy save for two or three felicities which he possessed to an extraordinary degree. But one excellence suggests the presence of others, and young ladies never failed to respond to his most casual fancy, enduring his fickleness of heart and never convinced that his fundamental indifference might not be overcome. They were dazzled by his flashing self-confidence, by his cherubic ingenuousness, which concealed a shrewd talent for getting around people, and by his extraordinary physical grace. Long-legged, beautifully proportioned, he had that tumbler's balance usually characteristic only of men 'built near the ground.' He was in constant motion that was a delight to watch, and Evelyn Beebe was not the only older girl who had found in him a mysterious promise and watched him for a long time with something more than curiosity.

He stood in the doorway now with an expression of bogus reverence on his round pert face.

'Excuse me,' he said. 'Is this the First Methodist Episcopal Church?' Everybody laughed—even Basil. 'I didn't know. I thought maybe I was in the right church, but in the wrong pew.'

They laughed again, somewhat discouraged. Basil waited until Hubert had seated himself beside Evelyn Beebe. Then he began to read once more, while the others, fascinated, watched Hubert's efforts to balance a chair on its hind legs. This squeaky experiment continued as an undertone to the reading. Not until Basil's desperate 'Now, here's where you come in, Hube,' did attention swing back to the play.

Basil read for more than an hour. When, at the end, he closed the composition book and looked up shyly, there was a burst of spontaneous applause. He had followed his models closely, and for all its grotesqueries, the result was actually interesting—it was a play. Afterwards he lingered, talking to Miss Halliburton, and he walked home glowing with excitement and rehearsing a little by himself into the August night.

The first week of rehearsal was a matter of Basil climbing back and forth from auditorium to stage, crying, 'No! Look here, Connie; you come in more like this.' Then things began to happen. Mrs Van Schellinger came to rehearsal one day and, lingering afterwards, announced that she couldn't let Gladys be in 'a play about criminals.' Her theory was that this element could be removed; for instance, the two comic crooks could be changed to 'two funny farmers.'

Basil listened with horror. When she had gone he assured Miss Halliburton that he would change nothing.

Luckily Gladys played the cook, an interpolated part that could be summarily struck out, but her absence was felt in another way. She was tranquil and tractable, 'the most carefully brought-up girl in town,' and at her withdrawal rowdiness appeared during rehearsals. Those who had only such lines as 'I'll ask Mrs Van Baker, sir,' in Act I and 'No, ma'am,' in Act III showed a certain tendency to grow restless in between. So now it was:

'Please keep that dog quiet or else send him home!' or:

'Where's that maid? Wake up, Margaret, for heaven's sake!' or

'What is there to laugh at that's so darn funny?'

More and more the chief problem was the tactful management of Hubert Blair. Apart from his unwillingness to learn his lines, he was a satisfactory hero, but off the stage he became a nuisance. He gave an endless private performance for Evelyn Beebe, which took such forms as chasing her amorously around the hall or flipping peanuts over his shoulder to land mysteriously on the stage. Called to order, he would mutter, 'Aw, shut up yourself!' just loud enough for Basil to guess, but not to hear.

But Evelyn Beebe was all that Basil had expected. Once on the stage she compelled a breathless attention, and Basil recognized this by adding to her part. He envied the half-sentimental fun that she and Hubert derived from their scenes together and he felt a vague, impersonal jealousy that almost every night after rehearsal they drove around together in Hubert's car.

One afternoon when matters had progressed a fortnight, Hubert came in an hour late, loafed through the first act and then informed Miss Halliburton that he was going home.

'What for?' Basil demanded.

'I've got some things I got to do.'

'Are they important?'

'What business is that of yours?'

'Of course it's my business,' said Basil heatedly, where-upon Miss Halliburton interfered.

'There's no use of anybody getting angry. What Basil means, Hubert, is that if it's just some small thing—why, we're all giving up our pleasure to make this play a success.'

Hubert listened with obvious boredom.

'I've got to drive downtown and get father.'

He looked coolly at Basil, as if challenging him to deny the adequacy of this explanation.

'Then why did you come an hour late?' demanded Basil.

'Because I had to do something for mother.'

A group had gathered and he glanced around triumphantly. It was one of those sacred excuses, and only Basil saw that it was disingenuous.

'Oh, tripe!' he said.

'Maybe you think so—Bossy.'

Basil took a step towards him, his eyes blazing.

'What'd you say?'

'I said "Bossy." Isn't that what they call you at school?'

It was true. It had followed him home. Even as he went white with rage a vast impotence surged over him at the realization that the past was always lurking near. The faces of school were around him, sneering and watching. Hubert laughed.

'Get out!' said Basil in a strained voice. 'Go on! Get right out!'

Hubert laughed again, but as Basil took a step towards him he retreated.

'I don't want to be in your play anyhow. I never did.'

'Then go on out of this hall.'

'Now, Basil!' Miss Halliburton hovered breathlessly beside them. Hubert laughed again and looked about for his cap.

'I wouldn't be in your crazy old show,' he said. He turned slowly and jauntily, and sauntered out the door.

Riply Buckner read Hubert's part that afternoon, but

there was a cloud upon the rehearsal. Miss Beebe's performance lacked its customary verve and the others clustered and whispered, falling silent when Basil came near. After the rehearsal, Miss Halliburton, Riply, and Basil held a conference. Upon Basil flatly refusing to take the leading part, it was decided to enlist a certain Mayall De Bec, known slightly to Riply, who had made a name for himself in theatricals at the Central High School.

But next day a blow fell that was irreparable. Evelyn, flushed and uncomfortable, told Basil and Miss Halliburton that her family's plans had changed—they were going East next week and she couldn't be in the play after all. Basil understood. Only Hubert had held her this long.

'Good-bye,' he said gloomily.

His manifest despair shamed her and she tried to justify herself.

'Really, I can't help it. Oh, Basil, I'm so sorry!'

'Couldn't you stay over a week with me after your family goes?' Miss Halliburton asked innocently.

'Not possibly. Father wants us all to go together. That's the only reason. If it wasn't for that I'd stay.'

'All right,' Basil said. 'Good-bye.'

'Basil, you're not mad, are you?' A gust of repentance swept over her. 'I'll do anything to help. I'll come to rehearsals this week until you get someone else, and then I'll try to help her all I can. But father says we've got to go.'

In vain Riply tried to raise Basil's morale after the rehearsal that afternoon, making suggestions which he waved contemptuously away. Margaret Torrence? Connie Davies? They could hardly play the parts they had. It seemed to Basil as if the undertaking was falling to pieces before his eyes.

It was still early when he got home. He sat dispiritedly by his bedroom window, watching the little Barnfield boy playing a lonesome game by himself in the yard next door.

His mother came in at five, and immediately sensed his depression.

'Teddy Barnfield has the mumps,' she said, in an effort to distract him. 'That's why he's playing there all alone.'

'Has he?' he responded listlessly.

'It isn't at all dangerous, but it's very contagious. You had it when you were seven.'

'H'm.'

She hesitated.

'Are you worrying about your play? Has anything gone wrong?'

'No, mother. I just want to be alone.'

After a while he got up and started after a malted milk at the soda fountain around the corner. It was half in his mind to see Mr Beebe and ask him if he couldn't postpone his trip East. If he could only be sure that was Evelyn's real reason.

The sight of Evelyn's nine-year-old brother coming along the street broke in on his thoughts.

'Hello, Ham. I hear you're going away.'

Ham nodded.

'Going next week. To the seashore.'

Basil looked at him speculatively, as if, through his proximity to Evelyn, he held the key to the power of moving her.

'Where are you going now?' he asked.

'I'm going to play with Teddy Barnfield.'

'What!' Basil exclaimed. 'Why, didn't you know—' He stopped. A wild, criminal idea broke over him; his mother's words floated through his mind: 'It isn't at all dangerous, but it's very contagious.' If little Ham Beebe got the mumps, and Evelyn *couldn't* go away—

He came to a decision quickly and coolly.

'Teddy's playing in his back yard,' he said. 'If you want to see him without going through his house, why don't you go down this street and turn up the alley?'

'All right. Thanks,' said Ham trustingly.

Basil stood for a minute looking after him until he

turned the corner into the alley, fully aware that it was the worst thing he had ever done in his life.

III

A week later Mrs Lee had an early supper—all Basil's favourite things: chipped beef, French-fried potatoes, sliced peaches and cream, and devil's food.

Every few minutes Basil said, 'Gosh! I wonder what time it is,' and went out in the hall to look at the clock. 'Does that clock work right?' he demanded with sudden suspicion. It was the first time the matter had ever interested him.

'Perfectly all right. If you eat so fast you'll have indigestion and then you won't be able to act well.'

'What do you think of the programme?' he asked for the third time. 'Riply Buckner, Jr., presents Basil Duke Lee's comedy, "The Captured Shadow." '

'I think it's very nice.'

'He doesn't really present it.'

'It sounds very well though.'

'I wonder what time it is?' he inquired.

'You just said it was ten minutes after six.'

'Well, I guess I better be starting.'

'Eat your peaches, Basil. If you don't eat you won't be able to act.'

'I don't have to act,' he said patiently. 'All I am is a small part, and it wouldn't matter—' It was too much trouble to explain.

'Please don't smile at me when I come on, mother,' he requested. 'Just act as if I was anybody else.'

'Can't I even say how-do-you-do?'

'What?' Humour was lost on him. He said good-bye. Trying very hard to digest not his food but his heart, which had somehow slipped hard down into his stomach, he started off for the Martindale School.

As its yellow windows loomed out of the night his excitement became insupportable; it bore no resemblance to the building he had been entering so casually for three weeks. His footsteps echoed symbolically and portentously in its deserted hall; upstairs there was only the janitor setting out the chairs in rows, and Basil wondered about the vacant stage until someone came in.

It was Mayall De Bec, the tall, clever, not very likeable youth they had imported from Lower Crest Avenue to be the leading man. Mayall, far from being nervous, tried to engage Basil in casual conversation. He wanted to know if Basil thought Evelyn Beebe would mind if he went to see her sometime when the show was over. Basil supposed not. Mayall said he had a friend whose father owned a brewery who owned a twelve-cylinder car.

Basil said, 'Gee!'

At quarter to seven the participants arrived in groups —Riply Buckner with the six boys he had gathered to serve as ticket takers and ushers; Miss Halliburton, trying to seem very calm and reliable; Evelyn Beebe, who came in as if she were yielding herself up to something and whose glance at Basil seemed to say: 'Well, it looks as if I'm really going through with it after all.'

Mayall De Bec was to make up the boys and Miss Halliburton the girls. Basil soon came to the conclusion that Miss Halliburton knew nothing about make-up, but he judged it diplomatic, in that lady's overwrought condition, to say nothing, but to take each girl to Mayall for corrections when Miss Halliburton had done.

An exclamation from Bill Kampf, standing at a crack in the curtain, brought Basil to his side. A tall bald-headed man in spectacles had come in and was shown to a seat in the middle of the house, where he examined the programme. He was the public. Behind those waiting eyes, suddenly so mysterious and incalculable, was the secret of the play's failure or success. He finished the programme, took off his glasses and looked around. Two old ladies and two little boys came in, followed immediately by a dozen more.

'Hey, Riply,' Basil called softly. 'Tell them to put the children down in front.'

Riply, struggling into his policeman's uniform, looked up, and the long black moustache on his upper lip quivered indignantly.

'I thought of that long ago.'

That hall, filling rapidly, was now alive with the buzz of conversation. The children in front were jumping up and down in their seats, and everyone was talking and calling back and forth save the several dozen cooks and housemaids who sat in stiff and quiet pairs about the room.

Then, suddenly, everything was ready. It was incredible. 'Stop! Stop!' Basil wanted to say. 'It can't be ready. There must be something—there always has been something,' but the darkened auditorium and the piano and violin from Geyer's Orchestra playing *Meet Me in the Shadows* belied his words. Miss Saunders, Leilia Van Baker, and Leilia's friend, Estella Carrage, were already seated on the stage, and Miss Halliburton stood in the wings with the prompt book. Suddenly the music ended and the chatter in front died away.

'Oh, gosh!' Basil thought. 'Oh, my gosh!'

The curtain rose. A clear voice floated up from somewhere. Could it be from that unfamiliar group on the stage?

I will, Miss Saunders. I tell you I will!

But, Miss Leilia, I don't consider the newspapers proper for young ladies nowadays.

I don't care. I want to read about this wonderful gentleman burglar they call The Shadow.

It was actually going on. Almost before he realized it, a ripple of laughter passed over the audience as Evelyn gave her imitation of Miss Saunders behind her back.

'Get ready, Basil,' breathed Miss Halliburton.

Basil and Bill Kampf, the crooks, each took an elbow of Victor Van Baker, the dissolute son of the house, and made ready to aid him through the front door.

It was strangely natural to be out on the stage with all those eyes looking up encouragingly. His mother's face floated past him, other faces that he recognized and remembered.

Bill Kampf stumbled on a line and Basil picked him up quickly and went on.

MISS SAUNDERS: So you are alderman from the Sixth Ward?

RABBIT SIMMMONS: Yes, ma'am.

MISS SAUNDERS (*shaking her head kittenishly*): Just what is an alderman?

CHINAMAN RUDD: An alderman is half-way between a politician and a pirate.

This was one of Basil's lines that he was particularly proud of—but there was not a sound from the audience, not a smile. A moment later Bill Kampf absent-mindedly wiped his forehead with his handkerchief and then stared at it, startled by the red stains of make-up on it—and the audience roared. The theatre was like that.

MISS SAUNDERS: Then you believe in spirits, Mr Rudd?

CHINAMAN RUDD: Yes, ma'am, I certainly do believe in spirits. Have you got any?

The first big scene came. On the darkened stage a window rose slowly and Mayall De Bec, 'in a full evening dress,' climbed over the sill. He was tiptoeing cautiously from one side of the stage to the other, when Leilia Van Baker came in. For a moment she was frightened, but he assured her that he was a friend of her brother Victor. They talked. She told him naïvely yet feelingly of her admiration for The Shadow, of whose exploits she had read. She hoped, though, that The Shadow would not come here tonight, as the family jewels were all in that safe at the right.

The stranger was hungry. He had been late for his dinner and so had not been able to get any that night. Would he have some crackers and milk? That would be fine. Scarcely had she left the room when he was on his knees by the safe, fumbling at the catch, undeterred by the unpromising word 'Cake' stencilled on the safe's front. It swung open, but he heard footsteps outside and closed it just as Leilia came back with the crackers and milk.

They lingered, obviously attracted to each other. Miss Saunders came in, very kittenish, and was introduced. Again Evelyn mimicked her behind her back and the audience roared. Other members of the household appeared and were introduced to the stranger.

What's this? A banging at the door, and Mulligan, a policeman, rushes in.

We have just received word from the Central Office that the notorious Shadow has been seen climbing in the window! No one can leave this house tonight!

The curtain fell. The first rows of the audience—the younger brothers and sisters of the cast—were extravagant in their enthusiasm. The actors took a bow.

A moment later Basil found himself alone with Evelyn Beebe on the stage. A weary doll in her make-up she was leaning against a table.

'Heigh-ho, Basil,' she said.

She had not quite forgiven him for holding her to her promise after her little brother's mumps had postponed their trip East, and Basil had tactfully avoided her, but now they met in the genial glow of excitement and success.

'You were wonderful,' he said—'Wonderful!'

He lingered a moment. He could never please her, for she wanted someone like herself, someone who could

reach her through her senses, like Hubert Blair. Her in-
tuition told her that Basil was of a certain vague conse-
quence; beyond that his incessant attempts to make
people think and feel bothered and wearied her. But suddenly, in the glow of the evening, they leaned forward
and kissed peacefully, and from that moment, because
they had no common ground even to quarrel on, they
were friends for life.

When the curtain rose upon the second act Basil slipped
down a flight of stairs and up another to the back of the
hall, where he stood watching in the darkness. He laughed
silently when the audience laughed, enjoying it as if it
were a play he had never seen before.

There was a second and a third act scene that were very
similar. In each of them The Shadow, alone on the stage,
was interrupted by Miss Saunders. Mayall De Bec, having
had but ten days of rehearsal, was inclined to confuse the
two, but Basil was totally unprepared for what happened.
Upon Connie's entrance Mayall spoke his third-act line
and involuntarily Connie answered in kind.

Others coming on the stage were swept up in the nervousness and confusion, and suddenly they were playing
the third act in the middle of the second. It happened so
quickly that for a moment Basil had only a vague sense
that something was wrong. Then he dashed down one
stairs and up another and into the wings, crying:

'Let down the curtain! Let down the curtain!'

The boys who stood there aghast sprang to the rope.
In a minute Basil, breathless, was facing the audience.

'Ladies and gentlemen,' he said, 'there's been changes
in the cast and what just happened was a mistake. If
you'll excuse us we'd like to do that scene over.'

He stepped back in the wings to a flutter of laughter
and applause.

'All right, Mayall!' he called excitedly. 'On the stage
alone. Your line is: "I just want to see that the jewels are
all right," and Connie's is: "Go ahead, don't mind me."
All right! Curtain up!'

In a moment things righted themselves. Someone brought water for Miss Halliburton, who was in a state of collapse, and as the act ended they all took a curtain call once more. Twenty minutes later it was over. The hero clasped Leilia Van Baker to his breast, confessing that he was The Shadow, 'and a captured Shadow at that'; the curtain went up and down, up and down; Miss Halliburton was dragged unwillingly on the stage and the ushers came up the aisles laden with flowers. Then everything became informal and the actors mingled happily with the audience, laughing and important, congratulated from all sides. An old man whom Basil didn't know came up to him and shook his hand, saying, 'You're a young man that's going to be heard from some day,' and a reporter from the paper asked him if he was really only fifteen. It might all have been very bad and demoralizing for Basil, but it was already behind him. Even as the crowd melted away and the last few people spoke to him and went out, he felt a great vacancy come into his heart. It was over, it was done and gone—all that work, and interest, and absorption. It was a hollowness like fear.

'Good-night, Miss Halliburton. Good-night, Evelyn.'

'Good-night, Basil. Congratulations, Basil. Good-night.'

'Where's my coat? Good-night, Basil.'

'Leave your costumes on the stage, please. They've got to go back tomorrow.'

He was almost the last to leave, mounting to the stage for a moment and looking around the deserted hall. His mother was waiting and they strolled home together through the first cool night of the year.

'Well, I thought it went very well indeed. Were you satisfied?' He didn't answer for a moment. 'Weren't you satisfied with the way it went?'

'Yes.' He turned his head away.

'What's the matter?'

'Nothing,' and then, 'Nobody really cares, do they?'

'About what?'

'About anything.'

'Everybody cares about different things. I care about you, for instance.'

Instinctively he ducked away from a hand extended caressingly towards him: 'Oh, don't. I don't mean like that.'

'You're just overwrought, dear.'

'I am not overwrought. I just feel sort of sad.'

'You shouldn't feel sad. Why, people told me after the play—'

'Oh, that's all over. Don't talk about that—don't ever talk to me about that any more.'

'Then what are you sad about?'

'Oh, about a little boy.'

'What little boy?'

'Oh, little Ham—you wouldn't understand.'

'When we get home I want you to take a real hot bath and quiet your nerves.'

'All right.'

But when he got home he fell immediately into deep sleep on the sofa. She hesitated. Then covering him with a blanket and a comforter, she pushed a pillow under his protesting head and went upstairs.

She knelt for a long time beside her bed.

'God, help him! Help him,' she prayed, 'because he needs help that I can't give him any more.'

JOSEPHINE
FIRST BLOOD
[1930]

'I REMEMBER your coming to me in despair when Josephine was about three!' cried Mrs Bray. 'George was furious because he couldn't decide what to go to work at, so he used to spank little Josephine.'

'I remember,' said Josephine's mother.

'And so this is Josephine.'

This was, indeed, Josephine. She looked at Mrs Bray and smiled, and Mrs Bray's eyes hardened imperceptibly. Josephine kept on smiling.

'How old are you, Josephine?'

'Just sixteen.'

'Oh-h. I would have said you were older.'

At the first opportunity Josephine asked Mrs Perry, 'Can I go to the movies with Lillian this afternoon?'

'No, dear; you have to study.' She turned to Mrs Bray as if the matter were dismissed—but: 'You darn fool,' muttered Josephine audibly.

Mrs Bray said some words to cover the situation, but, of course, Mrs Perry could not let it pass unreproved.

'What did you call mother, Josephine?'

'I don't see why I can't go to the movies with Lillian.'

Her mother was content to let it go at this.

'Because you've got to study. You go somewhere every day, and your father wants it to stop.'

'How crazy!' said Josephine, and she added vehemently, 'How utterly insane! Father's got to be a maniac I think. Next thing he'll start tearing his hair and think he's Napoleon or something.'

'No,' interposed Mrs Bray jovially as Mrs Perry grew

rosy. 'Perhaps she's right. Maybe George *is* crazy—I'm sure my husband's crazy. It's this war.'

But she was not really amused; she thought Josephine ought to be beaten with sticks.

They were talking about Anthony Harker, a contemporary of Josephine's older sister.

'He's divine,' Josephine interposed—not rudely, for, despite the foregoing, she was not rude; it was seldom even that she appeared to talk too much, though she lost her temper, and swore sometimes when people were unreasonable. 'He's perfectly——'

'He's very popular. Personally, I don't see very much to him. He seems rather superficial.'

'Oh, no, mother,' said Josephine. 'He's far from it. Everybody says he has a great deal of personality—which is more than you can say of most of these jakes. Any girl would be glad to get their hands on him. I'd marry him in a minute.'

She had never thought of this before; in fact the phrase had been invented to express her feeling for Travis de Coppet. When, presently, tea was served, she excused herself and went to her room.

It was a new house, but the Perrys were far from being new people. They were Chicago Society, and almost very rich, and not uncultured as things went thereabouts in 1914. But Josephine was an unconscious pioneer of the generation that was destined to 'get out of hand.'

In her room she dressed herself for going to Lillian's house, thinking meanwhile of Travis de Coppet and of riding home from the Davidsons' dance last night. Over his tuxedo, Travis had worn a loose blue cape inherited from an old-fashioned uncle. He was tall and thin, an exquisite dancer, and his eyes had often been described by female contemporaries as 'very dark'—to an adult it appeared that he had two black eyes in the collisional sense, and that probably they were justifiably renewed every night; the area surrounding them was so purple, or brown, or crimson, that they were the first thing you noticed about his face, and, save for his white teeth, the last. Like Josephine, he was also something new. There were a lot of new things in Chicago then, but lest the interest of this narrative be divided, it should be remarked that Josephine was the newest of all.

Dressed, she went down the stairs and through a softly opening side door, out into the street. It was October and a harsh breeze blew her along under trees without leaves, past houses with cold corners, past caves of the wind that were the mouths of residential streets. From that time until April, Chicago is an indoor city, where entering by a door is like going into another world, for the cold of the lake is unfriendly and not like real northern cold—it serves only to accentuate the things that go on inside. There is no music outdoors, or love-making, and even in prosperous times the wealth that rolls by in limousines is less glamorous than embittering to those on the sidewalk. But in the houses there is a deep, warm quiet, or else an excited, singing noise, as if those within were inventing things like new dances. That is part of what people mean when they say they love Chicago.

Josephine was going to meet her friend Lillian Hammell, but their plan did not include attending the movies. In comparison to it, their mothers would have preferred the most objectionable, the most lurid movie. It was no less than to go for a long auto ride with Travis de Coppet and Howard Page, in the course of which they would kiss not once but a lot. The four of them had been planning this since the previous Saturday, when unkind circumstances had combined to prevent its fulfilment.

Travis and Howard were already there—not sitting down, but still in their overcoats, like symbols of action, hurrying the girls breathlessly into the future. Travis wore a fur collar on his overcoat and carried a gold-headed cane; he kissed Josephine's hand facetiously yet seriously, and she said, 'Hello, Travis!' with the warm affection of a politician greeting a prospective vote. But for a minute the two girls exchanged news aside.

'I saw him,' Lillian whispered, 'just now.'

'Did you?'

Their eyes blazed and fused together.

'Isn't he *divine*?' said Josephine.

They were referring to Mr Anthony Harker, who was twenty-two, and unconscious of their existence, save that in the Perry house he occasionally recognized Josephine as Constance's younger sister.

'He has the most beautiful nose,' cried Lillian, suddenly laughing. 'It's—' She drew it on the air with her finger and they both became hilarious. But Josephine's face composed itself as Travis's black eyes, conspicuous as if they had been freshly made the previous night, peered in from the hall.

'Well!' he said tensely.

The four young people went out, passed through fifty bitter feet of wind and entered Page's car. They were all very confident and knew exactly what they wanted. Both girls were expressly disobeying their parents, but they had no more sense of guilt about it than a soldier escaping from an enemy prison camp. In the back seat, Josephine and Travis looked at each other; she wailed as he burned darkly.

'Look,' he said to his hand; it was trembling. 'Up till five this morning. Girls from the Follies.'

'Oh, Travis!' she cried automatically, but for the first time a communication such as this failed to thrill her. She took his hand, wondering what the matter was inside herself.

It was quite dark, and he bent over her suddenly, but as suddenly she turned her face away. Annoyed, he made cynical nods with his head and lay back in the corner of the car. He became engaged in cherishing his dark secret —the secret that always made her yearn towards him. She could see it come into his eyes and fill them, down to the cheek bones and up to the brows, but she could not concentrate on him. The romantic mystery of the world had moved into another man.

Travis waited ten minutes for her capitulation; then he tried again, and with this second approach she saw him plain for the first time. It was enough. Josephine's imagination and her desires were easily exploited up to a certain point, but after that her very impulsiveness protected her. Now, suddenly, she found something real against Travis, and her voice was modulated with lowly sorrow.

'I heard what you did last night. I heard very well.'

'What's the matter?'

'You told Ed Bement you were in for a big time because you were going to take me home in your car.'

'Who told you that?' he demanded, guilty but belittling.

'Ed Bement did, and he told me he almost hit you in the face when you said it. He could hardly keep restraining himself.'

Once more Travis retired to his corner of the seat. He accepted this as the reason for her coolness, as in a measure it was. In view of Doctor Jung's theory that innumerable male voices argue in the subconscious of a woman, and even speak through her lips, then the absent Ed Bement was probably speaking through Josephine at that moment.

'I've decided not to kiss any more boys, because I won't have anything left to give the man I really love.'

'Bull!' replied Travis.

'It's true. There's been too much talk around Chicago about me. A man certainly doesn't respect a girl he can kiss whenever he wants to, and I want to be respected by the man I'm going to marry some day.'

Ed Bement would have been overwhelmed had he realized the extent of his dominance over her that afternoon.

Walking from the corner, where the youths discreetly left her, to her house, Josephine felt that agreeable lightness which comes with the end of a piece of work. She would be a good girl now forever, see less of boys, as her parents wished, try to be what Miss Benbower's school denominated An Ideal Benbower Girl. Then next year, at Brearley, she could be an Ideal Brearley Girl. But the first stars were out over Lake Shore Drive, and all about her she could feel Chicago swinging around its circle at a hundred miles an hour, and Josephine knew that she only wanted to want such wants for her soul's sake. Actually, she had no desire for achievement. Her grandfather had had that, her parents had had the consciousness of it, but Josephine accepted the proud world into which she was born. This was easy in Chicago, which, unlike New York, was a city state, where the old families formed a caste—intellect was represented by the university professors, and there were no ramifications, save that even the Perrys had to be nice to half a dozen families even richer and more important than themselves. Josephine loved to dance, but the field of feminine glory, the ballroom floor, was something you slipped away from with a man.

As Josephine came to the iron gate of her house, she saw her sister shivering on the top steps with a departing young man; then the front door closed and the man came down the walk. She knew who he was.

He was abstracted, but he recognized her for just a moment in passing.

'Oh, hello,' he said.

She turned all the way round so that he could see her face by the street lamp; she lifted her face full out of her fur collar and towards him, and then smiled.

'Hello,' she said modestly.

They passed. She drew in her head like a turtle.

'Well, now he knows what I look like, anyhow,' she told herself excitedly, as she went on into the house.

II

Several days later Constance Perry spoke to her mother in a serious tone:

'Josephine is so conceited that I really think she's a little crazy.'

'She's very conceited,' admitted Mrs Perry. 'Father and I were talking and we decided that after the first of the year she should go East to school. But you don't say a word about it until we know more definitely.'

'Heavens, mother, it's none too soon! She and that terrible Travis de Coppet running around with his cloak, as if they were about a thousand years old. They came into the Blackstone last week and my *spine* crawled. They looked just like two maniacs—Travis slinking along, and Josephine twisting her mouth around as if she had St Vitus dance. *Honestly*——'

'What did you begin to say about Anthony Harker?' interrupted Mrs Perry.

'That she's got a crush on him, and he's about old enough to be her grandfather.'

'Not quite.'

'Mother, he's twenty-two and she's sixteen. Every time Jo and Lillian go by him, they giggle and stare——'

'Come here, Josephine,' said Mrs Perry.

Josephine came into the room slowly and leaned her backbone against the edge of the opened door, teetering upon it calmly.

'What, mother?'

'Dear, you don't want to be laughed at, do you?'

Josephine turned sulkily to her sister. 'Who laughs at me? You do, I guess. You're the only one that does.'

'You're so conceited that you don't see it. When you and Travis de Coppet came into the Blackstone that afternoon, my *spine* crawled. Everybody at our table and most of the other tables laughed—the ones that weren't shocked.'

'I guess they were more shocked,' guessed Josephine complacently.

'You'll have a fine reputation by the time you come out.'

'Oh, shut your mouth!' said Josephine.

There was a moment's silence. Then Mrs Perry whispered solemnly, 'I'll have to tell your father about this as soon as he comes home.'

'Go on, tell him.' Suddenly Josephine began to cry. 'Oh, why can't anybody ever leave me alone? I wish I was dead.'

Her mother stood with her arm around her, saying, 'Josephine—now, Josephine'; but Josephine went on with deep, broken sobs that seemed to come from the bottom of her heart.

'Just a lot—of—of ugly and jealous girls who get mad when anybody looks at m-me, and make up all sorts of stories that are absolutely untrue, just because I can get anybody I want. I suppose that Constance is mad about it because I went in and sat for *five* minutes with Anthony Harker while he was waiting last night.'

'Yes, I was *terribly* jealous! I sat up and cried all night about it. Especially because he comes to talk to me about Marice Whaley. Why!—you got him so crazy about you in that five minutes that he couldn't stop laughing all the way to the Warrens.'

Josephine drew in her breath in one last gasp, and stopped crying. 'If you want to know, I've decided to give him up.'

'Ha-ha!' Constance exploded. 'Listen to *that*, mother! She's going to give him up—as if he ever looked at her or knew she was al*ive*! Of all the conceited——'

But Mrs Perry could stand no more. She put her arm around Josephine and hurried her to her room down the hall.

'All your sister meant was that she didn't like to see you laughed at,' she explained.

'Well, I've given him up,' said Josephine gloomily.

She had given him up, renouncing a thousand kisses she had never had, a hundred long, thrilling dances in his arms, a hundred evenings not to be recaptured. She did

not mention the letter she had written him last night—
and had not sent, and now would never send.

'You mustn't think about such things at your age,' said
Mrs Perry. 'You're just a child.'

Josephine got up and went to the mirror.

'I promised Lillian to come over to her house. I'm late
now.'

Back in her room, Mrs Perry thought: 'Two months to
February.' She was a pretty woman who wanted to be
loved by everyone around her; there was no power of
governing in her. She tied up her mind like a neat package
and put it in the post office, with Josephine inside it
safely addressed to the Brearley School.

An hour later, in the tea room at the Blackstone Hotel,
Anthony Harker and another young man lingered at table.
Anthony was a happy fellow, lazy, rich enough, pleased
with his current popularity. After a brief career in an
Eastern university, he had gone to a famous college in
Virginia and in its less exigent shadow completed his
education; at least, he had absorbed certain courtesies and
mannerisms that Chicago girls found charming.

'There's that guy Travis de Coppet,' his companion
had just remarked. 'What's he think he is, anyhow?'

Anthony looked remotely at the young people across
the room, recognizing the little Perry girl and other young
females whom he seemed to have encountered frequently
in the street of late. Although obviously much at home,
they seemed silly and loud; presently his eyes left them
and searched the room for the party he was due to join
for dancing, but he was still sitting there when the room
—it had a twilight quality, in spite of the lights within
and the full dark outside—woke up to confident and
exciting music. A thickening parade drifted past him.
The men in sack suits, as though they had just come from
portentous affairs, and the women in hats that seemed
about to take flight, gave a special impermanence to the

scene. This implication that this gathering, a little more than uncalculated, a little less clandestine, would shortly be broken into formal series, made him anxious to seize its last minutes, and he looked more and more intently into the crowd for the face of anyone he knew.

One face emerged suddenly around a man's upper arm not five feet away, and for a moment Anthony was the object of the saddest and most tragic regard that had ever been directed upon him. It was a smile and not a smile—two big grey eyes with bright triangles of colour underneath, and a mouth twisted into a universal sympathy that seemed to include both him and herself—yet withal, the expression not of a victim, but rather of the very demon of tender melancholy—and for the first time Anthony really saw Josephine.

His immediate instinct was to see with whom she was dancing. It was a young man he knew, and with this assurance he was on his feet giving a quick tug to his coat, and then out upon the floor.

'May I cut in, please?'

Josephine came close to him as they started, looked up into his eyes for an instant, and then down and away. She said nothing. Realizing that she could not possibly be more than sixteen, Anthony hoped that the party he was to join would not arrive in the middle of the dance.

When that was over, she raised eyes to him again; a sense of having been mistaken, of her being older than he had thought, possessed him. Just before he left her at her table, he was moved to say:

'Couldn't I have another later?'

'Oh, sure.'

She united her eyes with his, every glint a spike—perhaps from the railroads on which their family fortunes were founded, and upon which they depended. Anthony was disconcerted as he went back to his table.

One hour later, they left the Blackstone together in his car.

This had simply happened—Josephine's statement, at

5*

the end of their second dance, that she must leave, then her request, and his own extreme self-consciousness as he walked beside her across the empty floor. It was a favour to her sister to take her home—but he had that unmistakable feeling of expectation.

Nevertheless, once outside and shocked into reconsideration by the bitter cold, he tried again to allocate his responsibilities in the matter. This was hard going with Josephine's insistent dark and ivory youth pressed up against him. As they got in the car he tried to dominate the situation with a masculine stare, but her eyes, shining as if with fever, melted down his bogus austerity in a whittled second.

Idly he patted her hand—then suddenly he was inside the radius of her perfume and kissing her breathlessly.

'So that's that,' she whispered after a moment. Startled, he wondered if he had forgotten something—something he had said to her before.

'What a cruel remark,' he said, 'just when I was getting interested.'

'I only meant that any minute with you may be the last one,' she said miserably. 'The family are going to send me away to school—they think I haven't found that out yet.'

'Too bad.'

—and today they got together—and tried to tell me that you didn't know I was al*ive*!'

After a long pause, Anthony contributed feebly. 'I hope you didn't let them convince you.'

She laughed shortly. 'I just laughed and came down here.'

Her hand burrowed its way into his; when he pressed it, her eyes, bright now, not dark, rose until they were as high as his, and came towards him. A minute later he thought to himself: 'This is a rotten trick I'm doing.'

He was sure he was doing it.

'You're so sweet,' she said.

'You're a dear child.'

'I hate jealousy worse than anything in the world,' Josephine broke forth, 'and *I* have to suffer from it. And my own sister worse than all the rest.'

'Oh, no!' he protested.

'I couldn't help it if I fell in love with you. I tried to help it. I used to go out of the house when I knew you were coming.'

The force of her lies came from her sincerity and from her simple and superb confidence that whomsoever she loved must love her in return. Josephine was never either ashamed or plaintive. She was in the world of being alone with a male, a world through which she had moved surely since she was eight years old. She did not plan; she merely let herself go, and the overwhelming life in her did the rest. It is only when youth is gone and experience has given us a sort of cheap courage that most of us realize how simple such things are.

'But you couldn't be in love with me,' Anthony wanted to say, and couldn't. He fought with a desire to kiss her again, even tenderly, and began to tell her that she was being unwise, but before he got really started at his handsome project, she was in his arms again, and whispering something that he had to accept, since it was wrapped up in a kiss. Then he was alone, driving away from her door.

What had he agreed to? All they had said rang and beat in his ear like an unexpected temperature—tomorrow at four o'clock on that corner.

'Good God!' he thought uneasily. 'All that stuff about giving me up. She's a crazy kid, she'll get into trouble if somebody looking for trouble comes along. *Big* chance of my meeting her tomorrow!'

And neither at dinner nor at the dance that he went to that night could Anthony get the episode out of his mind; he kept looking around the ballroom regretfully, as if he missed someone who should be there.

III

Two weeks later, waiting for Marice Whaley in a meagre, indefinable downstairs 'sitting-room,' Anthony reached in his pocket for some half-forgotten mail. Three letters he replaced; the other—after a moment of listening—he opened quickly and read with his back to the door. It was the third of a series—for one had followed each of his meetings with Josephine—and it was exactly like the others—the letter of a child. Whatever maturity of emotion could accumulate in her expression, when once she set pen to paper was snowed under by ineptitude. There was much about 'your feeling for me' and 'my feeling for you,' and sentences began, 'Yes, I know I am sentimental,' or more gawkily, 'I have always been sort of pash, and I can't help that,' and inevitably much quoting of lines from current popular songs, as if they expressed the writer's state of mind more fully than verbal struggles of her own.

The letter disturbed Anthony. As he reached the post-script, which coolly made a rendezvous for five o'clock this afternoon, he heard Marice coming downstairs, and put it back in his pocket.

Marice hummed and moved about the room. Anthony smoked.

'I saw you Tuesday afternoon,' she said suddenly. 'You seemed to be having a fine time.'

'Tuesday,' he repeated, as if thinking. 'Oh, yeah. I ran into some kids and we went to a tea dance. It was amusing.'

'You were *al*most alone when I saw you.'

'What are you getting at?'

Marice hummed again. 'Let's go out. Let's go to a matinée.'

On the way Anthony explained how he had happened to be with Connie's little sister; the necessity of the explanation somehow angered him. When he had done, Marice said crisply:

'If you wanted to rob the cradle, why did you have to pick out that little devil? Her reputation's so bad already that Mrs McRae didn't want to invite her to dancing class this year—she only did it on account of Constance.'

'Why is she so awful?' asked Anthony, disturbed.

'I'd rather not discuss it.'

His five o'clock engagement was on his mind throughout the matinée. Though Marice's remarks served only to make him dangerously sorry for Josephine, he was nevertheless determined that this meeting should be the last. It was embarrassing to have been remarked in her company, even though he had tried honestly to avoid it. The matter could very easily develop into a rather dangerous little mess, with no benefit either to Josephine or to himself. About Marice's indignation he did not care; she had been his for the asking all autumn, but Anthony did not want to get married; did not want to get involved with anybody at all.

It was dark when he was free at 5:30, and turned his car towards the new Philanthropological Building in the maze of reconstruction in Grant Park. The bleakness of place and time depressed him, gave a further painfulness to the affair. Getting out of his car, he walked past a young man in a waiting roadster—a young man whom he seemed to recognize—and found Josephine in the half darkness of the little chamber that the storm doors formed.

With an indefinable sound of greeting, she walked determinedly into his arms, putting up her face.

'I can only stay for a sec,' she protested, just as if he had begged her to come. 'I'm supposed to go to a wedding with sister, but I had to see you.'

When Anthony spoke, his voice froze into a white mist, obvious in the darkness. He said things he had said to her before but this time firmly and finally. It was easier, because he could scarcely see her face and because somewhere in the middle she irritated him by starting to cry.

'I knew you were supposed to be fickle,' she whispered, 'but I didn't expect this. Anyhow, I've got enough pride not to bother you any further.' She hesitated. 'But I wish we could meet just once more to try and arrive at a more different settlement.'

'No.'

'Some jealous girl has been talking to you about me.'

'No.' Then, in despair, he struck at her heart. 'I'm *not* fickle. I've never loved you and I *never* told you I did.'

Guessing at the forlorn expression that would come into her face, Anthony turned away and took a purposeless step; when he wheeled nervously about, the storm door had just shut—she was gone.

'Josephine!' he shouted in helpless pity, but there was no answer. He waited, heart in his boots, until presently he heard a car drive away.

At home, Josephine thanked Ed Bement, whom she had used, with a tartlet of hope, went in by a side door and up to her room. The window was open and, as she dressed hurriedly for the wedding she stood close to it so that she would catch cold and die.

Seeing her face in the bathroom mirror, she broke down and sat on the edge of the tub, making a small choking sound like a struggle with a cough, and cleaning her finger nails. Later she could cry all night in bed when everyone else was asleep, but now it was still afternoon.

The two sisters and their mother stood side by side at the wedding of Mary Jackson and Jackson Dillon. It was a sad and sentimental wedding—an end to the fine, glamorous youth of a girl who was universally admired and loved. Perhaps to no onlooker there were its details symbolical of the end of a period, yet from the vantage point of a decade, certain things that happened are already powdered with yesterday's ridiculousness, and even tinted with the lavender of the day before. The bride raised her veil, smiling that grave sweet smile that made her 'adored,' but with tears pouring down her cheeks, and faced dozens of friends hands outheld as if embracing all of them for the last time. Then she turned to a husband as serious and immaculate as herself, at him as if to say, 'That's done. All this that I am is yours forever and ever.'

In her pew, Constance, who had been at school with Mary Jackson, was frankly weeping, from a heart that was a ringing vault. But the face of Josephine beside her was a more intricate study. Once or twice, though Josephine's eyes lost none of their level straight intensity, an isolated tear escaped, and, as if startled by the feel of it, the face hardened slightly and the mouth remained in defiant immobility, like a child well warned against making a disturbance. Only once did she move; hearing a voice behind her say: 'That's the little Perry girl. Isn't she lovely-looking?' she turned presently and gazed at a stained-glass window lest her unknown admirers miss the sight of the side face.

Josephine's family went on to the reception, so she dined alone—or rather with her little brother and his nurse, which was the same thing.

She felt empty. Tonight Anthony Harker, 'so deeply lovable—so sweetly lovable—so deeply, sweetly lovable,' was making love to someone new, kissing her ugly, jealous face; soon he would have disappeared forever, together with all the men of his generation, into a loveless matrimony, leaving only a world of Travis de Coppet and Ed Bements—people so easy as to scarcely be worth the effort of a smile.

Up in her room, she was excited again by the sight of herself in the bathroom mirror. Oh, what if she should die in her sleep tonight?

'Oh, what a shame!' she whispered.

She opened the window, and holding her only souvenir of Anthony, a big initialed linen handkerchief, crept desolately into bed. While the sheets were still cold, there was a knock at the door.

'Special delivery letter,' said the maid.

Putting on the light, Josephine opened it, turned to the signature, then back again, her breast rising and falling quickly under her nightgown.

> DARLING LITTLE JOSEPHINE: It's no use. I can't help it, I can't lie about it. I'm desperately, terribly in love with you. When you went away this afternoon, it all rushed over me, and I knew I couldn't give you up. I drove home, and I couldn't eat or sit still, but only walk up and down thinking of your darling face and your darling tears, there in that vestibule. And now I sit writing this letter——

It was four pages long. Somewhere it disposed of their disparate ages as unimportant, and the last words were:

> I know how miserable you must be, and I would give ten years of my life to be there to kiss your sweet lips good night.

When she had read it through, Josephine sat motionless for some minutes; grief was suddenly gone, and for a moment she was so overwhelmed that she supposed joy had come in its stead. On her face was a twinkling frown.

'Gosh!' she said to herself. She read over the letter once more.

Her first instinct was to call up Lillian, but she thought better of it. The image of the bride at the wedding popped out at her—the reproachless bride, unsullied, beloved and holy with a sweet glow. An adolescence of uprightness, a host of friends, then the appearance of the perfect lover, the Ideal. With an effort, she recalled her drifting mind to the present occasion. Certainly Mary Jackson would never have kept such a letter. Getting out of bed, Josephine tore it into little pieces and, with some difficulty, caused by an unexpected amount of smoke, burned it on a glass-topped table. No well-brought up girl would have answered such a letter; the proper thing was to simply ignore it.

She wiped up the table top with the man's linen handkerchief she held in her hand, threw it absently into a laundry basket and crept into bed. She suddenly was very sleepy.

IV

For what ensued, no one, not even Constance, blamed Josephine. If a man of twenty-two should so debase himself as to pay frantic court to a girl of sixteen against the wishes of her parents and herself, there was only one answer—he was a person who shouldn't be received by decent people. When Travis de Coppet made a controversial remark on the affair at a dance, Ed Bement beat him into what was described as 'a pulp,' down in the washroom, and Josephine's reputation rose to normal and stayed there. Accounts of how Anthony had called time and time again at the house, each time denied admittance, how he had threatened Mr Perry, how he had tried to bribe a maid to deliver letters, how he had attempted to waylay Josephine on her way back from school—these things pointed to the fact that he was a little mad. It was Anthony Harker's own family who insisted that he should go West.

All this was a trying time for Josephine. She saw how close she had come to disaster, and by constant consideration and implicit obedience tried to make up to her parents for the trouble she had unwittingly caused. At first she decided she didn't want to go to any Christmas dances, but she was persuaded by her mother, who hoped she would be distracted by boys and girls home from school for the holidays. Mrs Perry was taking her East to the Brearley School early in January, and in the buying of clothes and uniforms mother and daughter were much together, and Mrs Perry was delighted at Josephine's new feeling of responsibility and maturity.

As a matter of fact, it was sincere, and only once did Josephine do anything that she could not have told the world. The day after New Year's she put on her new travelling suit and her new fur coat and went out by her familiar egress, the side door, and walked down the block to the waiting car of Ed Bement. Downtown she left Ed waiting at a corner and entered a drug store opposite the old Union Station on LaSalle Street. A man with an unhappy mouth and desperate, baffled eyes was waiting for her there.

'Thank you for coming,' he said miserably.

She didn't answer. Her face was grave and polite.

'Here's what I want—just one thing,' he said quickly: 'Why did you change? What did I do that made you change so suddenly? Was it something that happened, something I did? Was it what I said in the vestibule that night?'

Still looking at him, she tried to think, but she could only think how unattractive and rather terrible she found him now, and try not to let him see it. There would have been no use saying the simple truth—that she could not help what she had done, that great beauty has a need, almost an obligation, of trying itself, that her ample cup of emotion had spilled over of its own accord, and it was an accident that it had destroyed him and not her. The eyes of pity might follow Anthony Harker in his journey West, but most certainly the eyes of destiny followed Josephine as she crossed the street through the falling snow to Ed Bement's car.

She sat quiet for a minute as they drove away, relieved and yet full of awe. Anthony Harker was twenty-two, handsome, popular and sought after—and how he had loved her—so much that he had to go away. She was as impressed as if they had been two other people.

Taking her silence for depression, Ed Bement said:

'Well, it did one thing anyhow—it stopped that other story they had around about you.'

She turned to him quickly: 'What story?'

'Oh, just some crazy story.'

'What was it?' she demanded.

'Oh, nothing much,' he said hesitantly, 'but there was a story around last August that you and Travis de Coppet were married.'

'Why, how perfectly terrible!' she exclaimed. 'Why, I never heard of such a lie. It—' She stopped herself short of saying the truth—that though she and Travis had adventurously driven twenty miles to New Ulm, they had been unable to find a minister willing to marry them. It all seemed ages behind her, childish, forgotten.

'Oh, how perfectly terrible!' she repeated. 'That's the kind of story that gets started by jealous girls.'

'I know,' agreed Ed. 'I'd just like to hear any boy try to repeat it to me. Nobody believed it anyhow.'

It was the work of ugly and jealous girls. Ed Bement, aware of her body next to him, and of her face shining like fire through the half darkness, knew that nobody so beautiful could ever do anything really wrong.

JOSEPHINE

A WOMAN WITH A PAST

[1930]

DRIVING slowly through New Haven, two of the young girls became alert. Josephine and Lillian darted soft frank glances into strolling groups of three or four under-graduates, into larger groups on corners, which swung about as one man to stare at their receding heads. Be-lieving that they recognized an acquaintance in a solitary loiterer, they waved wildly, whereupon the youth's mouth fell open, and as they turned the next corner he made a dazed dilatory gesture with his hand. They laughed. 'We'll send him a post card when we get back to school tonight, to see if it really was him.'

Adele Craw, sitting on one of the little seats, kept on talking to Miss Chambers, the chaperon. Glancing sideways at her, Lillian winked at Josephine without batting an eye, but Josephine had gone into a reverie.

This was New Haven—city of her adolescent dreams, of glittering proms where she would move on air among men as intangible as the tunes they danced to. City sacred as Mecca, shining as Paris, hidden as Timbuktu. Twice a year the life-blood of Chicago, her home, flowed into it, and twice a year flowed back, bringing Christmas or bringing summer. Bingo, bingo, bingo, that's the lingo; love of mine, I pine for one of your glances; the darling boy on the left there; underneath the stars I wait.

Seeing it for the first time, she found herself sur-prisingly unmoved—the men they passed seemed young and rather bored with the possibilities of the day, glad of anything to stare at; seemed undynamic and purpose-less against the background of bare elms, lakes of dirty snow and buildings crowded together under the February sky. A wisp of hope, a well-turned-out derby-crowned man, hurrying with stick and suitcase towards the station, caught her attention, but his reciprocal glance was too startled, too ingenuous. Josephine wondered at the extent of her own disillusionment.

She was exactly seventeen and she was blasé. Already she had been a sensation and a scandal; she had driven mature men to a state of disequilibrium; she had, it was said, killed her grandfather, but as he was over eighty at the time perhaps he just died. Here and there in the Middle West were discouraged little spots which upon inspection turned out to be the youths who had once looked full into her green and wistful eyes. But her love affair of last summer had ruined her faith in the all-sufficiency of men. She had grown bored with the waning September days—and it seemed as though it had happened once too often. Christmas with its provocative shortness, its travelling glee clubs, had brought no one new. There remained to her only a persistent, a physical hope; hope in her stomach that there was someone whom she would love more than he loved her.

They stopped at a sporting-goods store and Adele Craw, a pretty girl with clear honourable eyes and piano legs, purchased the sporting equipment which was the reason for their trip—they were the spring hockey committee for the school. Adele was in addition the president of the senior class and the school's ideal girl. She had lately seen a change for the better in Josephine Perry— rather as an honest citizen might guilelessly approve a peculator retired on his profits. On the other hand, Adele was simply incomprehensible to Josephine—admirable, without doubt, but a member of another species. Yet with the charming adaptability that she had hitherto reserved for men, Josephine was trying hard not to disillusion her, trying to be honestly interested in the small, neat, organized politics of the school.

Two men who had stood with their backs to them at another counter turned to leave the store, when they caught sight of Miss Chambers and Adele. Immediately they came forward. The one who spoke to Miss Chambers was thin and rigid of face. Josephine recognized him as Miss Brereton's nephew, a student at New Haven, who had spent several week-ends with his aunt at the school. The other man Josephine had never seen before. He was tall and broad, with blond curly hair and an open expression in which strength of purpose and a nice consideration were pleasantly mingled. It was not the sort of face that generally appealed to Josephine. The eyes were obviously without a secret, without a sidewise gambol, without a desperate flicker to show that they had a life of their own apart from the mouth's speech. The mouth itself was large and masculine; its smile was an act of kindness and control. It was rather with curiosity as to the sort of man who would be attentive to Adele Craw that Josephine continued to look at him, for his voice that obviously couldn't lie greeted Adele as if this meeting was the pleasant surprise of his day.

In a moment Josephine and Lillian were called over and introduced.

'This is Mr Waterbury'—that was Miss Brereton's nephew—'and Mr Dudley Knowleton.'

Glancing at Adele, Josephine saw on her face an expression of tranquil pride, even of possession. Mr Knowleton spoke politely, but it was obvious that though he looked at the younger girls he did not quite see them. But since they were friends of Adele's he made suitable remarks, eliciting the fact that they were both coming down to New Haven to their first prom the following week. Who were their hosts? Sophomores; he knew them slightly. Josephine thought that was unnecessarily superior. Why, they were the charter members of the Loving Brothers' Association—Ridgeway Saunders and George Davey—and on the glee-club trip the girls they picked out to rush in each city considered themselves a sort of élite, second only to the girls they asked to New Haven.

'And oh, I've got some bad news for you,' Knowleton

said to Adele. 'You may be leading the prom. Jack Coe
went to the infirmary with appendicitis, and against my
better judgment I'm the provisional chairman.' He looked
apologetic. 'Being one of those stoneage dancers, the two-
step king, I don't see how I ever got on the committee
at all.'

When the car was on its way back to Miss Brereton's
school, Josephine and Lillian bombarded Adele with
questions.

'He's an old friend from Cincinnati,' she explained
demurely. 'He's captain of the baseball team and he was
last man for Skull and Bones.'

'You're going to the prom with him?'

'Yes. You see, I've known him all my life.'

Was there a faint implication in this remark that only
those who had known Adele all her life knew her at her
true worth?

'Are you engaged?' Lillian demanded.

Adele laughed. 'Mercy, I don't think of such matters!
It doesn't seem to be time for that sort of thing yet,
does it?' ('Yes,' interpolated Josephine silently.) 'We're
just good friends. I think there can be a perfectly healthy
friendship between a man and a girl without a lot of—'

'Mush,' supplied Lillian helpfully.

'Well, yes, but I don't like that word. I was going to
say without a lot of sentimental romantic things that
ought to come later.'

'Bravo, Adele!' said Miss Chambers somewhat per-
functorily.

But Josephine's curiosity was unappeased.

'Doesn't he say he's in love with you, and all that sort
of thing?'

'Mercy, no! Dud doesn't believe in such stuff any
more than I do. He's got enough to do at New Haven,
serving on the committees and the team.'

'Oh!' said Josephine.

She was oddly interested. That two people who were
attracted to each other should never even say anything

about it but be content to 'not believe in such stuff,' was something new in her experience. She had known girls who had no beaux, others who seemed to have no emotions, and still others who lied about what they thought and did; but here was a girl who spoke of the attentions of the last man tapped for Skull and Bones as if they were two of the limestone gargoyles that Miss Chambers had pointed out on the just completed Harkness Hall. Yet Adele seemed happy—happier than Josephine, who had always believed that boys and girls were made for nothing but each other, and as soon as possible.

In the light of his popularity and achievements, Knowleton seemed more attractive. Josephine wondered if he would remember her and dance with her at the prom, or if that depended on how well he knew her escort, Ridgeway Saunders. She tried to remember whether she had smiled at him when he was looking at her. If she had really smiled he would remember her and dance with her. She was still trying to be sure of that over her two French irregular verbs and her ten stanzas of the Ancient Mariner that night; but she was still uncertain when she fell asleep.

II

Three gay young sophomores, the founders of the Loving Brothers' Association, took a house together for Josephine, Lillian and a girl from Farmington and their three mothers. For the girls it was a first prom, and they arrived at New Haven with all the nervousness of the condemned; but a Sheffield fraternity tea in the afternoon yielded up such a plethora of boys from home, and boys who had visited there and friends of those boys, and new boys with unknown possibilities but obvious eagerness, that they were glowing with self-confidence as they poured into the glittering crowd that thronged the armoury at ten.

It was impressive; for the first time Josephine was at a function run by men upon men's standards—an outward projection of the New Haven world from which women were excluded and which went on mysteriously behind the scenes. She perceived that their three escorts, who had once seemed the very embodiments of worldliness, were modest fry in this relentless microcosm of accomplishment and success. A man's world! Looking around her at the glee-club concert, Josephine had felt a grudging admiration for the good fellowship, the good feeling. She envied Adele Craw, barely glimpsed in the dressing-room, for the position she automatically occupied by being Dudley Knowleton's girl tonight. She envied her more stepping off under the draped bunting through a gateway of hydrangeas at the head of the grand march, very demure and faintly unpowdered in a plain white dress. She was temporarily the centre of all attention, and at the sight something that had long lain dormant in Josephine awakened—her sense of a problem, a scarcely defined possibility.

'Josephine,' Ridgeway Saunders began, 'you can't realize how happy I am now that it's come true. I've looked forward to this so long, and dreamed about it—'

She smiled up at him automatically, but her mind was elsewhere, and as the dance progressed the idea continued to obsess her. She was rushed from the beginning; to the men from the tea were added a dozen new faces, a dozen confident or timid voices, until, like all the more popular girls, she had her own queue trailing her about the room. Yet all this had happened to her before, and there was something missing. One might have ten men to Adele's two, but Josephine was abruptly aware that here a girl took on the importance of the man who had brought her.

She was discomforted by the unfairness of it. A girl earned her popularity by being beautiful and charming. The more beautiful and charming she was, the more she could afford to disregard public opinion. It seemed absurd that simply because Adele had managed to attach a baseball captain, who mightn't know anything about girls at all, or be able to judge their attractions, she should be thus elevated in spite of her thick ankles, her rather too pinkish face.

Josephine was dancing with Ed Bement from Chicago. He was her earliest beau, a flame of pigtail days in dancing school when one wore white cotton stockings, lace drawers with a waist attached and ruffled dresses with the inevitable sash.

'What's the matter with me?' she asked Ed, thinking aloud. 'For months I've felt as if I were a hundred years old, and I'm just seventeen and that party was only seven years ago.'

'You've been in love a lot since then,' Ed said.

'I haven't,' she protested indignantly. 'I've had a lot of silly stories started about me, without any foundation, usually by girls who were jealous.'

'Jealous of what?'

'Don't get fresh,' she said tartly. 'Dance me near Lillian.'

Dudley Knowleton had just cut in on Lillian. Josephine spoke to her friend; then waiting until their turns would bring them face to face over a space of seconds, she smiled at Knowleton. This time she made sure that smile intersected as well as met glance, that he passed beside the circumference of her fragrant charm. If this had been named like French perfume of a later day it might have been called 'Please.' He bowed and smiled back; a minute later he cut in on her.

It was in an eddy in a corner of the room and she danced slower so that he adapted himself, and for a moment they went around in a slow circle.

'You looked so sweet leading the march with Adele,' she told him. 'You seemed so serious and kind, as if the others were a lot of children. Adele looked sweet, too.' And she added on an inspiration, 'At school I've taken her for a model.'

'You have!' She saw him conceal his sharp surprise as he said, 'I'll have to tell her that.'

He was handsomer than she had thought, and behind his cordial good manners there was a sort of authority. Though he was correctly attentive to her, she saw his eyes search the room quickly to see if all went well; he spoke quietly, in passing, to the orchestra leader, who came down deferentially to the edge of his dais. Last man for Bones. Josephine knew what that meant—her father had been Bones. Ridgeway Saunders and the rest of the Loving Brothers' Association would certainly not be Bones. She wondered, if there had been a Bones for girls, whether she would be tapped—or Adele Craw with her ankles, symbol of solidity.

> Come on o-ver here,
> Want to have you near;
> Come on join the part-y,
> Get a wel-come heart-y.

'I wonder how many boys here have taken you for a model,' she said. 'If I were a boy you'd be exactly what I'd like to be. Except I'd be terribly bothered having girls falling in love with me all the time.'

'They don't,' he said simply. 'They never have.'

'Oh, yes—but they hide it because they're so impressed with you, and they're afraid of Adele.'

'Adele wouldn't object.' And he added hastily, '—if it ever happened. Adele doesn't believe in being serious about such things.'

'Are you engaged to her?'

He stiffened a little. 'I don't believe in being engaged till the right time comes.'

'Neither do I,' agreed Josephine readily. 'I'd rather have one good friend than a hundred people hanging around being mushy all the time.'

'Is that what that crowd does that keeps following you around tonight?'

'What crowd?' she asked innocently.

'The fifty per cent of the sophomore class that's rushing you.'

'A lot of parlour snakes,' she said ungratefully.

Josephine was radiantly happy now as she turned beautifully through the newly enchanted hall in the arms of the chairman of the prom committee. Even this extra time with him she owed to the awe which he inspired in her entourage; but a man cut in eventually and there was a sharp fall in her elation. The man was impressed that Dudley Knowleton had danced with her; he was more respectful, and his modulated admiration bored her. In a little while, she hoped, Dudley Knowleton would cut back, but as midnight passed, dragging on another hour with it, she wondered if after all it had only been a courtesy to a girl from Adele's school. Since then Adele had probably painted him a neat little landscape of Josephine's past. When finally he approached her she grew tense and watchful, a state which made her exteriorly pliant and tender and quiet. But instead of dancing he drew her into the edge of a row of boxes.

'Adele had an accident on the cloakroom steps. She turned her ankle a little and tore her stocking on a nail. She'd like to borrow a pair from you because you're staying near here and we're way out at the Lawn Club.'

'Of course.'

'I'll run over with you—I have a car outside.'

'But you're busy, you mustn't bother.'

'Of course I'll go with you.'

There was thaw in the air; a hint of thin and lucid spring hovered delicately around the elms and cornices of buildings whose bareness and coldness had so depressed her the week before. The night had a quality of asceticism, as if the essence of masculine struggle were seeping everywhere through the little city where men of three centuries had brought their energies and aspirations for winnowing. And Dudley Knowleton sitting beside her, dynamic and capable, was symbolic of it all. It seemed that she had never met a man before.

'Come in, please,' she said as he went up the steps of the house with her. 'They've made it very comfortable.'

There was an open fire burning in the dark parlour. When she came downstairs with the stockings she went in and stood beside him, very still for a moment, watching it with him. Then she looked up, still silent, looked down, looked at him again.

'Did you get the stockings?' he asked, moving a little.

'Yes,' she said breathlessly. 'Kiss me for being so quick.'

He laughed as if she said something witty and moved towards the door. She was smiling and her disappointment was deeply hidden as they got into the car.

'It's been wonderful meeting you,' she told him. 'I can't tell you how many ideas I've gotten from what you said.'

'But I haven't any ideas.'

'You have. All that about not getting engaged till the proper time comes. I haven't had much opportunity to talk to a man like you. Otherwise my ideas would be different, I guess. I've just realized that I've been wrong about a lot of things. I used to want to be exciting. Now I want to help people.'

'Yes,' he agreed, 'that's very nice.'

He seemed about to say more when they arrived at the armoury. In their absence supper had begun; and crossing the great floor by his side, conscious of many eyes regarding them, Josephine wondered if people thought that they had been up to something.

'We're late,' said Knowleton when Adele went off to put on the stockings. 'The man you're with has probably given you up long ago. You'd better let me get you something here.'

'That would be too divine.'

Afterwards, back on the floor again, she moved in a sweet aura of abstraction. The followers of several departed belles merged with hers until now no girl on the floor was cut in on with such frequency. Even Miss Brereton's nephew, Ernest Waterbury, danced with her in stiff approval. Danced? With a tentative change of pace she simply swung from man to man in a sort of hands-right-and-left around the floor. She felt a sudden need to relax, and as if in answer to her mood a new man was presented, a tall, sleek Southerner with a persuasive note:

'You lovely creacha. I been strainin my eyes watchin your cameo face floatin round. You stand out above all these othuz like an Amehken Beauty Rose over a lot of field daisies.'

Dancing with him a second time, Josephine hearkened to his pleadings.

'All right. Let's go outside.'

'It wasn't outdaws I was considering,' he explained as they left the floor. 'I happen to have a mortgage on a nook right hee in the building.'

'All right.'

Book Chaffee, of Alabama, led the way through the cloakroom, through a passage to an inconspicuous door.

'This is the private apartment of my friend Sergeant Boone, instructa of the battery. He wanted to be particularly sure it'd be used as a nook tonight and not a readin room or anything like that.'

Opening the door he turned on a dim light; she came in and he shut it behind her, and they faced each other.

'Mighty sweet,' he murmured. His tall face came down, his long arms wrapped around her tenderly, and very slowly so that their eyes met for quite a long time, he drew her up to him. Josephine kept thinking that she had never kissed a Southern boy before.

They started apart at the sudden sound of a key turning in the lock outside. Then there was a muffled snicker followed by retreating footsteps, and Book sprang for the door and wrenched at the handle just as Josephine noticed that this was not only Sergeant Boone's parlour; it was his bedroom as well.

'Who was it?' she demanded. 'Why did they lock us in?'

'Some funny boy. I'd like to get my hands on him.'

'Will he come back?'

Book sat down on the bed to think. 'I couldn't say. Don't even know who it was. But if somebody on the committee came along it wouldn't look too good, would it?'

Seeing her expression change, he came over and put his arm around her. 'Don't you worry, honey. We'll fix it.'

She returned his kiss, briefly but without distraction. Then she broke away and went into the next apartment, which was hung with boots, uniform coats and various military equipment.

'There's a window up here,' she said. It was high in the wall and had not been opened for a long time. Book mounted on a chair and forced it ajar.

'About ten feet down,' he reported, after a moment, 'but there's a big pile of snow just underneath. You might get a nasty fall and you'll sure soak your shoes and stockin's.'

'We've got to get out,' Josephine said sharply.

'We'd better wait and give this funny man a chance—'

'I won't wait. I want to get out. Look—throw out all the blankets from the bed and I'll jump on that: or you jump first and spread them over the pile of snow.'

After that it was merely exciting. Carefully Book Chaffee wiped the dust from the window to protect her dress; then they were struck silent by a footstep that approached—and passed the outer door. Book jumped, and she heard him kicking profanely as he waded out of the soft drift below. He spread the blankets. At the moment when Josephine swung her legs out the window, there was the sound of voices outside the door and the key turned again in the lock. She landed softly, reaching for his hand, and convulsed with laughter they ran and skidded down the half block towards the corner, and reaching the entrance to the armoury, they stood panting for a moment, breathing in the fresh night. Book was reluctant to go inside.

'Why don't you let me conduct you where you're stayin? We can sit around and sort of recuperate.'

She hesitated, drawn towards him by the community of their late predicament; but something was calling her inside, as if the fulfilment of her elation awaited her there.

'No,' she decided.

As they went in she collided with a man in a great hurry, and looked up to recognize Dudley Knowleton.

'So sorry,' he said. 'Oh hello—'

'Won't you dance me over to my box?' she begged him impulsively. 'I've torn my dress.'

As they started off he said abstractedly: 'The fact is, a little mischief has come up and the buck has been passed to me. I was going along to see about it.'

Her heart raced wildly and she felt the need of being another sort of person immediately.

'I can't tell you how much it's meant meeting you. It would be wonderful to have one friend I could be serious with without being all mushy and sentimental. Would you mind if I wrote you a letter—I mean, would Adele mind?'

'Lord, no!' His smile had become utterly unfathomable to her. As they reached the box she thought of one more thing:

'Is it true that the baseball team is training at Hot Springs during Easter?'

'Yes. You going there?'

'Yes. Good night, Mr Knowleton.'

But she was destined to see him once more. It was outside the men's coat room, where she waited among a crowd of other pale survivors and their paler mothers, whose wrinkles had doubled and tripled with the passing night. He was explaining something to Adele, and Josephine heard the phrase, 'The door was locked, and the window open—'

Suddenly it occurred to Josephine that, meeting her coming in damp and breathless, he must have guessed at the truth—and Adele would doubtless confirm his suspicion. Once again the spectre of her old enemy, the plain and jealous girl, arose before her. Shutting her mouth tight together she turned away.

But they had seen her, and Adele called to her in her cheerful ringing voice:

'Come say good night. You were so sweet about the stockings. Here's a girl you won't find doing shoddy, silly things, Dudlcy.' Impulsively she leaned and kissed Josephine on the cheek. 'You'll see I'm right, Dudley —next year she'll be the most respected girl in school.'

III

As things go in the interminable days of early March, what happened next happened quickly. The annual senior dance at Miss Brereton's school came on a night soaked through with spring, and all the junior girls lay awake listening to the sighing tunes from the gymnasium. Between the numbers, when boys up from New Haven and Princeton wandered about the grounds, cloistered glances looked down from dark open windows upon the vague figures.

Not Josephine, though she lay awake like the others. Such vicarious diversions had no place in the sober patterns she was spinning now from day to day; yet she might as well have been in the forefront of those who called down to the men and threw notes and entered into conversations, for destiny had suddenly turned against her and was spinning a dark web of its own.

> Lit-tle lady, don't be depressed and blue,
> After all, we're both in the same can-noo—

Dudley Knowleton was over in the gymnasium fifty yards away, but proximity to a man did not thrill her as it would have done a year ago—not, at least, in the same way. Life, she saw now, was a serious matter, and

6+S.F. 6

in the modest darkness a line of a novel ceaselessly re-
curred to her: 'He is a man fit to be the father of my
children.' What were the seductive graces, the fast lines
of a hundred parlour snakes compared to such realities.
One couldn't go on forever kissing comparative strangers
behind half-closed doors.

Under her pillow now were two letters, answers to
her letters. They spoke in a bold round hand of the
beginning of baseball practice; they were glad Josephine
felt as she did about things; and the writer certainly
looked forward to seeing her at Easter. Of all the letters
she had ever received they were the most difficult from
which to squeeze a single drop of heart's blood—one
couldn't even read the 'Yours' of the subscription as
'Your'—but Josephine knew them by heart. They were
precious because he had taken the time to write them;
they were eloquent in the very postage stamp because
he used so few.

She was restless in her bed—the music had begun
again in the gymnasium:

> Oh, my love, I've waited so long for you,
> Oh, my love, I'm singing this song for you—
>   Oh-h-h—

From the next room there was light laughter, and then
from below a male voice, and a long interchange of comic
whispers. Josephine recognized Lillian's laugh and the
voices of two other girls. She could imagine them as
they lay across the window in their nightgowns, their
heads just showing from the open window. 'Come right
down,' one boy kept saying. 'Don't be formal—come just
as you are.'

There was a sudden silence, then a quick crunching
of footsteps on gravel, a suppressed snicker and a scurry,
and the sharp, protesting groan of several beds in the
next room and the banging of a door down the hall.
Trouble for somebody, maybe. A few minutes later
Josephine's door half opened, she caught a glimpse of

Miss Kwain against the dim corridor light, and then the door closed.

The next afternoon Josephine and four other girls, all of whom denied having breathed so much as a word into the night, were placed on probation. There was absolutely nothing to do about it. Miss Kwain had recognized their faces in the window and they were all from two rooms. It was an injustice, but it was nothing compared to what happened next. One week before Easter vacation the school motored off on a one-day trip to inspect a milk farm—all save the ones on probation. Miss Chambers, who sympathized with Josephine's misfortune, enlisted her services in entertaining Mr Ernest Waterbury, who was spending a week-end with his aunt. This was only vaguely better than nothing, for Mr Waterbury was a very dull, very priggish young man. He was so dull and so priggish that the following morning Josephine was expelled from school.

It happened like this: they had strolled in the grounds, they had sat down at a garden table and had tea. Ernest Waterbury had expressed a desire to see something in the chapel, just a few minutes before his aunt's car rolled up the drive. The chapel was reached by descending winding mock-medieval stairs; and, her shoes still wet from the garden, Josephine had slipped on the top step and fallen five feet directly into Mr Waterbury's unwilling arms, where she lay helpless, convulsed with irresistible laughter. It was in this position that Miss Brereton and the visiting trustee had found them.

'But I had nothing to do with it!' declared the ungallant Mr Waterbury. Flustered and outraged, he was packed back to New Haven, and Miss Brereton, connecting this with last week's sin, proceeded to lose her head. Josephine, humiliated and furious, lost hers, and Mr Perry, who happened to be in New York, arrived at the school the same night. At his passionate indignation, Miss Brereton collapsed and retracted, but the damage was done, and Josephine packed her trunk. Unexpectedly, monstrously, just as it had begun to mean something, her school life was over.

For the moment all her feelings were directed against Miss Brereton, and the only tears she shed at leaving were of anger and resentment. Riding with her father up to New York, she saw that while at first he had instinctively and whole-heartedly taken her part, he felt also a certain annoyance with her misfortune.

'We'll all survive,' he said. 'Unfortunately, even that old idiot Miss Brereton will survive. She ought to be running a reform school.' He brooded for a moment. 'Anyhow, your mother arrives tomorrow and you and she go down to Hot Springs as you planned.'

'Hot Springs!' Josephine cried, in a choked voice. 'Oh, no!'

'Why not?' he demanded in surprise. 'It seems the best thing to do. Give it a chance to blow over before you go back to Chicago.'

'I'd rather go to Chicago,' said Josephine breathlessly. 'Daddy, I'd much rather go to Chicago.'

'That's absurd. Your mother's started East and the arrangements are all made. At Hot Springs you can get out and ride and play golf and forget that old she-devil—'

'Isn't there another place in the East we could go? There's people I know going to Hot Springs who'll know all about this, people that I don't want to meet—girls from school.'

'Now, Jo, you keep your chin up—this is one of those times. Sorry I said that about letting it blow over in Chicago; if we hadn't made other plans we'd go back and face every old shrew and gossip in town right away. When anybody slinks off in a corner they think you've been up to something bad. If anybody says anything to you, you tell them the truth—what I said to Miss Brereton. You tell them she said you could come back and I damn well wouldn't let you go back.'

'They won't believe it.'

There would be, at all events, four days of respite

at Hot Springs before the vacations of the schools. Josephine passed this time taking golf lessons from a professional so newly arrived from Scotland that he surely
knew nothing of her misadventure; she even went riding
with a young man one afternoon, feeling almost at home
with him after his admission that he had flunked out
of Princeton in February—a confidence, however, which
she did not reciprocate in kind. But in the evenings,
despite the young man's importunity, she stayed with
her mother, feeling nearer to her than she ever had before.

But one afternoon in the lobby Josephine saw by the
desk two dozen good-looking young men waiting by a
stack of bat cases and bags, and knew that what she
dreaded was at hand. She ran upstairs and with an invented headache dined there that night, but after dinner
she walked restlessly around their apartment. She was
ashamed not only of her situation but of her reaction
to it. She had never felt any pity for the unpopular girls
who skulked in dressing-rooms because they could attract
no partners on the floor, or for girls who were outsiders
at Lake Forest, and now she was like them—hiding
miserably out of life. Alarmed lest already the change
was written in her face, she paused in front of the
mirror, fascinated as ever by what she found there.

'The darn fools!' she said aloud. And as she said it
her chin went up and the faint cloud about her eyes
lifted. The phrases of the myriad love letters she had
received passed before her eyes; behind her, after all,
was the reassurance of a hundred lost and pleading faces,
of innumerable tender and pleading voices. Her pride
flooded back into her till she could see the warm blood
rushing up into her cheeks.

There was a knock at the door—it was the Princeton
boy.

'How about slipping downstairs?' he proposed. 'There's
a dance. It's full of E-lies, the whole Yale baseball team.
I'll pick up one of them and introduce you and you'll
have a big time. How about it?'

'All right, but I don't want to meet anybody. You'll just have to dance with me all evening.'

'You know that suits me.'

She hurried into a new spring evening dress of the frailest fairy blue. In the excitement of seeing herself in it, it seemed as if she had shed the old skin of winter and emerged a shining chrysalis with no stain; and going downstairs her feet fell softly just off the beat of the music from below. It was a tune from a play she had seen a week ago in New York, a tune with a future—ready for gaieties as yet unthought of, lovers not yet met. Dancing off, she was certain that life had innumerable beginnings. She had hardly gone ten steps when she was cut in upon by Dudley Knowleton.

'Why, Josephine!' He had never used her first name before—he stood holding her hand. 'Why, I'm so glad to see you! I've been hoping and hoping you'd be here.'

She soared skyward on a rocket of surprise and delight. He was actually glad to see her—the expression on his face was obviously sincere. Could it be possible that he hadn't heard?

'Adele wrote me you might be here. She wasn't sure.'

—Then he knew and didn't care; he liked her anyhow.

'I'm in sackcloth and ashes,' she said.

'Well, they're very becoming to you.'

'You know what happened—' she ventured.

'I do. I wasn't going to say anything, but it's generally agreed that Waterbury behaved like a fool—and it's not going to be much help to him in the elections next month. Look—I want you to dance with some men who are just starving for a touch of beauty.'

Presently she was dancing with, it seemed to her, the entire team at once. Intermittently Dudley Knowleton cut back in, as well as the Princeton man, who was somewhat indignant at this unexpected competition. There were many girls from many schools in the room, but with an admirable team spirit the Yale men displayed a sharp prejudice in Josephine's favour; already she was pointed out from the chairs along the wall.

But interiorly she was waiting for what was coming, for the moment when she would walk with Dudley Knowleton into the warm, Southern night. It came naturally, just at the end of a number, and they strolled along an avenue of early-blooming lilacs and turned a corner and another corner. . . .

'You were glad to see me, weren't you?' Josephine said.

'Of course.'

'I was afraid at first. I was sorriest about what happened at school because of you. I'd been trying so hard to be different—because of you.'

'You mustn't think of that school business any more. Everybody that matters knows you got a bad deal. Forget it and start over.'

'Yes,' she agreed tranquilly. She was happy. The breeze and the scent of lilacs—that was she, lovely and intangible; the rustic bench where they sat and the trees—that was he, rugged and strong beside her, protecting her.

'I'd thought so much of meeting you here,' she said after a minute. 'You'd been so good for me, that I thought maybe in a different way I could be good for you—I mean I know ways of having a good time that you don't know. For instance, we've certainly got to go horseback riding by moonlight some night. That'll be fun.'

He didn't answer.

'I can really be very nice when I like somebody—that's really not often,' she interpolated hastily, 'not seriously. But I mean when I do feel seriously that a boy and I are really friends I don't believe in having a whole mob of other boys hanging around taking up time. I like to be with him all the time, all day and all evening, don't you?'

He stirred a little on the bench; he leaned forward with his elbows on his knees, looking at his strong hands. Her gently modulated voice sank a note lower.

'When I like anyone I don't even like dancing. It's sweeter to be alone.'

Silence for a moment.

'Well, you know'—he hesitated, frowning—'as a matter of fact, I'm mixed up in a lot of engagements made some time ago with some people.' He floundered about unhappily. 'In fact, I won't even be at the hotel after tomorrow. I'll be at the house of some people down the valley—a sort of house party. As a matter of fact, Adele's getting here tomorrow.'

Absorbed in her own thoughts, she hardly heard him at first, but at the name she caught her breath sharply.

'We're both to be at this house party while we're here, and I imagine it's more or less arranged what we're going to do. Of course, in the daytime I'll be here for baseball practice.'

'I see.' Her lips were quivering. 'You won't be—you'll be with Adele.'

'I think that—more or less—I will. She'll—want to see you, of course.'

Another silence while he twisted his big fingers and she helplessly imitated the gesture.

'You were just sorry for me,' she said. 'You like Adele —much better.'

'Adele and I understand each other. She's been more or less my ideal since we were children together.'

'And I'm not your kind of girl?' Josephine's voice trembled with a sort of fright. 'I suppose because I've kissed a lot of boys and got a reputation for speed and raised the deuce.'

'It isn't that.'

'Yes, it is,' she declared passionately. 'I'm just paying for things.' She stood up. 'You'd better take me back inside so I can dance with the kind of boys that like me.'

She walked quickly down the path, tears of misery streaming from her eyes. He overtook her by the steps, but she only shook her head and said, 'Excuse me for being so fresh. I'll grow up—I got what was coming to me—it's all right.'

A little later when she looked around the floor for him he had gone—and Josephine realized with a shock that for the first time in her life, she had tried for a man and failed. But, save in the very young, only love begets love, and from the moment Josephine had perceived that his interest in her was merely kindness she realized the wound was not in her heart but in her pride. She would forget him quickly, but she would never forget what she had learned from him. There were two kinds of men, those you played with and those you might marry. And as this passed through her mind, her restless eyes wandered casually over the group of stags, resting very lightly on Mr Gordon Tinsley, the current catch of Chicago, reputedly the richest young man in the Middle West. He had never paid any attention to young Josephine until tonight. Ten minutes ago he had asked her to go driving with him tomorrow.

But he did not attract her—and she decided to refuse. One mustn't run through people, and, for the sake of a romantic half-hour, trade a possibility that might develop —quite seriously—later, at the proper time. She did not know that this was the first mature thought that she had ever had in her life, but it was.

The orchestra were packing their instruments and the Princeton man was still at her ear, still imploring her to walk out with him into the night. Josephine knew without cogitation which sort of man he was—and the moon was bright even on the windows. So with a certain sense of relaxation she took his arm and they strolled out to the pleasant bower she had so lately quitted, and their faces turned towards each other, like little moons under the great white ones which hovered high over the Blue Ridge; his arm dropped softly about her yielding shoulder.

'Well?' he whispered.

'Well.'

6*

IV
LAST ACT
AND EPILOGUE

EDITOR'S NOTE

THERE had been intimations of disaster—'faintly signalled, like a nervous beating of the feet'—in some of the stories Fitzgerald wrote in 1928 and 1929. By the middle of 1930 the disaster was upon him: Zelda was a patient in a Swiss sanatorium, where the doctors were unable to promise that she would recover, and Fitzgerald was beginning to think of himself as an alcoholic. One result of the new situation was a new type of story, more complicated emotionally, with less yearning for the past and more dignity in the face of real sorrow. I have placed 'Babylon Revisited' (1931) a little out of its chronological order, at the head of the stories in this group, since it confirms and illuminates the others. It shows how much has changed in two years. The hero, who might have figured in the background of earlier stories, is now a bewildered survivor wandering through Paris like a lonely bison. 'I lost everything I wanted in the boom,' he says to the head barman at the Ritz, and then he adds to himself, 'The snow of twenty-nine wasn't real snow. If you didn't want it to be snow, you just paid some money.'

The three stories that follow 'Babylon' were first published in the preceding year. Among them 'Two Wrongs' dates from a period when Fitzgerald was recovering from a mild attack of tuberculosis—his second or third—and Zelda was working frantically to become a professional dancer. 'What if she floated out of my life?' it seems to ask. . . . 'The Bridal Party' was suggested by the Paris wedding of Powell Fowler, much chronicled in the summer of 1930. Better than anything else I have read it gives us the atmosphere of that brief time when the spirit of the Wall Street boom still flourished after the crash. . . . 'One Trip Abroad,' written while Zelda was in the sanatorium, was an attempt to reconsider their years in Europe and was also an early sketch for *Tender Is the*

Night. It is another 'junked and dismantled' story, with many of the details saved out for use in the novel, including the heroine's name—Nicole—, the rainstorm over the Lake of Geneva, and the cannon booming to save the vineyards from hail.

Next in the group are two stories written in 1932 and later included in *Taps at Reveille.* 'Family in the Wind' is among the best—after 'Babylon'—of his many case histories of gifted alcoholics, and it is completely honest even in its mixture of self-justification and boozy goodness with a dash of self-contempt. . . . 'Crazy Sunday' is the fortunate result of a second brief and disastrous trip to Hollywood. Besides showing what Fitzgerald had learned about the movie-makers, it reveals his admiration for Irving Thalberg, who served as a model for the director in the story and would later become the hero of *The Last Tycoon.*

In 1933 Fitzgerald was too busy with the manuscript of *Tender Is the Night* to do much writing for magazines, and after the novel was published in 1934 he was distracted by worries about Zelda's third breakdown and what he called his 'lesion of vitality'; he began to fear that he had lost his talent. 'I can never write anything completely bad,' he said belligerently, and the boast was true to the extent that even the trivial stories he sold to *Liberty* and *Collier's* after the *Saturday Evening Post* stopped printing his work had something good in each of them, if only a scene or an incidental observation that gave dignity to his characters; but the plots were carelessly thrown together and the subjects were far from his own experience.

After 1937, when he settled in Hollywood, the type of energy he had formerly devoted to writing long magazine stories went into motion-picture scripts, but he was also writing shorter pieces for *Esquire,* and some of these —not all, but a few of the best—proved to be another development for Fitzgerald. 'At last I am mature,' he said in his ruin, and these are really mature stories— without the glitter and high spirits of his early work, without boasting or nostalgia, and even without the strong rhythms and incantatory words he had once used to intensify the emotions he was evoking. By this time the emotions had no need of being intensified. He was a tired man, as some of the stories show, but the best of them are so close to his personal tragedy that the emotion is in the events themselves, which have merely to be stated in the barest language.

In the present group there are ten very short stories from his last years. 'An Alcoholic Case' suggests his own débâcle, as does 'Design in Plaster,' and 'The Long Way Out' suggests Zelda's. 'Financing Finnegan' is a comedy, if a painful one, about the debts he owed to his agent Harold Ober and his editor Maxwell Perkins. It is a relief to learn that the debts were paid almost in full before Finnegan died. The four Pat Hobby sketches, not my favourites, are the best and the least self-contemptuous in a series of seventeen that Fitzgerald wrote for *Esquire* in 1939 and 1940. Pat wasn't the author himself, but in his farcical degradation he was what the author sometimes feared he might become. 'Three Hours between Planes' is simply a story honestly told, but 'The Lost Decade,' short as it is, has more to reveal. Written in the summer of 1939 when Fitzgerald was recovering from the long after-effects of his worst spree, it is his memorial to the years when he 'was taken drunk ... every-which-way drunk.' It is also his promise that the rest of his life, however brief, would be different—as indeed it was.

BABYLON REVISITED

[1931]

'AND WHERE'S Mr Campbell?' Charlie asked.

'Gone to Switzerland. Mr Campbell's a pretty sick man, Mr Wales.'

'I'm sorry to hear that. And George Hardt?' Charlie inquired.

'Back in America, gone to work.'

'And where is the Snow Bird?'

'He was in here last week. Anyway, his friend, Mr Schaeffer, is in Paris'.

Two familiar names from the long list of a year and a half ago. Charlie scribbled an address in his notebook and tore out the page.

'If you see Mr Schaeffer, give him this,' he said. 'It's my brother-in-law's address. I haven't settled on a hotel yet.'

He was not really disappointed to find Paris was so empty. But the stillness in the Ritz bar was strange and portentous. It was not an American bar any more—he felt polite in it, and not as if he owned it. It had gone back into France. He felt the stillness from the moment he got out of the taxi and saw the doorman, usually in a frenzy of activity at this hour, gossiping with a *chasseur* by the servants' entrance.

Passing through the corridor, he heard only a single, bored voice in the once-clamorous women's room. When he turned into the bar he travelled the twenty feet of green carpet with his eyes fixed straight ahead by old habit; and then, with his foot firmly on the rail, he turned and surveyed the room, encountering only a single pair of eyes that fluttered up from a newspaper in the corner. Charlie asked for the head barman, Paul, who in the latter days of the bull market had come to work in his own custom-built car—disembarking, however, with due nicety at the nearest corner. But Paul was at his country house today and Alix giving him information.

'No, no more,' Charlie said, 'I'm going slow these days.'

Alix congratulated him: 'You were going pretty strong a couple of years ago.'

'I'll stick to it all right,' Charlie assured him. 'I've stuck to it for over a year and a half now.'

'How do you find conditions in America?'

'I haven't been to America for months. I'm in business in Prague, representing a couple of concerns there. They don't know about me down there.'

Alix smiled.

'Remember the night of George Hardt's bachelor dinner here?' said Charlie. 'By the way, what's become of Claude Fessenden?'

Alix lowered his voice confidentially: 'He's in Paris, but he doesn't come here any more. Paul doesn't allow it. He ran up a bill of thirty thousand francs, charging all his drinks and his lunches, and usually his dinner, for more than a year. And when Paul finally told him he had to pay, he gave him a bad cheque.'

Alix shook his head sadly.

'I don't understand it, such a dandy fellow. Now he's all bloated up—' He made a plump apple of his hands.

Charlie watched a group of strident queens installing themselves in a corner.

'Nothing affects them,' he thought. 'Stocks rise and fall, people loaf or work, but they go on forever.' The place oppressed him. He called for the dice and shook with Alix for the drink.

'Here for long, Mr. Wales?'

'I'm here for four or five days to see my little girl.'

'Oh-h! You have a little girl?'

Outside, the fire-red, gas-blue, ghost-green signs shone smokily through the tranquil rain. It was late afternoon and the streets were in movement; the *bistros* gleamed. At the corner of the Boulevard des Capucines he took a taxi. The Place de la Concorde moved by in pink majesty; they crossed the logical Seine, and Charlie felt the sudden provincial quality of the left bank.

Charlie directed his taxi to the Avenue de l'Opéra, which was out of his way. But he wanted to see the blue hour spread over the magnificent façade, and imagine that the cab horns, playing endlessly the first few bars of Le Plus que Lent, were the trumpets of the Second Empire. They were closing the iron grill in front of Brentano's Book-store, and people were already at dinner behind the trim little bourgeois hedge of Duval's. He had never eaten at a really cheap restaurant in Paris. Five-course dinner, four francs fifty, eighteen cents, wine included. For some odd reason he wished that he had.

As they rolled on to the Left Bank and he felt its sudden provincialism, he thought, 'I spoiled this city for myself. I didn't realise it, but the days came along one after another, and then two years were gone, and everything was gone, and I was gone.'

He was thirty-five, and good to look at. The Irish mobility of his face was sobered by a deep wrinkle between his eyes. As he rang his brother-in-law's bell in the Rue Palatine, the wrinkle deepened till it pulled down his brow; he felt a cramping sensation in his belly. From behind the maid who opened the door darted a lovely little girl of nine who shrieked 'Daddy!' and flew up, struggling like a fish into his arms. She pulled his head around by one ear and set her cheek against his.

'My old pie,' he said.

'Oh, daddy, daddy, daddy, daddy, dads, dads, dads!'

She drew him into the salon, where the family waited, a boy and a girl his daughter's age, his sister-in-law and her husband. He greeted Marion with his voice pitched carefully to avoid either feigned enthusiasm or dislike, but her response was more frankly tepid, though she minimized her expression of unalterable distrust by directing her regard toward his child. The two men clasped hands in a friendly way and Lincoln Peters rested his for a moment on Charlie's shoulder.

The room was warm and comfortably American. The three children moved intimately about, playing through the yellow oblongs that led to other rooms; the cheer of six o'clock spoke in the eager smacks of the fire and the sounds of French activity in the kitchen. But Charlie did not relax; his heart sat up rigidly in his body and he drew confidence from his daughter, who from time to time came close to him, holding in her arms the doll he had brought.

'Really extremely well,' he declared in answer to Lincoln's question. 'There's a lot of business there that isn't moving at all, but we're doing even better than ever. In fact, damn well. I'm bringing my sister over from America next month to keep house for me. My income last year was bigger than it was when I had money. You see, the Czechs——'

His boasting was for a specific purpose; but after a moment, seeing a faint restiveness in Lincoln's eye, he changed the subject:

'Those are fine children of yours, well brought up, good manners.'

'We think Honoria's a great little girl too.'

Marion Peters came back from the kitchen. She was a tall woman with worried eyes, who had once possessed a fresh American loveliness. Charlie had never been sensitive to it and was always surprised when people spoke of how pretty she had been. From the first there had been an instinctive antipathy between them.

'Well, how do you find Honoria?' she asked.

'Wonderful. I was astonished how much she's grown in ten months. All the children are looking well.'

'We haven't had a doctor for a year. How do you like being back in Paris?'

'It seems very funny to see so few Americans around.'

'I'm delighted,' Marion said vehemently. 'Now at least you can go into a store without their assuming you're a millionaire. We've suffered like everybody, but on the whole it's a good deal pleasanter.'

'But it was nice while it lasted,' Charlie said. 'We were a sort of royalty, almost infallible, with a sort of magic around us. In the bar this afternoon'—he stumbled, seeing his mistake—'there wasn't a man I knew.'

She looked at him keenly. 'I should think you'd have had enough of bars.'

'I only stayed a minute. I take one drink every afternoon, and no more.'

'Don't you want a cocktail before dinner?' Lincoln asked.

'I take only one drink every afternoon, and I've had that.'

'I hope you keep to it,' said Marion.

Her dislike was evident in the coldness with which she spoke, but Charlie only smiled; he had larger plans. Her very aggressiveness gave him an advantage, and he knew enough to wait. He wanted them to initiate the discussion of what they knew had brought him to Paris.

At dinner he couldn't decide whether Honoria was most like him or her mother. Fortunate if she didn't combine the traits of both that had brought them to disaster. A great wave of protectiveness went over him. He thought he knew what to do for her. He believed in character; he wanted to jump back a whole generation and trust in character again as the eternally valuable element. Everything else wore out.

He left soon after dinner, but not to go home. He was curious to see Paris by night with clearer and more judicious eyes than those of other days. He bought a *strapontin* for the Casino and watched Josephine Baker go through her chocolate arabesques.

After an hour he left and stolled toward Montmartre, up the Rue Pigalle into the Place Blanche. The rain had stopped and there were a few people in evening clothes disembarking from taxis in front of cabarets, and *cocottes* prowling singly or in pairs, and many Negroes. He passed a lighted door from which issued music, and stopped with

the sense of familiarity; it was Bricktop's, where he had
parted with so many hours and so much money. A few doors
farther on he found another ancient rendezvous and in-
cautiously put his head inside. Immediately an eager
orchestra burst into sound, a pair of professional dancers
leaped to their feet and a maître d'hôtel swooped toward
him, crying, 'Crowd just arriving, sir!' But he withdrew
quickly.

'You have to be damn drunk,' he thought.

Zelli's was closed, the bleak and sinister cheap hotels
surrounding it were dark; up in the Rue Blanche there was
more light and a local, colloquial French crowd. The Poet's
Cave had disappeared, but the two great mouths of the
Café of Heaven and the Café of Hell still yawned—even
devoured, as he watched, the meagre contents of a tourist
bus—a German, a Japanese, and an American couple who
glanced at him with frightened eyes.

So much for the effort and ingenuity of Montmartre. All
the catering to vice and waste was on an utterly childish
scale, and he suddenly realized the meaning of the word
'dissipate'—to dissipate into thin air; to make nothing out
of something. In the little hours of the night every move
from place to place was an enormous human jump, an
increase of paying for the privilege of slower and slower
motion.

He remembered thousand-franc notes given to an
orchestra for playing a single number, hundred-franc notes
tossed to a doorman for calling a cab.

But it hadn't been given for nothing.

It had been given, even the most wildly squandered sum,
as an offering to destiny that he might not remember the
things most worth remembering, the things that now he
would always remember—his child taken from his control,
his wife escaped to a grave in Vermont.

In the glare of a *brasserie* a woman spoke to him. He
bought her some eggs and coffee, and then, eluding her
encouraging stare, gave her a twenty-franc note and took
a taxi to his hotel.

II

He woke upon a fine fall day—football weather. The depression of yesterday was gone and he liked the people on the streets. At noon he sat opposite Honoria at Le Grand Vatel, the only restaurant he could think of not reminiscent of champagne dinners and long luncheons that began at two and ended in a blurred and vague twilight.

'Now, how about vegetables? Oughtn't you to have some vegetables?'

'Well, yes.'

'Here's *épinards* and *chou-fleur* and carrots and *haricots*.'

'I'd like *chou-fleur*.'

'Wouldn't you like to have two vegetables?'

'I usually only have one at lunch.'

The waiter was pretending to be inordinately fond of children.

'*Qu'elle est mignonne la petite! Elle parle exactement comme une Française.*'

'How about dessert? Shall we wait and see?'

The waiter disappeared. Honoria looked at her father expectantly.

'What are you going to do?'

'First, we're going to that toy store in the Rue Saint-Honoré and buy you anything you like. And then we're going to the vaudeville at the Empire.'

She hesitated. 'I like it about the vaudeville, but not the toy store.'

'Why not?'

'Well, you brought me this doll.' She had it with her. 'And I've got lots of things. And we're not rich any more, are we?'

'We never were. But today you are to have anything you want.'

'All right,' she agreed resignedly.

When there had been her mother and a French nurse he had been inclined to be strict; now he extended himself, reached out for a new tolerance; he must be both parents to her and not shut any of her out of communication.

'I want to get to know you,' he said gravely. 'First let me introduce myself. My name is Charles J. Wales, of Prague.'

'Oh, daddy!' her voice cracked with laughter.

'And who are you, please?' he persisted, and she accepted a rôle immediately: 'Honoria Wales, Rue Palatine, Paris.'

'Married or single?'

'No, not married. Single.'

He indicated the doll. 'But I see you have a child, madame.'

Unwilling to disinherit it, she took it to her heart and thought quickly: 'Yes, I've been married, but I'm not married now. My husband is dead.'

He went on quickly, 'And the child's name?'

'Simone. That's after my best friend at school.'

'I'm very pleased that you're doing so well at school.'

'I'm third this month,' she boasted. 'Elsie'—that was her cousin—'is only about eighteenth, and Richard is about at the bottom.'

'You like Richard and Elsie, don't you?'

'Oh, yes. I like Richard quite well and I like her all right.'

Cautiously and casually he asked: 'And Aunt Marion and Uncle Lincoln—which do you like best?'

'Oh, Uncle Lincoln, I guess.'

He was increasingly aware of her presence. As they came in, a murmur of ' . . . adorable' followed them, and now the people at the next table bent all their silences upon her, staring as if she were something no more conscious than a flower.

'Why don't I live with you?' she asked suddenly. 'Because mamma's dead?'

'You must stay here and learn more French. It would have been hard for daddy to take care of you so well.'

'I don't really need much taking care of any more. I do everything for myself.'

Going out of the restaurant, a man and a woman unexpectedly hailed him.

'Well, the old Wales!'

'Hello there, Lorraine. . . . Dunc.'

Sudden ghosts out of the past: Duncan Schaeffer, a friend from college. Lorraine Quarrles, a lovely, pale blonde of thirty; one of a crowd who had helped them make months into days in the lavish times of three years ago.

'My husband couldn't come this year,' she said, in answer to his question. 'We're poor as hell. So he gave me two hundred a month and told me I could do my worst on that. . . . This your little girl?'

'What about coming back and sitting down?' Duncan asked.

'Can't do it.' He was glad for an excuse. As always, he felt Lorraine's passionate, provocative attraction, but his own rhythm was different now.

'Well, how about dinner?' she asked.

'I'm not free. Give me your address and let me call you.'

'Charlie, I believe you're sober,' she said judicially. 'I honestly believe he's sober, Dunc. Pinch him and see if he's sober.'

Charlie indicated Honoria with his head. They both laughed.

'What's your address?' said Duncan sceptically.

He hesitated, unwilling to give the name of his hotel.

'I'm not settled yet. I'd better call you. We're going to see the vaudeville at the Empire.'

'There! That's what I want to do,' Lorraine said. 'I want to see some clowns and acrobats and jugglers. That's just what we'll do, Dunc.'

'We've got to do an errand first,' said Charlie. 'Perhaps we'll see you there.'

'All right, you snob. . . . Good-bye, beautiful little girl.'

'Good-bye.'

Honoria bobbed politely.

Somehow, an unwelcome encounter. They liked him because he was functioning, because he was serious; they wanted to see him, because he was stronger than they were now, because they wanted to draw a certain sustenance from his strength.

At the Empire, Honoria proudly refused to sit upon her father's folded coat. She was already an individual with a code of her own, and Charlie was more and more absorbed by the desire of putting a little of himself into her before she crystallized utterly. It was hopeless to try to know her in so short a time.

Between the acts they came upon Duncan and Lorraine in the lobby where the band was playing.

'Have a drink?'

'All right, but not up at the bar. We'll take a table.'

'The perfect father.'

Listening abstractedly to Lorraine, Charlie watched Honoria's eyes leave their table, and he followed them wistfully about the room, wondering what they saw. He met her glance and she smiled. 'I liked that lemonade,' she said.

What had she said? What had he expected? Going home in a taxi afterward, he pulled her over until her head rested against his chest.

'Darling, do you ever think about your mother?'

'Yes, sometimes,' she answered vaguely.

'I don't want you to forget her. Have you got a picture of her?'

'Yes, I think so. Anyhow, Aunt Marion has. Why don't you want me to forget her?'

'She loved you very much.'

'I loved her too.'

They were silent for a moment.

'Daddy, I want to come and live with you,' she said suddenly.

His heart leaped; he had wanted it to come like this.

'Aren't you perfectly happy?'

'Yes, but I love you better than anybody. And you love me better than anybody, don't you, now that mummy's dead?'

'Of course I do. But you won't always like me best,

honey. You'll grow up and meet somebody your own age and go marry him and forget you ever had a daddy.'

'Yes, that's true,' she agreed tranquilly.

He didn't go in. He was coming back at nine o'clock and he wanted to keep himself fresh and new for the thing he must say then.

'When you're safe inside, just show yourself in that window.'

'All right. Good-bye, dads, dads, dads, dads.'

He waited in the dark street until she appeared, all warm and glowing, in the window above and kissed her fingers out into the night.

III

They were waiting. Marion sat behind the coffee service in a dignified black dinner dress that just faintly suggested mourning. Lincoln was walking up and down with the animation of one who had already been talking. They were as anxious as he was to get into the question. He opened it almost immediately:

'I suppose you know what I want to see you about—why I really came to Paris.'

Marion played with the black stars on her necklace and frowned.

'I'm awfully anxious to have a home,' he continued. 'And I'm awfully anxious to have Honoria in it. I appreciate your taking in Honoria for her mother's sake, but things have changed now'—he hesitated and then continued more forcibly—'changed radically with me, and I want to ask you to reconsider the matter. It would be silly for me to deny that about three years ago I was acting badly——'

Marion looked up at him with hard eyes.

'—but all that's over. As I told you, I haven't had more than a drink a day for over a year, and I take that drink deliberately, so that the idea of alcohol won't get too big in my imagination. You see the idea?'

'No,' said Marion succinctly.

'It's a sort of stunt I set myself. It keeps the matter in proportion.'

'I get you,' said Lincoln. 'You don't want to admit it's got any attraction for you.'

'Something like that. Sometimes I forget and don't take it. But I try to take it. Anyhow, I couldn't afford to drink in my position. The people I represent are more than satisfied with what I've done, and I'm bringing my sister over from Burlington to keep house for me, and I want awfully to have Honoria too. You know that even when her mother and I weren't getting along well we never let anything that happened touch Honoria. I know she's fond of me and I know I'm able to take care of her and—well, there you are. How do you feel about it?'

He knew that now he would have to take a beating. It would last an hour or two hours, and it would be difficult, but if he modulated his inevitable resentment to the chastened attitude of the reformed sinner, he might win his point in the end.

Keep your temper, he told himself. You don't want to be justified. You want Honoria.

Lincoln spoke first: 'We've been talking it over ever since we got your letter last month. We're happy to have Honoria here. She's a dear little thing, and we're glad to be able to help her, but of course that isn't the question——'

Marion interrupted suddenly. 'How long are you going to stay sober, Charlie?' she asked.

'Permanently, I hope.'

'How can anybody count on that?'

'You know I never did drink heavily until I gave up business and came over here with nothing to do. Then Helen and I began to run around with——'

'Please leave Helen out of it. I can't bear to hear you talk about her like that.'

He stared at her grimly; he had never been certain how fond of each other the sisters were in life.

'My drinking only lasted about a year and a half—from the time we came over until I—collapsed.'

'It was time enough.'

'It was time enough,' he agreed.

'My duty is entirely to Helen," she said. 'I try to think what she would have wanted me to do. Frankly, from the night you did that terrible thing you haven't really existed for me. I can't help that. She was my sister.'

'Yes.'

'When she was dying she asked me to look out for Honoria. If you hadn't been in a sanatorium then, it might have helped matters.'

He had no answer.

'I'll never in my life be able to forget the morning when Helen knocked at my door, soaked to the skin and shivering and said you'd locked her out.'

Charlie gripped the sides of the chair. This was more difficult than he expected; he wanted to launch out into a long expostulation and explanation, but he only said: 'The night I locked her out—' and she interrupted, 'I don't feel up to going over that again.'

After a moment's silence Lincoln said: 'We're getting off the subject. You want Marion to set aside her legal guardianship and give you Honoria. I think the main point for her is whether she has confidence in you or not.'

'I don't blame Marion,' Charlie said slowly, 'but I think she can have entire confidence in me. I had a good record up to three years ago. Of course, it's within human possibilities I might go wrong any time. But if we wait much longer I'll lose Honoria's childhood and my chance for a home.' He shook his head, 'I'll simply lose her, don't you see?'

'Yes, I see,' said Lincoln.

'Why didn't you think of all this before?' Marion asked.

'I suppose I did, from time to time, but Helen and I were getting along badly. When I consented to the guardianship, I was flat on my back in a sanatorium and the market had cleaned me out. I knew I'd acted badly, and I thought if it would bring any peace to Helen, I'd agree to anything.

But now it's different. I'm functioning, I'm behaving damn well, so far as——'

'Please don't swear at me,' Marion said.

He looked at her, startled. With each remark the force of her dislike became more and more apparent. She had built up all her fear of life into one wall and faced it toward him. This trivial reproof was possibly the result of some trouble with the cook several hours before. Charlie became increasingly alarmed at leaving Honoria in this atmosphere of hostility against himself; sooner or later it would come out in a word here, a shake of the head there, and some of that distrust would be irrevocably implanted in Honoria. But he pulled his temper down out of his face and shut it up inside him; he had won a point, for Lincoln realized the absurdity of Marion's remark and asked her lightly since when she had objected to the word 'damn.'

'Another thing,' Charlie said: 'I'm able to give her certain advantages now. I'm going to take a French governess to Prague with me. I've got a lease on a new apartment——'

He stopped, realizing that he was blundering. They couldn't be expected to accept with equanimity the fact that his income was again twice as large as their own.

'I suppose you can give her more luxuries than we can,' said Marion. 'When you were throwing away money we were living along watching every ten francs. . . . I suppose you'll start doing it again.'

'Oh, no,' he said. 'I've learned. I worked hard for ten years, you know—until I got lucky in the market, like so many people. Terribly lucky. It won't happen again.'

There was a long silence. All of them felt their nerves straining, and for the first time in a year Charlie wanted a drink. He was sure now that Lincoln Peters wanted him to have his child.

Marion shuddered suddenly; part of her saw that Charlie's feet were planted on the earth now, and her own maternal feeling recognised the naturalness of his desire; but she had lived for a long time with a prejudice—a prejudice founded on a curious disbelief in her sister's happiness, and which, in the shock of one terrible night, had turned to hatred for him. It had all happened at a point in her life where the discouragement of ill health and adverse circumstances made it necessary for her to believe in tangible villainy and a tangible villain.

'I can't help what I think!' she cried out suddenly. 'How much you were responsible for Helen's death, I don't know. It's something you'll have to square with your own conscience.'

An electric current of agony surged through him; for a moment he was almost on his feet, an unuttered sound echoing in his throat. He hung on to himself for a moment, another moment.

'Hold on there,' said Lincoln uncomfortably. 'I never thought you were responsible for that.'

'Helen died of heart trouble,' Charlie said dully.

'Yes, heart trouble.' Marion spoke as if the phrase had another meaning for her.

Then, in the flatness that followed her outburst, she saw him plainly and she knew he had somehow arrived at control over the situation. Glancing at her husband, she found no help from him, and as abruptly as if it were a matter of no importance, she threw up the sponge.

'Do what you like!' she cried, springing up from her chair. 'She's your child. I'm not the person to stand in your way. I think if it were my child I'd rather see her—' She managed to check herself. 'You two decide it. I can't stand this, I'm sick. I'm going to bed.'

She hurried from the room; after a moment Lincoln said:

'This has been a hard day for her. You know how strongly she feels—' His voice was almost apologetic: 'When a woman gets an idea in her head.'

'Of course.'

'It's going to be all right. I think she sees now that you—can provide for the child, and so we can't very well stand in your way or Honoria's way.'

'Thank you, Lincoln.'

'I'd better go along and see how she is.'

'I'm going.'

He was still trembling when he reached the street, but a walk down the Rue Bonaparte to the *quais* set him up, and as he crossed the Seine, fresh and new by the *quai* lamps, he felt exultant. But back in his room he couldn't sleep. The image of Helen haunted him. Helen whom he had loved so until they had senselessly begun to abuse each other's love, tear it into shreds. On that terrible February night that Marion remembered so vividly, a slow quarrel had gone on for hours. There was a scene at the Florida, and then he attempted to take her home, and then she kissed young Webb at a table; after that there was what she had hysterically said. When he arrived home alone he turned the key in the lock in wild anger. How could he know she would arrive an hour later alone, that there would be a snowstorm in which she wandered about in slippers, too confused to find a taxi? Then the aftermath, her escaping pneumonia by a miracle, and all the attendant horror. They were 'reconciled,' but that was the beginning of the end, and Marion, who had seen with her own eyes and who imagined it to be one of many scenes from her sister's martyrdom, never forgot.

Going over it again brought Helen nearer, and in the white, soft light that steals upon half sleep near morning he found himself talking to her again. She said that he was perfectly right about Honoria and that she wanted Honoria to be with him. She said she was glad he was being good and doing better. She said a lot of other things—very friendly things—but she was in a swing in a white dress, and swinging faster and faster all the time, so that at the end he could not hear clearly all that she said.

IV

He woke up feeling happy. The door of the world was open again. He made plans, vistas, futures for Honoria and himself, but suddenly he grew sad, remembering all the plans he and Helen had made. She had not planned to die. The present was the thing—work to do and someone to love. But not to love too much, for he knew the injury that a father can do to a daughter or a mother to a son by attaching them too closely: afterward, out in the world, the child would seek in the marriage partner the same blind tenderness and, failing probably to find it, turn against love and life.

It was another bright, crisp day. He called Lincoln Peters at the bank where he worked and asked if he could count on taking Honoria when he left for Prague. Lincoln agreed that there was no reason for delay. One thing—the legal guardianship. Marion wanted to retain that a while longer. She was upset by the whole matter, and it would oil things if she felt that the situation was still in her control for another year. Charlie agreed, wanting only the tangible, visible child.

Then the question of a governess. Charles sat in a gloomy agency and talked to a cross Béarnaise and to a buxom Breton peasant, neither of whom he could have endured. There were others whom he would see tomorrow.

He lunched with Lincoln Peters at Griffons, trying to keep down his exultation.

'There's nothing quite like your own child,' Lincoln said. 'But you understand how Marion feels too.'

'She's forgotten how hard I worked for seven years there,' Charlie said. 'She just remembers one night.'

'There's another thing.' Lincoln hesitated. 'While you and Helen were tearing around Europe throwing money away, we were just getting along. I didn't touch any of the prosperity because I never got ahead enough to carry anything but my insurance. I think Marion felt there was some kind of injustice in it—you not even working toward the end, and getting richer and richer.'

'It went just as quick as it came,' said Charlie.

'Yes, a lot of it stayed in the hands of *chasseurs* and saxophone players and maîtres d'hôtel—well, the big party's over now. I just said that to explain Marion's feeling about those crazy years. If you drop in about six o'clock tonight before Marion's too tired, we'll settle the details on the spot.'

Back at his hotel, Charlie found a *pneumatique* that had been re-directed from the Ritz bar where Charlie had left his address for the purpose of finding a certain man.

'DEAR CHARLIE:

You were so strange when we saw you the other day that I wondered if I did something to offend you. If so, I'm not conscious of it. In fact, I have thought about you too much for the last year, and it's always been in the back of my mind that I might see you if I came over here. We *did* have such good times that crazy spring, like the night you and I stole the butcher's tricycle, and the time we tried to call on the president and you had the old derby rim and the wire cane. Everybody seems so old lately, but I don't feel old a bit. Couldn't we get together some time today for old time's sake? I've got a vile hang-over for the moment, but will be feeling better this afternoon and will look for you about five in the sweat-shop at the Ritz.

'Always devotedly,

LORRAINE.'

His first feeling was one of awe that he had actually, in his mature years, stolen a tricycle and pedalled Lorraine all over the Étoile between the small hours and dawn. In retrospect it was a nightmare. Locking out Helen didn't fit in with any other act of his life, but the tricycle incident did—it was one of many. How many weeks or months of dissipation to arrive at that condition of utter irresponsibility?

He tried to picture how Lorraine had appeared to him then—very attractive; Helen was unhappy about it, though she said nothing. Yesterday, in the restaurant, Lorraine had seemed trite, blurred, worn away. He emphatically did not want to see her, and he was glad Alix had not given away his hotel address. It was a relief to think instead of Honoria, to think of Sundays spent with her and of saying good morning to her and of knowing she was there in his house at night, drawing her breath in the darkness.

At five he took a taxi and bought presents for all the Peters—a piquant cloth doll, a box of Roman soldiers, flowers for Marion, big linen handkerchiefs for Lincoln.

He saw, when he arrived in the apartment, that Marion had accepted the inevitable. She greeted him now as though he were a recalcitrant member of the family, rather than a menacing outsider. Honoria had been told she was going; Charlie was glad to see that her tact made her conceal her excessive happiness. Only on his lap did she whisper her delight and the question 'When?' before she slipped away with the other children.

He and Marion were alone for a minute in the room, and on an impulse he spoke out boldly:

'Family quarrels are bitter things. They don't go according to any rules. They're not like aches or wounds; they're more like splits in the skin that won't heal because there's not enough material. I wish you and I could be on better terms.'

'Some things are hard to forget,' she answered. 'It's a question of confidence.' There was no answer to this and presently she asked, 'When do you propose to take her?'

'As soon as I can get a governess. I hoped the day after tomorrow.'

'That's impossible. I've got to get her things in shape. Not before Saturday.'

He yielded. Coming back into the room, Lincoln offered him a drink.

'I'll take my daily whisky,' he said.

It was warm here, it was a home, people together by a fire. The children felt very safe and important; the mother and father were serious, watchful. They had things to do for the children more important than his visit here. A spoonful of medicine was, after all, more important than the strained relations between Marion and himself. They were not dull people, but they were very much in the grip of life and circumstances. He wondered if he couldn't do something to get Lincoln out of his rut at the bank.

A long peal at the door-bell; the *bonne à tout faire* passed

through and went down the corridor. The door opened
upon another long ring, and then voices, and the three in
the salon looked up expectantly; Richard moved to bring
the corridor within his range of vision, and Marion rose.
Then the maid came back along the corridor, closely followed by the voices, which developed under the light into
Duncan Schaeffer and Lorraine Quarrles.

They were gay, they were hilarious, they were roaring
with laughter. For a moment Charlie was astounded; unable
to understand how they ferreted out the Peters' address.

'Ah-h-h!' Duncan wagged his finger roguishly at Charlie.
'Ah-h-h!'

They both slid down another cascade of laughter. Anxious and at a loss, Charlie shook hands with them quickly
and presented them to Lincoln and Marion. Marion
nodded, scarcely speaking. She had drawn back a step
toward the fire; her little girl stood beside her, and Marion
put an arm about her shoulder.

With growing annoyance at the intrusion, Charlie waited
for them to explain themselves. After some concentration
Duncan said:

'We came to invite you out to dinner. Lorraine and I
insist that all this shishi, cagey business 'bout your address
got to stop.'

Charlie came closer to them, as if to force them backward down the corridor.

'Sorry, but I can't. Tell me where you'll be and I'll phone
you in half an hour'.

This made no impression. Lorraine sat down suddenly
on the side of a chair, and focusing her eyes on Richard,
cried, 'Oh, what a nice little boy! Come here, little boy'.
Richard glanced at his mother, but did not move. With a
perceptible shrug of her shoulders, Lorraine turned back
to Charlie:

'Come and dine. Sure your cousins won' mine. See you
so sel'om. Or solemn.'

'I can't,' said Charlie sharply. 'you two have dinner and
I'll phone you.'

Her voice became suddenly unpleasant. 'All right, we'll go. But I remember once when you hammered on my door at four A.M. I was enough of a good sport to give you a drink. Come on, Dunc.'

Still in slow motion, with blurred, angry faces, with uncertain feet, they retired along the corridor.

'Good night,' Charlie said.

'Good night!' responded Lorraine emphatically.

When he went back into the salon Marion had not moved, only now her son was standing in the circle of her other arm. Lincoln was still swinging Honoria back and forth like a pendulum from side to side.

'What an outrage!' Charlie broke out. 'What an absolute outrage!'

Neither of them answered. Charlie dropped into an arm-chair, picked up his drink, set it down again and said:

'People I haven't seen for two years having the colossal nerve——'

He broke off. Marion had made the sound 'Oh!' in one swift, furious breath, turned her body from him with a jerk and left the room.

Lincoln set down Honoria carefully.

'You children go in and start your soup,' he said, and when they obeyed, he said to Charlie:

'Marion's not well and she can't stand shocks. That kind of people make her really physically sick.'

'I didn't tell them to come here. They wormed your name out of somebody. They deliberately——'

'Well, it's too bad. It doesn't help matters. Excuse me a minute.'

Left alone, Charlie sat tense in his chair. In the next room he could hear the children eating, talking in mono-syllables, already oblivious to the scene between their elders. He heard a murmur of conversation from a farther room and then the ticking bell of a telephone receiver picked up, and in a panic he moved to the other side of the room and out of earshot.

In a minute Lincoln came back. 'Look here, Charlie. I

think we'd better call off dinner for tonight. Marion's in bad shape.'

'Is she angry with me?'

'Sort of,' he said, almost roughly. 'She's not strong and——'

'You mean she's changed her mind about Honoria?'

'She's pretty bitter right now. I don't know. You phone me at the bank tomorrow.'

'I wish you'd explain to her I never dreamed these people would come here. I'm just as sore as you are.'

'I couldn't explain anything to her now.'

Charlie got up. He took his coat and hat and started down the corridor. Then he opened the door of the dining-room and said in a strange voice, 'Good night, children.'

Honoria rose and ran around the table to hug him.

'Good night, sweetheart,' he said vaguely, and then trying to make his voice more tender, trying to conciliate something, 'Good night, dear children.'

V

Charlie went directly to the Ritz bar with the furious idea of finding Lorraine and Duncan, but they were not there, and he realized that in any case there was nothing he could do. He had not touched his drink at the Peters', and now he ordered a whisky-and-soda. Paul came over to say hello.

'It's a great change,' he said sadly. 'We do about half the business we did. So many fellows I hear about back in the States lost everything, maybe not in the first crash, but then in the second. Your friend George Hardt lost every cent, I hear. Are you back in the States?'

'No, I'm in business in Prague.'

'I heard that you lost a lot in the crash.'

'I did,' and he added grimly, 'but I lost everything I wanted in the boom.'

'Selling short.'

'Something like that.'

Again the memory of those days swept over him like a

nightmare—the people they had met travelling; then people who couldn't add a row of figures or speak a coherent sentence. The little man Helen had consented to dance with at the ship's party, who had insulted her ten feet from the table; the women and girls carried screaming with drink or drugs out of public places——

—The men who locked their wives out in the snow, because the snow of twenty-nine wasn't real snow. If you didn't want it to be snow, you just paid some money.

He went to the phone and called the Peters' apartment; Lincoln answered.

'I called up because this thing is on my mind. Has Marion said anything definite?'

'Marion's sick,' Lincoln answered shortly. 'I know this thing isn't altogether your fault, but I can't have her go to pieces about it. I'm afraid we'll have to let it slide for six months; I can't take the chance of working her up to this state again.'

'I see.'

'I'm sorry, Charlie.'

He went back to his table. His whisky glass was empty, but he shook his head when Alix looked at it questioningly. There wasn't much he could do now except send Honoria some things; he would send her a lot of things tomorrow. He thought rather angrily that this was just money—he had given so many people money. . . .

'No, no more,' he said to another waiter. 'What do I owe you?'

He would come back some day; they couldn't make him pay forever. But he wanted his child, and nothing was much good now, beside that fact. He wasn't young any more, with a lot of nice thoughts and dreams to have by himself. He was absolutely sure Helen wouldn't have wanted him to be so alone.

TWO WRONGS

[1930]

'Look at those shoes,' said Bill—'twenty-eight dollars.'

Mr Brancusi looked. 'Purty.'

'Made to order.'

'I knew you were a great swell. You didn't get me up here to show me those shoes, did you?'

'I am not a great swell. Who said I was a great swell?' demanded Bill. 'Just because I've got more education than most people in show business.'

'And then, you know, you're a handsome young fellow,' said Brancusi dryly.

'Sure I am—compared to you anyhow. The girls think I must be an actor, till they find out. . . . Got a cigarette? What's more, I look like a man—which is more than some of these pretty boys round Times Square do.'

'Good-looking. Gentleman. Good shoes. Shot with luck.'

'You're wrong there,' objected Bill. 'Brains. Three years—nine shows—four big hits—only one flop. Where do you see any luck in that?'

A little bored, Brancusi just gazed. What he would have seen—had he not made his eyes opaque and taken to thinking about something else—was a fresh-faced young Irishman exuding aggressiveness and self-confidence until the air of his office was thick with it. Presently, Brancusi knew, Bill would hear the sound of his own voice and be ashamed and retire into his other humour—the quietly superior, sensitive one, the patron of the arts, modelled on the intellectuals of the Theatre Guild. Bill McChesney had not quite decided between the two, such blends are seldom complete before thirty.

'Take Ames, take Hopkins, take Harris—take any of
them,' Bill insisted. 'What have they got on me? What's
the matter? Do you want a drink?'—seeing Brancusi's
glance wander towards the cabinet on the opposite wall.

'I never drink in the morning. I just wondered who it
was keeps on knocking. You ought to make it stop. I get
a nervous fidgets, kind of half crazy, with that kind of
thing.'

Bill went quickly to the door and threw it open.

'Nobody,' he said. . . . 'Hello! What do you want?'

'Oh, I'm so sorry,' a voice answered; 'I'm terribly sorry.
I got so excited and I didn't realize I had this pencil in
my hand.'

'What is it you want?'

'I want to see you, and the clerk said you were busy.
I have a letter for you from Alan Rogers, the playwright
—and I wanted to give it to you personally.'

'I'm busy,' said Bill. 'See Mr Cadorna.'

'I did, but he wasn't very encouraging, and Mr Rogers
said——'

Brancusi, edging over restlessly, took a quick look at
her. She was very young, with beautiful red hair, and
more character in her face than her chatter would indicate;
it did not occur to Mr Brancusi that this was due to her
origin in Delaney, South Carolina.

'What shall I do?' she inquired, quietly laying her
future in Bill's hands. 'I had a letter to Mr Rogers, and
he just gave me this one to you.'

'Well, what do you want me to do—marry you?' exploded Bill.

'I'd like to get a part in one of your plays.'

'Then sit down and wait. I'm busy. . . . Where's Miss
Cohalan?' He rang a bell, looked once more, crossly, at
the girl and closed the door of his office. But during the
interruption his other mood had come over him, and he
resumed his conversation with Brancusi in the key of
one who was hand in glove with Reinhardt for the artistic
future of the theatre.

7*

By 12.30 he had forgotten everything except that he
was going to be the greatest producer in the world and
that he had an engagement to tell Sol Lincoln about it at
lunch. Emerging from his office, he looked expectantly at
Miss Cohalan.

'Mr Lincoln won't be able to meet you,' she said. 'He
jus' 'is minute called.'

'Just this minute,' repeated Bill, shocked. 'All right.
Just cross him off that list for Thursday night.'

Miss Cohalan drew a line on a sheet of paper before
her.

'Mr McChesney, now you haven't forgotten me, have
you?'

He turned to the red-headed girl.

'No,' he said vaguely, and then to Miss Cohalan:
'That's all right: ask him for Thursday anyhow. To hell
with him!'

He did not want to lunch alone. He did not like to do
anything alone now, because contacts were too much fun
when one had prominence and power.

'If you would just let me talk to you two minutes——'
she began.

'Afraid I can't now.' Suddenly he realized that she was
the most beautiful person he had ever seen in his life.

He stared at her.

'Mr Rogers told me——'

'Come and have a spot of lunch with me,' he said, and
then, with an air of great hurry, he gave Miss Cohalan
some quick and contradictory instructions and held open
the door.

They stood on Forty-second Street and he breathed his
pre-empted air—there is only enough air there for a few
people at a time. It was November and the first exhilar-
ating rush of the season was over, but he could look east
and see the electric sign of one of his plays, and west and
see another. Around the corner was the one he had put
on with Brancusi—the last time he would produce anything except alone.

They went to the Bedford, where there was a to-do of waiters and captains as he came in.

'This is ver' tractive restaurant,' she said, impressed and on company behaviour.

'This is hams' paradise.' He nodded to several people. 'Hello, Jimmy—Bill. . . . Hello there, Jack. . . . That's Jack Dempsey. . . . I don't eat here much. I usually eat up at the Harvard Club.'

'Oh, did you go to Harvard? I used to know——'

'Yes.' He hesitated; there were two versions about Harvard, and he decided suddenly on the true one. 'Yes, and they had me down for a hick there, but not any more. About a week ago I was out on Long Island at the Gouverneer Haights—very fashionable people—and a couple of Gold Coast boys that never knew I was alive up in Cambridge began pulling this "Hello, Bill, old boy" on me.'

He hesitated and suddenly decided to leave the story there.

'What do you want—a job?' he demanded. He remembered suddenly that she had holes in her stockings. Holes in stockings always moved him, softened him.

'Yes, or else I've got to go home,' she said. 'I want to be a dancer—you know, Russian Ballet. But the lessons cost so much, so I've got to get a job. I thought it'd give me stage presence anyhow.'

'Hoofer, eh?'

'Oh, no, serious.'

'Well, Pavlova's a hoofer, isn't she?'

'Oh, no.' She was shocked at this profanity, but after a moment she continued: 'I took with Miss Campbell— Georgia Berriman Campbell—back home—maybe you know her. She took from New Wayburn, and she's really wonderful. She——'

'Yeah?' he said abstractedly. 'Well, it's a tough business—casting agencies bursting with people that can all do anything, till I give them a try. How old are you?'

'Eighteen.'

'I'm twenty-six. Came here four years ago without a cent.'

'My!'

'I could quit now and be comfortable the rest of my life.'

'My!'

'Going to take a year off next year—get married. . . . Ever hear of Irene Rikker?'

'I should say! She's about my favourite of all.'

'We're engaged.'

'My!'

When they went out into Times Square after a while he said carelessly, 'What are you doing now?'

'Why, I'm trying to get a job.'

'I mean right this minute.'

'Why, nothing.'

'Do you want to come up to my apartment on Forty-sixth Street and have some coffee?'

Their eyes met, and Emmy Pinkard made up her mind she could take care of herself.

It was a great bright studio apartment with a ten-foot divan, and after she had coffee and he a highball, his arm dropped round her shoulder.

'Why should I kiss you?' she demanded. 'I hardly know you, and besides, you're engaged to somebody else.'

'Oh, that! She doesn't care.'

'No, really!'

'You're a good girl.'

'Well, I'm certainly not an idiot.'

'All right, go on being a good girl.'

She stood up, but lingered a minute, very fresh and cool, and not upset at all.

'I suppose this means you won't give me a job?' she asked pleasantly.

He was already thinking about something else—about an interview and a rehearsal—but now he looked at her again and saw that she still had holes in her stockings. He telephoned:

'Joe, this is the Fresh Boy. . . . You didn't think I knew you called me that, did you? . . . It's all right. . . . Say, have you got those three girls for the party scene? Well, listen; save one for a Southern kid I'm sending around today.'

He looked at her jauntily, conscious of being such a good fellow.

'Well, I don't know how to thank you. And Mr Rogers,' she added audaciously. 'Good-bye, Mr McChesney.'

II

During rehearsal he used to come around a great deal and stand watching with a wise expression, as if he knew everything in people's minds; but actually he was in a haze about his own good fortune and didn't see much and didn't for the moment care. He spent most of his week-ends on Long Island with the fashionable people who had 'taken him up.' When Brancusi referred to him as the 'big social butterfly,' he would answer, 'Well, what about it? Didn't I go to Harvard? You think they found me in a Grand Street apple-cart, like you?' He was well liked among his new friends for his good looks and good nature, as well as his success.

His engagement to Irene Rikker was the most unsatisfactory thing in his life; they were tired of each other but unwilling to put an end to it. Just as, often, the two richest young people in a town are drawn together by the fact, so Bill McChesney and Irene Rikker, borne side by side on waves of triumph, could not spare each other's nice appreciation of what was due such success. Nevertheless, they indulged in fiercer and more frequent quarrels, and the end was approaching. It was embodied in one Frank Llewellen, a big, fine-looking actor playing opposite Irene. Seeing the situation at once, Bill became bitterly humorous about it; from the second week of rehearsals there was tension in the air.

Meanwhile Emmy Pinkard, with enough money for

crackers and milk, and a friend who took her out to dinner, was being happy. Her friend, Easton Hughes from Delaney, was studying at Columbia to be a dentist. He sometimes brought along other lonesome young men studying to be dentists, and at the price, if it can be called that, of a few casual kisses in taxicabs, Emmy dined when hungry. One afternoon she introduced Easton to Bill McChesney at the stage door, and afterwards Bill made his facetious jealousy the basis of their relationship.

'I see that dental number has been slipping it over on me again. Well, don't let him give you any laughing gas is my advice.'

Though their encounters were few, they always looked at each other. When Bill looked at her he stared for an instant as if he had not seen her before, and then remembered suddenly that she was to be teased. When she looked at him she saw many things—a bright day outside, with great crowds of people hurrying through the streets; a very good new limousine that waited at the curb for two people with very good new clothes, who got in and went somewhere that was just like New York, only away, and more fun there. Many times she had wished she had kissed him, but just as many times she was glad she hadn't; since, as the weeks passed he grew less romantic, tied up, like the rest of them, to the play's laborious evolution.

They were opening in Atlantic City. A sudden moodiness, apparent to everyone, came over Bill. He was short with the director and sarcastic with the actors. This, it was rumoured, was because Irene Rikker had come down with Frank Llewellen on a different train. Sitting beside the author on the night of the dress rehearsal, he was an almost sinister figure in the twilight of the auditorium; but he said nothing until the end of the second act, when, with Llewellen and Irene Rikker on the stage alone, he suddenly called:

'We'll go over that again—and cut out the mush!'

Llewellen came down to the footlights.

'What do you mean—cut out the mush?' he inquired. 'Those are the lines, aren't they?'

'You know what I mean—stick to business.'

'I don't know what you mean.'

Bill stood up. 'I mean all that damn whispering.'

'There wasn't any whispering. I simply asked——'

'That'll do—take it over.'

Llewellen turned away furiously and was about to proceed, when Bill added audibly: 'Even a ham has got to do his stuff.'

Llewellen whipped about. 'I don't have to stand that kind of talk, Mr McChesney.'

'Why not? You're a ham, aren't you? When did you get ashamed of being a ham? I'm putting on this play and I want you to stick to your stuff.' Bill got up and walked down the aisle. 'And when you don't do it, I'm going to call you just like anybody else.'

'Well, you watch out for your tone of voice——'

'What'll you do about it?'

Llewellen jumped down into the orchestra pit.

'I'm not taking anything from you!' he shouted.

Irene Rikker called to them from the stage, 'For heaven's sake, are you two crazy?' And then Llewellen swung at him, one short, mighty blow. Bill pitched back across a row of seats, fell through one, splintering it, and lay wedged there. There was a moment's wild confusion, then people holding Llewellen, then the author, with a white face, pulling Bill up, and the stage manager crying: 'Shall I kill him, chief? Shall I break his fat face?' and Llewellen panting and Irene Rikker frightened.

'Get back there!' Bill cried, holding a handkerchief to his face and teetering into the author's supporting arms. 'Everybody get back! Take that scene again, and no talk! Get back, Llewellen!'

Before they realized it they were all back on the stage, Irene pulling Llewellen's arm and talking to him fast. Someone put on the auditorium lights and then dimmed them again hurriedly. When Emmy came out presently for her scene, she saw in a quick glance that Bill was sitting with a whole mask of handkerchiefs over his bleeding face. She hated Llewellen and was afraid that presently they would break up and go back to New York. But Bill had saved the show from his own folly, since for Llewellen to take the further initiative of quitting would hurt his professional standing. The act ended and the next one began without an interval. When it was over, Bill was gone.

Next night, during the performance, he sat on a chair in the wings in view of everyone coming on or off. His face was swollen and bruised, but he neglected to seem conscious of the fact and there were no comments. Once he went around in front, and when he returned, word leaked out that two of the New York agencies were making big buys. He had a hit—they all had a hit.

At the sight of him to whom Emmy felt they all owed so much, a great wave of gratitude swept over her. She went up and thanked him.

'I'm a good picker, red-head,' he agreed grimly.

'Thank you for picking me.'

And suddenly Emmy was moved to a rash remark.

'You've hurt your face so badly!' she exclaimed. 'Oh, I think it was so brave of you not to let everything go to pieces last night.'

He looked at her hard for a moment and then an ironic smile tried unsuccessfully to settle on his swollen face.

'Do you admire me, baby?'

'Yes.'

'Even when I fell in the seats, did you admire me?'

'You got control of everything so quick.'

'That's loyalty for you. You found something to admire in that fool mess.'

And her happiness bubbled up into, 'Anyhow, you behaved just wonderfully.' She looked so fresh and young that Bill, who had had a wretched day, wanted to rest his swollen cheek against her cheek.

He took both the bruise and the desire with him to

New York next morning; the bruise faded, but the desire remained. And when they opened in the city, no sooner did he see other men begin to crowd around her beauty than she became this play for him, this success, the thing that he came to see when he came to the theatre. After a good run it closed just as he was drinking too much and needed someone on the grey days of reaction. They were married suddenly in Connecticut, early in June.

III

Two men sat in the Savoy Grill in London, waiting for the Fourth of July. It was already late in May.

'Is he a nice guy?' asked Hubbel.

'Very nice,' answered Brancusi; 'very nice, very handsome, very popular.' After a moment, he added: 'I want to get him to come home.'

'That's what I don't get about him,' said Hubbel. 'Show business over here is nothing compared to home. What does he want to stay here for?'

'He goes around with a lot of dukes and ladies.'

'Oh?'

'Last week when I met him he was with three ladies— Lady this, Lady that, Lady the other thing.'

'I thought he was married.'

'Married three years,' said Brancusi, 'got a fine child, going to have another.'

He broke off as McChesney came in, his very American face staring about boldly over the collar of a box-shouldered topcoat.

'Hello, Mac; meet my friend Mr Hubbel.'

'J'doo,' said Bill. He sat down, continuing to stare around the bar to see who was present. After a few minutes Hubbel left, and Bill asked:

'Who's that bird?'

'He's only been here a month. He ain't got a title yet. You been here six months, remember.'

Bill grinned.

'You think I'm high-hat, don't you? Well, I'm not kidding myself anyhow. I like it; it gets me. I'd like to be the Marquis of McChesney.'

'Maybe you can drink yourself into it,' suggested Brancusi.

'Shut your trap. Who said I was drinking? Is that what they say now? Look here; if you can tell me any American manager in the history of the theatre who's had the success that I've had in London in less than eight months, I'll go back to America with you tomorrow. If you'll just tell me——'

'It was with your old shows. You had two flops in New York.'

Bill stood up, his face hardening.

'Who do you think you are?' he demanded. 'Did you come over here to talk to me like that?'

'Don't get sore now, Bill. I just want you to come back. I'd say anything for that. Put over three seasons like you had in '22 and '23, and you're fixed for life.'

'New York makes me sick,' said Bill moodily. 'One minute you're a king; then you have two flops, they go around saying you're on the toboggan.'

Brancusi shook his head.

'That wasn't why they said it. It was because you had that quarrel with Aronstael, your best friend.'

'Friend hell!'

'Your best friend in business anyhow. Then——'

'I don't want to talk about it.' He looked at his watch. 'Look here; Emmy's feeling bad so I'm afraid I can't have dinner with you tonight. Come around to the office before you sail.'

Five minutes later, standing by the cigar counter, Brancusi saw Bill enter the Savoy again and descend the steps that led to the tea room.

'Grown to be a great diplomat,' thought Brancusi; 'he used to just say when he had a date. Going with these dukes and ladies is polishing him up even more.'

Perhaps he was a little hurt, though it was not typical

of him to be hurt. At any rate he made a decision, then and there, that McChesney was on the down-grade; it was quite typical of him that at that point he erased him from his mind forever.

There was no outward indication that Bill was on the down-grade; a hit at the New Strand, a hit at the Prince of Wales, and the weekly grosses pouring in almost as well as they had two or three years before in New York. Certainly a man of action was justified in changing his base. And the man who, an hour later, turned into his Hyde Park house for dinner had all the vitality of the late twenties. Emmy, very tired and clumsy, lay on a couch in the upstairs sitting-room. He held her for a moment in his arms.

'Almost over now,' he said. 'You're beautiful.'

'Don't be ridiculous.'

'It's true. You're always beautiful. I don't know why. Perhaps because you've got character, and that's always in your face, even when you're like this.'

She was pleased; she ran her hand through his hair.

'Character is the greatest thing in the world,' he declared, 'and you've got more than anybody I know.'

'Did you see Brancusi?'

'I did, the little louse! I decided not to bring him home to dinner.'

'What was the matter?'

'Oh, just snooty—talking about my row with Aronstael, as if it was my fault.'

She hesitated, closed her mouth tight and then said quietly, 'You got into that fight with Aronstael because you were drinking.'

He rose impatiently.

'Are you going to start——'

'No, Bill, but you're drinking too much now. You know you are.'

Aware that she was right, he evaded the matter and they went in to dinner. On the glow of a bottle of claret he decided he would go on the wagon tomorrow till after the baby was born.

'I always stop when I want, don't I? I always do what I say. You never saw me quit yet.'

'Never yet.'

They had coffee together, and afterwards he got up.

'Come back early,' said Emmy.

'Oh, sure. . . . What's the matter, baby?'

'I'm just crying. Don't mind me. Oh, go on; don't just stand there like a big idiot.'

'But I'm worried, naturally. I don't like to see you cry.'

'Oh, I don't know where you go in the evenings; I don't know who you're with. And that Lady Sybil Combrinck who kept phoning. It's all right, I suppose, but I wake up in the night and I feel so alone, Bill. Because we've always been together, haven't we, until recently?'

'But we're together still. . . . What's happened to you, Emmy?'

'I know—I'm just crazy. We'd never let each other down, would we? We never have——'

'Of course not.'

'Come back early, or when you can.'

He looked in for a minute at the Prince of Wales Theatre; then he went into the hotel next door and called a number.

'I'd like to speak to her Ladyship. Mr McChesney calling.'

It was some time before Lady Sybil answered:

'This is rather a surprise. It's been several weeks since I've been lucky enough to hear from you.'

Her voice was flip as a whip and cold as automatic refrigeration, in the mode grown familiar since British ladies took to piecing themselves together out of literature. It had fascinated Bill for a while, but just for a while. He had kept his head.

'I haven't had a minute,' he explained easily. 'You're not sore, are you?'

'I could scarcely say "sore." '

'I was afraid you might be; you didn't send me an invitation to your party tonight. My idea was that after we talked it all over we agreed——'

'You talked a great deal,' she said; 'possibly a little too much.'

Suddenly, to Bill's astonishment, she hung up.

'Going British on me,' he thought. 'A little skit entitled The Daughter of a Thousand Earls.'

The snub roused him, the indifference revived his waning interest. Usually women forgave his changes of heart because of his obvious devotion to Emmy, and he was remembered by various ladies with a not unpleasant sigh. But he had detected no such sigh upon the phone.

'I'd like to clear up this mess,' he thought. Had he been wearing evening clothes, he might have dropped in at the dance and talked it over with her, still he didn't want to go home. Upon consideration it seemed important that the misunderstanding should be fixed up at once, and presently he began to entertain the idea of going as he was; Americans were excused unconventionalities of dress. In any case, it was not nearly time, and, in the company of several highballs, he considered the matter for an hour.

At midnight he walked up the steps of her Mayfair house. The coat-room attendants scrutinized his tweeds disapprovingly and a footman peered in vain for his name on the list of guests. Fortunately his friend Sir Humphrey Dunn arrived at the same time and convinced the footman it must be a mistake.

Inside, Bill immediately looked about for his hostess.

She was a very tall young woman, half American and all the more intensely English. In a sense, she had discovered Bill McChesney, vouched for his savage charms; his retirement was one of her most humiliating experiences since she had begun being bad.

She stood with her husband at the head of the receiving line—Bill had never seen them together before. He decided to choose a less formal moment for presenting himself.

As the receiving went on interminably, he became increasingly uncomfortable. He saw a few people he knew, but not many, and he was conscious that his clothes were attracting a certain attention; he was aware also that Lady Sybil saw him and could have relieved his embarrassment with a wave of her hand, but she made no sign. He was sorry he had come, but to withdraw now would be absurd, and going to a buffet table, he took a glass of champagne.

When he turned around she was alone at last, and he was about to approach her when the butler spoke to him:

'Pardon me, sir. Have you a card?'

'I'm a friend of Lady Sybil's,' said Bill impatiently. He turned away, but the butler followed.

'I'm sorry, sir, but I'll have to ask you to step aside with me and straighten this up.'

'There's no need. I'm just about to speak to Lady Sybil now.'

'My orders are different sir,' said the butler firmly.

Then, before Bill realized what was happening, his arms were pressed quietly to his sides and he was propelled into a little ante-room back of the buffet.

There he faced a man in a pince-nez in whom he recognized the Combrincks' private secretary.

The secretary nodded to the butler, saying, 'This is the man'; whereupon Bill was released.

'Mr McChesney,' said the secretary, 'you have seen fit to force your way here without a card, and His Lordship requests that you leave his house at once. Will you kindly give me the check for your coat?'

Then Bill understood, and the single word that he found applicable to Lady Sybil sprang to his lips; whereupon the secretary gave a sign to two footmen, and in a furious struggle Bill was carried through a pantry where busy bus boys stared at the scene, down a long hall, and pushed out a door into the night. The door closed; a moment later it was opened again to let his coat billow forth and his cane clatter down the steps.

As he stood there, overwhelmed, stricken aghast, a taxi-cab stopped beside him and the driver called:

'Feeling ill, gov'nor?'

'What?'

'I know where you can get a good pick-me-up, gov'nor. Never too late.' The door of the taxi opened on a nightmare. There was a cabaret that broke the closing hours; there was being with strangers he had picked up somewhere; then there were arguments, and trying to cash a cheque, and suddenly proclaiming over and over that he was William McChesney, the producer, and convincing no one of the fact, not even himself. It seemed important to see Lady Sybil right away and call her to account; but presently nothing was important at all. He was in a taxi-cab whose driver had just shaken him awake in front of his own home.

The telephone was ringing as he went in, but he walked stonily past the maid and only heard her voice when his foot was on the stair.

'Mr McChesney, it's the hospital calling again. Mrs McChesney's there, and they've been phoning every hour.'

Still in a daze, he held the receiver up to his ear.

'We're calling from the Midland Hospital, for your wife. She was delivered of a still-born child at nine this morning.'

'Wait a minute.' His voice was dry and cracking. 'I don't understand.'

After a while he understood that Emmy's child was dead and she wanted him. His knees sagged groggily as he walked down the street, looking for a taxi.

The room was dark; Emmy looked up and saw him from a rumpled bed.

'It's you!' she cried. 'I thought you were dead! Where did you go?'

He threw himself down on his knees beside the bed, but she turned away.

'Oh, you smell awful,' she said. 'It makes me sick.'

But she kept her hand in his hair, and he knelt there motionless for a long time.

'I'm done with you,' she muttered, 'but it was awful when I thought you were dead. Everybody's dead. I wish I was dead.'

A curtain parted with the wind, and as he rose to arrange it, she saw him in the full morning light, pale and terrible, with rumpled clothes and bruises on his face. This time she hated him instead of those who had hurt him. She could feel him slipping out of her heart, feel the space he left, and all at once he was gone, and she could even forgive him and be sorry for him. All this in a minute.

She had fallen down at the door of the hospital, trying to get out of the taxicab alone.

IV

When Emmy was well, physically and mentally, her incessant idea was to learn to dance; the old dream inculcated by Miss Georgia Berriman Campbell of South Carolina persisted as a bright avenue leading back to first youth and days of hope in New York. To her, dancing meant that elaborate blend of tortuous attitudes and formal pirouettes that evolved out of Italy several hundred years ago and reached its apogee in Russia at the beginning of this century. She wanted to use herself on something she could believe in, and it seemed to her that the dance was woman's interpretation of music; instead of strong fingers, one had limbs with which to render Tschaikowsky and Stravinski; and feet could be as eloquent in Chopiniana as voices in 'The Ring.' At the bottom, it was something sandwiched in between the acrobats and the trained seals; at the top it was Pavlova and art.

Once they were settled in an apartment back in New York, she plunged into her work like a girl of sixteen— four hours a day at bar exercises, attitudes, sauts, arabesques, and pirouettes. It became the realest part of her life, and her only worry was whether or not she was too old. At twenty-six she had ten years to make up, but she was a natural dancer with a fine body—and that lovely face.

Bill encouraged it; when she was ready he was going to build the first real American ballet around her. There were even times when he envied her her absorption; for affairs in his own line were more difficult since they had come home. For one thing, he had made enemies in those early days of self-confidence; there were exaggerated stories of his drinking and of his being hard on actors and difficult to work with.

It was against him that he had always been unable to save money and must beg a backing for each play. Then, too, in a curious way, he was intelligent, as he was brave enough to prove in several uncommercial ventures, but he had no Theatre Guild behind him, and what money he lost was charged against him.

There were successes, too, but he worked harder for them, or it seemed so, for he had begun to pay a price for his irregular life. He always intended to take a rest or give up his incessant cigarettes, but there was so much competition now—new men coming up, with new reputations for infallibility—and besides, he wasn't used to regularity. He liked to do his work in those great spurts, inspired by black coffee, that seem so inevitable in show business, but which took so much out of a man after thirty. He had come to lean, in a way, on Emmy's fine health and vitality. They were always together, and if he felt a vague dissatisfaction that he had grown to need her more than she needed him, there was always the hope that things would break better for him next month, next season.

Coming home from ballet school one November evening, Emmy swung her little grey bag, pulled her hat far
down over her still damp hair, and gave herself up to
pleasant speculation. For a month she had been aware of
people who had come to the studio especially to watch
her—she was ready to dance. Once she had worked just
as hard and for as long a time on something else—her
relations with Bill—only to reach a climax and misery,
but here there was nothing to fail her except herself. Yet
even now she felt a little rash in thinking: 'Now it's come.
I'm going to be happy.'

She hurried, for something had come up today that she
must talk over with Bill.

Finding him in the living-room, she called him to come
back while she dressed. She began to talk without looking
around:

'Listen what happened!' Her voice was loud, to com-
pete with the water running in the tub. 'Paul Makova
wants me to dance with him at the Metropolitan this
season; only it's not sure, so it's a secret—even I'm not
supposed to know.'

'That's great.'

'The only thing is whether it wouldn't be far better
for me to make a début abroad? Anyhow Donilof says
I'm ready to appear. What do you think?'

'I don't know.'

'You don't sound very enthusiastic.'

'I've got something on my mind. I'll tell you about it
later. Go on.'

'That's all, dear. If you still feel like going to Germany
for a month, like you said, Donilof would arrange a début
for me in Berlin, but I'd rather open here and dance with
Paul Makova. Just imagine——' She broke off, feeling
suddenly through the thick skin of her elation how
abstracted he was. 'Tell me what you've got on your
mind.'

'I went to Doctor Kearns this afternoon.'

'What did he say?' Her mind was still singing with her

own happiness. Bill's intermittent attacks of hypochondria had long ceased to worry her.

'I told him about that blood this morning, and he said what he said last year—it was probably a little broken vein in my throat. But since I'd been coughing and was worried, perhaps it was safer to take an X-ray and clear the matter up. Well, we cleared it up all right. My left lung is practically gone.'

'Bill!'

'Luckily there are no spots on the other.'

She waited, horribly afraid.

'It's come at a bad time for me,' he went on steadily, 'but it's got to be faced. He thinks I ought to go to the Adirondacks or to Denver for the winter, and his idea is Denver. That way it'll probably clear up in five or six months.'

'Of course we'll have to——' she stopped suddenly.

'I wouldn't expect you to go—especially if you have this opportunity.'

'Of course I'll go,' she said quickly. 'Your health comes first. We've always gone everywhere together.'

'Oh, no.'

'Why, of course.' She made her voice strong and decisive. 'We've always been together. I couldn't stay here without you. When do you have to go?'

'As soon as possible. I went in to see Brancusi to find out if he wanted to take over the Richmond piece, but he didn't seem enthusiastic.' His face hardened. 'Of course there won't be anything else for the present, but I'll have enough, with what's owing——'

'Oh, if I was only making some money!' Emmy cried. 'You work so hard and here I've been spending two hundred dollars a week for just my dancing lessons alone —more than I'll be able to earn for years.'

'Of course in six months I'll be as well as ever—he says.'

'Sure, dearest; we'll get you well. We'll start as soon as we can.'

She put an arm around him and kissed him.

'I'm just an old parasite,' she said. 'I should have known my darling wasn't well.'

He reached automatically for a cigarette, and then stopped.

'I forgot—I've got to start cutting down smoking.' He rose to the occasion suddenly: 'No, baby, I've decided to go alone. You'd go crazy with boredom out there, and I'd just be thinking I was keeping you away from your dancing.'

'Don't think about that. The thing is to get you well.'

They discussed the matter hour after hour for the next week, each of them saying everything except the truth—that he wanted her to go with him and that she wanted passionately to stay in New York. She talked it over guardedly with Donilof, her ballet master, and found that he thought any postponement would be a terrible mistake. Seeing other girls in the ballet school making plans for the winter, she wanted to die rather than go, and Bill saw all the involuntary indications of her misery. For a while they talked of compromising on the Adirondacks, whither she would commute by aeroplane for the week-ends, but he was running a little fever now and he was definitely ordered West.

Bill settled it all one gloomy Sunday night, with that rough, generous justice that had first made her admire him, that made him rather tragic in his adversity, as he had always been bearable in his overweening success:

'It's just up to me, baby. I got into this mess because I didn't have any self-control—you seem to have all of that in this family—and now it's only me that can get me out. You've worked hard at your stuff for three years and you deserve your chance—and if you came out there now you'd have it on me the rest of my life.' He grinned. 'And I couldn't stand that. Besides, it wouldn't be good for the kid.'

Eventually she gave in, ashamed of herself, miserable—

and glad. For the world of her work, where she existed without Bill, was bigger to her now than the world in which they existed together. There was more room to be glad in one than to be sorry in the other.

Two days later, with his ticket bought for that afternoon at five, they passed the last hours together, talking of everything hopeful. She protested still, and sincerely; had he weakened for a moment she would have gone. But the shock had done something to him, and he showed more character under it than he had for years. Perhaps it would be good for him to work it out alone.

'In the spring!' they said.

Then in the station with little Billy, and Bill saying: 'I hate these graveside partings. You leave me here. I've got to make a phone call from the train before it goes.'

They had never spent more than a night apart in six years, save when Emmy was in the hospital; save for the time in England they had a good record of faithfulness and of tenderness towards each other, even though she had been alarmed and often unhappy at this insecure bravado from the first. After he went through the gate alone, Emmy was glad he had a phone call to make and tried to picture him making it.

She was a good woman; she had loved him with all her heart. When she went out into Thirty-third Street, it was just as dead as dead for a while, and the apartment he paid for would be empty of him, and she was here, about to do something that would make her happy.

She stopped after a few blocks, thinking: 'Why, this is terrible—what I'm doing! I'm letting him down like the worst person I ever heard of. I'm leaving him flat and going off to dinner with Donilof and Paul Makova, whom I like for being beautiful and for having the same colour eyes and hair. Bill's on the train alone.'

She swung little Billy around suddenly as if to go back to the station. She could see him sitting in the train, with his face so pale and tired, and no Emmy.

'I can't let him down,' she cried to herself as wave after wave of sentiment washed over her. But only sentiment—hadn't he let her down—hadn't he done what he wanted in London?

'Oh, poor Bill!'

She stood irresolute, realizing for the last honest moment how quickly she would forget this and find excuses for what she was doing. She had to think hard of London, and her conscience cleared. But with Bill all alone in the train it seemed terrible to think that way. Even now she could turn and go back to the station and tell him that she was coming, but she still waited, with life very strong in her, fighting for her. The sidewalk was narrow where she stood; presently a great wave of people, pouring out of the theatre, came flooding along it, and she and little Billy were swept along with the crowd.

In the train, Bill telephoned up to the last minute, postponed going back to his state-room, because he knew it was almost certain that he would not find her there. After the train started he went back and, of course, there was nothing but his bags in the rack and some magazines on the seat.

He knew then that he had lost her. He saw the set-up without any illusions—this Paul Makova, and months of proximity, and loneliness—afterwards nothing would ever be the same. When he had thought about it all a long time, reading *Variety* and *Zit's* in between, it began to seem, each time he came back to it, as if Emmy somehow were dead.

'She was a fine girl—one of the best. She had character.' He realized perfectly that he had brought all this on himself and that there was some law of compensation involved. He saw, too, that by going away he had again become as good as she was; it was all evened up at last.

He felt beyond everything, even beyond his grief, an almost comfortable sensation of being in the hands of something bigger than himself; and grown a little tired and unconfident—two qualities he could never for a moment tolerate—it did not seem so terrible if he were going West for a definite finish. He was sure that Emmy would come at the end, no matter what she was doing or how good an engagement she had.

THE BRIDAL PARTY

[1930]

THERE was the usual insincere little note saying: 'I wanted you to be the first to know.' It was a double shock to Michael, announcing, as it did, both the engagement and the imminent marriage; which, moreover, was to be held, not in New York, decently and far away, but here in Paris under his very nose, if that could be said to extend over the Protestant Episcopal Church of the Holy Trinity, Avenue George-Cinq. The date was two weeks off, early in June.

At first Michael was afraid and his stomach felt hollow. When he left the hotel that morning, the *femme de chambre*, who was in love with his fine, sharp profile and his pleasant buoyancy, scented the hard abstraction that had settled over him. He walked in a daze to his bank, he bought a detective story at Smith's on the Rue de Rivoli, he sympathetically stared for a while at a faded panorama of the battlefields in a tourist-office window and cursed a Greek tout who followed him with a half-displayed packet of innocuous post cards warranted to be very dirty indeed.

But the fear stayed with him, and after a while he recognized it as the fear that now he would never be happy. He had met Caroline Dandy when she was seventeen, possessed her young heart all through her first season in New York, and then lost her, slowly, tragically, uselessly, because he had no money and could make no money; because, with all the energy and goodwill in the world, he could not find himself; because, loving him still, Caroline had lost faith and begun to see him as something pathetic, futile, and shabby, outside the great, shining stream of life towards which she was inevitably drawn.

Since his only support was that she loved him, he leaned weakly on that; the support broke, but still he held on to it and was carried out to sea and washed up on the French coast with its broken pieces still in his hands. He carried them around with him in the form of photographs and packets of correspondence and a liking for a maudlin popular song called *Among My Souvenirs*. He kept clear of other girls, as if Caroline would somehow know it and reciprocate with a faithful heart. Her note informed him that he had lost her forever.

It was a fine morning. In front of the shops in the Rue de Castiglioni, proprietors and patrons were on the sidewalk gazing upward, for the Graf Zeppelin, shining and glorious, symbol of escape and destruction—of escape, if necessary, through destruction—glided in the Paris sky. He heard a woman say in French that it would not astonish her if that commenced to let fall the bombs. Then he heard another voice, full of husky laughter, and the void in his stomach froze. Jerking about, he was face to face with Caroline Dandy and her fiancé.

'Why, Michael! Why, we were wondering where you were. I asked at the Guaranty Trust, and Morgan and Company, and finally sent a note to the National City——'

Why didn't they back away? Why didn't they back right up, walking backwards down the Rue de Castiglione, across the Rue de Rivoli, through the Tuileries Gardens, still walking backwards as fast as they could till they grew vague and faded out across the river?

'This is Hamilton Rutherford, my fiancé.'

'We've met before.'

'At Pat's, wasn't it?'

'And last spring in the Ritz Bar.'

'Michael, where have you been keeping yourself?'

'Around here.' This agony. Previews of Hamilton Rutherford flashed before his eyes—a quick series of

8+s.f. 6

pictures, sentences. He remembered hearing that he had bought a seat in 1920 for a hundred and twenty-five thousand of borrowed money, and just before the break sold it for more than half a million. Not handsome like Michael, but vitally attractive, confident, authoritative, just the right height over Caroline there—Michael had always been too short for Caroline when they danced.

Rutherford was saying: 'No, I'd like it very much if you'd come to the bachelor dinner. I'm taking the Ritz Bar from nine o'clock on. Then right after the wedding there'll be a reception and breakfast at the Hôtel George-Cinq.'

'And, Michael, George Packman is giving a party day after tomorrow at Chez Victor, and I want you to be sure and come. And also to tea Friday at Jebby West's; she'd want to have you if she knew where you were. Where's your hotel, so we can send you an invitation? You see, the reason we decided to have it over here is because mother has been sick in a nursing home here and the whole clan is in Paris. Then Hamilton's mother's being here too——'

The entire clan; they had always hated him, except her mother; always discouraged his courtship. What a little counter he was in this game of families and money! Under his hat his brow sweated with the humiliation of the fact that for all his misery he was worth just exactly so many invitations. Frantically he began to mumble something about going away.

Then it happened—Caroline saw deep into him, and Michael knew that she saw. She saw through to his profound woundedness, and something quivered inside her, died out along the curve of her mouth and in her eyes. He had moved her. All the unforgettable impulses of first love had surged up once more; their hearts had in some way touched across two feet of Paris sunlight. She took her fiancé's arm suddenly, as if to steady herself with the feel of it.

They parted. Michael walked quickly for a minute;

then he stopped, pretending to look in a window, and saw them farther up the street, walking fast into the Place Vendôme, people with much to do.

He had things to do also—he had to get his laundry.

'Nothing will ever be the same again,' he said to himself. 'She will never be happy in her marriage and I will never be happy at all any more.'

The two vivid years of his love for Caroline moved back around him like years in Einstein's physics. Intolerable memories arose—of rides in the Long Island moonlight; of a happy time at Lake Placid with her cheeks so cold there, but warm just underneath the surface; of a despairing afternoon in a little café on Forty-eighth Street in the last sad months when their marriage had come to seem impossible.

'Come in,' he said aloud.

The concierge with a telegram; brusque, because Mr Curly's clothes were a little shabby. Mr Curly gave few tips; Mr Curly was obviously a *petit client*.

Michael read the telegram.

'An answer?' the concierge asked.

'No,' said Michael, and then, on an impulse: 'Look.'

'Too bad—too bad,' said the concierge. 'Your grandfather is dead.'

'Not too bad,' said Michael. 'It means that I come into a quarter of a million dollars.'

Too late by a single month; after the first flush of the news his misery was deeper than ever. Lying awake in bed that night, he listened endlessly to the long caravan of a circus moving through the street from one Paris fair to another.

When the last van had rumbled out of hearing and the corners of the furniture were pastel blue with the dawn, he was still thinking of the look in Caroline's eyes that morning—the look that seemed to say: 'Oh, why couldn't you have done something about it? Why couldn't you have been stronger, made me marry you? Don't you see how sad I am?'

Michael's fists clenched.

'Well, I won't give up till the last moment,' he whispered. 'I've had all the bad luck so far, and maybe it's turned at last. One takes what one can get, up to the limit of one's strength, and if I can't have her, at least she'll go into this marriage with some of me in her heart.'

II

Accordingly he went to the party at Chez Victor two days later, upstairs and into the little salon off the bar where the party was to assemble for cocktails. He was early; the only other occupant was a tall lean man of fifty. They spoke.

'You waiting for George Packman's party?'

'Yes. My name's Michael Curly.'

'My name's——'

Michael failed to catch the name. They ordered a drink, and Michael supposed that the bride and groom were having a gay time.

'Too much so,' the other agreed, frowning. 'I don't see how they stand it. We all crossed on the boat together; five days of that crazy life and then two weeks of Paris. You'—he hesitated, smiling faintly—'you'll excuse me for saying that your generation drinks too much.'

'Not Caroline.'

'No, not Caroline. She seems to take only a cocktail and a glass of champagne, and then she's had enough, thank God. But Hamilton drinks too much and all this crowd of young people drink too much. Do you live in Paris?'

'For the moment,' said Michael.

'I don't like Paris. My wife—that is to say, my ex-wife, Hamilton's mother—lives in Paris.'

'You're Hamilton Rutherford's father?'

'I have that honour. And I'm not denying that I'm proud of what he's done; it was just a general comment.'

'Of course.'

Michael glanced up nervously as four people came in. He felt suddenly that his dinner coat was old and shiny; he had ordered a new one that morning. The people who had come in were rich and at home in their richness with one another—a dark, lovely girl with a hysterical little laugh whom he had met before; two confident men whose jokes referred invariably to last night's scandal and tonight's potentialities, as if they had important rôles in a play that extended indefinitely into the past and the future. When Caroline arrived, Michael had scarcely a moment of her, but it was enough to note that, like all the others, she was strained and tired. She was pale beneath her rouge; there were shadows under her eyes. With a mixture of relief and wounded vanity, he found himself placed far from her and at another table; he needed a moment to adjust himself to his surroundings. This was not like the immature set in which he and Caroline had moved; the men were more than thirty and had an air of sharing the best of this world's goods. Next to him was Jebby West, whom he knew; and, on the other side, a jovial man who immediately began to talk to Michael about a stunt for the bachelor dinner: They were going to hire a French girl to appear with an actual baby in her arms, crying: 'Hamilton, you can't desert me now!' The idea seemed stale and unamusing to Michael, but its originator shook with anticipatory laughter.

Farther up the table there was talk of the market— another drop today, the most appreciable since the crash; people were kidding Rutherford about it: 'Too bad, old man. You better not get married, after all.'

Michael asked the man on his left, 'Has he lost a lot?'

'Nobody knows. He's heavily involved, but he's one of the smartest young men in Wall Street. Anyhow, nobody ever tells you the truth.'

It was a champagne dinner from the start, and towards the end it reached a pleasant level of conviviality, but Michael saw that all these people were too weary to be

exhilarated by any ordinary stimulant; for weeks they
had drunk cocktails before meals like Americans, wines
and brandies like Frenchmen, beer like Germans, whisky-
and-soda like the English, and as they were no longer
in the twenties, this preposterous *mélange,* that was like
some gigantic cocktail in a nightmare, served only to
make them temporarily less conscious of the mistakes of
the night before. Which is to say that it was not really
a gay party; what gaiety existed was displayed in the
few who drank nothing at all.

But Michael was not tired, and the champagne stimu-
lated him and made his misery less acute. He had been
away from New York for more than eight months and
most of the dance music was unfamiliar to him, but at
the first bars of the 'Painted Doll,' to which he and
Caroline had moved through so much happiness and
despair the previous summer, he crossed to Caroline's
table and asked her to dance.

She was lovely in a dress of thin ethereal blue, and
the proximity of her crackly yellow hair, of her cool
and tender grey eyes, turned his body clumsy and rigid;
he stumbled with their first step on the floor. For a
moment it seemed that there was nothing to say; he
wanted to tell her about his inheritance, but the idea
seemed abrupt, unprepared for.

'Michael, it's so nice to be dancing with you again.'

He smiled grimly.

'I'm so happy you came,' she continued. 'I was afraid
maybe you'd be silly and stay away. Now we can be
just good friends and natural together. Michael, I want
you and Hamilton to like each other.'

The engagement was making her stupid; he had never
heard her make such a series of obvious remarks before.

'I could kill him without a qualm,' he said pleasantly,
'but he looks like a good man. He's fine. What I want
to know is, what happens to people like me who aren't
able to forget?'

As he said this he could not prevent his mouth from

drooping suddenly, and glancing up, Caroline saw, and her heart quivered violently, as it had the other morning.

'Do you mind so much, Michael?'

'Yes.'

For a second as he said this, in a voice that seemed to have come up from his shoes, they were not dancing; they were simply clinging together. Then she leaned away from him and twisted her mouth into a lovely smile.

'I didn't know what to do at first, Michael. I told Hamilton about you—that I'd cared for you an awful lot—but it didn't worry him, and he was right. Because I'm over you now—yes, I am. And you'll wake up some sunny morning and be over me just like that.'

He shook his head stubbornly.

'Oh, yes. We weren't for each other. I'm pretty flighty, and I need somebody like Hamilton to decide things. It was that more than the question of—of——'

'Of money.' Again he was on the point of telling her what had happened, but again something told him it was not the time.

'Then how do you account for what happened when we met the other day,' he demanded helplessly—'what happened just now? When we just pour towards each other like we used to—as if we were one person, as if the same blood was flowing through both of us?'

'Oh, don't!' she begged him. 'You mustn't talk like that; everything's decided now. I love Hamilton with all my heart. It's just that I remember certain things in the past and I feel sorry for you—for us—for the way we were.'

Over her shoulder, Michael saw a man come towards them to cut in. In a panic he danced her away, but inevitably the man came on.

'I've got to see you alone, if only for a minute,' Michael said quickly. 'When can I?'

'I'll be at Jebby West's tea tomorrow,' she whispered as a hand fell politely upon Michael's shoulder.

But he did not talk to her at Jebby West's tea. Rutherford stood next to her, and each brought the other into all conversations. They left early. The next morning the wedding cards arrived in the first mail.

Then Michael, grown desperate with pacing up and down his room, determined on a bold stroke; he wrote to Hamilton Rutherford, asking him for a rendezvous the following afternoon. In a short telephone communication Rutherford agreed, but for a day later than Michael had asked. And the wedding was only six days away.

They were to meet in the bar of the Hôtel Jéna. Michael knew what he would say: 'See here, Rutherford, do you realize the responsibility you're taking in going through with this marriage? Do you realize the harvest of trouble and regret you're sowing in persuading a girl into something contrary to the instincts of her heart?' He would explain that the barrier between Caroline and himself had been an artificial one and was now removed, and demand that the matter be put up to Caroline frankly before it was too late.

Rutherford would be angry, conceivably there would be a scene, but Michael felt that he was fighting for his life now.

He found Rutherford in conversation with an older man, whom Michael had met at several of the wedding parties.

'I saw what happened to most of my friends,' Rutherford was saying, 'and I decided it wasn't going to happen to me. It isn't so difficult; if you take a girl with common sense, and tell her what's what, and do your stuff damn well, and play decently square with her, it's a marriage. If you stand for any nonsense at the beginning, it's one of these arrangements—within five years the man gets out, or else the girl gobbles him up and you have the usual mess.'

'Right!' agreed his companion enthusiastically. 'Hamilton, boy, you're right.'

Michael's blood boiled slowly.

'Doesn't it strike you,' he inquired coldly, 'that your attitude went out of fashion about a hundred years ago?'

'No, it didn't,' said Rutherford pleasantly, but impatiently. 'I'm as modern as anybody. I'd get married in an aeroplane next Saturday if it'd please my girl.'

'I don't mean that way of being modern. You can't take a sensitive woman——'

'Sensitive? Women aren't so darn sensitive. It's fellows like you who are sensitive; it's fellows like you that they exploit—all your devotion and kindness and all that. They read a couple of books and see a few pictures because they haven't got anything else to do, and then they say they're finer in grain than you are, and to prove it they take the bit in their teeth and tear off for a fare-you-well—just about as sensitive as a fire horse.'

'Caroline happens to be sensitive,' said Michael in a clipped voice.

At this point the other man got up to go; when the dispute about the check had been settled and they were alone, Rutherford leaned back to Michael as if a question had been asked him.

'Caroline's more than sensitive,' he said. 'She's got sense.'

His combative eyes, meeting Michael's, flickered with a grey light. 'This all sounds pretty crude to you, Mr. Curly, but it seems to me that the average man nowadays just asks to be made a monkey of by some woman who doesn't even get any fun out of reducing him to that level. There are darn few men who possess their wives any more, but I am going to be one of them.'

To Michael it seemed time to bring the talk back to the actual situation: 'Do you realize the responsibility you're taking?'

'I certainly do,' interrupted Rutherford. 'I'm not afraid of responsibility. I'll make the decisions—fairly, I hope, but anyhow they'll be final.'

8*

'What if you didn't start right?' said Michael impetuously. 'What if your marriage isn't founded on mutual love?'

'I think I see what you mean,' Rutherford said, still pleasant. 'And since you've brought it up, let me say that if you and Caroline had married, it wouldn't have lasted three years. Do you know what your affair was founded on? On sorrow. You got sorry for each other. Sorrow's a lot of fun for most women and for some men, but it seems to me that a marriage ought to be based on hope.' He looked at his watch and stood up.

'I've got to meet Caroline. Remember, you're coming to the bachelor dinner day after tomorrow.'

Michael felt the moment slipping away. 'Then Caroline's personal feelings don't count with you?' he demanded fiercely.

'Caroline's tired and upset. But she has what she wants, and that's the main thing.'

'Are you referring to yourself?' demanded Michael incredulously.

'Yes.'

'May I ask how long she's wanted you?'

'About two years.' Before Michael could answer, he was gone.

During the next two days Michael floated in an abyss of helplessness. The idea haunted him that he had left something undone that would sever this knot drawn tight under his eyes. He phoned Caroline, but she insisted that it was physically impossible for her to see him until the day before the wedding, for which day she granted him a tentative rendezvous. Then he went to the bachelor dinner, partly in fear of an evening alone at his hotel, partly from a feeling that by his presence at that function he was somehow nearer to Caroline, keeping her in sight.

The Ritz Bar had been prepared for the occasion by French and American banners and by a great canvas covering one wall, against which the guests were invited to concentrate their proclivities in breaking glasses.

At the first cocktail, taken at the bar, there were many slight spillings from many trembling hands, but later, with the champagne, there was a rising tide of laughter and occasional bursts of song.

Michael was surprised to find what a difference his new dinner coat, his new silk hat, his new, proud linen made in his estimate of himself; he felt less resentment towards all these people for being so rich and assured. For the first time since he had left college he felt rich and assured himself; he felt that he was part of all this, and even entered into the scheme of Johnson, the practical joker, for the appearance of the woman betrayed, now waiting tranquilly in the room across the hall.

'We don't want to go too heavy,' Johnson said, 'because I imagine Ham's had a pretty anxious day already. Did you see Fullman Oil's sixteen points off this morning?'

'Will that matter to him?' Michael asked, trying to keep the interest out of his voice.

'Naturally. He's in heavily; he's always in everything heavily. So far he's had luck; anyhow, up to a month ago.'

The glasses were filled and emptied faster now, and men were shouting at one another across the narrow table. Against the bar a group of ushers was being photographed, and the flash light surged through the room in a stifling cloud.

'Now's the time,' Johnson said. 'You're to stand by the door, remember, and we're both to try and keep her from coming in—just till we get everybody's attention.'

He went on out into the corridor, and Michael waited obediently by the door. Several minutes passed. Then Johnson reappeared with a curious expression on his face.

'There's something funny about this.'

'Isn't the girl there?'

'She's there all right, but there's another woman there, too; and it's nobody we engaged either. She wants to see Hamilton Rutherford, and she looks as if she had something on her mind.'

They went out into the hall. Planted firmly in a chair near the door sat an American girl a little the worse for liquor, but with a determined expression on her face. She looked up at them with a jerk of her head.

'Well, j'tell him?' she demanded. 'The name is Marjorie Collins, and he'll know it. I've come a long way, and I want to see him now and quick, or there's going to be more trouble than you ever saw.' She rose unsteadily to her feet.

'You go in and tell Ham,' whispered Johnson to Michael. 'Maybe he'd better get out. I'll keep her here.'

Back at the table, Michael leaned close to Rutherford's ear and, with a certain grimness, whispered:

'A girl outside named Marjorie Collins says she wants to see you. She looks as if she wanted to make trouble.'

Hamilton Rutherford blinked and his mouth fell ajar; then slowly the lips came together in a straight line and he said in a crisp voice:

'Please keep her there. And send the head barman to me right away.'

Michael spoke to the barman, and then, without returning to the table, asked quietly for his coat and hat. Out in the hall again, he passed Johnson and the girl without speaking and went out into the Rue Cambon. Calling a cab, he gave the address of Caroline's hotel.

His place was beside her now. Not to bring bad news, but simply to be with her when her house of cards came falling around her head.

Rutherford had implied that he was soft—well, he was hard enough not to give up the girl he loved without taking advantage of every chance within the pale of honour. Should she turn away from Rutherford, she would find him there.

She was in; she was surprised when he called, but she was still dressed and would be down immediately. Presently she appeared in a dinner gown, holding two blue telegrams in her hand. They sat down in armchairs in the deserted lobby.

'But, Michael, is the dinner over?'

'I wanted to see you, so I came away.'

'I'm glad.' Her voice was friendly, but matter-of-fact. 'Because I'd just phoned your hotel that I had fittings and rehearsals all day tomorrow. Now we can have our talk after all.'

'You're tired,' he guessed. 'Perhaps I shouldn't have come.'

'No. I was waiting up for Hamilton. Telegrams that may be important. He said he might go on somewhere, and that may mean any hour, so I'm glad I have someone to talk to.'

Michael winced at the impersonality in the last phrase.

'Don't you care when he gets home?'

'Naturally,' she said, laughing, 'but I haven't got much say about it, have it?'

'Why not?'

'I couldn't start by telling him what he could and couldn't do.'

'Why not?'

'He wouldn't stand for it.'

'He seems to want merely a housekeeper,' said Michael ironically.

'Tell me about your plans, Michael,' she asked quickly.

'My plans? I can't see any future after the day after tomorrow. The only real plan I ever had was to love you.'

Their eyes brushed past each other's, and the look he knew so well was staring out at him from hers. Words flowed quickly from his heart:

'Let me tell you just once more how well I've loved you, never wavering for a moment, never thinking of another girl. And now when I think of all the years ahead without you, without any hope, I don't want to live, Caroline darling. I used to dream about our home, our children, about holding you in my arms and touching your face and hands and hair that used to belong to me, and now I just can't wake up.'

Caroline was crying softly. 'Poor Michael—poor Michael.' Her hand reached out and her fingers brushed the lapel of his dinner coat. 'I was so sorry for you the other night. You looked so thin, and as if you needed a new suit and somebody to take care of you.' She sniffled and looked more closely at his coat. 'Why, you've got a new suit! And a new silk hat! Why, Michael, how swell!' She laughed, suddenly cheerful through her tears. 'You must have come into money, Michael; I never saw you so well turned out.'

For a moment, at her reaction, he hated his new clothes.

'I have come into money,' he said. 'My grandfather left me about a quarter of a million dollars.'

'Why, Michael,' she cried, 'how perfectly swell! I can't tell you how glad I am. I've always thought you were the sort of person who ought to have money.'

'Yes, just too late to make a difference.'

The revolving door from the street groaned around and Hamilton Rutherford came into the lobby. His face was flushed, his eyes were restless and impatient.

'Hello, darling; hello, Mr Curly.' He bent and kissed Caroline. 'I broke away for a minute to find out if I had any telegrams. I see you've got them there.' Taking them from her, he remarked to Curly, 'That was an odd business there in the bar, wasn't it? Especially as I understand some of you had a joke fixed up in the same line.' He opened one of the telegrams, closed it and turned to Caroline with the divided expression of a man carrying two things in his head at once.

'A girl I haven't seen for two years turned up,' he said. 'It seemed to be some clumsy form of blackmail, for I haven't and never have had any sort of obligation towards her whatever.'

'What happened?'

'The head barman had a Sûreté Générale man there

in ten minutes and it was settled in the hall. The French blackmail laws make ours look like a sweet wish, and I gather they threw a scare into her that she'll remember. But it seems wiser to tell you.'

'Are you implying that I mentioned the matter?' said Michael stiffly.

'No,' Rutherford said slowly. 'No, you were just going to be on hand. And since you're here, I'll tell you some news that will interest you even more.'

He handed Michael one telegram and opened the other.

'This is in code,' Michael said.

'So is this. But I've got to know all the words pretty well this last week. The two of them together mean I'm due to start life all over.'

Michael saw Caroline's face grow a shade paler, but she sat quiet as a mouse.

'It was a mistake and I stuck to it too long,' continued Rutherford. 'So you see I don't have all the luck, Mr Curly. By the way, they tell me you've come into money.'

'Yes,' said Michael.

'There we are, then.' Rutherford turned to Caroline. 'You understand, darling, that I'm not joking or exaggerating. I've lost almost every cent I had and I'm starting life over.'

Two pairs of eyes were regarding her—Rutherford's noncommittal and unrequiring, Michael's hungry, tragic, pleading. In a minute she had raised herself from the chair and with a little cry thrown herself into Hamilton Rutherford's arms.

'Oh, darling,' she cried, 'what does it matter! It's better; I like it better, honestly I do! I want to start that way; I want to! Oh, please don't worry or be sad even for a minute!'

'All right, baby,' said Rutherford. His hand stroked her hair gently for a moment; then he took his arm from around her.

'I promised to join the party for an hour,' he said. 'So I'll say good night, and I want you to go to bed soon and get a good sleep. Good night, Mr Curly. I'm sorry to have let you in for all these financial matters.'

But Michael had already picked up his hat and cane. 'I'll go along with you,' he said.

III

It was such a fine morning. Michael's cutaway hadn't been delivered, so he felt rather uncomfortable passing before the cameras and moving-picture machines in front of the little church on the Avenue George-Cinq.

It was such a clean, new church that it seemed unforgivable not to be dressed properly, and Michael, white and shaky after a sleepless night, decided to stand in the rear. From there he looked at the back of Hamilton Rutherford, and the lacy, filmy back of Caroline, and the fat back of George Packman, which looked unsteady, as if it wanted to lean against the bride and groom.

The ceremony went on for a long time under the gay flags and pennons overhead, under the thick beams of June sunlight slanting down through the tall windows upon the well-dressed people.

As the procession, headed by the bride and groom, started down the aisle, Michael realized with alarm he was just where everyone would dispense with the parade stiffness, become informal and speak to him.

So it turned out. Rutherford and Caroline spoke first to him; Rutherford grim with the strain of being married, and Caroline lovelier than he had ever seen her, floating all softly down through the friends and relatives of her youth, down through the past and forward to the future by the sunlit door.

Michael managed to murmur, 'Beautiful, simply beautiful,' and then other people passed and spoke to him— old Mrs Dandy, straight from her sickbed and looking remarkably well, or carrying it off like the very fine old lady she was; and Rutherford's father and mother, ten years divorced, but walking side by side and looking made for each other and proud. Then all Caroline's sisters and their husbands and her little nephews in Eton suits, and then a long parade, all speaking to Michael because he was still standing paralysed just at that point where the procession broke.

He wondered what would happen now. Cards had been issued for a reception at the George-Cinq; an expensive enough place, heaven knew. Would Rutherford try to go through with that on top of those disastrous telegrams? Evidently, for the procession outside was streaming up there through the June morning, three by three and four by four. On the corner the long dresses of girls, five abreast, fluttered many-coloured in the wind. Girls had become gossamer again, perambulatory flora; such lovely fluttering dresses in the bright noon wind.

Michael needed a drink; he couldn't face that reception line without a drink. Diving into a side doorway of the hotel, he asked for the bar, whither a *chasseur* led him through half a kilometre of new American-looking passages.

But—how did it happen?—the bar was full. There were ten—fifteen men and two—four girls, all from the wedding, all needing a drink. There were cocktails and champagne in the bar; Rutherford's cocktails and champagne, as it turned out, for he had engaged the whole bar and the ballroom and the two great reception rooms and all the stairways leading up and down, and windows looking out over the whole square block of Paris. By and by Michael went and joined the long, slow drift of the receiving line. Through a flowery mist of 'Such a lovely wedding,' 'My dear, you were simply lovely,' 'You're a lucky man, Rutherford' he passed down the line. When Michael came to Caroline, she took a single step forward and kissed him on the lips, but he felt no contact in the kiss; it was unreal and he floated on away from it. Old Mrs Dandy, who had always liked him, held his hand for a minute and thanked him for the flowers he had sent when he heard she was ill.

'I'm so sorry not to have written; you know, we old ladies are grateful for——' The flowers, the fact that she had not written, the wedding—Michael saw that they all had the same relative importance to her now; she had married off five other children and seen two of the marriages go to pieces, and this scene, so poignant, so confusing to Michael, appeared to her simply a familiar charade in which she had played her part before.

A buffet luncheon with champagne was already being served at small tables and there was an orchestra playing in the empty ballroom. Michael sat down with Jebby West; he was still a little embarrassed at not wearing a morning coat, but he perceived now that he was not alone in the omission and felt better. 'Wasn't Caroline divine?' Jebby West said. 'So entirely self-possessed. I asked her this morning if she wasn't a little nervous at stepping off like this. And she said, "Why should I be? I've been after him for two years, and now I'm just happy, that's all."'

'It must be true,' said Michael gloomily.

'What?'

'What you just said.'

He had been stabbed, but, rather to his distress, he did not feel the wound.

He asked Jebby to dance. Out on the floor, Rutherford's father and mother were dancing together.

'It makes me a little sad, that,' she said. 'Those two hadn't met for years; both of them were married again and she divorced again. She went to the station to meet him when he came over for Caroline's wedding, and invited him to stay at her house in the Avenue du Bois with a whole lot of other people, perfectly proper, but he was afraid his wife would hear about it and not like it, so he went to a hotel. Don't you think that's sort of sad?'

An hour or so later Michael realized suddenly that it was afternoon. In one corner of the ballroom an arrangement of screens like a moving-picture stage had been set up and photographers were taking official pictures of the bridal party. The bridal party, still as death and pale as wax under the bright lights, appeared, to the dancers circling the modulated semidarkness of the ball-room, like those jovial or sinister groups that one comes upon in The Old Mill at an amusement park.

After the bridal party had been photographed, there was a group of the ushers; then the bridesmaids, the families, the children. Later Caroline, active and excited, having long since abandoned the repose implicit in her flowing dress and great bouquet, came and plucked Michael off the floor.

'Now we'll have them take one of just old friends.' Her voice implied that this was best, most intimate of all. 'Come here, Jebby, George—not you, Hamilton; this is just my friends—Sally——'

A little after that, what remained of formality disappeared and the hours flowed easily down the profuse stream of champagne. In the modern fashion, Hamilton Rutherford sat at the table with his arm about an old girl of his and assured his guests, which included not a few bewildered but enthusiastic Europeans, that the party was not nearly at an end; it was to reassemble at Zelli's after midnight. Michael saw Mrs Dandy, not quite over her illness, rise to go and become caught in polite group after group, and he spoke of it to one of her daughters, who thereupon forcibly abducted her mother and called her car. Michael felt very considerate and proud of himself after having done this, and drank much more champagne.

'It's amazing,' George Packman was telling him enthusiastically. 'This show will cost Ham about five thousand dollars, and I understand they'll be just about his last. But did he countermand a bottle of champagne or a flower? Not he! He happens to have it—that young man. Do you know that T. G. Vance offered him a salary of fifty thousand dollars a year ten minutes before the wedding this morning? In another year he'll be back with the millionaires.'

The conversation was interrupted by a plan to carry Rutherford out on communal shoulders—a plan which six of them put into effect, and then stood in the four-o'clock sunshine waving good-bye to the bride and groom. But there must have been a mistake somewhere, for five minutes later Michael saw both bride and groom descending the stairway to the reception, each with a glass of champagne held defiantly on high.

'This is our way of doing things,' he thought. 'Generous and fresh and free; a sort of Virginia-plantation hospitality, but at a different pace now, nervous as a ticker tape.'

Standing unselfconsciously in the middle of the room to see which was the American ambassador, he realized with a start that he hadn't really thought of Caroline for hours. He looked about him with a sort of alarm, and then he saw her across the room, very bright and young, and radiantly happy. He saw Rutherford near her, looking at her as if he could never look long enough, and as Michael watched them they seemed to recede as he had wished them to do that day in the Rue de Castiglione—recede and fade off into joys and griefs of their own, into the years that would take the toll of Rutherford's fine pride and Caroline's young, moving beauty; fade far away, so that now he could scarcely see them, as if they were shrouded in something as misty as her white, billowing dress.

Michael was cured. The ceremonial function, with its pomp and its revelry, had stood for a sort of initiation into a life where even his regret could not follow them. All the bitterness melted out of him suddenly and the world reconstituted itself out of the youth and happiness that was all around him, profligate as the spring sunshine. He was trying to remember which one of the bridesmaids he had made a date to dine with tonight as he walked forward to bid Hamilton and Caroline Rutherford good-bye.

ONE TRIP ABROAD
[1930]

IN THE AFTERNOON the air became black with locusts, and some of the women shrieked, sinking to the floor of the motorbus and covering their hair with travelling rugs. The locusts were coming north, eating everything in their path, which was not so much in that part of the world; they were flying silently and in straight lines, flakes of black snow. But none struck the windshield or tumbled into the car, and presently humorists began holding out their hands, trying to catch some. After ten minutes the cloud thinned out, passed, and the women emerged from the blankets, dishevelled and feeling silly. And everyone talked together.

Everyone talked; it would have been absurd not to talk after having been through a swarm of locusts on the edge of the Sahara. The Smyrna-American talked to the British widow going down to Biskra to have one last fling with an as-yet-unencountered sheik. The member of the San Francisco Stock Exchange talked shyly to the author. 'Aren't you an author?' he said. The father and daughter from Wilmington talked to the cockney airman who was going to fly to Timbuctoo. Even the French chauffeur turned about and explained in a loud, clear voice: 'Bumble-Bees,' which sent the trained nurse from New York into shriek after shriek of hysterical laughter.

Amongst the unsubtle rushing together of the travellers there was one interchange more carefully considered. Mr and Mrs Liddell Miles, turning as one person, smiled and spoke to the young American couple in the seat behind:

'Didn't catch any in your hair?'

The young couple smiled back politely.

'No. We survived that plague.'

They were in their twenties, and there was still a pleasant touch of bride and groom upon them. A handsome couple; the man rather intense and sensitive, the girl arrestingly light of hue in eyes and hair, her face without shadows, its living freshness modulated by a lovely confident calm. Mr and Mrs Miles did not fail to notice their air of good breeding, of a specifically 'swell' background, expressed both by their unsophistication and by their ingrained reticence that was not stiffness. If they held aloof, it was because they were sufficient to each other, while Mr and Mrs Miles's aloofness toward the other passengers was a conscious mask, a social attitude, quite as public an affair in its essence as the ubiquitous advances of the Smyrna-American, who was snubbed by all.

The Mileses had, in fact, decided that the young couple were 'possible' and, bored with themselves, were frankly approaching them.

'Have you been to Africa before? It's been so utterly fascinating! Are you going on to Tunis?'

The Mileses, if somewhat worn away inside by fifteen years of a particular set in Paris, had undeniable style, even charm, and before the evening arrival at the little oasis town of Bou Saada they had all four become companionable. They uncovered mutual friends in New York and, meeting for a cocktail in the bar of the Hôtel Transatlantique, decided to have dinner together.

As the young Kellys came downstairs later, Nicole was conscious of a certain regret that they had accepted, realizing that now they were probably committed to seeing a certain amount of their new acquaintances as far as Constantine, where their routes diverged.

In the eight months of their marriage she had been so very happy that it seemed like spoiling something. On the Italian liner that had brought them to Gibraltar they had not joined the groups that leaned desperately on one another in the bar; instead, they seriously studied French, and Nelson worked on business contingent on his recent inheritance of half a million dollars. Also he painted a picture of a smokestack. When one member of the gay crowd in the bar disappeared permanently into the Atlantic just this side of the Azores, the young Kellys were almost glad, for it justified their aloof attitude.

But there was another reason Nicole was sorry they had committed themselves. She spoke to Nelson about it: 'I passed that couple in the hall just now.'

'Who—the Mileses?'

'No, that young couple—about our age—the ones that were on the other motorbus, that we thought looked so nice, in Bir Rabalou after lunch, in the camel market.'

'They did look nice.'

'Charming,' she said emphatically; 'the girl and man, both. I'm almost sure I've met the girl somewhere before.'

The couple referred to were sitting across the room at dinner, and Nicole found her eyes drawn irresistibly toward them. They, too, now had companions, and again Nicole, who had not talked to a girl of her own age for two months, felt a faint regret. The Mileses, being formally sophisticated and frankly snobbish, were a different matter. They had been to an alarming number of places and seemed to know all the flashing phantoms of the newspapers.

They dined on the hotel veranda under a sky that was low and full of the presence of a strange and watchful God; around the corners of the hotel the night already stirred with the sounds of which they had so often read but that were even so hysterically unfamiliar—drums from Senegal, a native flute, the selfish, effeminate whine of a camel, the Arabs pattering past in shoes made of old automobile tires, the wail of Magian prayer.

At the desk in the hotel, a fellow passenger was arguing monotonously with the clerk about the rate of exchange, and the inappropriateness added to the detachment which had increased steadily as they went south.

Mrs Miles was the first to break the lingering silence;

with a sort of impatience she pulled them with her, in from the night and up to the table.

'We really should have dressed. Dinner's more amusing if people dress, because they feel differently in formal clothes. The English know that.'

'Dress here?' her husband objected. 'I'd feel like that man in the ragged dress suit we passed today, driving the flock of sheep.'

'I always feel like a tourist if I'm not dressed.'

'Well, we are, aren't we?' asked Nelson.

'I don't consider myself a tourist. A tourist is somebody who gets up early and goes to cathedrals and talks about scenery.'

Nicole and Nelson, having seen all the official sights from Fez to Algiers, and taken reels of moving pictures and felt improved, confessed themselves, but decided that their experiences on the trip would not interest Mrs Miles.

'Every place is the same,' Mrs Miles continued. 'The only thing then that matters is who's there. New scenery is fine for half an hour, but after that you want your own kind to see. That's why some places have a certain vogue, and then the vogue changes and the people move on somewhere else. The place itself really never matters.'

'But doesn't somebody first decide that the place is nice?' objected Nelson. 'The first ones go there because they like the place.'

'Where were you going this spring?' Mrs Miles asked.

'We thought of San Remo, or maybe Sorrento. We've never been to Europe before.'

'My children, I know both Sorrento and San Remo, and you won't stand either of them for a week. They're full of the most awful English, reading the *Daily Mail* and waiting for letters and talking about the most incredibly dull things. You might as well go to Brighton or Bournemouth and buy a white poodle and a sunshade and walk on the pier. How long are you staying in Europe?'

'We don't know; perhaps several years.' Nicole hesitated. 'Nelson came into a little money, and we wanted a change. When I was young, my father had asthma and I had to live in the most depressing health resorts with him for years; and Nelson was in the fur business in Alaska and he loathed it; so when we were free we came abroad. Nelson's going to paint and I'm going to study singing.' She looked triumphantly at her husband. 'So far, it's been absolutely gorgeous.'

Mrs Miles decided, from the evidence of the younger woman's clothes, that it was quite a bit of money, and their enthusiasm was infectious.

'You really must go to Biarritz,' she advised them. 'Or else come to Monte Carlo.'

'They tell me there's a great show here,' said Miles, ordering champagne. 'The Ouled Naïls. The concierge says they're some kind of tribe of girls who come down from the mountains and learn to be dancers, and what not, till they've collected enough gold to go back to their mountains and marry. Well, they give a performance tonight.'

Walking over to the Café of the Ouled Naïls afterward, Nicole regretted that she and Nelson were not strolling alone through the ever-lower, ever-softer, ever-brighter night. Nelson had reciprocated the bottle of champagne at dinner, and neither of them was accustomed to so much. As they drew near the sad flute she didn't want to go inside, but rather to climb to the top of a low hill where a white mosque shone clear as a planet through the night. Life was better than any show; closing in toward Nelson, she pressed his hand.

The little cave of a café was filled with the passengers from the two buses. The girls—light-brown, flat-nosed Berbers with fine, deep-shaded eyes—were already doing each one her solo on the platform. They wore cotton dresses, faintly reminiscent of Southern mammies; under these their bodies writhed in a slow nautch, culminating in a stomach dance, with silver belts bobbing wildly and their strings of real gold coins tinkling on their necks and arms. The flute player was also a comedian; he danced, burlesquing the girls. The drummer, swathed in goatskins like a witch doctor, was a true black from the Sudan.

Through the smoke of cigarettes each girl went in turn through the finger movement, like piano playing in the air—outwardly facile, yet, after a few moments, so obviously exacting—and then through the very simple, languid, yet equally precise steps of the feet—these were but preparation to the wild sensuality of the culminated dance.

Afterwards there was a lull. Though the performance seemed not quite over, most of the audience gradually got up to go, but there was a whispering in the air.

'What is it?' Nicole asked her husband.

'Why, I believe—it appears that for a consideration the Ouled Naïls dance in more or less—ah—Oriental style —in very little except jewellery.'

'Oh.'

'We're all staying,' Mr Miles assured her jovially. 'After all, we're here to see the real customs and manners of the country; a little prudishness shouldn't stand in our way.'

Most of the men remained, and several of the women. Nicole stood up suddenly.

'I'll wait outside,' she said.

'Why not stay, Nicole? After all, Mrs Miles is staying.'

The flute player was making preliminary flourishes. Upon the raised dais two pale brown children of perhaps fourteen were taking off their cotton dresses. For an instant Nicole hesitated, torn between repulsion and the desire not to appear to be a prig. Then she saw another American woman get up quickly and start for the door. Recognizing the attractive young wife from the other bus, her own decision came quickly and she followed.

Nelson hurried after her. 'I'm going if you go,' he said, but with evident reluctance.

'Please don't bother. I'll wait with the guide outside.'

'Well—' The drum was starting. He compromised: 'I'll only stay a minute. I want to see what it's like.'

Waiting in the fresh night, she found that the incident had hurt her—Nelson's not coming with her at once, giving as an argument the fact that Mrs Miles was staying. From being hurt, she grew angry and made signs to the guide that she wanted to return to the hotel.

Twenty minutes later, Nelson appeared, angry with the anxiety at finding her gone, as well as to hide his guilt at having left her. Incredulous with themselves, they were suddenly in a quarrel.

Much later, when there were no sounds at all in Bou Saada and the nomads in the market place were only motionless bundles rolled up in their burnouses, she was asleep upon his shoulder. Life is progressive, no matter what our intentions, but something was harmed, some precedent of possible non-agreement was set. It was a love match, though, and it could stand a great deal. She and Nelson had passed lonely youths, and now they wanted the taste and smell of the living world; for the present they were finding it in each other.

A month later they were in Sorrento, where Nicole took singing lessons and Nelson tried to paint something new into the Bay of Naples. It was the existence they had planned and often read about. But they found, as so many have found, that the charm of idyllic interludes depends upon one person's 'giving the party'—which is to say, furnishing the background, the experience, the patience, against which the other seems to enjoy again the spells of pastoral tranquillity recollected from childhood. Nicole and Nelson were at once too old and too young, and too American, to fall into immediate soft agreement with a strange land. Their vitality made them restless, for as yet his painting had no direction and her singing no immediate prospect of becoming serious. They said they were not 'getting anywhere'—the evenings were long, so they began to drink a lot of *vin de Capri* at dinner.

The English owned the hotel. They were aged, come South for good weather and tranquillity; Nelson and

Nicole resented the mild tenor of their days. Could people be content to talk eternally about the weather, promenade the same walks, face the same variant of macaroni at dinner month after month? They grew bored, and Americans bored are already in sight of excitement. Things came to a head all in one night.

Over a flask of wine at dinner they decided to go to Paris, settle in an apartment and work seriously. Paris promised metropolitan diversion, friends of their own age, a general intensity that Italy lacked. Eager with new hopes, they strolled into the salon after dinner, when, for the tenth time, Nelson noticed an ancient and enormous mechanical piano and was moved to try it.

Across the salon sat the only English people with whom they had had any connection—Gen. Sir Evelyne Fragelle and Lady Fragelle. The connection had been brief and unpleasant—seeing them walking out of the hotel in peignoirs to swim, Lady Fragelle had announced, over quite a few yards of floor space, that it was disgusting and shouldn't be allowed.

But that was nothing compared with her response to the first terrific bursts of sound from the electric piano. As the dust of years trembled off the keyboard at the vibration, she shot galvanically forward with the sort of jerk associated with the electric chair. Somewhat stunned himself by the sudden din of 'Waiting for the Robert E. Lee', Nelson had scarcely sat down when she projected herself across the room, her train quivering behind her, and, without glancing at the Kellys, turned off the instrument.

It was one of those gestures that are either plainly justified, or else outrageous. For a moment Nelson hesitated uncertainly; then, remembering Lady Fragelle's arrogant remark about his bathing suit, he returned to the instrument in her still-billowing wake and turned it on again.

The incident had become international. The eyes of the entire salon fell eagerly upon the protagonists, watching for the next move. Nicole hurried after Nelson, urging him to let the matter pass, but it was too late. From the outraged English table there arose, joint by joint, Gen. Sir Evelyne Fragelle, faced with perhaps his most crucial situation since the relief of Ladysmith.

' 'T'lee outrageous!—'t'lee outrageous!'

'I beg your pardon,' said Nelson.

'Here for fifteen years!' screamed Sir Evelyne to himself. 'Never heard of anyone doing such a thing before!'

'I gathered that this was put here for the amusement of the guests.'

Scorning to answer, Sir Evelyne knelt, reached for the catch, pushed it the wrong way, whereupon the speed and volume of the instrument tripled until they stood in a wild pandemonium of sound; Sir Evelyne livid with military emotions, Nelson on the point of maniacal laughter.

In a moment the firm hand of the hotel manager settled the matter; the instrument gulped and stopped, trembling a little from its unaccustomed outburst, leaving behind it a great silence in which Sir Evelyne turned to the manager.

'Most outrageous affair ever heard of in my life. My wife turned it off once, and he'—this was his first acknowledgement of Nelson's identity as distinct from the instrument—'he put it on again!'

'This is a public room in a hotel,' Nelson protested. 'The instrument is apparently here to be used.'

'Don't get in an argument,' Nicole whispered. 'They're old.'

But Nelson said, 'If there's any apology, it's certainly due to me.'

Sir Evelyne's eye was fixed menacingly upon the manager, waiting for him to do his duty. The latter thought of Sir Evelyne's fifteen years of residence, and cringed.

'It is not the habitude to play the instrument in the evening. The clients are each one quiet on his or her table.'

'American cheek!' snapped Sir Evelyne.

'Very well,' Nelson said; 'we'll relieve the hotel of our presence tomorrow.'

As a reaction from this incident, as a sort of protest against Sir Evelyne Fragelle, they went not to Paris but to Monte Carlo after all. They were through with being alone.

II

A little more than two years after the Kellys' first visit to Monte Carlo, Nicole woke up one morning into what, though it bore the same name, had become to her a different place altogether.

It spite of hurried months in Paris or Biarritz, it was now home to them. They had a villa, they had a large acquaintance among the spring and summer crowd—a crowd which, naturally, did not include people on charted trips or the short parties from Mediterranean cruises; these latter had become for them 'tourists.'

They loved the Riviera in full summer with many friends there and the night open and full of music. Before the maid drew the curtains this morning to shut out the glare, Nicole saw from her window the yacht of T. E. Golding, placid among the swells of the Monacan Bay, as if constantly bound on a romantic voyage not dependent upon actual motion.

The yacht had taken the slow tempo of the coast; it had gone no farther than to Cannes and back all summer, though it might have toured the world. The Kellys were dining on board that night.

Nicole spoke excellent French; she had five new evening dresses and four others that would do; she had her husband; she had two men in love with her, and she felt sad for one of them. She had her pretty face. At 10.30 she was meeting a third man, who was just beginning to be in love with her 'in a harmless way.' At one she was having a dozen charming people to luncheon. All that.

'I'm happy,' she brooded towards the bright blinds. 'I'm young and good-looking, and my name is often in the paper as having been here and there, but really I don't care about chichi. I think it's all awfully silly, but if you do want to see people, you might as well see the chic, amusing ones; and if people call you a snob, it's envy, and they know it and everybody knows it.'

She repeated the substance of this to Oscar Dane on the Mont Agel golf course two hours later, and he cursed her quietly.

'Not at all,' he said. 'You're just getting to be an old snob. Do you call that crowd of drunks you run with amusing people? Why, they're not even very swell. They're so hard that they've shifted down through Europe like nails in a sack of wheat, till they stick out of it a little into the Mediterranean Sea.'

Annoyed, Nicole fired a name at him, but he answered: 'Class C. A good solid article for beginners.'

'The Colbys—anyway, her.'

'Third flight.'

'Marquis and Marquise de Kalb.'

'If she didn't happen to take dope and he didn't have other peculiarities.'

'Well, then, where are the amusing people?' she demanded impatiently.

'Off by themselves somewhere. They don't hunt in herds, except occasionally.'

'How about you? You'd snap up an invitation from every person I named. I've heard stories about you wilder than any you can make up. There's not a man that's known you six months that would take your cheque for ten dollars. You're a sponge and a parasite and everything——'

'Shut up for a minute,' he interrupted. 'I don't want to spoil this drive. . . . I just don't like to see you kid yourself,' he continued. 'What passes with you for international society is just about as hard to enter nowadays as the public rooms at the Casino; and if I can make my living by sponging off it, I'm still giving twenty times more than I get. We dead beats are about the only people in it with any stuff, and we stay with it because we have to.'

She laughed, liking him immensely, wondering how angry Nelson would be when he found Oscar had walked off with his nail scissors and his copy of the *New York Herald* this morning.

'Anyhow,' she thought afterward, as she drove home toward luncheon, 'we're getting out of it all soon, and we'll be serious and have a baby. After this last summer.'

Stopping for a moment at a florist's, she saw a young woman coming out with an armful of flowers. The young woman glanced at her over the heap of colour, and Nicole perceived that she was extremely smart, and then that her face was familiar. It was someone she had known once, but only slightly; the name had escaped her, so she did not nod, and forgot the incident until that afternoon.

They were twelve for luncheon: the Goldings' party from the yacht, Liddell and Cardine Miles, Mr Dane— seven different nationalities she counted; among them an exquisite young Frenchwoman, Madame Delauney, whom Nicole referred to lightly as 'Nelson's girl.' Noel Delauney was perhaps her closest friend; when they made up four-somes for golf or for trips, she paired off with Nelson; but today, as Nicole introduced her to someone as 'Nelson's girl,' the bantering phrase filled Nicole with distaste.

She said aloud at luncheon: 'Nelson and I are going to get away from it all.'

Everybody agreed that they, too, were going to get away from it all.

'It's all right for the English,' someone said, 'because they're doing a sort of dance of death—you know, gaiety in the doomed fort, with the Sepoys at the gate. You can see it by their faces when they dance—the intensity. They know it and they want it, and they don't see any future. But you Americans, you're having a rotten time. If you want to wear the green hat or the crushed hat, or whatever it is, you always have to get a little tipsy.'

'We're going to get away from it all,' Nicole said firmly,

but something within her argued: 'What a pity—this lovely blue sea, this happy time.' What came afterward? Did one just accept a lessening of tension? It was somehow Nelson's business to answer that. His growing discontent that he wasn't getting anywhere ought to explode into a new life for both of them, or rather a new hope and content with life. That secret should be his masculine contribution.

'Well, children, good-bye.'

'It was a great luncheon.'

'Don't forget about getting away from it all.'

'See you when——'

The guests walked down the path toward their cars. Only Oscar, just faintly flushed on liqueurs, stood with Nicole on the veranda, talking on and on about the girl he had invited up to see his stamp collection. Momentarily tired of people, impatient to be alone, Nicole listened for a moment and then, taking a glass vase of flowers from the luncheon table, went through the French windows into the dark, shadowy villa, his voice following her as he talked on and on out there.

It was when she crossed the first salon, still hearing Oscar's monologue on the veranda, that she began to hear another voice in the next room, cutting sharply across Oscar's voice.

'Ah, but kiss me again,' it said, stopped; Nicole stopped, too, rigid in the silence, now broken only by the voice on the porch.

'Be careful.' Nicole recognized the faint French accent of Noel Delauney.

'I'm tired of being careful. Anyhow, they're on the veranda.'

'No, better the usual place.'

'Darling, sweet darling.'

The voice of Oscar Dane on the veranda grew weary and stopped and, as if thereby released from her paralysis, Nicole took a step—forward or backward, she did not know which. At the sound of her heel on the floor, she heard the two people in the next room breaking swiftly apart.

Then she went in. Nelson was lighting a cigarette; Noel, with her back turned, was apparently hunting for hat or purse on a chair. With blind horror rather than anger, Nicole threw, or rather pushed away from her, the glass vase which she carried. If at anyone, it was at Nelson she threw it, but the force of her feeling had entered the inanimate thing; it flew past him, and Noel Delauney, just turning about, was struck full on the side of her head and face.

'Say, there!' Nelson cried. Noel sank slowly into the chair before which she stood, her hand slowly rising to cover the side of her face. The jar rolled unbroken on the thick carpet, scattering its flowers.

'You look out!' Nelson was at Noel's side, trying to take the hand away to see what had happened.

'*C'est liquide*', gasped Noel in a whisper. '*Est-ce que c'est le sang?*'

He forced her hand away, and cried breathlessly, 'No, it's just water!' and then, to Oscar, who had appeared in the doorway: 'Get some cognac!' and to Nicole: 'You fool, you must be crazy!'

Nicole, breathing hard, said nothing. When the brandy arrived, there was a continuing silence, like that of people watching an operation, while Nelson poured a glass down Noel's throat. Nicole signalled to Oscar for a drink, and, as if afraid to break the silence without it, they all had a brandy. Then Noel and Nelson spoke at once:

'If you can find my hat——'

'This is the silliest——'

'—I shall go immediately.'

'—thing I ever saw; I——'

They all looked at Nicole, who said: 'Have her car drive right up to the door.' Oscar departed quickly.

'Are you sure you don't want to see a doctor?' asked Nelson anxiously.

'I want to go.'

A minute later, when the car had driven away, Nelson came in and poured himself another glass of brandy. A wave of subsiding tension flowed over him, showing in his face; Nicole saw it, and saw also his gathering will to make the best he could of it.

'I want to know just why you did that,' he demanded. 'No, don't go, Oscar.' He saw the story starting out into the world.

'What possible reason——'

'Oh, shut up!' snapped Nicole.

'If I kissed Noel, there's nothing so terrible about it. It's of absolutely no significance.'

She made a contemptuous sound. 'I heard what you said to her.'

'You're crazy.'

He said it as if she were crazy, and wild rage filled her.

'You liar! All this time pretending to be so square, and so particular what I did, and all the time behind my back you've been playing around with that little——'

She used a serious word, and as if maddened with the sound of it, she sprang toward his chair. In protection against this sudden attack, he flung up his arm quickly, and the knuckles of his open hand struck across the socket of her eye. Covering her face with her hand as Noel had done ten minutes previously, she fell sobbing to the floor.

'Hasn't this gone far enough?' Oscar cried.

'Yes,' admitted Nelson, 'I guess it has.'

'You go out on the veranda and cool off.'

He got Nicole to a couch and sat beside her, holding her hand.

'Brace up—brace up, baby,' he said, over and over. 'What are you—Jack Dempsey? You can't go around hitting French women; they'll sue you.'

'He told her he loved her,' she gasped hysterically. 'She said she'd meet him at the same place.... Has he gone there now?'

'He's out on the porch, walking up and down, sorry as

the devil that he accidentally hit you, and sorry he ever saw Noel Delauney.'

'Oh, yes!'

'You might have heard wrong, and it doesn't prove a thing, anyhow.'

After twenty minutes, Nelson came in suddenly and sank down on his knees by the side of his wife. Mr Oscar Dane, reinforced in his idea that he gave much more than he got, backed discreetly and far from unwillingly to the door.

In another hour, Nelson and Nicole, arm in arm, emerged from their villa and walked slowly down to the Café de Paris. They walked instead of driving, as if trying to return to the simplicity they had once possessed, as if they were trying to unwind something that had become visibly tangled. Nicole accepted his explanations, not because they were credible, but because she wanted passionately to believe them. They were both very quiet and sorry.

The Café de Paris was pleasant at that hour, with sunset drooping through the yellow awnings and the red parasols as through stained glass. Glancing about, Nicole saw the young woman she had encountered that morning. She was with a man now, and Nelson placed them immediately as the young couple they had seen in Algeria, almost three years ago.

'They've changed,' he commented. 'I suppose we have, too, but not so much. They're harder-looking and he looks dissipated. Dissipation always shows in light eyes rather than in dark ones. The girl is *tout ce qu'il y a de chic*, as they say, but there's a hard look in her face too.'

'I like her.'

'Do you want me to go and ask them if they are that same couple?'

'No! That'd be like lonesome tourists do. They have their own friends.'

At that moment people were joining them at their table.

'Nelson, how about tonight?' Nicole asked a little later.

'Do you think we can appear at the Goldings' after what's happened?'

'We not only can but we've got to. If the story's around and we're not there, we'll just be handing them a nice juicy subject of conversation. . . . Hello! What on earth——'

Something strident and violent had happened across the café; a woman screamed and the people at one table were all on their feet, surging back and forth like one person. Then the people at the other tables were standing and crowding forward; for just a moment the Kellys saw the face of the girl they had been watching, pale now, and distorted with anger. Panic-stricken, Nicole plucked at Nelson's sleeve.

'I want to get out, I can't stand any more today. Take me home. Is everybody going crazy?'

On the way home, Nelson glanced at Nicole's face and perceived with a start that they were not going to dinner on the Goldings' yacht after all. For Nicole had the beginnings of a well-defined and unmistakable black eye—an eye that by eleven o'clock would be beyond the aid of all the cosmetics in the principality. His heart sank and he decided to say nothing about it until they reached home.

III

There is some wise advice in the catechism about avoiding the occasions of sin, and when the Kellys went up to Paris a month later they made a conscientious list of the places they wouldn't visit any more and the people they didn't want to see again. The places included several famous bars, all the night clubs except one or two that were highly decorous, all the early-morning clubs of every description, and all summer resorts that made whoopee for its own sake—whoopee triumphant and unrestrained—the main attraction of the season.

The people they were through with included three-fourths of those with whom they had passed the last two years. They did this not in snobbishness, but for self-preservation, and not without a certain fear in their hearts that they were cutting themselves off from human contacts forever.

But the world is always curious, and people become valuable merely for their inaccessibility. They found that there were others in Paris who were only interested in those who had separated from the many. The first crowd they had known was largely American, salted with Europeans; the second was largely European, peppered with Americans. This latter crowd was 'society,' and here and there it touched the ultimate *milieu*, made up of individuals of high position, of great fortune, very occasionally of genius, and always of power. Without being intimate with the great, they made new friends of a more conservative type. Moreover, Nelson began to paint again; he had a studio, and they visited the studios of Brancusi and Léger and Duchamp. It seemed that they were more part of something than before, and when certain gaudy rendezvous were mentioned, they felt a contempt for their first two years in Europe, speaking of their former acquaintances as 'that crowd' and as 'people who waste your time.'

So, although they kept their rules, they entertained frequently at home and they went out to the houses of others. They were young and handsome and intelligent; they came to know what did go and what did not go, and adapted themselves accordingly. Moreover, they were naturally generous and willing, within the limits of common sense, to pay.

When one went out one generally drank. This meant little to Nicole, who had a horror of losing her *soigné* air, losing a touch of bloom or a ray of admiration, but Nelson, thwarted somewhere, found himself quite as tempted to drink at these small dinners as in the more frankly rowdy world. He was not a drunk, he did nothing conspicuous or sodden, but he was no longer willing to go out socially without the stimulus of liquor. It was with the idea of bringing him to a serious and responsible attitude that

Nicole decided after a year in Paris, that the time had come to have a baby.

This was coincidental with their meeting Count Chiki Sarolai. He was an attractive relic of the Austrian court, with no fortune or pretence to any, but with solid social and financial connections in France. His sister was married to the Marquis de la Clos d'Hirondelle, who, in addition to being of the ancient noblesse, was a successful banker in Paris. Count Chiki roved here and there, frankly sponging, rather like Oscar Dane, but in a different sphere.

His penchant was Americans; he hung on their words with a pathetic eagerness, as if they would sooner or later let slip their mysterious formula for making money. After a casual meeting, his interest gravitated to the Kellys. During Nicole's months of waiting he was in the house continually, tirelessly interested in anything that concerned American crime, slang, finance, or manners. He came in for a luncheon or dinner when he had no other place to go, and with tacit gratitude he persuaded his sister to call on Nicole, who was immensely flattered.

It was arranged that when Nicole went to the hospital he would stay at the *appartement* and keep Nelson company—an arrangement of which Nicole didn't approve, since they were inclined to drink together. But the day on which it was decided, he arrived with news of one of his brother-in-law's famous canal-boat parties on the Seine, to which the Kellys were to be invited and which, conveniently enough, was to occur three weeks after the arrival of the baby. So, when Nicole moved out to the American Hospital Count Chiki moved in.

The baby was a boy. For a while Nicole forgot all about people and their human status and their value. She even wondered at the fact that she had become such a snob, since everything seemed trivial compared with the new individual that, eight times a day, they carried to her breast.

After two weeks she and the baby went back to the

apartment, but Chiki and his valet stayed on. It was understood, with that subtlety the Kellys had only recently begun to appreciate, that he was merely staying until after his brother-in-law's party, but the apartment was crowded and Nicole wished him gone. But her old idea, that if one had to see people they might as well be the best, was carried out in being invited to the de la Clos d'Hirondelles'.

As she lay in her chaise longue the day before the event, Chiki explained the arrangements, in which he had evidently aided.

'Everyone who arrives must drink two cocktails in the American style before they can come aboard—as a ticket of admission.'

'But I thought that very fashionable French—Faubourg St Germain and all that—didn't drink cocktails.'

'Oh, but my family is very modern. We adopt many American customs.'

'Who'll be there?'

'Everyone! Everyone in Paris.'

Great names swam before her eyes. Next day she could not resist dragging the affair into conversation with her doctor. But she was rather offended at the look of astonishment and incredulity that came into his eyes.

'Did I understand you aright?' he demanded. 'Did I understand you to say that you were going to a ball tomorrow?'

'Why, yes,' she faltered. 'Why not?'

'My dear lady, you are not going to stir out of the house for two more weeks; you are not going to dance or do anything strenuous for two more after that.'

'That's ridiculous!' she cried. 'It's been three weeks already! Esther Sherman went to America after——'

'Never mind,' he interrupted. 'Every case is different. There is a complication which makes it positively necessary for you to follow my orders.'

'But the idea is that I'll just go for two hours, because of course I'll have to come home to Sonny——'

'You'll not go for two minutes.'

She knew, from the seriousness of his tone, that he was right, but, perversely, she did not mention the matter to Nelson. She said, instead, that she was tired, that possibly she might not go, and lay awake that night measuring her disappointment against her fear. She woke up for Sonny's first feeding, thinking to herself: 'But if I just take ten steps from a limousine to a chair and just sit half an hour——'

At the last minute the pale green evening dress from Callets, draped across a chair in her bedroom, decided her. She went.

Somewhere, during the shuffle and delay on the gang-plank while the guests went aboard and were challenged and drank down their cocktails with attendant gaiety, Nicole realized that she had made a mistake. There was, at any rate, no formal receiving line and, after greeting their hosts, Nelson found her a chair on deck, where presently the faintness disappeared.

Then she was glad she had come. The boat was hung with fragile lanterns, which blended with the pastels of the bridges and the reflected stars in the dark Seine, like a child's dream out of the Arabian Nights. A crowd of hungry-eyed spectators were gathered on the banks. Champagne moved past in platoons like a drill of bottles, while the music, instead of being loud and obtrusive, drifted down from the upper deck like frosting dripping over a cake. She became aware presently that they were not the only Americans there—across the deck were the Liddell Mileses, whom she had not seen for several years.

Other people from that crowd were present, and she felt a faint disappointment. What if this was not the marquis's best party? She remembered her mother's second days at home. She asked Chiki, who was at her side, to point out celebrities, but when she inquired about several people whom she associated with that set, he replied vaguely that they were away, or coming later, or could not be there. It seemed to her that she saw across the room the girl who had made the scene in the Café de Paris at Monte Carlo,

9*

but she could not be sure, for with the faint almost imperceptible movement of the boat, she realized that she was growing faint again. She sent for Nelson to take her home.

'You can come right back, of course. You needn't wait for me, because I'm going right to bed.'

He left her in the hands of the nurse, who helped her upstairs and aided her to undress quickly.

'I'm desperately tired,' Nicole said. 'Will you put my pearls away?'

'Where?'

'In the jewel-box on the dressing-table.'

'I don't see it,' said the nurse after a minute.

'Then it's in a drawer.'

There was a thorough rummaging of the dressing-table, without result.

'But of course it's there.' Nicole attempted to rise, but fell back, exhausted. 'Look for it, please, again. Everything is in it—all my mother's things and my engagement things.'

'I'm sorry, Mrs Kelly. There's nothing in this room that answers to that description.'

'Wake up the maid.'

The maid knew nothing; then, after a persistent cross-examination, she did know something. Count Sarolai's valet had gone out, carrying his suitcase, half an hour after madame left the house.

Writhing in sharp and sudden pain, with a hastily summoned doctor at her side, it seemed to Nicole hours before Nelson came home. When he arrived, his face was deathly pale and his eyes were wild. He came directly into her room.

'What do you think?' he said savagely. Then he saw the doctor. 'Why, what's the matter?'

'Oh, Nelson, I'm sick as a dog and my jewel box is gone, and Chiki's valet has gone. I've told the police. . . . Perhaps Chiki would know where the man——'

'Chiki will never come in this house again,' he said slowly. 'Do you know whose party that was? Have you got

any idea whose party that was?' He burst into wild
laughter. 'It was our party—our party, do you understand? We gave it—we didn't know it, but we did.'

'*Maintenant, monsieur, il ne faut pas exciter madame*——'
the doctor began.

'I thought it was odd when the marquis went home
early, but I didn't suspect till the end. They were just
guests—Chiki invited all the people. After it was all over,
the caterers and musicians began to come up and ask me
where to send their bills. And that damn Chiki had the
nerve to tell me he thought I knew all the time. He said
that all he'd promised was that it would be his brother-in-
law's sort of party, and that his sister would be there. He
said perhaps I was drunk, or perhaps I didn't understand
French—as if we'd ever talked anything but English to
him.'

'Don't pay!' she said. 'I wouldn't think of paying.'

'So I said, but they're going to sue—the boat people
and the others. They want twelve thousand dollars.'

She relaxed suddenly. 'Oh, go away!' she cried. 'I don't
care! I've lost my jewels and I'm sick, sick!'

IV

This is the story of a trip abroad, and the geographical
element must not be slighted. Having visited North Africa,
Italy, the Riviera, Paris, and points in between, it was not
surprising that eventually the Kellys should go to Switzerland. Switzerland is a country where very few things begin,
but many things end.

Though there was an element of choice in their other
ports of call, the Kellys went to Switzerland because they
had to. They had been married a little more than four
years when they arrived one spring day at the lake that is
the centre of Europe—a placid, smiling spot with pastoral
hillsides, a backdrop of mountains, and waters of postcard
blue, waters that are a little sinister beneath the surface
with all the misery that has dragged itself here from every

corner of Europe. Weariness to recuperate and death to
die. There are schools, too, and young people splashing at
the sunny plages; there is Bonnivard's dungeon and
Calvin's city, and the ghosts of Byron and Shelley still sail
the dim shores by night; but the Lake Geneva that Nelson
and Nicole came to was the dreary one of sanatoriums and
rest hotels.

For, as if by some profound sympathy that had continued to exist beneath the unlucky destiny that had pursued their affairs, health had failed them both at the same
time; Nicole lay on the balcony of a hotel coming slowly
back to life after two successive operations, while Nelson
fought for life against jaundice in a hospital two miles
away. Even after the reserve force of twenty-nine years
had pulled him through, there were months ahead during
which he must live quietly. Often they wondered why, of
all those who sought pleasure over the face of Europe, this
misfortune should have come to them.

'There've been too many people in our lives,' Nelson
said. 'We've never been able to resist people. We were so
happy the first year when there weren't any people.'

Nicole agreed. 'If we could ever be alone—really alone—
we could make up some kind of life for ourselves. We'll
try, won't we, Nelson?'

But there were other days when they both wanted company desperately, concealing it from each other. Days
when they eyed the obese, the wasted, the crippled and
the broken of all nationalities who filled the hotel, seeking
for one who might be amusing. It was a new life for them,
turning on the daily visits of their two doctors, the arrival
of the mail and newspapers from Paris, the little walk into
the hillside village or occasionally the descent by funicular
to the pale resort on the lake, with its *Kursaal*, its grass
beach, its tennis clubs, and sight-seeing buses. They read
Tauchnitz editions and yellow-jacketed Edgar Wallaces;
at a certain hour each day they watched the baby being
given its bath; three nights a week there was a tired and
patient orchestra in the lounge after dinner, that was all.

And sometimes there was a booming from the vine-covered hills on the other side of the lake, which meant that cannons were shooting at hail-bearing clouds, to save the vineyards from an approaching storm; it came swiftly, first falling from the heavens and then falling again in torrents from the mountains, washing loudly down the roads and stone ditches; it came with a dark, frightening sky and savage filaments of lightning and crashing, world-splitting thunder, while ragged and destroyed clouds fled along before the wind past the hotel. The mountains and the lake disappeared completely; the hotel crouched alone amid tumult and chaos and darkness.

It was during such a storm, when the mere opening of a door admitted a tornado of rain and wind into the hall, that the Kellys for the first time in months saw someone they knew. Sitting downstairs with other victims of frayed nerves, they became aware of two new arrivals—a man and woman whom they recognized as the couple, first seen in Algiers, who had crossed their path several times since. A single unexpressed thought flashed through Nelson and Nicole. It seemed like destiny that at last here in this desolate place they should know them, and watching, they saw other couples eyeing them in the same tentative way. Yet something held the Kellys back. Had they not just been complaining that there were too many people in their lives?

Later, when the storm had dozed off into a quiet rain, Nicole found herself near the girl on the glass veranda. Under cover of reading a book, she inspected the face closely. It was an inquisitive face, she saw at once, possibly calculating; the eyes, intelligent enough, but with no peace in them, swept over people in a single quick glance as though estimating their value. 'Terrible egoist,' Nicole thought, with a certain distaste. For the rest, the cheeks were wan, and there were little pouches of ill health under the eyes; these combining with a certain flabbiness of arms and legs to give an impression of unwholesomeness. She was dressed expensively, but with a hint of slovenliness, as if she did not consider the people of the hotel important.

On the whole, Nicole decided she did not like her; she was glad that they had not spoken, but she was rather surprised that she had not noticed these things when the girl crossed her path before.

Telling Nelson her impression at dinner, he agreed with her.

'I ran into the man in the bar, and I noticed we both took nothing but mineral water, so I started to say something. But I got a good look at his face in the mirror and I decided not to. His face is so weak and self-indulgent that it's almost mean—the kind of face that needs half a dozen drinks really to open the eyes and stiffen the mouth up to normal.'

After dinner the rain stopped and the night was fine outside. Eager for the air, the Kellys wandered down into the dark garden; on their way they passed the subjects of their late discussion, who withdrew abruptly down a side path.

'I don't think they want to know us any more than we do them,' Nicole laughed.

They loitered among the wild rose-bushes and the beds of damp-sweet, indistinguishable flowers. Below the hotel, where the terrace fell a thousand feet to the lake, stretched a necklace of lights that was Montreux and Vevey, and then, in a dim pendant, Lausanne; a blurred twinkling across the lake was Evian and France. From somewhere below—probably the *Kursaal*—came the sound of full-bodied dance music—American, they guessed, though now they heard American tunes months late, mere distant echoes of what was happening far away.

Over the Dent du Midi, over a black bank of clouds that was the rearguard of the receding storm, the moon lifted itself and the lake brightened; the music and the far-away lights were like hope, like the enchanted distance from which children see things. In their separate hearts Nelson and Nicole gazed backward to a time when life was all like this. Her arm went through his quietly and drew him close.

'We can have it all again,' she whispered. 'Can't we try, Nelson?'

She paused as two dark forms came into the shadows nearby and stood looking down at the lake below.

Nelson put his arm round Nicole and pulled her closer.

'It's just that we don't understand what's the matter,' she said. 'Why did we lose peace and love and health, one after the other? If we knew, if there was anybody to tell us, I believe we could try. I'd try so hard.'

The last clouds were lifting themselves over the Bernese Alps. Suddenly, with a final intensity, the west flared with pale white lightning. Nelson and Nicole turned, and simultaneously the other couple turned, while for an instant the night was as bright as day. Then darkness and a last low peal of thunder, and from Nicole a sharp, terrified cry. She flung herself against Nelson; even in the darkness she saw that his face was as white and strained as her own.

'Did you see?' she cried in a whisper. 'Did you see them?'

'Yes!'

'They're us! They're us! Don't you see?'

Trembling, they clung together. The clouds merged into the dark mass of mountains; looking around after a moment, Nelson and Nicole saw that they were alone together in the tranquil moonlight.

FAMILY IN THE WIND

[1932]

THE TWO men drove up the hill toward the blood-red sun. The cotton fields bordering the road were thin and withered, and no breeze stirred in the pines.

'When I am totally sober,' the doctor was saying—'I mean when I am totally sober—I don't see the same world that you do. I'm like a friend of mine who had one good eye and got glasses made to correct his bad eye; the result was that he kept seeing elliptical suns and falling off tilted curbs, until he had to throw the glasses away. Granted that I am thoroughly anaesthetized the greater part of the day—well, I only undertake work that I know I can do when I am in that condition.'

'Yeah,' agreed his brother Gene uncomfortably. The doctor was a little tight at the moment and Gene could find no opening for what he had to say. Like so many Southerners of the humbler classes, he had a deep-seated courtesy, characteristic of all violent and passionate lands —he could not change the subject until there was a moment's silence, and Forrest would not shut up.

'I'm very happy,' he continued, 'or very miserable. I chuckle or I weep alcoholically and, as I continue to slow up, life accommodatingly goes faster, so that the less there is of myself inside, the more diverting becomes the moving picture without. I have cut myself off from the respect of my fellow man, but I am aware of a compensatory cirrhosis of the emotions. And because my sensitivity, my pity, no longer has direction, but fixes itself on whatever is at hand, I have become an exceptionally good fellow—much more so than when I was a good doctor.'

As the road straightened after the next bend and Gene

saw his house in the distance, he remembered his wife's face as she had made him promise, and he could wait no longer: 'Forrest, I got a thing——'

But at that moment the doctor brought his car to a sudden stop in front of a small house just beyond a grove of pines. On the front steps a girl of eight was playing with a stray cat.

'This is the sweetest little kid I ever saw,' the doctor said to Gene, and then to the child, in a grave voice: 'Helen, do you need any pills for kitty?'

The little girl laughed.

'Well, I don't know,' she said doubtfully. She was playing another game with the cat now and this came as rather an interruption.

'Because kitty telephoned me this morning,' the doctor continued, 'and said her mother was neglecting her and couldn't I get her a trained nurse from Montgomery.'

'She did not.' The little girl grabbed the cat close indignantly; the doctor took a nickel from his pocket and tossed it to the steps.

'I recommend a good dose of milk,' he said as he put the car into gear. 'Good night, Helen.'

'Good night, doctor.'

As they drove off, Gene tried again: 'Listen; stop,' he said. 'Stop here a little way down . . . Here.'

The doctor stopped the car and the brothers faced each other. They were alike as to robustness of figure and a certain asceticism of feature and they were both in their middle forties; they were unlike in that the doctor's glasses failed to conceal the veined, weeping eyes of a soak, and that he wore corrugated city wrinkles; Gene's wrinkles bounded fields, followed the lines of rooftrees, of poles propping up sheds. His eyes were a fine, furry blue. But the sharpest contrast lay in the fact that Gene Janney was a country man while Dr Forrest Janney was obviously a man of education.

'Well?' the doctor asked.

'You know Pinky's at home,' Gene said looking down
the road.

'So I hear,' the doctor answered noncommittally.

'He got in a row in Birmingham and somebody shot
him in the head.' Gene hesitated. 'We got Doc Behrer
because we thought maybe you wouldn't—maybe you
wouldn't——'

'I wouldn't,' agreed Doctor Janney blandly.

'But look, Forrest; here's the thing,' Gene insisted. 'You
know how it is—you often say Doc Behrer doesn't know
nothing. Shucks, I never thought he was much either. He
says the bullet's pressing on the—pressing on the brain,
and he can't take it out without causin' a hemmering, and
he says he doesn't know whether we could get him to
Birmingham or Montgomery, or not, he's so low. Doc
wasn't no help. What we want——'

'No,' said his brother, shaking his head. 'No.'

'I just want you to look at him and tell us what to do,'
Gene begged. 'He's unconscious, Forrest. He wouldn't
know you; you'd hardly know him. Thing is his mother's
about crazy.'

'She's in the grip of a purely animal instinct.' The
doctor took from his hip a flask containing half water and
half Alabama corn, and drank. 'You and I know that boy
ought to been drowned the day he was born.'

Gene flinched. 'He's bad,' he admitted, 'but I don't
know—You see him lying there——'

As the liquor spread over the doctor's insides he felt an
instinct to do something, not to violate his prejudices but
simply to make some gesture, to assert his own moribund
but still struggling will to power.

'All right, I'll see him,' he said. 'I'll do nothing myself
to help him, because he ought to be dead. And even his
death wouldn't make up for what he did to Mary Decker.'

Gene Janney pursed his lips. 'Forrest, you sure about
that?'

'Sure about it!' exclaimed the doctor. 'Of course I'm
sure. She died of starvation; she hadn't had more than a

couple cups of coffee in a week. And if you looked at her shoes, you could see she'd walked for miles.'

'Doc Behrer says——'

'What does he know? I performed the autopsy the day they found her on the Birmingham Highway. There was nothing the matter with her but starvation. That—that'—his voice shook with feeling—'that Pinky got tired of her and turned her out, and she was trying to get home. It suits me fine that he was invalided home himself a couple of weeks later.'

As he talked, the doctor had plunged the car savagely into gear and let the clutch out with a jump; in a moment they drew up before Janney's home.

It was a square frame house with a brick foundation and a well-kept lawn blocked off from the farm, a house rather superior to the buildings that composed the town of Bending and the surrounding agricultural area, yet not essentially different in type or in its interior economy. The last of the plantation houses in this section of Alabama had long disappeared, the proud pillars yielding to poverty, rot, and rain.

Gene's wife, Rose, got up from her rocking-chair on the porch.

'Hello, doc.' She greeted him a little nervously and without meeting his eyes. 'You been a stranger here lately.'

The doctor met her eyes for several seconds. 'How do you do, Rose,' he said. 'Hi, Edith . . . Hi, Eugene'—this to the little boy and girl who stood beside their mother; and then: 'Hi, Butch!' to the stocky youth of nineteen who came around the corner of the house hugging a round stone.

'Goin' to have a sort of low wall along the front here—kind of neater,' Gene explained.

All of them had a lingering respect for the doctor. They felt reproachful toward him because they could no longer refer to him as the celebrated relative—'one of the bess surgeons up in Montgomery, yes suh'—but there was his learning and the position he had once occupied in the larger world, before he had committed professional suicide by taking to cynicism and drink. He had come home to Bending and bought a half interest in the local drug store two years ago, keeping up his licence, but practising only when sorely needed.

'Rose,' said Gene, 'doc says he'll take a look at Pinky.'

Pinky Janney, his lips curved mean and white under a new beard, lay in bed in a darkened room. When the doctor removed the bandage from his head, his breath blew into a low groan, but his paunchy body did not move. After a few minutes, the doctor replaced the bandage and, with Gene and Rose, returned to the porch.

'Behrer wouldn't operate?' he asked.

'No.'

'Why didn't they operate in Birmingham?'

'I don't know.'

'H'm.' The doctor put on his hat. 'That bullet ought to come out, and soon. It's pressing against the carotid sheath. That's the—anyhow, you can't get him to Montgomery with that pulse.'

'What'll we do?' Gene's question carried a little tail of silence as he sucked his breath back.

'Get Behrer to think it over. Or else get somebody in Montgomery. There's about a 25 per cent chance that the operation would save him; without the operation he hasn't any chance at all.'

'Who'll we get in Montgomery?' asked Gene.

'Any good surgeon would do it. Even Behrer could do it if he had any nerve.'

Suddenly Rose Janney came close to him, her eyes straining and burning with an animal maternalism. She seized his coat where it hung upen.

'Doc, you do it! You can do it. You know you were as good a surgeon as any of em once. Please, doc, you go on do it.'

He stepped back a little so that her hands fell from his coat, and held out his own hands in front of him.

'See how they tremble?' he said with elaborate irony. 'Look close and you'll see. I wouldn't dare operate.'

'You could do it all right,' said Gene hastily, 'with a drink to stiffen you up.'

The doctor shook his head and said, looking at Rose: 'No. You see, my decisions are not reliable, and if anything went wrong, it would seem to be my fault.' He was acting a little now—he chose his words carefully. 'I hear that when I found that Mary Decker died of starvation, my opinion was questioned on the ground that I was a drunkard.'

'I didn't say that,' lied Rose breathlessly.

'Certainly not. I just mention it to show how careful I've got to be.' He moved down the steps. 'Well, my advice is to see Behrer again, or, failing that, get somebody from the city. Good night.'

But before he had reached the gate, Rose came tearing after him, her eyes white with fury.

'I did say you were a drunkard!' she cried. 'When you said Mary Decker died of starvation, you made it out as if it was Pinky's fault—you, swilling yourself full of corn all day! How can anybody tell whether you know what you're doing or not? Why did you think so much about Mary Decker, anyhow—a girl half your age? Everybody saw how she used to come in your drug store and talk to you——'

Gene, who had followed, seized her arms. 'Shut up now, Rose . . . Drive along, Forrest.'

Forrest drove along, stopping at the next bend to drink from his flask. Across the fallow cotton fields he could see the house where Mary Decker had lived, and had it been six months before, he might have detoured to ask why she hadn't come into the store that day for her free soda, or to delight her with a sample cosmetic left by a salesman that morning. He had not told Mary Decker how he felt about her; never intended to—she was seventeen, he was forty-five, and he no longer dealt in futures—but only after she ran away to Birmingham with Pinky Janney, did he realize how much his love for her had counted in his lonely life.

His thoughts went back to his brother's house.

'Now, if I were a gentleman,' he thought, 'I wouldn't have done like that. And another person might have been sacrificed to that dirty dog, because if he died afterward Rose would say I killed him.'

Yet he felt pretty bad as he put his car away; not that he could have acted differently, but just that it was all so ugly.

He had been home scarcely ten minutes when a car creaked to rest outside and Butch Janney came in. His mouth was set tight and his eyes were narrowed as though to permit of no escape to the temper that possessed him until it should be unleashed upon its proper objective.

'Hi, Butch.'

'I want to tell you, Uncle Forrest, you can't talk to my mother thataway. I'll kill you, you talk to my mother like that!'

'Now shut up, Butch, and sit down,' said the doctor sharply.

'She's already 'bout sick on account of Pinky, and you come over and talk to her like that.'

'Your mother did all the insulting that was done, Butch. I just took it.'

'She doesn't know what she's saying and you ought to understand that.'

The doctor thought a minute. 'Butch, what do you think of Pinky?'

Butch hesitated uncomfortably. 'Well, I can't say I ever thought so much of him'—his tone changed defiantly—'but after all, he's my own brother——'

'Wait a minute, Butch. What do you think of the way he treated Mary Decker?'

But Butch had shaken himself free, and now he let go the artillery of his rage:

'That ain't the point; the point is anybody that doesn't

do right to my mother has me to answer to. It's only fair
when you got all the education——'

'I got my education myself, Butch.'

'I don't care. We're going to try again to get Doc
Behrer to operate or get us some fellow from the city. But
if we can't I'm coming and get you, and you're going to
take the bullet out if I have to hold a gun to you while
you do it.' He nodded, panting a little; then he turned and
went out and drove away.

'Something tells me,' said the doctor to himself, 'that
there's no more peace for me in Chilton County.' He
called to his coloured boy to put supper on the table. Then
he rolled himself a cigarette and went out on the back
stoop.

The weather had changed. The sky was now overcast
and the grass stirred restlessly and there was a sudden
flurry of drops without a sequel. A minute ago it had been
warm, but now the moisture on his forehead was suddenly
cool, and he wiped it away with his handkerchief. There
was a buzzing in his ears and he swallowed and shook
his head. For a moment he thought he must be sick; then
suddenly the buzzing detached itself from him, grew into
a swelling sound, louder and ever nearer, that might have
been the roar of an approaching train.

II

Butch Janney was halfway home when he saw it—a huge,
black, approaching cloud whose lower edge bumped the
ground. Even as he stared at it vaguely, it seemed to
spread until it included the whole southern sky, and he
saw pale electric fire in it and heard an increasing roar.
He was in a strong wind now; blown debris, bits of
broken branches, splinters, larger objects unidentifiable in
the growing darkness, flew by him. Instinctively he got
out of his car and, by now hardly able to stand against
the wind, ran for a bank, or rather found himself thrown

and pinned against a bank. Then for a minute, two minutes, he was in the black centre of pandemonium.

First there was the sound, and he was part of the sound, so engulfed in it and possessed by it that he had no existence apart from it. It was not a collection of sounds, it was just Sound itself; a great screeching bow drawn across the chords of the universe. The sound and force were inseparable. The sound as well as the force held him to what he felt was the bank like a man crucified. Somewhere in this first moment his face, pinned sideways, saw his automobile make a little jump, spin halfway around and then go bobbing off over a field in a series of great helpless leaps. Then began the bombardment, the sound dividing its sustained cannon note into the cracks of a gigantic machine gun. He was only half-conscious as he felt himself become part of one of those cracks, felt himself lifted away from the bank to tear through space, through a blinding, lacerating mass of twigs and branches, and then, for an incalculable time, he knew nothing at all.

His body hurt him. He was lying between two branches in the top of a tree; the air was full of dust and rain, and he could hear nothing; it was a long time before he realized that the tree he was in had been blown down and that his involuntary perch among the pine needles was only five feet from the ground.

'Say, man!' he cried, aloud, outraged. 'Say, man! Say, what a wind! Say, man!'

Made acute by pain and fear, he guessed that he had been standing on the tree's root and had been catapulted by the terrific wrench as the big pine was torn from the earth. Feeling over himself, he found that his left ear was caked full of dirt, as if someone had wanted to take an impression of the inside. His clothes were in rags, his coat had torn on the back seam, and he could feel where, as some stray gust tried to undress him, it had cut into him under his arms.

Reaching the ground, he set off in the direction of his

father's house, but it was a new and unfamiliar landscape he traversed. The Thing—he did not know it was a tornado—had cut a path a quarter of a mile wide, and he was confused, as the dust slowly settled, by vistas he had never seen before. It was unreal that Bending church tower should be visible from here; there had been groves of trees between.

But where was here? For he should be close to the Baldwin house; only as he tripped over great piles of boards, like a carelessly kept lumberyard, did Butch realize that there was no more Baldwin house, and then, looking around wildly, that there was no Necrawney house on the hill, no Peltzer house below it. There was not a light, not a sound, save the rain falling on the fallen trees.

He broke into a run. When he saw the bulk of his father's house in the distance, he gave a 'Hey!' of relief, but coming closer, he realized that something was missing. There were no outhouses and the built-on wing that held Pinky's room had been sheared completely away.

'Mother!' he called. 'Dad!' There was no answer; a dog bounded out of the yard and licked his hand. . . .

. . . It was full dark twenty minutes later when Doc Janney stopped his car in front of his own drug store in Bending. The electric lights had gone out, but there were men with lanterns in the street, and in a minute a small crowd had collected around him. He unlocked the door hurriedly.

'Somebody break open the old Wiggins Hospital.' He pointed across the street. 'I've got six badly injured in my car. I want some fellows to carry em in. Is Doc Behrer here?'

'Here he is,' offered eager voices out of the darkness as the doctor, case in hand, came through the crowd. The two men stood face to face by lantern light, forgetting that they disliked each other.

'God knows how many more there's going to be,' said Doc Janney. 'I'm getting dressing and disinfectant.

There'll be a lot of fractures—' He raised his voice, 'Somebody bring me a barrel!'

'I'll get started over there,' said Doc Behrer. 'There's about half a dozen more crawled in.'

'What's been done?' demanded Doc Janney of the men who followed him into the drug store. 'Have they called Birmingham and Montgomery?'

'The telephone wires are down, but the telegraph got through.'

'Well, somebody get Doctor Cohen from Wettala, and tell any people who have automobiles to go up the Willard Pike and cut across toward Corsica and all through those roads there. There's not a house left at the crossroads by the nigger store. I passed a lot of folks walking in, all of them hurt, but I didn't have room for anybody else.' As he talked he was throwing bandages, disinfectant and drugs into a blanket. 'I thought I had a lot more stuff than this in stock. And wait!' he called. 'Somebody drive out and look down in that hollow where the Wooleys live. Drive right across the fields—the road's blocked. . . . Now, you with the cap—Ed Jenks, aint it?'

'Yes, doc.'

'You see what I got here? You collect everything in the store that looks like this and bring it across the way, understand?'

'Yes, doc.'

As the doctor went out into the street, the victims were streaming into town—a woman on foot with a badly injured child, a buckboard full of groaning Negroes, frantic men gasping terrible stories. Everywhere confusion and hysteria mounted in the dimly illuminated darkness. A mud-covered reporter from Birmingham drove up in a side-car, the wheels crossing the fallen wires and brushwood that clogged the street, and there was the siren of a police car from Cooper, thirty miles away.

Already a crowd pressed around the doors of the hospital, closed these three months for lack of patients. The doctor squeezed past the mêleé of white faces and established himself in the nearest ward, grateful for the waiting row of old iron beds. Doctor Behrer was already at work across the hall.

'Get me half a dozen lanterns,' he ordered.

'Doctor Behrer wants iodine and adhesive.'

'All right, there it is. . . . Here, you Shinkey, stand by the door and keep everybody out except cases that can't walk. Somebody run over and see if there ain't some candles in the grocery store.'

The street outside was full of sound now—the cries of women, the contrary directions of volunteer gangs trying to clear the highway, the tense staccato of people rising to an emergency. A little before midnight arrived the first unit of the Red Cross. But the three doctors, presently joined by two others from near-by villages, had lost track of time long before that. The dead began to be brought in by ten o'clock; there were twenty, twenty-five, thirty, forty—the list grew. Having no more needs, these waited, as became simple husbandmen, in a garage behind, while the stream of injured—hundreds of them—flowed through the old hospital built to house only a score. The storm had dealt out fractures of the leg, collar bone, ribs and hip, lacerations of the back, elbows, ears, eyelids, nose; there were wounds from flying planks, and odd splinters in odd places, and a scalped man, who would recover to grow a new head of hair. Living or dead, Doc Janney knew every face, almost every name.

'Don't you fret now. Billy's all right. Hold still and let me tie this. People are drifting in every minute, but it's so consarned dark they can't find 'em—All right, Mrs Oakley. That's nothing. Ev here'll touch it with iodine . . . Now let's see this man.'

Two o'clock. The old doctor from Wettala gave out, but now there were fresh men from Montgomery to take his place. Upon the air of the room, heavy with disinfectant, floated the ceaseless babble of human speech reaching the doctor dimly through layer after layer of increasing fatigue:

'. . . Over and over—just rolled me over and over. Got hold of a bush and the bush came along too.'

Jeff! Where's Jeff?'

'. . . I bet that pig sailed a hundred yards——'

'—just stopped the train in time. All the passengers got out and helped pull the poles——'

'Where's Jeff?'

'He says, "Let's get down cellar," and I says, "We ain't got no cellar"——'

'—If there's no more stretchers, find some light doors.'

'. . . Five seconds? Say, it was more like five minutes!'

At some time he heard that Gene and Rose had been seen with their two youngest children. He had passed their house on the way in and, seeing it standing, hurried on. The Janney family had been lucky; the doctor's own house was outside the sweep of the storm.

Only as he saw the electric lights go on suddenly in the streets and glimpsed the crowd waiting for hot coffee in front of the Red Cross did the doctor realize how tired he was.

'You better go rest,' a young man was saying. 'I'll take this side of the room. I've got two nurses with me.'

'All right—all right. I'll finish this row.'

The injured were being evacuated to the cities by train as fast as their wounds were dressed, and their places taken by others. He had only two beds to go—in the first one he found Pinky Janney.

He put his stethoscope to the heart. It was beating feebly. That he, so weak, so nearly gone, had survived this storm at all was remarkable. How he had got there, who had found him and carried him, was a mystery in itself. The doctor went over the body; there were small contusions and lacerations, two broken fingers, the dirt-filled ears that marked every case—nothing else. For a moment the doctor hesitated, but even when he closed his eyes, the image of Mary Decker seemed to have receded, eluding him. Something purely professional that had noth-ing to do with human sensibilities had been set in motion inside him, and he was powerless to head it off. He held out his hands before him; they were trembling slightly.

'Hell's bells!' he muttered.

He went out of the room and around the corner of the hall, where he drew from his pocket the flask containing the last of the corn and water he had had in the afternoon. He emptied it. Returning to the ward, he disinfected two instruments and applied a local anaesthetic to a square section at the base of Pinky's skull where the wound had healed over the bullet. He called a nurse to his side and then, scalpel in hand, knelt on one knee beside his nephew's bed.

III

Two days later the doctor drove slowly around the mournful countryside. He had withdrawn from the emergency work after the first desperate night, feeling that his status as a pharmacist might embarrass his collaborators. But there was much to be done in bringing the damage to outlying sections under the aegis of the Red Cross, and he devoted himself to that.

The path of the demon was easy to follow. It had pursued an irregular course on its seven-league boots, cutting cross country, through woods, or even urbanely keeping to roads until they curved, when it went off on its own again. Sometimes the trail could be traced by cotton fields, apparently in full bloom, but this cotton came from the insides of hundreds of quilts and mattresses redistributed in the fields by the storm.

At a lumber pile that had lately been a Negro cabin, he stopped a moment to listen to a dialogue between two reporters and two shy pickaninnies. The old grandmother, her head bandaged, sat among the ruins, gnawing some vague meat and moving her rocker ceaselessly.

'But where is the river you were blown across?' one of the reporters demanded.

'There.'

'Where?'

The pickaninnies looked to their grandmother for aid. 'Right there behind you-all,' spoke up the old woman.

The newspapermen looked disgustedly at a muddy stream four yards wide.

'That's no river.'

'That's a Menada River, we always calls it ever since I was a gull. Yes, suh, that's a Menada River. An' them two boys was blowed right across it an set down on the othah side just as pretty, 'thout any hurt at all. Chimney fell on me,' she concluded, feeling her head.

'Do you mean to say that's all it was?' demanded the younger reporter indignantly. 'That's the river they were blown across! And one hundred and twenty million people have been led to believe——'

'That's all right, boys,' interrupted Doc Janney. 'That's a right good river for these parts, And it'll get bigger as those little fellahs get older.'

He tossed a quarter to the old woman and drove on.

Passing a country church, he stopped and counted the new brown mounds that marred the graveyard. He was nearing the centre of the holocaust now. There was the Howden house where three had been killed; there remained a gaunt chimney, a rubbish heap and a scarecrow surviving ironically in the kitchen garden. In the ruins of the house across the way a rooster strutted on top of a piano, reigning vociferously over an estate of trunks, boots, cans, books, calendars, rugs, chairs and window frames, a twisted radio and a legless sewing machine. Everywhere there was bedding—blankets, mattresses, bent springs, shredded padding—he had not realized how much of people's lives was spent in bed. Here and there, cows and horses, often stained with disinfectant, were grazing again in the fields. At intervals there were Red Cross tents, and sitting by one of these, with the grey cat in her arms, the doctor came upon little Helen Kilrain. The usual lumber pile, like a child's building game knocked down in a fit of temper, told the story.

'Hello, dear,' he greeted her, his heart sinking. 'How did kitty like the tornado?'

'She didn't.'

'What did she do?'

'She meowed.'

'Oh.'

'She wanted to get away, but I hanged on to her and she scratched me—see?'

He glanced at the Red Cross tent.

'Who's taking care of you?'

'The lady from the Red Cross and Mrs Wells,' she answered. 'My father got hurt. He stood over me so it wouldn't fall on me, and I stood over kitty. He's in the hospital in Birmingham. When he comes back, I guess he'll build our house again.'

The doctor winced. He knew that her father would build no more houses; he had died that morning. She was alone, and she did not know she was alone. Around her stretched the dark universe, impersonal, inconscient. Her lovely little face looked up at him confidently as he asked: 'You got any kin anywhere, Helen?'

'I don't know.'

'You've got kitty, anyhow, haven't you?'

'It's just a cat,' she admitted calmly, but anguished by her own betrayal of her love, she hugged it closer.

'Taking care of a cat must be pretty hard.'

'Oh, no,' she said hurriedly. 'It isn't any trouble at all. It doesn't eat hardly anything.'

He put his hand in his pocket, and then changed his mind suddenly.

'Dear, I'm coming back and see you later—later today. You take good care of kitty now, won't you?'

'Oh, yes,' she answered lightly.

The doctor drove on. He stopped next at a house that had escaped damage. Walt Cupps, the owner, was cleaning a shotgun on his front porch.

'What's that, Walt? Going to shoot up the next tornado?'

'Ain't going to be a next tornado.'

'You can't tell. Just take a look at that sky now. It's getting mighty dark.'

Walt laughed and slapped his gun. 'Not for a hundred years, anyhow. This here is for looters. There's a lot of 'em around, and not all black either. Wish when you go to town that you'd tell 'em to scatter some militia out here.'

'I'll tell em now. You come out all right?'

'I did, thank God. With six of us in the house. It took off one hen, and probably it's still carrying it around somewhere.'

The doctor drove on towards town, overcome by a feeling of uneasiness he could not define.

'It's the weather,' he thought. 'It's the same kind of feel in the air there was last Saturday.'

For a month the doctor had felt an urge to go away permanently. Once this countryside had seemed to promise peace. When the impetus that had lifted him temporarily out of tired old stock was exhausted, he had come back here to rest, to watch the earth put forth, and live on simple, pleasant terms with his neighbours. Peace! He knew that the present family quarrel would never heal, nothing would ever be the same, it would all be bitter forever. And he had seen the placid countryside turned into a land of mourning. There was no peace here. Move on!

On the road he overtook Butch Janney walking to town.

'I was coming to see you,' said Butch, frowning. 'You operated on Pinky after all, didn't you?'

'Jump in. . . . Yes, I did. How did you know?'

'Doc Behrer told us.' He shot a quick look at the doctor, who did not miss the quality of suspicion in it. 'They don't think he'll last out the day.'

'I'm sorry for your mother.'

Butch laughed unpleasantly. 'Yes, you are.'

'I said I'm sorry for your mother,' said the doctor sharply.

'I heard you.'

They drove for a moment in silence.

'Did you find your automobile?'

'Did I?' Butch laughed ruefully. 'I found something—I don't know whether you'd call it a car any more. And, you know, I could of had tornado insurance for twenty-five cents.' His voice trembled indignantly: 'Twenty-five cents—but who would ever of thought of getting tornado insurance?'

It was growing darker; there was a thin crackle of thunder far to the southward.

'Well, all I hope,' said Butch with narrowed glance, 'is that you hadn't been drinking anything when you operated on Pinky.'

'You know, Butch,' the doctor said slowly, 'that was a pretty dirty trick of mine to bring that tornado here.'

He had not expected the sarcasm to hit home, but he expected a retort—when suddenly he caught sight of Butch's face. It was fish-white, the mouth was open, the eyes fixed and staring, and from the throat came a mewling sound. Limply he raised one hand before him, and then the doctor saw.

Less than a mile away, an enormous, top-shaped black cloud filled the sky and bore towards them, dipping and swirling, and in front of it sailed already a heavy, singing wind.

'It's come back!' the doctor yelled.

Fifty yards ahead of them was the old iron bridge spanning Bilby Creek. He stepped hard on the accelerator and drove for it. The fields were full of running figures headed in the same direction. Reaching the bridge, he jumped out and yanked Butch's arm.

'Get out, you fool! Get out!'

A nerveless mass stumbled from the car; in a moment they were in a group of half a dozen, huddled in the triangular space that the bridge made with the shore.

'Is it coming here?'

'No, it's turning!'

10+s.f.6

'We had to leave grampa!'

'Oh, save me, save me! Jesus save me! Help me!'

'Jesus save my soul!'

There was a quick rush of wind outside, sending little tentacles under the bridge with a curious tension in them that made the doctor's skin crawl. Then immediately there was a vacuum, with no more wind, but a sudden thresh of rain. The doctor crawled to the edge of the bridge and put his head up cautiously.

'It's passed,' he said. 'We only felt the edge; the centre went way to the right of us.'

He could see it plainly; for a second he could even distinguish objects in it—shrubbery and small trees, planks and loose earth. Crawling farther out, he produced his watch and tried to time it, but the thick curtain of rain blotted it from sight.

Soaked to the skin, he crawled back underneath. Butch lay shivering in the farthest corner, and the doctor shook him.

'It went in the direction of your house!' the doctor cried. 'Pull yourself together! Who's there?'

'No one,' Butch groaned. 'They're all down with Pinky.'

The rain had changed to hail now; first small pellets, then larger ones, and larger, until the sound of the fall upon the iron bridge was an ear-splitting tattoo.

The spared wretches under the bridge were slowly recovering, and in the relief there were titters of hysterical laughter. After a certain point of strain, the nervous system makes its transitions without dignity or reason. Even the doctor felt the contagion.

'This is worse than a calamity,' he said dryly. 'It's getting to a nuisance.'

IV

There were to be no more tornadoes in Alabama that spring. The second one—it was popularly thought to be the first one come back; for to the people of Chilton County it had become a personified force, definite as a pagan god—took a dozen houses, Gene Janney's among them, and injured about thirty people. But this time—perhaps because everyone had developed some scheme of self-protection—there were no fatalities. It made its last dramatic bow by sailing down the main street of Bending, prostrating the telephone poles and crushing in the fronts of three shops, including Doc Janney's drug store.

At the end of a week, houses were going up again, made of the old boards; and before the end of the long, lush Alabama summer the grass would be green again on all the graves. But it would be years before the people of the country ceased to reckon events as happening 'before the tornado' or 'after the tornado,'—and for many families thing would never be the same.

Doctor Janney decided that this was as good a time to leave as any. He sold the remains of his drug store, gutted alike by charity and catastrophe, and turned over his house to his brother until Gene could rebuild his own. He was going up to the city by train, for his car had been rammed against a tree and couldn't be counted on for much more than the trip to the station.

Several times on the way in he stopped by the roadside to say good-bye—once it was to Walter Cupps.

'So it hit you, after all,' he said, looking at the melancholy back house which alone marked the site.

'It's pretty bad,' Walter answered. 'But just think; they was six of us in or about the house and not one was injured. I'm content to give thanks to God for that.'

'You were lucky there, Walt,' the doctor agreed. 'Do you happen to have heard whether the Red Cross took little Helen Kilrain to Montgomery or to Birmingham?'

'To Montgomery. Say, I was there when she came into town with that cat, tryin' to get somebody to bandage up its paw. She must of walked miles through that rain and hail but all that mattered to her was her kitty. Bad as I felt, I couldn't help laughin' at how spunky she was.'

The doctor was silent for a moment. 'Do you happen to recollect if she has any people left?'

'I don't, suh,' Walter replied, 'but I think as not.'

At his brother's place, the doctor made his last stop. They were all there, even the youngest, working among the ruins; already Butch had a shed erected to house the salvage of their goods. Save for this the most orderly thing surviving was the pattern of round white stone which was to have enclosed the garden.

The doctor took a hundred dollars in bills from his pocket and handed it to Gene.

'You can pay it back sometime, but don't strain yourself,' he said, 'It's money I got from the store.' He cut off Gene's thanks: 'Pack up my books carefully when I send for 'em.'

'You reckon to practise medicine up there, Forrest?'

'I'll maybe try it.'

The brothers held on to each other's hands for a moment, the two youngest children came up to say good-bye. Rose stood in the background in an old blue dress—she had no money to wear black for her eldest son.

'Good-bye, Rose,' said the doctor.

'Good-bye,' she responded, and then added in a dead voice, 'Good luck to you, Forrest.'

For a moment he was tempted to say something conciliatory, but he saw it was no use. He was up against the maternal instinct, the same face that had sent little Helen through the storm with her injured cat.

At the station he bought a one-way ticket to Montgomery. The village was drab under the sky of a retarded spring, and as the train pulled out, it was odd to think that six months ago it had seemed to him as good a place as any other.

He was alone in the white section of the day coach; presently he felt for a bottle on his hip and drew it forth. 'After all, a man of forty-five is entitled to more artificial courage when he starts over again.' He began thinking of

Helen. 'She hasn't got any kin. I guess she's my little girl now.'

He patted the bottle, then looked down at it as if in surprise.

'Well, we'll have to put you aside for a while, old friend. Any cat that's worth all that trouble and care is going to need a lot of grade-B milk.'

He settled down in his seat, looking out the window. In his memory of the terrible week the winds still sailed about him, came in as draughts through the corridor of the car —winds of the world—cyclones, hurricanes, tornadoes— grey and black, expected or unforeseen, some from the sky, some from the caves of hell.

But he would not let them touch Helen again—if he could help it.

He dozed momentarily, but a haunting dream woke him: *'Daddy stood over me and I stood over kitty.'*

'All right, Helen,' he said aloud, for he often talked to himself, 'I guess the old brig can keep afloat a little longer —in any wind.'

CRAZY SUNDAY

[1932]

IT WAS SUNDAY—not a day, but rather a gap between two other days. Behind, for all of them, lay sets and sequences, the long waits under the crane that swung the microphone, the hundred miles a day by automobiles to and fro across a county, the struggles of rival ingenuities in the conference rooms, the ceaseless compromise, the clash and strain of many personalities fighting for their lives. And now Sunday, with individual life starting up again, with a glow kindling in eyes that had been glazed with monotony the afternoon before. Slowly as the hours waned they came awake like 'Puppenfeen' in a toy shop: an intense colloquy in a corner, lovers disappearing to neck in a hall. And the feeling of 'Hurry, it's not too late, but for God's sake hurry before the blessed forty hours of leisure are over.'

Joel Coles was writing continuity. He was twenty-eight and not yet broken by Hollywood. He had had what were considered nice assignments since his arrival six months before and he submitted his scenes and sequences with enthusiasm. He referred to himself modestly as a hack but really did not think of it that way. His mother had been a successful actress; Joel had spent his childhood between London and New York trying to separate the real from the unreal, or at least to keep one guess ahead. He was a handsome man with the pleasant cow-brown eyes that in 1913 had gazed out at Broadway audiences from his mother's face.

When the invitation came it made him sure that he was getting somewhere. Ordinarily he did not go out on

Sundays but stayed sober and took work home with him. Recently they had given him a Eugene O'Neill play destined for a very important lady indeed. Everything he had done so far had pleased Miles Calman, and Miles Calman was the only director on the lot who did not work under a supervisor and was responsible to the money men alone. Everything was clicking into place in Joel's career. ('This is Mr Calman's secretary. Will you come to tea from four to six Sunday—he lives in Beverly Hills, number ——.')

Joel was flattered. It would be a party out of the top-drawer. It was a tribute to himself as a young man of promise. The Marion Davies crowd, the high-hats, the big currency numbers, perhaps even Dietrich and Garbo and the Marquis, people who were not seen everywhere, would probably be at Calman's.

'I won't take anything to drink,' he assured himself. Calman was audibly tired of rummies, and thought it was a pity the industry could not get along without them.

Joel agreed that writers drank too much—he did himself, but he wouldn't this afternoon. He wished Miles would be within hearing when the cocktails were passed to hear his succinct, unobtrusive, 'No, thank you.'

Miles Calman's house was built for great emotional moments—there was an air of listening, as if the far silences of its vistas hid an audience, but this afternoon it was thronged, as though people had been bidden rather than asked. Joel noted with pride that only two other writers from the studio were in the crowd, an ennobled limey and, somewhat to his surprise, Nat Keogh, who had evoked Calman's impatient comment on drunks.

Stella Calman (Stella Walker, of course) did not move on to her other guests after she spoke to Joel. She lingered—she looked at him with the sort of beautiful look that demands some sort of acknowledgment and Joel drew quickly on the dramatic adequacy inherited from his mother:

'Well, you look about sixteen! Where's your kiddy car?'

She was visibly pleased; she lingered. He felt that he should say something more, something confident and easy —he had first met her when she was struggling for bits in New York. At the moment a tray slid up and Stella put a cocktail glass into his hand.

'Everybody's afraid, aren't they?' he said, looking at it absently. 'Everybody watches for everybody else's blunders, or tries to make sure they're with people that'll do them credit. Of course that's not true in your house,' he covered himself hastily. 'I just meant generally in Hollywood.'

Stella agreed. She presented several people to Joel as if he were very important. Reassuring himself that Miles was at the other side of the room, Joel drank the cocktail.

'So you have a baby?' he said. 'That's the time to look out. After a pretty woman has had her first child, she's very vulnerable, because she wants to be reassured about her own charm. She's got to have some new man's unqualified devotion to prove to herself she hasn't lost anything.'

'I never get anybody's unqualified devotion,' Stella said rather resentfully.

'They're afraid of your husband.'

'You think that's it?' She wrinkled her brow over the idea; then the conversation was interrupted at the exact moment Joel would have chosen.

Her attentions had given him confidence. Not for him to join safe groups, to slink to refuge under the wings of such acquaintances as he saw about the room. He walked to the window and looked out towards the Pacific, colourless under its sluggish sunset. It was good here—the American Riviera and all that, if there were ever time to enjoy it. The handsome, well-dressed people in the room, the lovely girls, and the—well, the lovely girls. You couldn't have everything.

He saw Stella's fresh boyish face, with the tired eyelid that always drooped a little over one eye, moving about among her guests and he wanted to sit with her and talk a long time as if she were a girl instead of a name; he followed her to see if she paid anyone as much attention as she had paid him. He took another cocktail—not because he needed confidence but because she had given him so much of it. Then he sat down beside the director's mother.

'Your son's gotten to be a legend, Mrs Calman—Oracle and a Man of Destiny and all that. Personally, I'm against him but I'm in a minority. What do you think of him? Are you impressed? Are you surprised how far he's gone?'

'No, I'm not surprised,' she said calmly. 'We always expected a lot from Miles.'

'Well now, that's unusual,' remarked Joel. 'I always think all mothers are like Napoleon's mother. My mother didn't want me to have anything to do with the entertainment business. She wanted me to go to West Point and be safe.'

'We always had every confidence in Miles.' . . .

He stood by the built-in bar of the dining-room with the good-humoured, heavy-drinking, highly paid Nat Keogh.

'—I made a hundred grand during the year and lost forty grand gambling, so now I've hired a manager.'

'You mean an agent,' suggested Joel.

'No, I've got that too. I mean a manager. I make over everything to my wife and then he and my wife get together and hand me out the money. I pay him five thousand a year to hand me out my money.'

'You mean your agent.'

'No, I mean my manager, and I'm not the only one—a lot of other irresponsible people have him.'

'Well, if you're irresponsible why are you responsible enough to hire a manager?'

'I'm just irresponsible about gambling. Look here——'

A singer performed; Joel and Nat went forward with the others to listen.

II

The singing reached Joel vaguely; he felt happy and friendly towards all the people gathered there, people of

10*

bravery and industry, superior to bourgeoisie that outdid them in ignorance and loose living, risen to a position of the highest prominence in a nation that for a decade had wanted only to be entertained. He liked them—he loved them. Great waves of good feeling flowed through him.

As the singer finished his number and there was a drift towards the hostess to say good-bye, Joel had an idea. He would give them 'Building It Up,' his own composition. It was his only parlour trick, it had amused several parties and it might please Stella Walker. Possessed by the hunch, his blood throbbing with the scarlet corpuscles of exhibitionism, he sought her.

'Of course,' she cried. 'Please! Do you need anything?'

'Someone has to be the secretary that I'm supposed to be dictating to.'

'I'll be her.'

As the word spread, the guests in the hall, already putting on their coats to leave, drifted back and Joel faced the eyes of many strangers. He had a dim foreboding, realizing that the man who had just performed was a famous radio entertainer. Then someone said 'Sh!' and he was alone with Stella, the centre of a sinister Indian-like half-circle. Stella smiled up at him expectantly—he began.

His burlesque was based upon the cultural limitations of Mr Dave Silverstein, an independent producer; Silverstein was presumed to be dictating a letter outlining a treatment of a story he had bought.

'—a story of divorce, the younger generators and the Foreign Legion,' he heard his voice saying, with the intonations of Mr Silverstein. 'But we got to build it up, see?'

A sharp pang of doubt struck through him. The faces surrounding him in the gently moulded light were intent and curious, but there was no ghost of a smile anywhere; directly in front the Great Lover of the screen glared at him with an eye as keen as the eye of a potato. Only Stella Walker look up at him with a radiant, never faltering smile.

'If we make him a Menjou type, then we get a sort of Michael Arlen only with a Honolulu atmosphere.'

Still not a ripple in front, but in the rear a rustling, a perceptible shift towards the left, towards the front door.

'—then she says she feels this sex appil for him and he burns out and says, "Oh, go on destroy yourself——"'

At some point he heard Nat Keogh snicker and here and there were a few encouraging faces, but as he finished he had the sickening realization that he had made a fool of himself in view of an important section of the picture world, upon whose favour depended his career.

For a moment he existed in the midst of a confused silence, broken by a general trek for the door. He felt the undercurrent of derision that rolled through the gossip; then—all this was in the space of ten seconds—the Great Lover, his eye hard and empty as the eye of a needle, shouted 'Boo! Boo!' voicing in an overtone what he felt was the mood of the crowd. It was the resentment of the professional towards the amateur, of the community towards the stranger, the thumbs-down of the clan.

Only Stella Walker was still standing near and thanking him as if he had been an unparalleled success, as if it hadn't occurred to her that anyone hadn't liked it. As Nat Keogh helped him into his overcoat, a great wave of self-disgust swept over him and he clung desperately to his rule of never betraying an inferior emotion until he no longer felt it.

'I was a flop,' he said lightly, to Stella. 'Never mind, it's a good number when appreciated. Thanks for your co-operation.'

The smile did not leave her face—he bowed rather drunkenly and Nat drew him towards the door. . . .

The arrival of his breakfast awakened him into a broken and ruined world. Yesterday he was himself, a point of fire against an industry, to-day he felt that he was pitted under an enormous disadvantage, against those faces, against individual contempt and collective sneer. Worse than that, to Miles Calman he was become one of those rummies, stripped of dignity, whom Calman regretted he was compelled to use. To Stella Walker on whom he had forced a martyrdom to preserve the courtesy of her house—her opinion he did not dare to guess. His gastric juices ceased to flow and he set his poached eggs back on the telephone table. He wrote:

> DEAR MILES: You can imagine my profound self-disgust. I confess to a taint of exhibitionism, but at six o'clock in the afternoon, in broad daylight! Good God! My apologies to your wife.
>
> Yours ever,
>
> JOEL COLES.

Joel emerged from his office on the lot only to slink like a malefactor to the tobacco store. So suspicious was his manner that one of the studio police asked to see his admission card. He had decided to eat lunch outside when Nat Keogh, confident and cheerful, overtook him.

'What do you mean you're in permanent retirement? What if that Three-Piece Suit did boo you?'

'Why, listen,' he continued, drawing Joel into the studio restaurant. 'The night of one of his premières at Grauman's, Joe Squires kicked his tail while he was bowing to the crowd. The ham said Joe'd hear from him later but when Joe called him up at eight o'clock next day and said, "I thought I was going to hear from you," he hung up the phone.'

The preposterous story cheered Joel, and he found a gloomy consolation in staring at the group at the next table, the sad, lovely Siamese twins, the mean dwarfs, the proud giant from the circus picture. But looking beyond at the yellow-stained faces of pretty women, their eyes all melancholy and startling with mascara, their ball gowns garish in full day, he saw a group who had been at Calman's and winced.

'Never again,' he exclaimed aloud, 'absolutely my last social appearance in Hollywood!'

The following morning a telegram was waiting for him at his office:

> You were one of the most agreeable people at our party. Expect you at my sister June's buffet supper next Sunday.
>
> STELLA WALKER CALMAN.

The blood rushed fast through his veins for a feverish minute. Incredulously he read the telegram over.

'Well, that's the sweetest thing I ever heard of in my life!'

III

Crazy Sunday again. Joel slept until eleven, then he read a newspaper to catch up with the past week. He lunched in his room on trout, avocado salad and a pint of California wine. Dressing for the tea, he selected a pin-check suit, a blue shirt, a burnt orange tie. There were dark circles of fatigue under his eyes. In his second-hand car he drove to the Riviera apartments. As he was introducing himself to Stella's sister, Miles and Stella arrived in riding clothes— they had been quarrelling fiercely most of the afternoon on all the dirt roads back of Beverly Hills.

Miles Calman, tall, nervous, with a desperate humour and the unhappiest eyes Joel ever saw, was an artist from the top of his curiously shaped head to his niggerish feet. Upon these last he stood firmly—he had never made a cheap picture though he had sometimes paid heavily for the luxury of making experimental flops. In spite of his excellent company, one could not be with him long without realizing that he was not a well man.

From the moment of their entrance Joel's day bound itself up inextricably with theirs. As he joined the group around them Stella turned away from it with an impatient little tongue click—and Miles Calman said to the man who happened to be next to him:

'Go easy on Eva Goebel. There's hell to pay about her at home.' Miles turned to Joel, 'I'm sorry I missed you at the office yesterday. I spent the afternoon at the analyst's.'

'You being psychoanalysed?'

'I have been for months. First I went for claustrophobia, now I'm trying to get my whole life cleared up. They say it'll take over a year.'

'There's nothing the matter with your life,' Joel assured him.

'Oh, no? Well, Stella seems to think so. Ask anybody—they can all tell you about it,' he said bitterly.

A girl perched herself on the arm of Miles's chair; Joel crossed to Stella, who stood disconsolately by the fire.

'Thank you for your telegram,' he said. 'It was darn sweet. I can't imagine anybody as good-looking as you are being so good-humoured.'

She was a little lovelier than he had ever seen her and perhaps the unstinted admiration in his eyes prompted her to unload on him—it did not take long, for she was obviously at the emotional bursting point.

'—and Miles has been carrying on this thing for two years, and I never knew. Why, she was one of my best friends, always in the house. Finally when people began to come to me, Miles had to admit it.'

She sat down vehemently on the arm of Joel's chair. Her riding breeches were the colour of the chair and Joel saw that the mass of her hair was made up of some strands of red gold and some of pale gold, so that it could not be dyed, and that she had on no make-up. She was that good-looking——

Still quivering with the shock of her discovery, Stella found unbearable the spectacle of a new girl hovering over Miles; she led Joel into a bedroom, and seated at either end of a big bed they went on talking. People on their way to the washroom glanced in and made wisecracks, but Stella, emptying out her story, paid no attention. After a while Miles stuck his head in the door and said, 'There's no use trying to explain something to Joel in half an hour that I don't understand myself and the psychoanalyst says will take a whole year to understand.'

She talked on as if Miles were not there. She loved Miles, she said—under considerable difficulties she had always been faithful to him.

'The psychoanalyst told Miles that he had a mother complex. In his first marriage he transferred his mother complex to his wife, you see—and then his sex turned to me. But when we married the thing repeated itself—he transferred his mother complex to me and all his libido turned towards this other woman.'

Joel knew that this probably wasn't gibberish—yet it sounded like gibberish. He knew Eva Goebel; she was a motherly person, older and probably wiser than Stella, who was a golden child.

Miles now suggested impatiently that Joel come back with them since Stella had so much to say, so they drove out to the mansion in Beverly Hills. Under the high ceilings the situation seemed more dignified and tragic. It was an eerie bright night with the dark very clear outside of all the windows and Stella all rose-gold raging and crying around the room. Joel did not quite believe in picture actresses' grief. They have other preoccupations—they are beautiful rose-gold figures blown full of life by writers and directors, and after hours they sit around and talk in whispers and giggle innuendoes, and the ends of many adventures flow through them.

Sometimes he pretended to listen and instead thought how well she was got up—sleek breeches with a matched set of legs in them, an Italian-coloured sweater with a little high neck, and a short brown chamois coat. He couldn't decide whether she was an imitation of an English lady or an English lady was an imitation of her. She hovered somewhere between the realest of realities and the most blatant of impersonations.

'Miles is so jealous of me that he questions everything I do,' she cried scornfully. 'When I was in New York I wrote him that I'd been to the theatre with Eddie Baker. Miles was so jealous he phoned me ten times in one day.'

'I was wild,' Miles snuffled sharply, a habit he had in times of stress. 'The analyst couldn't get any results for a week.'

Stella shook her head despairingly. 'Did you expect me just to sit in the hotel for three weeks?'

'I don't expect anything. I admit that I'm jealous. I try not to be. I worked on that with Dr Bridgebane, but it didn't do any good. I was jealous of Joel this afternoon when you sat on the arm of his chair.'

'You were?' She started up. 'You were! Wasn't there somebody on the arm of your chair? And did you speak to me for two hours?'

'You were telling your troubles to Joel in the bedroom.'

'When I think that that woman'—she seemed to believe that to omit Eva Goebel's name would be to lessen her reality—'used to come here——'

'All right—all right,' said Miles wearily. 'I've admitted everything and I feel as bad about it as you do.' Turning to Joel he began talking about pictures, while Stella moved restlessly along the far walls, her hands in her breeches pockets.

'They've treated Miles terribly,' she said, coming suddenly back into the conversation as if they'd never discussed her personal affairs. 'Dear, tell him about old Beltzer trying to change your picture.'

As she stood hovering protectively over Miles, her eyes flashing with indignation in his behalf, Joel realized that he was in love with her. Stifled with excitement he got up to say good night.

With Monday the week resumed its workaday rhythm, in sharp contrast to the theoretical discussions, the gossip and scandal of Sunday; there was the endless detail of script revision—'Instead of a lousy dissolve, we can leave her voice on the sound track and cut to a medium shot of the taxi from Bell's angle or we can simply pull the camera back to include the station, hold it a minute and then pam to the row of taxis'—by Monday afternoon Joel had again forgotten that people whose business was to provide entertainment were ever privileged to be entertained. In the evening he phoned Miles's house. He asked for Miles but Stella came to the phone.

'Do things seem better?'

'Not particularly. What are you doing next Saturday evening?'

'Nothing.'

'The Perrys are giving a dinner and theatre party and Miles won't be here—he's flying to South Bend to see the Notre Dame-California game. I thought you might go with me in his place.'

After a long moment Joel said, 'Why—surely. If there's a conference I can't make dinner but I can get to the theatre.'

'Then I'll say we can come.'

Joel walked to his office. In view of the strained relations of the Calmans, would Miles be pleased, or did she intend that Miles shouldn't know of it? That would be out of the question—if Miles didn't mention it Joel would. But it was an hour or more before he could get down to work again.

Wednesday there was a four-hour wrangle in a conference room crowded with planets and nebulæ of cigarette smoke. Three men and a woman paced the carpet in turn, suggesting or condemning, speaking sharply or persuasively, confidently or despairingly. At the end Joel lingered to talk to Miles.

The man was tired—not with the exaltation of fatigue but life-tired, with his lids sagging and his beard prominent over the blue shadows near his mouth.

'I hear you're flying to the Notre Dame game.'

Miles looked beyond him and shook his head.

'I've given up the idea.'

'Why?'

'On account of you.' Still he did not look at Joel.

'What the hell, Miles?'

'That's why I've given it up.' He broke into a perfunctory laugh at himself. 'I can't tell what Stella might do just out of spite—she's invited you to take her to the Perrys', hasn't she? I wouldn't enjoy the game.'

The fine instinct that moved swiftly and confidently on the set muddled so weakly and helplessly through his personal life.

'Look, Miles,' Joel said frowning. 'I've never made any passes whatsoever at Stella. If you're really seriously cancelling your trip on account of me, I won't go to the Perrys' with her. I won't see her. You can trust me absolutely.'

Miles looked at him, carefully now.

'Maybe.' He shrugged his shoulders. 'Anyhow there'd just be somebody else. I wouldn't have any fun.'

'You don't seem to have much confidence in Stella. She told me she'd always been true to you.'

'Maybe she has.' In the last few minutes several more muscles had sagged around Miles's mouth. 'But how can I ask anything of her after what's happened? How can I expect her—' He broke off and his face grew harder as he said, 'I'll tell you one thing, right or wrong and no matter what I've done, if I ever had anything on her I'd divorce her. I can't have my pride hurt—that would be the last straw.'

His tone annoyed Joel, but he said:

'Hasn't she calmed down about the Eva Goebel thing?'

'No.' Miles snuffled pessimistically. 'I can't get over it either.'

'I thought it was finished.'

'I'm trying not to see Eva again, but you know it isn't easy just to drop something like that—it isn't some girl I kissed last night in a taxi. The psychoanalyst says——'

'I know,' Joel interrupted. 'Stella told me.' This was depressing. 'Well, as far as I'm concerned if you go to the game I won't see Stella. And I'm sure Stella has nothing on her conscience about anybody.'

'Maybe not,' Miles repeated listlessly. 'Anyhow I'll stay and take her to the party. Say,' he said suddenly, 'I wish you'd come too. I've got to have somebody sympathetic to talk to. That's the trouble—I've influenced Stella in everything. Especially I've influenced her so that she likes all the men I like—it's very difficult.'

'It must be,' Joel agreed.

IV

Joel could not get to the dinner. Self-conscious in his silk hat against the unemployment, he waited for the others in front of the Hollywood Theatre and watched the evening parade: obscure replicas of bright, particular picture stars, spavined men in polo coats, a stomping dervish with the beard and staff of an apostle, a pair of chic Filipinos in collegiate clothes, reminder that this corner of the Republic opened to the seven seas, a long fantastic carnival of young shouts which proved to be a fraternity initiation. The line split to pass two smart limousines that stopped at the curb.

There she was, in a dress like ice-water, made in a thousand pale-blue pieces, with icicles trickling at the throat. He started forward.

'So you like my dress?'

'Where's Miles?'

'He flew to the game after all. He left yesterday morning—at least I think—' She broke off. 'I just got a telegram from South Bend saying that he's starting back. I forgot—you know all these people?'

The party of eight moved into the theatre.

Miles had gone after all and Joel wondered if he should have come. But during the performance, with Stella a profile under the pure grain of light hair, he thought no more about Miles. Once he turned and looked at her and she looked back at him, smiling and meeting his eyes for as long as he wanted. Between the acts they smoked in the lobby and she whispered:

'They're all going to the opening of Jack Johnson's night club—I don't want to go, do you?'

'Do we have to?'

'I suppose not.' She hesitated. 'I'd like to talk to you. I suppose we could go to our house—if I were only sure ——'

Again she hesitated and Joel asked:

'Sure of what?'

'Sure that—oh, I'm haywire I know, but how can I be sure Miles went to the game?'

'You mean you think he's with Eva Goebel?'

'No, not so much that—but supposing he was here watching everything I do. You know Miles does odd things sometimes. Once he wanted a man with a long beard to drink tea with him and he sent down to the casting agency for one, and drank tea with him all afternoon.'

'That's different. He sent you a wire from South Bend —that proves he's at the game.'

After the play they said good night to the others at the curb and were answered by looks of amusement. They slid off along the golden garish thoroughfare through the crowd that had gathered around Stella.

'You see he could arrange the telegrams,' Stella said, 'very easily.'

That was true. And with the idea that perhaps her uneasiness was justified, Joel grew angry : if Miles had trained a camera on them he felt no obligations towards Miles. Aloud he said :

'That's nonsense.'

There were Christmas trees already in the shop windows and the full moon over the boulevard was only a prop, as scenic as the giant boudoir lamps of the corners. On into the dark foliage of Beverly Hills that flamed as eucalyptus by day, Joel saw only the flash of a white face under his own, the arc of her shoulder. She pulled away suddenly and looked up at him.

'Your eyes are like your mother's,' she said. 'I used to have a scrap book full of pictures of her.'

'Your eyes are like your own and not a bit like any other eyes,' he answered.

Something made Joel look out into the grounds as they went into the house, as if Miles were lurking in the shubbery. A telegram waited on the hall table. She read aloud :

CHICAGO.
'Home tomorrow night. Thinking of you. Love.
MILES.

'You see,' she said, throwing the slip back on the table, 'he could easily have faked that.' She asked the butler for drinks and sandwiches and ran upstairs, while Joel walked into the empty receptions rooms. Strolling about he wandered to the piano where he had stood in disgrace two Sundays before.

'Then we could put over,' he said aloud, 'a story of divorce, the younger generation and the Foreign Legion.'

His thoughts jumped to another telegram.

'You were one of the most agreeable people at our party——'

An idea occurred to him. If Stella's telegram had been purely a gesture of courtesy then it was likely that Miles had inspired it, for it was Miles who had invited him. Probably Miles had said:

'Send him a wire—he's miserable—he thinks he's queered himself.'

It fitted in with 'I've influenced Stella in everything. Especially I've influenced her so that she likes all the men I like.' A woman would do a thing like that because she felt sympathetic—only a man would do it because he felt responsible.

When Stella came back into the room he took both her hands.

'I have a strange feeling that I'm a sort of pawn in a spite game you're playing against Miles,' he said.

'Help yourself to a drink.'

'And the odd thing is that I'm in love with you anyhow.'

The telephone rang and she freed herself to answer it.

'Another wire from Miles,' she announced. 'He dropped it, or it says he dropped it, from the aeroplane at Kansas City.'

'I suppose he asked to be remembered to me.'

'No, he just said he loved me. I believe he does. He's so very weak.'

'Come sit beside me,' Joel urged her.

It was early. And it was still a few minutes short of midnight a half-hour later, when Joel walked to the cold hearth, and said tersely:

'Meaning that you haven't any curiosity about me?'

'Not at all. You attract me a lot and you know it. The point is that I suppose I really do love Miles.'

'Obviously.'

'And to-night I feel uneasy about everything.'

He wasn't angry—he was even faintly relieved that a possible entanglement was avoided. Still as he looked at her, the warmth and softness of her body thawing her cold blue costume, he knew she was one of the things he would always regret.

'I've got to go,' he said. 'I'll phone a taxi.'

'Nonsense—there's a chauffeur on duty.'

He winced at her readiness to have him go, and seeing this she kissed him lightly and said, 'You're sweet, Joel.' Then suddenly three things happened: he took down his drink at a gulp, the phone rang loud through the house and a clock in the hall struck in trumpet notes.

Nine—ten—eleven—twelve——

V

It was Sunday again. Joel realized that he had come to the theatre this evening with the work of the week still hanging about him like cerements. He had made love to Stella as he might attack some matter to be cleaned up hurriedly before the day's end. But this was Sunday—the lovely, lazy perspective of the next twenty-four hours unrolled before him—every minute was something to be approached with lulling indirection, every moment held the germ of innumerable possibilities. Nothing was impossible—everything was just beginning. He poured himself another drink.

With a sharp moan, Stella slipped forward inertly by the telephone. Joel picked her up and laid her on the sofa. He squirted soda-water on a handkerchief and slapped it over her face. The telephone mouthpiece was still grinding and he put it to his ear.

'—the plane fell just this side of Kansas City. The body of Miles Calman has been identified and——'

He hung up the receiver.

'Lie still,' he said, stalling, as Stella opened her eyes.

'Oh, what's happened?' she whispered. 'Call them back. Oh, what's happened?'

'I'll call them right away. What's your doctor's name?'

'Did they say Miles was dead?'

'Lie quiet—is there a servant still up?'

'Hold me—I'm frightened.'

He put his arm around her.

'I want the name of your doctor,' he said sternly. 'It may be a mistake but I want someone here.'

'It's Doctor—Oh, God, is Miles dead?'

Joel ran upstairs and searched through strange medicine cabinets for spirits of ammonia. When he came down Stella cried:

'He isn't dead—I know he isn't. This is part of his scheme. He's torturing me. I know he's alive. I can feel he's alive.'

'I want to get hold of some close friend of yours, Stella. You can't stay here alone to-night.'

'Oh, no,' she cried. 'I can't see anybody. You stay, I haven't got any friend.' She got up, tears streaming down her face. 'Oh, Miles is my only friend. He's not dead—he can't be dead. I'm going there right away and see. Get a train. You'll have to come with me.'

'You can't. There's nothing to do to-night. I want you to tell me the name of some woman I can call: Lois? Joan? Carmel? Isn't there somebody?'

Stella stared at him blindly.

'Eva Goebel was my best friend,' she said.

Joel thought of Miles, his sad and desperate face in the office two days before. In the awful silence of his death all was clear about him. He was the only American-born director with both an interesting temperament and an artistic conscience. Meshed in an industry, he had paid with his ruined nerves for having no resilience, no healthy cynicism, no refuge—only a pitiful and precarious escape.

There was a sound at the outer door—it opened suddenly, and there were footsteps in the hall.

'Miles!' Stella screamed. 'Is it you, Miles? Oh, it's Miles.'

A telegraph boy appeared in the doorway.

'I couldn't find the bell. I heard you talking inside.'

The telegram was a duplicate of the one that had been phoned. While Stella read it over and over, as though it were a black lie, Joel telephoned. It was still early and he had difficulty getting anyone; when finally he succeeded in finding some friends he made Stella take a stiff drink.

'You'll stay here, Joel,' she whispered, as though she were half-asleep. 'You won't go away. Miles liked you—he said you—' She shivered violently, 'Oh, my God, you don't know how alone I feel!' Her eyes closed, 'Put your arms around me. Miles had a suit like that.' She started bolt upright. 'Think of what he must have felt. He was afraid of almost everything, anyhow.'

She shook her head dazedly. Suddenly she seized Joel's face and held it close to hers.

'You won't go. You like me—you love me, don't you? Don't call up anybody. To-morrow's time enough. You stay here with me to-night.'

He stared at her, at first incredulously, and then with shocked understanding. In her dark groping Stella was trying to keep Miles alive by sustaining a situation in which he had figured—as if Miles's mind could not die so long as the possibilities that had worried him still existed. It was a distraught and tortured effort to stave off the realization that he was dead.

Resolutely Joel went to the phone and called a doctor.

'Don't, oh, don't call anybody!' Stella cried. 'Come back here and put your arms around me.'

'Is Doctor Bales in?'

'Joel,' Stella cried. 'I thought I could count on you. Miles liked you. He was jealous of you—Joel, come here.'

Ah then—if he betrayed Miles she would be keeping him alive—for if he were really dead how could he be betrayed?

'—has just had a very severe shock. Can you come at once, and get hold of a nurse?'

'Joel!'

Now the door-bell and the telephone began to ring intermittently, and automobiles were stopping in front of the door.

'But you're not going,' Stella begged him. 'You're going to stay, aren't you?'

'No,' he answered. 'But I'll be back, if you need me.'

Standing on the steps of the house which now hummed and palpitated with the life that flutters around death like protective leaves, he began to sob a little in his throat.

'Everything he touched he did something magical to,' he thought. 'He even brought that little gamine alive and made her a sort of masterpiece.'

And then:

'What a hell of a hole he leaves in this damn wilderness —already!'

And then with a certain bitterness, 'Oh, yes, I'll be back —I'll be back!'

AN ALCOHOLIC CASE

[1937]

'Let—go—that—oh-h-h! Please, now, will you? *Don't*
start drinking again! Come on—give me the bottle. I told
you I'd stay awake givin' it to you. Come on. If you do like
that a-way—then what are you going to be like when you
go home. Come on—leave it with me—I'll leave half in the
bottle. Pul-lease. You know what Dr Carter says—I'll
stay awake and give it to you, or else fix some of it in the
bottle—come on—like I told you, I'm too tired to be
fightin' you all night. . . . All right, drink your fool self to
death.'

'Would you like some beer?' he asked.

'No, I don't want any beer. Oh, to think that I have to
look at you drunk again. My God!'

'Then I'll drink the Coca-Cola.'

The girl sat down panting on the bed.

'Don't you believe in anything?' she demanded.

'Nothing you believe in—please—it'll spill.'

She had no business there, she thought, no business
trying to help him. Again they struggled, but after this time
he sat with his head in his hands awhile, before he turned
around once more.

'Once more you try to get it I'll throw it down,' she said
quickly. 'I will—on the tiles in the bathroom.'

'Then I'll step on the broken glass—or you'll step on it.'

'Then let go—oh you promised——'

Suddenly she dropped it like a torpedo, sliding underneath her hand and slithering with a flash of red and black and
the words: Sir Galahad, distilled Louisville

314

GIN. He took it by the neck and tossed it through the open door to the bathroom.

It was on the floor in pieces and everything was silent for a while and she read *Gone With the Wind* about things so lovely that had happened long ago. She began to worry that he would have to go into the bathroom and might cut his feet, and looked up from time to time to see if he would go in. She was very sleepy—the last time she looked up he was crying and he looked like an old Jewish man she had nursed once in California; he had had to go to the bathroom many times. On this case she was unhappy all the time but she thought:

'I guess if I hadn't liked him I wouldn't have stayed on the case.'

With a sudden resurgence of conscience she got up and put a chair in front of the bathroom door. She had wanted to sleep because he had got her up early that morning to get a paper with the story of the Yale-Dartmouth game in it and she hadn't been home all day. That afternoon a relative of his had come to see him and she had waited outside in the hall where there was a draught with no sweater to put over her uniform.

As well as she could she arranged him for sleeping, put a robe over his shoulders as he sat slumped over his writing table, and one on his knees. She sat down in the rocker but she was no longer sleepy; there was plenty to enter on the chart and treading lightly about she found a pencil and put it down:

Pulse 120
Respiration 25
Temp. 98—98.4—98.2
Remarks—
—She could make so many:
Tried to get bottle of gin. Threw it away and broke it.
She corrected it to read:
In the struggle it dropped and was broken. Patient was generally difficult.
She started to add as part of her report: *I never want to*

go on an alcoholic case again, but that wasn't in the picture. She knew she could wake herself at seven and clean up everything before his niece awakened. It was all part of the game. But when she sat down in the chair she looked at his face, white and exhausted, and counted his breathing again, wondering why it had all happened. He had been so nice to-day, drawn her a whole strip of his cartoon just for fun and given it to her. She was going to have it framed and hang it in her room. She felt again his thin wrists wrestling against her wrist and remembered the awful things he had said, and she thought too of what the doctor had said to him yesterday:

'You're too good a man to do this to yourself.'

She was tired and didn't want to clean up the glass on the bathroom floor, because as soon as he breathed evenly she wanted to get him over to the bed. But she decided finally to clean up the glass first; on her knees, searching a last piece of it, she thought:

—This isn't what I ought to be doing. And this isn't what *he* ought to be doing.

Resentfully she stood up and regarded him. Through the thin delicate profile of his nose came a light snore, sighing, remote, inconsolable. The doctor had shaken his head in a certain way, and she knew that really it was a case that was beyond her. Besides, on her card at the agency was written, on the advice of her elders, 'No Alcoholics.'

She had done her whole duty, but all she could think of was that when she was struggling about the room with him with that gin bottle there had been a pause when he asked her if she had hurt her elbow against a door and that she had answered: 'You don't know how people talk about you, no matter how you think of yourself——' when she knew he had a long time ceased to care about such things.

The glass was all collected—as she got out a broom to make sure, she realized that the glass, in its fragments, was less than a window through which they had seen each other for a moment. He did not know about her sister, and Bill Markoe whom she had almost married, and she did not know what had brought him to this pitch, when there was a picture on his bureau of his young wife and his two sons and him, all trim and handsome as he must have been five years ago. It was so utterly senseless—as she put a bandage on her finger where she had cut it while picking up the glass she made up her mind she would never take an alcoholic case again.

II

It was early the next evening. Some Halloween jokester had split the side windows of the bus and she shifted back to the Negro section in the rear for fear the glass might fall out. She had her patient's cheque but no way to cash it at this hour; there was a quarter and a penny in her purse.

Two nurses she knew were waiting in the hall of Mrs Hixson's Agency.

'What kind of case have you been on?'

'Alcoholic,' she said.

'Oh yes—Gretta Hawks told me about it—you were on with that cartoonist who lives at the Forest Park Inn.'

'Yes, I was.'

'I hear he's pretty fresh.'

'He's never done anything to bother me,' she lied. 'You can't treat them as if they were committed——'

'Oh, don't get bothered—I just heard that around town —oh, you know—they want you to play around with them——'

'Oh, be quiet!' she said, surprised at her own rising resentment.

In a moment Mrs Hixson came out and, asking the other two to wait, signalled her into the office.

'I don't like to put young girls on such cases,' she began. 'I got your call from the hotel.'

'Oh, it wasn't bad, Mrs Hixson. He didn't know what he was doing and he didn't hurt me in any way. I was thinking much more of my reputation with you. He was really nice all day yesterday. He drew me——'

'I didn't want to send you on that case.' Mrs Hixson thumbed through the registration cards. 'You take T.B. cases, don't you? Yes, I see you do. Now here's one——'

The phone rang in a continuous chime. The nurse listened as Mrs Hixson's voice said precisely:

'I will do what I can—that is simply up to the doctor. . . . That is beyond my jurisdiction. . . . Oh, hello, Hattie, no, I can't now. Look, have you got any nurse that's good with alcoholics? There's somebody up at the Forest Park Inn who needs somebody. Call back will you?'

She put down the receiver. 'Suppose you wait outside. What sort of man is this, anyhow? Did he act indecently?'

'He held my hand away,' she said, 'so I couldn't give him an injection.'

'Oh, an invalid he-man,' Mrs Hixson grumbled. 'They belong in sanatoria. I've got a case coming along in two minutes that you can get a little rest on. It's an old woman——'

The phone rang again. 'Oh, hello, Hattie. . . . Well, how about that big Svensen girl? She ought to be able to take care of any alcoholic. . . How about Josephine Markham? Doesn't she live in your apartment house? . . . Get her to the phone.' Then after a moment, 'Joe, would you care to take the case of a well-known cartoonist, or artist, whatever they call themselves, at Forest Park Inn? . . . No, I don't know, but Dr Carter is in charge and will be around about ten o'clock.'

There was a long pause; from time to time Mrs Hixson spoke:

'I see. . . . Of course, I understand your point of view. Yes, but this isn't supposed to be dangerous—just a little difficult. I never like to send girls to a hotel because I know what riff-raff you're liable to run into. . . . No, I'll find somebody. Even at this hour. Never mind and thanks. Tell Hattie I hope that the hat matches the negligee. . . .'

Mrs Hixson hung up the receiver and made notations on the pad before her. She was a very efficient woman. She had been a nurse and had gone through the worst of it, had been a proud, idealistic, overworked probationer, suffered the abuse of smart internes and the insolence of her first patients, who thought that she was something to be taken into camp immediately for premature commitment to the service of old age. She swung around suddenly from the desk.

'What kind of cases do you want? I told you I have a nice old woman——'

The nurse's brown eyes were alight with a mixture of thoughts—the movie she had just seen about Pasteur and the book they had all read about Florence Nightingale when they were student nurses. And their pride, swinging across the streets in the cold weather at Philadelphia General, as proud of their new capes as débutantes in their furs going in to balls at the hotels.

'I—I think I would like to try the case again,' she said amid a cacophony of telephone bells. 'I'd just as soon go back if you can't find anybody else.'

'But one minute you say you'll never go on an alcoholic case again and the next minute you say you want to go back to one.'

'I think I overestimated how difficult it was. Really, I think I could help him.'

'That's up to you. But if he tried to grab your wrists.'

'But he couldn't,' the nurse said. 'Look at my wrists: I played basketball at Waynesboro High for two years. I'm quite able to take care of him.'

Mrs Hixson looked at her for a long minute. 'Well, all right,' she said. 'But just remember that nothing they say when they're drunk is what they mean when they're sober —I've been all through that; arrange with one of the servants that you can call on him, because you never can tell —some alcoholics are pleasant and some of them are not, but all of them can be rotten.'

'I'll remember,' the nurse said.

It was an oddly clear night when she went out, with slanting particles of thin sleet making white of a blue-black sky. The bus was the same that had taken her into town.

but there seemed to be more windows broken now and the bus driver was irritated and talked about what terrible things he would do if he caught any kids. She knew he was just talking about the annoyance in general, just as she had been thinking about the annoyance of an alcoholic. When she came up to the suite and found him all helpless and distraught she would despise him and be sorry for him.

Getting off the bus, she went down the long steps to the hotel, feeling a little exalted by the chill in the air. She was going to take care of him because nobody else would, and because the best people of her profession had been interested in taking care of the cases that nobody else wanted.

She knocked at his study door, knowing just what she was going to say.

He answered it himself. He was in dinner clothes even to a derby hat—but minus his studs and tie.

'Oh, hello,' he said casually. 'Glad you're back. I woke up a while ago and decided I'd go out. Did you get a night nurse?'

'I'm the night nurse too,' she said. 'I decided to stay on twenty-four hour duty.'

He broke into a genial, indifferent smile.

'I saw you were gone, but something told me you'd come back. Please find my studs. They ought to be either in a little tortoise-shell box or——'

He shook himself a little more into his clothes, and hoisted the cuffs up inside his coat sleeves.

'I thought you had quit me,' he said casually.

'I thought I had, too.'

'If you look on that table,' he said, 'you'll find a whole strip of cartoons that I drew you.'

'Who are you going to see?' she asked.

'It's the President's secretary,' he said. 'I had an awful time trying to get ready. I was about to give up when you came in. Will you order me some sherry?'

'One glass,' she agreed wearily.

From the bathroom he called presently:

'Oh, Nurse, Nurse, Light of my Life, where is another stud?'

'I'll put it in.'

In the bathroom she saw the pallor and the fever on his face and smelled the mixed peppermint and gin on his breath.

'You'll come up soon?' she asked. 'Dr Carter's coming at ten.'

'What nonsense! You're coming down with me.'

'Me?' she exclaimed. 'In a sweater and skirt? Imagine!'

'Then I won't go.'

'All right then, go to bed. That's where you belong anyhow. Can't you see these people to-morrow?'

'No, of course not!'

She went behind him and reaching over his shoulder tied his tie—his shirt was already thumbed out of press where he had put in the studs, and she suggested:

'Won't you put on another one, if you've got to meet some people you like?'

'All right, but I want to do it myself.'

'Why can't you let me help you?' she demanded in exasperation. 'Why can't you let me help you with your clothes? What's a nurse for—what good am I doing?'

He sat down suddenly on the toilet seat.

'All right—go on.'

'Now don't grab my wrist,' she said, and then, 'Excuse me.'

'Don't worry. It didn't hurt. You'll see in a minute.'

She had the coat, vest and stiff shirt off him but before she could pull his undershirt over his head he dragged at his cigarette, delaying her.

'Now watch this,' he said. 'One—two—three.'

She pulled up the undershirt; simultaneously he thrust the crimson-grey point of the cigarette like a dagger against his heart. It crushed out against a copper plate on his left rib about the size of a silver dollar, and he said 'Ouch!' as a stray spark fluttered down against his stomach.

Now was the time to be hard-boiled, she thought. She

knew there were three medals from the war in his jewel box, but she had risked many things herself: tuberculosis among them and one time something worse, though she had not known it and had never quite forgiven the doctor for not telling her.

'You've had a hard time with that, I guess,' she said lightly as she sponged him. 'Won't it ever heal?'

'Never. That's a copper plate.'

'Well, it's no excuse for what you're doing to yourself.'

He bent his great brown eyes on her, shrewd—aloof, confused. He signalled to her, in one second, his Will to Die, and for all her training and experience she knew she could never do anything constructive with him. He stood up, steadying himself on the wash-basin and fixing his eyes on some place just ahead.

'Now, if I'm going to stay here you're not going to get at that liquor,' she said.

Suddenly she knew he wasn't looking for that. He was looking at the corner where he had thrown the bottle the night before. She stared at his handsome face, weak and defiant—afraid to turn even halfway because she knew that death was in that corner where he was looking. She knew death—she had heard it, smelt its unmistakable odour, but she had never seen it before it entered into anyone, and she knew this man saw it in the corner of his bathroom; that it was standing there looking at him while he spat from a feeble cough and rubbed the result into the braid of his trousers. It shone there crackling for a moment as evidence of the last gesture he ever made.

She tried to express it next day to Mrs Hixson:

'It's not like anything you can beat—no matter how hard you try. This one could have twisted my wrists until he strained them and that wouldn't matter so much to me. It's just that you can't really help them and it's so discouraging—it's all for nothing.'

THE LONG WAY OUT

[1937]

WE WERE talking about some of the older castles in Touraine and we touched upon the iron cage in which Louis XI imprisoned Cardinal Balue for six years, then upon oubliettes and such horrors. I had seen several of the latter, simply dry wells thirty or forty feet deep where a man was thrown to wait for nothing; since I have such a tendency to claustrophobia that a Pullman berth is a certain nightmare, they had made a lasting impression. So it was rather a relief when a doctor told this story—that is, it was a relief when he began it, for it seemed to have nothing to do with the tortures long ago.

There was a young woman named Mrs King who was very happy with her husband. They were well-to-do and deeply in love, but at the birth of her second child she went into a long coma and emerged with a clear case of schizophrenia or 'split personality.' Her delusion, which had something to do with the Declaration of Independence, had little bearing on the case and as she regained her health it began to disappear. At the end of ten months she was a convalescent patient scarcely marked by what had happened to her and very eager to go back into the world.

She was only twenty-one, rather girlish in an appealing way and a favourite with the staff of the sanatorium. When she became well enough so that she could take an experimental trip with her husband there was a general interest in the venture. One nurse had gone into Philadelphia with her to get a dress, another knew the story of her rather romantic courtship in Mexico and everyone

323

had seen her two babies on visits to the hospital. The trip
was to Virginia Beach for five days.

It was a joy to watch her make ready, dressing and
packing meticulously and living in the gay trivialities of
hair waves and such things. She was ready half an hour
before the time of departure and she paid some visits
on the floor in her powder-blue gown and her hat that
looked like one minute after an April shower. Her frail
lovely face, with just that touch of startled sadness that
often lingers after an illness, was alight with anticipation.

'We'll just do nothing,' she said. 'That's my ambition.
To get up when I want to for three straight mornings and
stay up late for three straight nights. To buy a bathing
suit by myself and order a meal.'

When the time approached Mrs King decided to wait
downstairs instead of in her room and as she passed along
the corridors, with an orderly carrying her suitcase, she
waved to the other patients, sorry that they too were not
going on a gorgeous holiday. The superintendent wished
her well, two nurses found excuses to linger and share
her infectious joy.

'What a beautiful tan you'll get, Mrs King!'

'Be sure and send a postcard.'

About the time she left her room her husband's car
was hit by a truck on his way from the city—he was hurt
internally and was not expected to live more than a few
hours. The information was received at the hospital in a
glassed-in office adjoining the hall where Mrs King waited.
The operator, seeing Mrs King and knowing that the
glass was not sound-proof, asked the head nurse to come
immediately. The head nurse hurried aghast to a doctor
and he decided what to do. So long as the husband was
still alive it was best to tell her nothing, but of course she
must know that he was not coming today.

Mrs King was greatly disappointed.

'I suppose it's silly to feel that way,' she said. 'After all
these months what's one more day? He said he'd come
tomorrow, didn't he?'

The nurse was having a difficult time but she managed to pass it off until the patient was back in her room. Then they assigned a very experienced and phlegmatic nurse to keep Mrs King away from other patients and from newspapers. By the next day the matter would be decided one way or another.

But her husband lingered on and they continued to prevaricate. A little before noon next day one of the nurses was passing along the corridor when she met Mrs King, dressed as she had been the day before but this time carrying her own suitcase.

'I'm going to meet my husband,' she explained. 'He couldn't come yesterday but he's coming today at the same time.'

The nurse walked along with her. Mrs King had the freedom of the building and it was difficult to simply steer her back to her room, and the nurse did not want to tell a story that would contradict what the authorities were telling her. When they reached the front hall she signalled to the operator, who fortunately understood. Mrs King gave herself a last inspection in the mirror and said:

'I'd like to have a dozen hats just like this to remind me to be this happy always.'

When the head nurse came in frowning a minute later she demanded:

'Don't tell me George is delayed?'

'I'm afraid he is. There is nothing much to do but be patient.'

Mrs King laughed ruefully. 'I wanted him to see my costume when it was absolutely new.'

'Why, there isn't a wrinkle in it.'

'I guess it'll last till tomorrow. I oughtn't to be blue about waiting one more day when I'm so utterly happy.'

'Certainly not.'

That night her husband died and at a conference of doctors next morning there was some discussion about what to do—it was a risk to tell her and a risk to keep it from her. It was decided finally to say that Mr King had been called away and thus destroy her hope of an immediate meeting; when she was reconciled to this they could tell her the truth.

As the doctors came out of the conference one of them stopped and pointed. Down the corridor towards the outer hall walked Mrs King carrying her suitcase.

Dr Pirie, who had been in special charge of Mrs King, caught his breath.

'This is awful,' he said. 'I think perhaps I'd better tell her now. There's no use saying he's away when she usually hears from him twice a week, and if we say he's sick she'll want to go to him. Anybody else like the job?'

II

One of the doctors in the conference went on a fortnight's vacation that afternoon. On the day of his return in the same corridor at the same hour, he stopped at the sight of a little procession coming towards him—an orderly carrying a suitcase, a nurse and Mrs King dressed in the powder-blue suit and wearing the spring hat.

'Good morning, Doctor,' she said. 'I'm going to meet my husband and we're going to Virginia Beach. I'm going to the hall because I don't want to keep him waiting.'

He looked into her face, clear and happy as a child's. The nurse signalled to him that it was as ordered, so he merely bowed and spoke of the pleasant weather.

'It's a beautiful day,' said Mrs King, 'but of course even if it was raining it would be a beautiful day for me.'

The doctor looked after her, puzzled and annoyed— why are they letting this go on, he thought. What possible good can it do?

Meeting Dr Pirie, he put the question to him.

'We tried to tell her,' Dr Pirie said. 'She laughed and said we were trying to see whether she's still sick. You could use the word unthinkable in an exact sense here— his death is unthinkable to her.'

'But you can't just go on like this.'

'Theoretically no,' said Dr Pirie. 'A few days ago when she packed up as usual the nurse tried to keep her from going. From out in the hall I could see her face, see her begin to go to pieces—for the first time, mind you. Her muscles were tense and her eyes glazed and her voice was thick and shrill when she very politely called the nurse a liar. It was touch and go there for a minute whether we had a tractable patient or a restraint case—and I stepped in and told the nurse to take her down to the reception room.'

He broke off as the procession that had just passed appeared again, headed back to the ward. Mrs King stopped and spoke to Dr Pirie.

'My husband's been delayed,' she said. 'Of course I'm disappointed but they tell me he's coming tomorrow and after waiting so long one more day doesn't seem to matter. Don't you agree with me, Doctor?'

'I certainly do, Mrs King.'

She took off her hat.

'I've got to put aside these clothes—I want them to be as fresh tomorrow as they are today.' She looked closely at the hat. 'There's a speck of dust on it, but I think I can get it off. Perhaps he won't notice.'

'I'm sure he won't.'

'Really I don't mind waiting another day. It'll be this time tomorrow before I know it, won't it?'

When she had gone along the younger doctor said:

'There are still the two children.'

'I don't think the children are going to matter. When she "went under," she tied up this trip with the idea of getting well. If we took it away she'd have to go to the bottom and start over.'

'Could she?'

'There's no prognosis,' said Dr Pirie. 'I was simply explaining why she was allowed to go to the hall this morning.'

'But there's tomorrow morning and the next morning.'

'There's always the chance,' said Dr Pirie, 'that some day he will be there.'

The doctor ended his story here, rather abruptly. When we pressed him to tell what happened he protested that the rest was anticlimax—that all sympathy eventually wears out and that finally the staff of the sanatorium had simply accepted the fact.

'But does she still go to meet her husband?'

'Oh yes, it's always the same—but the other patients, except new ones, hardly look up when she passes along the hall. The nurses manage to substitute a new hat every year or so but she still wears the same suit. She's always a little disappointed but she makes the best of it, very sweetly too. It's not an unhappy life as far as we know, and in some funny way it seems to set an example of tranquillity to the other patients. For God's sake let's talk about something else—let's go back to oubliettes!'

FINANCING FINNEGAN

[1938]

FINNEGAN AND I have the same literary agent to sell our
writings for us, but though I'd often been in Mr Cannon's
office just before and just after Finnegan's visits, I had
never met him. Likewise we had the same publisher and
often when I arrived there Finnegan had just departed.
I gathered from a thoughtful sighing way in which they
spoke of him—

'Ah—Finnegan——'

'Oh yes, Finnegan was here.'

—that the distinguished author's visit had been not
uneventful. Certain remarks implied that he had taken
something with him when he went—manuscripts, I supposed, one of those great successful novels of his. He had
taken 'it' off for a final revision, a last draft, of which he
was rumoured to make ten in order to achieve that facile
flow, that ready wit, which distinguished his work. I
discovered only gradually that most of Finnegan's visits
had to do with money.

'I'm sorry you're leaving,' Mr Cannon would tell me,
'Finnegan will be here to-morrow.' Then after a thoughtful
pause, 'I'll probably have to spend some time with him.'

I don't know what note in his voice reminded me of a
talk with a nervous bank president when Dillinger was
reported in the vicinity. His eyes looked out into the distance
and he spoke as to himself.

'Of course he may be bringing a manuscript. He has a
novel he's working on, you know. And a play too.' He spoke
as though he were talking about some interesting but remote

events of the cinquecento; but his eyes became more hopeful as he added: 'Or maybe a short story.'

'He's very versatile, isn't he?' I said.

'Oh yes,' Mr Cannon perked up. 'He can do anything
—anything when he puts his mind to it. There's never
been such a talent.'

'I haven't seen much of his work lately.'

'Oh, but he's working hard. Some of the magazines have
stories of his that they're holding.'

'Holding for what?'

'Oh, for a more appropriate time—an upswing. They
like to think they have something of Finnegan's.'

His was indeed a name with ingots in it. His career had
started brilliantly, and if it had not kept up to its first
exalted level, at least it started brilliantly all over again
every few years. He was the perennial man of promise in
American letters—what he could actually do with words
was astounding, they glowed and coruscated—he wrote
sentences, paragraphs, chapters that were masterpieces
of fine weaving and spinning. It was only when I met some
poor devil of a screen writer who had been trying to make
a logical story out of one of his books that I realized he had
his enemies.

'It's all beautiful when you read it,' this man said disgustedly, 'but when you write it down plain it's like a week
in the nut-house.'

From Mr Cannon's office I went over to my publishers
on Fifth Avenue, and there too I learned in no time that
Finnegan was expected to-morrow. Indeed he had thrown
such a long shadow before him that the luncheon where
I expected to discuss my own work was largely devoted to
Finnegan. Again I had the feeling that my host, Mr
George Jaggers, was talking not to me but to himself.

'Finnegan's a great writer,' he said.

'Undoubtedly.'

'And he's really quite all right, you know.'

As I hadn't questioned the fact I inquired whether there
was any doubt about it.

'Oh, no,' he said hurriedly. 'It's just that he's had such a run of hard luck lately——'

I shook my head sympathetically. 'I know. That diving into a half-empty pool was a tough break.'

'Oh, it wasn't half-empty. It was full of water. Full to the brim. You ought to hear Finnegan on the subject—he makes a side-splitting story of it. It seems he was in a run-down condition and just diving from the side of the pool, you know——' Mr Jaggers pointed his knife and fork at the table, 'and he saw some young girls diving from the fifteen-foot board. He says he thought of his lost youth and went up to do the same and made a beautiful swan-dive—but his shoulder broke while he was still in the air.' He looked at me rather anxiously. 'Haven't you heard of cases like that—a ball player throwing his arm out of joint?'

I couldn't think of any orthopaedic parallels at the moment.

'And then,' he continued dreamily, 'Finnegan had to write on the ceiling.'

'On the ceiling?'

'Practically. He didn't give up writing—he has plenty of guts, that fellow, though you may not believe it. He had some sort of arrangement built that was suspended from the ceiling and he lay on his back and wrote in the air.'

I had to grant that it was a courageous arrangement.

'Did it affect his work?' I inquired. 'Did you have to read his stories backward—like Chinese?'

'They were rather confused for a while,' he admitted, 'but he's all right now. I got several letters from him that sounded more like the old Finnegan—full of life and hope and plans for the future——'

The far-away look came into his face and I turned the discussion to affairs closer to my heart. Only when we were back in his office did the subject recur—and I blush as I write this because it included confessing something I seldom do—reading another man's telegram. It happened because Mr Jaggers was intercepted in the hall and when

I went into his office and sat down it was stretched out open before me:

> With fifty I could at least pay typist and get haircut and pencils life has become impossible and I exist on dream of good news desperately. FINNEGAN

I couldn't believe my eyes—fifty dollars, and I happened to know that Finnegan's price for short stories was somewhere around three thousand. George Jaggers found me still staring dazedly at the telegram. After he read it he stared at me with stricken eyes.

'I don't see how I can conscientiously do it,' he said.

I started and glanced around to make sure I was in the prosperous publishing office in New York. Then I understood—I had misread the telegram. Finnegan was asking for fifty thousand as an advance—a demand that would have staggered any publisher no matter who the writer was.

'Only last week,' said Mr Jaggers disconsolately, 'I sent him a hundred dollars. It puts my department in the red every season, so I don't dare tell my partners any more. I take it out of my own pocket—give up a suit and a pair of shoes.'

'You mean Finnegan's broke?'

'Broke!' He looked at me and laughed soundlessly—in fact I didn't exactly like the way that he laughed. My brother had a nervous—but that is afield from this story. After a minute he pulled himself together. 'You won't say anything about this, will you? The truth is Finnegan's been in a slump, he's had blow after blow in the past few years, but now he's snapping out of it and I know we'll get back every cent we've——' He tried to think of a word but 'given him' slipped out. This time it was he who was eager to change the subject.

Don't let me give the impression that Finnegan's affairs absorbed me during a whole week in New York—it was inevitable, though, that being much in the offices of my agent and my publisher, I happened in on a lot. For instance, two days later, using the telephone in Mr Cannon's office, I was accidentally switched in on a conversation he was having with George Jaggers. It was only partly eavesdropping, you see, because I could only hear one end of the conversation and that isn't as bad as hearing it all.

'But I got the impression he was in good health . . . he did say something about his heart a few months ago but I understood it got well . . . yes, and he talked about some operation he wanted to have—I think he said it was cancer. . . . Well, I felt like telling him I had a little operation up my sleeve, too, that I'd have had by now if I could afford it. . . . No, I didn't say it. He seemed in such good spirits that it seemed a shame to bring him down. He's starting a story today, he read me some of it on the phone . . .

'. . . I did give him twenty-five because he didn't have a cent in his pocket . . . oh, yes—I'm sure he'll be all right now. He sounds as if he means business.'

I understood it all now. The two men had entered into a silent conspiracy to cheer each other up about Finnegan. Their investment in him, in his future, had reached a sum so considerable that Finnegan belonged to them. They could not bear to hear a word against him—even from themselves.

II

I spoke my mind to Mr Cannon.

'If this Finnegan is a four-flusher you can't go on indefinitely giving him money. If he's through he's through and there's nothing to be done about it. It's absurd that you should put off an operation when Finnegan's out somewhere diving into half-empty swimming pools.'

'It was full,' said Mr Cannon patiently—'full to the brim.'

'Well, full or empty the man sounds like a nuisance to me.'

'Look here,' said Cannon, 'I've got a call from Hollywood due on the wire. Meanwhile you might glance over that.' He threw a manuscript into my lap. 'Maybe it'll help you understand. He brought it in yesterday.'

It was a short story. I began it in a mood of disgust, but before I'd read five minutes I was completely immersed in it, utterly charmed, utterly convinced, and wishing to God I could write like that. When Cannon finished his phone call I kept him waiting while I finished it and when I did there were tears in these hard old professional eyes. Any magazine in the country would have run it first in any issue.

But then nobody had ever denied that Finnegan could write.

III

Months passed before I went again to New York, and then, so far as the offices of my agent and my publisher were concerned, I descended upon a quieter, more stable world. There was at last time to talk about my own conscientious if uninspired literary pursuits, to visit Mr Cannon in the country, and to kill summer evenings with George Jaggers where the vertical New York starlight falls like lingering lightning into restaurant gardens. Finnegan might have been at the North Pole—and as a matter of fact he was. He had quite a group with him, including three Bryn Mawr anthropologists, and it sounded as if he might collect a lot of material there. They were going to stay several months, and if the thing had somehow the ring of a promising little house-party about it, that was probably due to my jealous, cynical disposition.

'We're all just delighted,' said Cannon. 'It's a godsend for him. He was fed up and he needed just this—this——'

'Ice and snow,' I supplied.

'Yes, ice and snow. The last thing he said was characteristic of him. Whatever he writes is going to be pure white—it's going to have a blinding glare about it.'

'I can imagine it will. But tell me—who's financing it? Last time I was here I gathered the man was insolvent.'

'Oh, he was really very decent about that. He owed me some money and I believe he owed George Jaggers a little too.' He 'believed', the old hypocrite. He knew damn well.

'So before he left he made most of his life insurance over to us. That's in case he doesn't come back—those trips are dangerous of course.'

'I should think so,' I said, 'especially with three anthropologists.'

'So Jaggers and I are absolutely covered in case anything happens—it's as simple as that.'

'Did the life-insurance company finance the trip?'

He fidgeted perceptibly.

'Oh, no. In fact when they learned the reason for the assignments they were a little upset. George Jaggers and I felt that when he had a specific plan like this with a specific book at the end of it, we were justified in backing him a little further.'

'I don't see it,' I said flatly.

'You don't?' The old harassed look came back into his eyes. 'Well, I'll admit we hesitated. In principle I know it's wrong. I used to advance authors small sums from time to time, but lately I've made a rule against it—and kept it. It's only been waived once in the last two years and that was for a woman who has having a bad struggle—Margaret Trahill, do you know her? She was an old girl of Finnegan's by the way.'

'Remember I don't even know Finnegan.'

'That's right. You must meet him when he comes back —if he does come back. You'd like him—he's utterly charming.'

Again I departed from New York, to imaginative North Poles of my own, while the year rolled through summer and fall. When the first snap of November was in the air, I thought of the Finnegan expedition with a sort of shiver and any envy of the man departed. He was probably earning any loot, literary or anthropological, he might bring back. Then, when I hadn't been back in New York three days, I read in the paper that he and some other members of his party had walked off into a snowstorm when the food supply gave out, and the Arctic had claimed another sacrifice of intrepid man.

I was sorry for him, but practical enough to be glad that Cannon and Jaggers were well protected. Of course, with Finnegan scarcely cold—if such a simile is not too harrowing—they did not talk about it but I gathered that the insurance companies had waived *habeas corpus* or whatever it is in their lingo, just as if he had fallen overboard into the Atlantic, and it seemed quite sure that they would collect.

His son, a fine-looking young fellow, came into George Jaggers's office while I was there and from him I could guess at Finnegan's charm—a shy frankness together with an impression of a very quiet, brave battle going on inside of him that he couldn't quite bring himself to talk about—but that showed as heat lightning in his work.

'The boy writes well too,' said George after he had gone. 'He's brought in some remarkable poems. He's not ready to step into his father's shoes, but there's a definite promise.'

'Can I see one of his things?'

'Certainly—here's one he left just as he went out.'

George took a paper from his desk, opened it and cleared his throat. Then he squinted and bent over a little in his chair.

'*Dear Mr Jaggers,*' he began, '*I didn't like to ask you this in person——*' Jaggers stopped, his eyes reading ahead rapidly.

'How much does he want?' I inquired.

He sighed.

'He gave me the impression that this was some of his work,' he said in a pained voice.

'But it is,' I consoled him. 'Of course he isn't quite ready to step into his father's shoes.'

I was sorry afterwards to have said this, for after all Finnegan had paid his debts, and it was nice to be alive now that better times were back and books were no longer rated as unnecessary luxuries. Many authors I knew who had skimped along during the depression were now making long-deferred trips or paying off mortgages or turning out the more finished kind of work that can only be done with a certain leisure and security. I had just got a thousand dollars advance for a venture in Hollywood and was going to fly out with all the verve of the old days when there was chicken feed in every pot. Going in to say good-bye to Cannon and collect the money, it was nice to find he too was profiting—wanted me to go along and see a motor-boat he was buying.

But some last-minute stuff came up to delay him and I grew impatient and decided to skip it. Getting no response to a knock on the door of his sanctum, I opened it anyhow.

The inner office seemed in some confusion. Mr Cannon was on several telephones at once and dictating something about an insurance company to a stenographer. One secretary was getting hurriedly into her hat and coat as upon an errand and another was counting bills from her purse upon a table.

'It'll be only a minute,' said Cannon, 'it's just a little office riot—you never saw us like this.'

'Is it Finnegan's insurance?' I couldn't help asking. 'Isn't it any good?'

'His insurance—oh, perfectly all right, perfectly. This is just a matter of trying to raise a few hundred in a hurry. The banks are closed and we're all contributing.'

'I've got that money you just gave me,' I said. 'I don't need all of it to get to the coast.' I peeled off a couple of hundred. 'Will this be enough?'

'That'll be fine—it just saves us. Never mind, Miss Carlsen. Mrs Mapes, you needn't go now.'

'I think I'll be running along,' I said.

'Just wait two minutes,' he urged. 'I've only got to take care of this wire. It's really splendid news. Bucks you up.'

It was a cablegram from Oslo, Norway—before I began to read I was full of a premonition.

Am miraculously safe here but detained by authorities please wire passage money for four people and two hundred extra I am bringing back plenty greetings from the dead. FINNEGAN

'Yes, that's splendid,' I agreed. 'He'll have a story to tell now.'

'Won't he though!' said Cannon. 'Miss Carlsen, will you wire the parents of those girls—and you'd better inform Mr Jaggers.'

As we walked along the street a few minutes later, I saw that Mr Cannon, as if stunned by the wonder of this news, had fallen into a brown study, and I did not disturb him, for after all I did not know Finnegan and could not whole-heartedly share his joy. His mood of silence continued until we arrived at the door of the motor-boat show. Just under the sign he stopped and stared upward, as if aware for the first time where we were going.

'Oh, my!' he said stepping back. 'There's no use going in here now. I thought we were going to get a drink.'

We did. Mr Cannon was still a little vague, a little under the spell of the vast surprise—he fumbled so long for the money to pay his round that I insisted it was on me.

I think he was in a daze during that whole time because, though he is a man of the most punctilious accuracy, the two hundred I handed him in his office has never shown to my credit in the statements he has sent me. I imagine, though, that some day I will surely get it because some day Finnegan will click again and I know that people will clamour to read what he writes. Recently I've taken it upon myself to investigate some of the stories about him and I've found that they're mostly as false as the half-empty pool. That pool was full to the brim.

So far there's only been a short story about the polar expedition, a love story. Perhaps it wasn't as big a subject as he expected. But the movies are interested in him—if they can get a good long look at him first and I have every reason to think that he will come through. He'd better!

DESIGN IN PLASTER
[1939]

'How long does the doctor think now?' Mary asked. With his good arm Martin threw back the top of the sheet, disclosing that the plaster armour had been cut away in front in the form of a square, so that his abdomen and the lower part of his diaphragm bulged a little from the aperture. His dislocated arm was still high over his head in an involuntary salute.

'This was a great advance,' he told her. 'But it took the heat wave to make Ottinger put in this window. I can't say much for the view but—have you seen the wire collection?'

'Yes, I've seen it,' his wife answered, trying to look amused.

It was laid out on the bureau like a set of surgeons' tools—wires bent to every length and shape so that the nurse could reach any point inside the plaster cast when perspiration made the itching unbearable.

Martin was ashamed at repeating himself.

'I apologize,' he said. 'After two months you get medical psychology. All this stuff is fascinating to me. In fact—' he added, and with only faint irony, '—it is in a way of becoming my life.'

Mary came over and sat beside the bed, raising him, cast and all, into her slender arms. He was chief electrical engineer at the studio and his thirty-foot fall wasn't costing a penny in doctor's bills. But that—and the fact that the catastrophe had swung them together after a four months' separation—was its only bright spot.

'I feel so close,' she whispered. 'Even through this plaster.'

'Do you think that's a nice way to talk?'

'Yes.'

'So do I.'

Presently she stood up and rearranged her bright hair in the mirror. He had seen her do it half a thousand times but suddenly there was a quality of remoteness about it that made him sad.

'What are you doing tonight?' he asked.

Mary turned, almost with surprise.

'It seems strange to have you ask me.'

'Why? You almost always tell me. You're my contact with the world of glamour.'

'But you like to keep bargains. That was our arrangement when we began to live apart.'

'You're being very technical.'

'No—but that *was* the arrangement. As a matter of fact I'm not doing anything. Bieman asked me to go to a preview, but he bores me. And that French crowd called up.'

'Which member of it?'

She came close and looked at him.

'Why, I believe you're jealous,' she said. 'The wife of course. Or *he* did, to be exact, but he was calling for his wife—she'd be there. I've never seen you like this before.'

Martin was wise enough to wink as if it meant nothing and let it die away, but Mary said an unfortunate last word.

'I thought you liked me to go with them.'

'That's it,' Martin tried to go slow, '—with "them," but now it's "he".'

'They're all leaving Monday,' she said almost impatiently. 'I'll probably never see him again.'

Silence for a minute. Since his accident there were not an unlimited number of things to talk about, except when there was love between them. Or even pity—he was accepting even pity in the past fortnight. Especially their uncertain plans about the future were in need of being preceded by a mood of love.

'I'm going to get up for a minute,' he said suddenly. 'No, don't help me—don't call the nurse. I've got it figured out.'

The cast extended half way to his knee on one side but with a snake-like motion he managed to get to the side of the bed—then rise with a gigantic heave. He tied on a dressing-gown, still without assistance, and went to the window. Young people were splashing and calling in the outdoor pool of the hotel.

'I'll go along,' said Mary. 'Can I bring you anything tomorrow? Or tonight if you feel lonely?'

'Not tonight. You know I'm always cross at night—and I don't like you making that long drive twice a day. Go along—be happy.'

'Shall I ring for the nurse?'

'I'll ring presently.'

He didn't though—he just stood. He knew that Mary was wearing out, that this resurgence of her love was wearing out. His accident was a very temporary dam of a stream that had begun to overflow months before.

When the pains began at six with their customary regularity the nurse gave him something with codeine in it, shook him a cocktail and ordered dinner, one of those dinners it was a struggle to digest since he had been sealed up in his individual bomb-shelter. Then she was off duty four hours and he was alone. Alone with Mary and the Frenchman.

He didn't know the Frenchman except by name but Mary had said once:

'Joris is rather like you—only naturally not formed—rather immature.'

Since she said that, the company of Mary and Joris had grown increasingly unattractive in the long hours between seven and eleven. He had talked with them, driven around with them, gone to pictures and parties with them—sometimes with the half comforting ghost of Joris's wife along. He had been near as they made love and even that was endurable as long as he could seem to hear and see them.

It was when they became hushed and secret that his stomach winced inside the plaster cast. That was when he had pictures of the Frenchman going toward Mary and Mary waiting. Because he was not sure just how Joris felt about her or about the whole situation.

'I told him I loved you,' Mary said—and he believed her, 'I told him that I could never love anyone but you.'

Still he could not be sure how Mary felt as she waited in her apartment for Joris. He could not tell if, when she said good night at her door, she turned away relieved, or whether she walked around her living-room a little and later, reading her book, dropped it in her lap and looked up at the ceiling. Or whether her phone rang once more for one more good night.

Martin hadn't worried about any of these things in the first two months of their separation when he had been on his feet and well.

At half-past eight he took up the phone and called her; the line was busy and still busy at a quarter to nine. At nine it was out of order; at nine-fifteen it didn't answer and at a little before nine-thirty it was busy again. Martin got up, slowly drew on his trousers and with the help of a bellboy put on a shirt and coat.

'Don't you want me to come, Mr Harris?' asked the bellboy.

'No thanks. Tell the taxi I'll be right down.'

When the boy had gone he tripped on the slightly raised floor of the bathroom, swung about on one arm and cut his head against the wash bowl. It was not so much, but he did a clumsy repair job with the adhesive and, feeling ridiculous at his image in the mirror, sat down and called Mary's number a last time—for no answer. Then he went out, not because he wanted to go to Mary's but because he had to go somewhere towards the flame, and he didn't know any other place to go.

At ten-thirty Mary, in her nightgown, was at the phone.

'Thanks for calling. But, Joris, if you want to know the truth I have a splitting headache. I'm turning in.'

'Mary, listen,' Joris insisted. 'It happens Marianne has a headache too and has turned in. This is the last night I'll have a chance to see you alone. Besides, you told me you'd *never* had a headache.'

Mary laughed.

'That's true—but I *am* tired.'

'I would promise to stay one half-hour—word of honour. I am only just around the corner.'

'No,' she said and a faint touch of annoyance gave firmness to the word. 'Tomorrow I'll have either lunch or dinner if you like, but now I'm going to bed.'

She stopped. She had heard a sound, a weight crunching against the outer door of her apartment. Then three odd, short bell rings.

'There's someone—call me in the morning,' she said. Hurriedly hanging up the phone she got into a dressing-gown.

By the door of her apartment she asked cautiously.

'Who's there?'

No answer—only a heavier sound—a human slipping to the floor.

'Who is it?'

She drew back and away from a frightening moan. There was a little shutter high in the door, like the peep-hole of a speakeasy, and feeling sure from the sound that whoever it was, wounded or drunk, was on the floor Mary reached up and peeped out. She could see only a hand covered with freshly ripening blood, and shut the trap hurriedly. After a shaken moment, she peered once more.

This time she recognized something—afterwards she could not have said what—a way the arm lay, a corner of the plaster cast—but it was enough to make her open the door quickly and duck down to Martin's side.

'Get doctor,' he whispered. 'Fell on the steps and broke.'

His eyes closed as she ran for the phone.

Doctor and ambulance came at the same time. What Martin had done was simple enough, a little triumph of misfortune. On the first flight of stairs that he had gone up for eight weeks, he had stumbled, tried to save himself with the arm that was no good for anything, then spun down catching and ripping on the stairs rail. After that a five minute drag up to her door.

Mary wanted to exclaim, 'Why? Why?' but there was no one to hear. He came awake as the stretcher was put under him to carry him to the hospital, repair the new breakage with a new cast, start it over again. Seeing Mary he called quickly. 'Don't you come. I don't like any-one around when—when—Promise on your word of honour not to come?'

The orthopaedist said he would phone her in an hour. And five minutes later it was with the confused thought that he was already calling that Mary answered the phone.

'I can't talk, Joris,' she said. 'There was an awful acci-dent—'

'Can I help?'

'It's gone now. It was my husband—'

Suddenly Mary knew she wanted to do anything but wait alone for word from the hospital.

'Come over then,' she said. 'You can take me up there if I'm needed.'

She sat in place by the phone until he came—jumped to her feet with an exclamation at his ring.

'Why? Why?' she sobbed at last. 'I offered to go see him at his hotel.'

'Not drunk?'

'No, no—he almost never takes a drink. Will you wait right outside my door while I dress and get ready?'

The news came half an hour later that Martin's shoulder was set again, that he was sleeping under the ethylene gas and would sleep till morning. Joris Deglen was very gentle, swinging her feet up on the sofa, putting a pillow at her back and answering her incessant 'Why?' with a different response every time—Martin had been delirious; he was lonely; then at a certain moment telling the truth he had long guessed at: Martin was jealous.

'That was it,' Mary said bitterly. 'We were to be free—only I wasn't free. Only free to sneak about behind his back.'

She was free now though, free as air. And later, when he said he wouldn't go just yet, but would sit in the living-room reading until she quieted down, Mary went into her room with her head clear as morning. After she undressed for the second time that night she stayed for a few minutes before the mirror arranging her hair and keeping her mind free of all thoughts about Martin except that he was sleeping and at the moment felt no pain.

Then she opened her bedroom door and called down the corridor into the living-room:

'Do you want to come and tell me good night?'

BOIL SOME WATER—LOTS OF IT

PAT HOBBY sat in his office in the Writer's Building and looked at his morning's work, just come back from the script department. He was on a 'polish job,' about the only kind he ever got nowadays. He was to repair a messy sequence in a hurry, but the word 'hurry' neither frightened nor inspired him, for Pat had been in Hollywood since he was thirty—now he was forty-nine. All the work he had done this morning (except a little changing around of lines so he could claim them as his own)—all he had actually invented was a single imperative sentence, spoken by a doctor.

'Boil some water—lots of it.'

It was a good line. It had sprung into his mind full grown as soon as he had read the script. In the old silent days Pat would have used it as a spoken title and ended his dialogue worries for a space, but he needed some spoken words for other people in the scene. Nothing came.

Boil some water, he repeated to himself, lots of it.

The word boil brought a quick glad thought of the commissary. A reverent thought too—for an old-timer like Pat, what people you sat with at lunch was more important in getting along than what you dictated in your office. This was no art, as he often said—this was an industry.

'This is no art,' he remarked to Max Leam, who was leisurely drinking at a corridor water-cooler. 'This is an industry.'

346

Max had flung him this timely bone of three weeks at three-fifty.

'Say look, Pat! Have you got anything down on paper yet?'

'Say I've got some stuff already that'll make 'em—' He named a familiar biological function with the somewhat startling assurance that it would take place in the theatre.

Max tried to gauge his sincerity.

'Want to read it to me now?' he asked

'Not yet. But it's got the old guts if you know what I mean.'

Max was full of doubts.

'Well, go to it. And if you run into any medical snags check with the doctor over at the First Aid Station. It's got to be right.'

The spirit of Pasteur shone firmly in Pat's eyes.

'It will be.'

He felt good walking across the lot with Max—so good that he decided to glue himself to the producer and sit down with him at the Big Table. But Max foiled his intention by cooing, 'See you later,' and slipping into the barbershop.

Once Pat had been a familiar figure at the Big Table; often in his golden prime he had dined in the private canteens of executives. Being of the older Hollywood he understood their jokes, their vanities, their social system with its swift fluctuations. But there were too many new faces at the Big Table now—faces that looked at him with the universal Hollywood suspicion. And at the little tables where the young writers sat they seemed to take work so seriously. As for just sitting down anywhere, even with secretaries or extras—Pat would rather catch a sandwich at the corner.

Detouring to the Red Cross Station he asked for the doctor. A girl, a nurse, answered from a wall mirror where she was hastily drawing her lips. 'He's out. What is it?'

'Oh. Then I'll come back.'

She had finished, and now she turned—vivid and young and with a bright consoling smile.

'Miss Stacey will help you. I'm about to go to lunch.'

He was aware of an old, old feeling that to invite this little beauty to lunch might cause trouble. But he remembered quickly that he didn't have any wives now—they had both given up asking for alimony.

'I'm working on a medical,' he said. 'I need some help.'

'A medical?'

'Writing it—idea about a doc. Listen—let me buy you lunch. I want to ask you some medical questions.'

The nurse hesitated.

'I don't know. It's my first day out here.'

'It's all right,' he assured her. 'Studios are democratic; everybody is just 'Joe' or 'Mary'—from the big shots right down to the prop boys.'

He proved it magnificently on their way to lunch by greeting a male star and getting his own name back in return. And in the commissary, where they were placed hard by the Big Table, his producer, Max Leam, looked up, did a little 'takem' and winked.

The nurse—her name was Helen Earle—peered about eagerly.

'I don't see anybody,' she said. 'Except, oh, there's Ronald Colman. I didn't know Ronald Colman looked like that.'

Pat pointed suddenly to the floor.

'And there's Mickey Mouse!'

She jumped and Pat laughed at his joke—but Helen Earle was already staring starry-eyed at the costume extras who filled the hall with the colours of the First Empire. Pat was piqued to see her interest go out to these nonentities.

'The big shots are at the next table,' he said solemnly, wistfully, 'directors and all except the biggest executives. They could have Ronald Colman pressing pants. I usually sit over there but they don't want ladies. At lunch, that is, they don't want ladies.'

'Oh,' said Helen Earle, polite but unimpressed. 'It must be wonderful to be a writer too. It's so very interesting.'

'It has its points,' he said . . . he had thought for years it was a dog's life.

'What is it you want to ask me about a doctor?'

Here was toil again. Something in Pat's mind snapped off when he thought of the story.

'Well, Max Leam—that man facing us—Max Leam and I have a script about a doc. You know? Like a hospital picture?'

'I know.' And she added after a moment, 'That's the reason that I went in training.'

'And we've got to have it *right* because a hundred million people would check on it. So this doctor in the script he tells them to boil some water. He says, "Boil some water—lots of it." And we were wondering what the people would do then.'

'Why—they'd probably boil it,' Helen said, and then, somewhat confused by the question. 'What people?'

'Well somebody's daughter and the man that lived there and an attorney and the man that was hurt.'

Helen tried to digest this before answering.

'—and some other guy I'm going to cut out,' he finished.

There was a pause. The waitress set down tuna fish sandwiches.

'Well, when a doctor gives orders they're orders', Helen decided.

'Him.' Pat's interest had wandered to an odd little scene at the Big Table while he inquired absently, 'You married?'

'No.'

'Neither am I.'

Beside the Big Table stood an extra. A Russian Cossack with a fierce moustache. He stood resting his hand on the back of an empty chair between Director Paterson and Producer Leam.

'Is this taken?' he asked, with a thick Central European accent.

All along the Big Table faces stared suddenly at him. Until after the first look the supposition was that he must be some well-known actor. But he was not—he was dressed in one of the many-coloured uniforms that dotted the room.

Someone at the table said: 'That's taken.' But the man drew out the chair and sat down.

'Got to eat somewhere,' he remarked with a grin.

A shiver went over the near-by tables. Pat Hobby stared with his mouth ajar. It was as if someone had crayoned Donald Duck into the *Last Supper*.

'Look at that,' he advised Helen. 'What they'll do to him! Boy!'

The flabbergasted silence at the Big Table was broken by Ned Harman, the Production Manager.

'This table is reserved,' he said.

The extra looked up from a menu.

'They told me sit anywhere.'

He beckoned a waitress—who hesitated, looking for an answer in the faces of her superiors.

'Extras don't eat here,' said Max Leam, still politely. 'This is a—'

'I got to eat,' said the Cossack doggedly. 'I been standing around six hours while they shoot this stinking mess and now I got to eat.'

The silence had extended—from Pat's angle all within range seemed to be poised in mid-air.

The extra shook his head wearily.

'I dunno who cooked it up—' he said—and Max Leam sat forward in his chair—'but it's the lousiest tripe I ever seen shot in Hollywood.'

—At his table Pat was thinking why didn't they do something? Knock him down, draw him away. If they were yellow themselves they could call the studio police.

'Who is that?' Helen Earle was following his eyes innocently. 'Somebody I ought to know?'

He was listening attentively to Max Leam's voice, raised in anger.

'Get up and get out of here, buddy, and get out quick!'

The extra frowned.

'Who's telling me?' he demanded.

'You'll see.' Max appealed to the table at large, 'Where's Cushman—where's the Personnel man?'

'You try to move me,' said the extra, lifting the hilt of his scabbard above the level of the table. 'And I'll hang this on your ear. I know my rights.'

The dozen men at the table, representing a thousand dollars an hour in salaries, sat stunned. Far down by the door one of the studio police caught wind of what was happening and started to elbow through the crowded room. And Big Jack Wilson, another director, was on his feet in an instant coming around the table.

But they were too late—Pat Hobby could stand no more. He had jumped up, seizing a big heavy tray from the serving stand nearby. In two springs he reached the scene of action—lifting the tray he brought it down upon the extra's head with all the strength of his forty-nine years. The extra, who had been in the act of rising to meet Wilson's threatened assault, got the blow full on his face and temple and as he collapsed a dozen red streaks sprang into sight through the heavy grease paint. He crashed sideways between the chairs.

Pat stood over him panting—the tray in his hand.

'The dirty rat!' he cried. 'Where does he think—'

The studio policeman brushed past; Wilson pushed past —two aghast men from another table rushed up to survey the situation.

'It was a gag!' one of them shouted. 'That's Walter Herrick, the writer. It's his picture.'

'My God!'

'He was kidding Max Leam. It was a gag I tell you!'

'Pull him out . . . Get a doctor . . . Look out, there!'

Now Helen Earle hurried over; Walter Herrick was

dragged out into a cleared space on the floor and there
were yells of 'Who did it?—Who beaned him?'

Pat let the tray lapse to a chair, its sound unnoticed in
the confusion.

He saw Helen Earle working swiftly at the man's head
with a pile of clean napkins.

'Why did they have to do this to him?' someone
shouted.

Pat caught Max Leam's eye but Max happened to look
away at the moment and a sense of injustice came over
Pat. He alone in this crisis, real or imaginary, had *acted*.
He alone had played the man, while those stuffed shirts
let themselves be insulted and abused. And now he would
have to take the rap—because Walter Herrick was powerful and popular, a three-thousand-a-week man who wrote
hit shows in New York. How could anyone have guessed
that it was a gag?

There was a doctor now. Pat saw him say something
to the manageress and her shrill voice sent the waitresses
scattering like leaves towards the kitchen.

'Boil some water! Lots of it!'

The words fell wild and unreal on Pat's burdened soul,
But even though he now knew at first-hand what came
next, he did not think that he could go on from there.

TEAMED WITH GENIUS

'I TOOK a chance in sending for you,' said Jack Berners.
'But there's a job that you just *may* be able to help out
with.'

Though Pat Hobby was not offended, either as man
or writer, a formal protest was called for.

'I been in the industry fifteen years, Jack. I've got more
screen credits than a dog has got fleas.'

'Maybe I chose the wrong word,' said Jack. 'What I
mean is, that was a long time ago. About money we'll pay

you just what Republic paid you last month—three-fifty a week. Now—did you ever hear of a writer named René Wilcox?'

The name was unfamiliar. Pat had scarcely opened a book in a decade.

'She's pretty good,' he ventured.

'It's a man, an English playwright. He's only here in L.A. for his health. Well—we've had a Russian Ballet picture kicking around for a year—three bad scripts on it. So last week we signed up René Wilcox—he seemed just the person.

Pat considered.

'You mean he's—'

'I don't know and I don't care,' interrupted Berners sharply. 'We think we can borrow Zorina, so we want to hurry things up—do a shooting script instead of just a treatment. Wilcox is inexperienced and that's where you come in. You used to be a good man for structure.'

'*Used* to be!'

'All right, maybe you still are.' Jack beamed with momentary encouragement. 'Find yourself an office and get together with René Wilcox.' As Pat started out he called him back and put a bill in his hand. 'First of all, get a new hat. You used to be quite a boy around the secretaries in the old days. Don't give up at forty-nine!'

Over in the Writers' Building Pat glanced at the direc‚ tory in the hall and knocked at the door of 216. No answer, but he went in to discover a blond, willowy youth of twenty-five staring moodily out the window.

'Hello, René!' Pat said. 'I'm your partner.'

Wilcox's regard questioned even his existence, but Pat continued heartily, 'I hear we're going to lick some stuff into shape. Ever collaborate before?'

'I have never written for the cinema before.'

While this increased Pat's chance for a screen credit he badly needed, it meant that he might have to do some work. The very thought made him thirsty.

12+s.f. 6

'This is different from playwriting,' he suggested, with suitable gravity.

'Yes—I read a book about it.'

Pat wanted to laugh. In 1928 he and another man had concocted such a sucker-trap, *Secrets of Film Writing*. It would have made money if pictures hadn't started to talk.

'It all seems simple enough,' said Wilcox. Suddenly he took his hat from the rack. 'I'll be running along now.'

'Don't you want to talk about the script?' demanded Pat. 'What have you done so far?'

'I've not done anything,' said Wilcox deliberately. 'That idiot, Berners, gave me some trash and told me to go on from here. But it's too dismal.' His blue eyes narrowed. 'I say, what's a boom shot?'

'A boom shot? Why, that's when the camera's on a crane.'

Pat leaned over the desk and picked up a blue-jacketed 'Treatment.' On the cover he read:

BALLET SHOES
A Treatment
by
Consuela Martin

An Original from an idea by Consuela Martin

Pat glanced at the beginning and then at the end.

'I'd like it better if we could get the war in somewhere,' he said frowning. 'Have the dancer go as a Red Cross nurse and then she could get regenerated. See what I mean?'

There was no answer. Pat turned and saw the door softly closing.

What is this? he exclaimed. What kind of collaborating can a man do if he walks out? Wilcox had not even given the legitimate excuse—the races at Santa Anita!

The door opened again, a pretty girl's face, rather frightened, showed itself momentarily, said 'Oh,' and disappeared. Then it returned.

'Why it's Mr Hobby!' she exclaimed. 'I was looking for Mr Wilcox.'

He fumbled for her name but she supplied it.

'Katherine Hodge. I was your secretary when I worked here three years ago.'

Pat knew she had once worked with him, but for the moment could not remember whether there had been a deeper relation. It did not seem to him that it had been love—but looking at her now, that appeared rather too bad.

'Sit down,' said Pat. 'You assigned to Wilcox?'

'I thought so—but he hasn't given me any work yet.'

'I think he's nuts,' Pat said gloomily. 'He asked me what a boom shot was. Maybe he's sick—that's why he's out here. He'll probably start throwing up all over the office.'

'He's well now,' Katherine ventured.

'He doesn't look it to me. Come on in my office. You can work for *me* this afternoon.'

Pat lay on his couch while Miss Katherine Hodge read the script of *Ballet Shoes* aloud to him. About midway in the second sequence he fell asleep with his new hat on his chest.

Except for the hat, that was the identical position in which he found René next day at eleven. And it was that way for three straight days—one was asleep or else the other—and sometimes both. On the fourth day they had several conferences in which Pat again put forward his idea about the war as a regenerating force for ballet dancers.

'Couldn't we *not* talk about the war?' suggested René. 'I have two brothers in the Guards.'

'You're lucky to be here in Hollywood.'

'That's as it may be.'

'Well, what's your idea of the start of the picture?'

'I do not like the present beginning. It gives me an almost physical nausea.'

'So then, we got to have something in its place. That's why I want to plant the war—'

'I'm late to luncheon,' said René Wilcox. 'Good-bye, Mike.'

Pat grumbled to Katherine Hodge:

'He can call me anything he likes, but somebody's got to write this picture. I'd go to Jack Berners and tell him —but I think we'd both be out on our ears.'

For two days more he camped in René's office, trying to rouse him to action, but with no avail. Desperate on the following day—when the playwright did not even come to the studio—Pat took a benzedrine tablet and attacked the story alone. Pacing his office with the treatment in his hand he dictated to Katherine—interspersing the dictation with a short, biased history of his life in Hollywood. At the day's end he had two pages of script.

The ensuing week was the toughest in his life—not even a moment to make a pass at Katherine Hodge. Gradually with many creaks, his battered hulk got in motion. Benzedrine and great draughts of coffee woke him in the morning, whisky anaesthetized him at night. Into his feet crept an old neuritis and as his nerves began to crackle he developed a hatred against René Wilcox, which served him as a sort of *ersatz* fuel. He was going to finish the script by himself and hand it to Berners with the statement that Wilcox had not contributed a single line.

But it was too much—Pat was too far gone. He blew up when he was half through and went on a twenty-four-hour bat—and next morning arrived back at the studio to find a message that Mr Berners wanted to see the script at four. Pat was in a sick and confused state when his door opened and René Wilcox came in with a type-script in one hand, and a copy of Berners's note in the other.

'It's all right,' said Wilcox. 'I've finished it.'

'*What?* Have you been *working?*'

'I always work at night.'

'What've you done? A treatment?'

'No, a shooting script. At first I was held back by

personal worries, but once I got started it was very simple. You just get behind the camera and dream.'

Pat stood up aghast.

'But we were supposed to collaborate. Jack'll be wild.'

'I've always worked alone,' said Wilcox gently. 'I'll explain to Berners this afternoon.'

Pat sat in a daze. If Wilcox's script was good—but how could a first script be good? Wilcox should have fed it to him as he wrote; then they might have *had* something.

Fear started his mind working—he was struck by his first original idea since he had been on the job. He phoned to the script department for Katherine Hodge and when she came over told her what he wanted. Katherine hesitated.

'I just want to *read* it,' Pat said hastily. 'If Wilcox is there you can't take it, of course. But he just might be out.'

He waited nervously. In five minutes she was back with the script.

'It isn't mimeographed or even bound,' she said.

He was at the typewriter, trembling as he picked out a letter with two fingers.

'Can I help?' she asked.

'Find me a plain envelope and a used stamp and some paste.'

Pat sealed the letter himself and then gave directions:

'Listen outside Wilcox's office. If he's in, push it under his door. If he's out get a call boy to deliver it to him, wherever he is. Say it's from the mail room. Then you better go off the lot for the afternoon. So he won't catch on, see?'

As she went out Pat wished he had kept a copy of the note. He was proud of it—there was a ring of factual sincerity in it too often missing from his work.

'*Dear Mr Wilcox:*
I am sorry to tell you your two brothers were killed

*in action today by a long-range Tommy-gun. You are
wanted at home in England right away.*

John Smythe
The British Consulate, New York'

But Pat realized that this was no time for self-applause.
He opened Wilcox's script.

To his vast surprise it was technically proficient—the
dissolves, fades, cuts, pans and trucking shots were
correctly detailed. This simplified everything. Turning
back to the first page he wrote at the top:

BALLET SHOES
First Revise
From Pat Hobby and René Wilcox—presently changing
this to read: *From René Wilcox and Pat Hobby.*

Then, working frantically, he made several dozen small
changes. He substituted the word 'Scram!' for 'Get out
of my sight!,' he put 'Behind the eight-ball' instead of
'in trouble,' and replaced 'you'll be sorry' with the apt
coinage 'Or else!' Then he phoned the script department.

'This is Pat Hobby. I've been working on a script
with René Wilcox, and Mr Berners would like to have
it mimeographed by half-past three.'

This would give him an hour's start on his unconscious
collaborator.

'Is it an emergency?'

'I'll say.'

'We'll have to split it up between several girls.'

Pat continued to improve the script till the call boy
arrived. He wanted to put in his war idea but time was
short—still, he finally told the call boy to sit down, while
he wrote laboriously in pencil on the last page.

Close shot: Boris and Rita
RITA: What does anything matter now! I have enlisted
as a trained nurse in the war.
BORIS: (*moved*) War purifies and regenerates!
(*He puts his arms around her in a wild embrace as the
music soars way up and we fade out*)

Limp and exhausted by his efforts he needed a drink, so he left the lot and slipped cautiously into the bar across from the studio where he ordered gin and water.

With the glow, he thought warm thoughts. He had done *almost* what he had been hired to do—though his hand had accidentally fallen upon the dialogue rather than the structure. But how could Berners tell that the structure wasn't Pat's? Katherine Hodge would say nothing, for fear of implicating herself. They were all guilty but guiltiest of all was René Wilcox for refusing to play the game. Always, according to his lights, Pat had played the game.

He had another drink, bought breath tablets and for a while amused himself at the nickel machine in the drugstore. Louie, the studio bookie, asked if he was interested in wagers on a bigger scale.

'Not today, Louie.'

'What are they paying you, Pat?'

'Thousand a week.'

'Not so bad.'

'Oh, a lot of us old-timers are coming back,' Pat prophesied. 'In silent days was where you got real training—with directors shooting off the cuff and needing a gag in a split second. Now it's a sis job. They got English teachers working in pictures! What do they know?'

'How about a little something on "Quaker Girl"?'

'No,' said Pat. 'This afternoon I got an important angle to work on. I don't want to worry about horses.'

At three-fifteen he returned to his office to find two copies of his script in bright new covers.

BALLET SHOES
from
René Wilcox and Pat Hobby
First Revise

It reassured him to see his name in type. As he waited in Jack Berners's anteroom he almost wished he had reversed the names. With the right director this might be another *It Happened One Night,* and if he got his name on something like that it meant a three or four year gravy ride. But this time he'd save his money—go to Santa Anita only once a week—get himself a girl along the type of Katherine Hodge, who wouldn't expect a mansion in Beverly Hills.

Berners's secretary interrupted his reverie, telling him to go in. As he entered he saw with gratification that a copy of the new script lay on Berners's desk.

'Did you ever—' asked Berners suddenly '—go to a psychoanalyst?'

'No,' admitted Pat. 'But I suppose I could get up on it. Is it a new assignment?'

'Not exactly. It's just that I think you've lost your grip. Even larceny requires a certain cunning. I've just talked to Wilcox on the phone.'

'Wilcox must be nuts,' said Pat, aggressively. 'I didn't steal anything from him. His name's on it, isn't it? Two weeks ago I laid out all his structure—every scene. I even wrote one whole scene—at the end about the war.'

'Oh yes, the war,' said Berners as if he was thinking of something else.

'But if you like Wilcox's ending better—'

'Yes, I like his ending better. I never saw a man pick up this work so fast.' He paused. 'Pat, you've told the truth just once since you came in this room—that you didn't steal anything from Wilcox.'

'I certainly did not. I *gave* him stuff.'

But a certain dreariness, a grey *malaise,* crept over him as Berners continued:

'I told you we had three scripts. You used an old one we discarded a year ago. Wilcox was in when your secretary arrived, and he sent one of them to you. Clever, eh?'

Pat was speechless.

'You see, he and that girl like each other. Seems she typed a play for him this summer.'

'They like each other,' said Pat incredulously. 'Why, he—'

'Hold it, Pat. You've had trouble enough today.'

'He's responsible,' Pat cried. 'He wouldn't collaborate —and all the time—'

'—he was writing a swell script. And he can write his own ticket if we can persuade him to stay here and do another.'

Pat could stand no more. He stood up.

'Anyhow thank you, Jack,' he faltered. 'Call my agent if anything turns up.' Then he bolted suddenly and surprisingly for the door.

Jack Berners signalled on the Dictograph for the President's office.

'Get a chance to read it?' he asked in a tone of eagerness.

'It's swell. Better than you said. Wilcox is with me now.'

'Have you signed him up?'

'I'm going to. Seems he wants to work with Hobby. Here, you talk to him.'

Wilcox's rather high voice came over the wire.

'Must have Mike Hobby,' he said. 'Grateful to him. Had a quarrel with a certain young lady just before he came, but today Hobby brought us together. Besides I want to write a play about him. So give him to me— you fellows don't want him any more.'

Berners picked up his secretary's phone.

'Go after Pat Hobby. He's probably in the bar across the street. We're putting him on salary again but we'll be sorry.'

He switched off, switched on again.

'Oh! Take him his hat. He forgot his hat.'

A PATRIOTIC SHORT

PAT HOBBY, the Writer and the Man, had his great success in Hollywood in an era described by Irving Cobb as 'when you had to have a shin-bone of St Sebastian for a clutch lever.' You had to have a pool too and Pat had one—at least he had one for the first few hours after it was filled every week, before it stubbornly seeped away through the cracks in the cement.

'But it was a pool,' he assured himself one afternoon more than ten years later. Now he was more than grateful for a small chore at two-fifty a week, but all the years of failure could not take the beautiful memory away.

He was working on an humble 'short.' It was precariously based on the career of General Fitzhugh Lee who fought for the Confederacy and later for the U.S. against Spain—so it would offend neither North nor South. In conference Pat had tried to co-operate.

'I was thinking—' he suggested to Jack Berners, '—that it might be a good thing nowadays if we could give it a Jewish touch.'

'What do you mean?' demanded Jack Berners quickly.

'Well I thought—the way things are and all, it would be a sort of good thing to show that there were Jews in it too.'

'In what?'

'In the Civil War.' Quickly Pat reviewed his meagre history. 'They were, weren't they?'

'I suppose so,' said Berners, with some impatience, 'I suppose everybody was in it—except Quakers.'

'Well, my idea was that we could have this Fitzhugh Lee in love with a Jewish girl. He is going to be shot at curfew so she grabs the church bell—'

Jack Berners leaned forward earnestly.

'Say, Pat, you want this job, don't you?'

'Sure, I do.'

'Well, I told you the story we want. The Jews can

take care of themselves, and if you thought up this tripe to please me you're losing your grip.'

Was that a way to treat a man who had once owned a pool? The reason Pat kept thinking about his long-lost pool was because of the President of the United States. Pat was remembering a certain day, a decade ago, in every detail. On that day word had gone around that the President was going to visit the lot. It seemed to mark a new era in pictures because the President of the United States had never visited a studio before. The executives of the company were all dressed up with ties and there were flags over the commissary door . . .

The voice of Ben Brown, the head of the shorts department, broke in on Pat's reverie.

'Jack Berners just phoned me,' he said, 'We don't want any new angles, Pat. We got a history. Fitzhugh Lee was in the cavalry. He was a nephew of Robert E. Lee and we want to show him surrendering at Appomattox, pretty sore and all that. And then show how he got reconciled—we'll have to be careful because Virginia is still lousy with Lees—and how he finally accepts a U.S. commission from McKinley. And clean up the stuff about Spain—the guy that wrote it was a Red and he's got all the Spanish officers having ants in their pants.'

In his office Pat looked at the script of 'True to Two Flags.' The first scene showed General Fitzhugh Lee at the head of his cavalry receiving word that Petersburg had been evacuated. In the script Lee took the blow in lively pantomime, but Pat was getting two-fifty a week —so, casually and without effort, he wrote in one of his favourite lines of dialogue.

LEE: (*To his officers*)
Well, what are you standing here gawking for? Do something!
6. *Medium Shot. Officers—pepping up, slapping each other on back etc.*
Dissolve to:

Dissolve to what? Pat's mind dissolved once more into the glamorous past. On that great day ten years before, his phone in his office had rung at noon. It was Mr Moskin.

'Pat, the President is lunching in the Executives' Dining Room. Doug Fairbanks can't come so there's a place empty and anyhow we think there ought to be one writer there.'

His memory of the luncheon was palpitant with glamour. The great man had asked questions about pictures and told a joke, and Pat had laughed uproariously with the others—all of them solid men together—rich, happy, successful.

Afterwards the President was to see some scenes taken on a set, and still later he was going to Mr Moskin's house to meet several women stars at tea. Pat was not invited to that party, but his Beverly Hills home was next door to Mr Moskin's mansion and he went home early. From his veranda he saw the cortège drive up, with Mr Moskin beside the President in the back seat. He was proud of pictures then—of the position he had won in them—of the President of the happy country where pictures were born...

Pat sighed. Returning once more to reality he looked down at the script of 'True to Two Flags' and wrote slowly and thoughtfully:

Insert: A calendar—with the years plainly marked and the sheets blowing off in a cold wind, to indicate that Fitzhugh Lee is growing older and older.

Pat's labours had made him thirsty—not for water, but he knew better than to take anything else his first day on the job. He went out into the hall and along the corridor to the cooler—and as he walked he slipped back into his reverie of things past...

It had been a lovely California afternoon so Mr Moskin had taken his exalted guest and the coterie of stars into his garden, adjoining Pat's garden. Pat went out his back door and followed a low privet hedge keeping out of sight—and then accidentally came face to face with the Presidential party.

The President smiled and nodded. Mr Moskin smiled and nodded.

'You met Mr Hobby at lunch,' Mr Moskin said to the President. 'He's one of our writers.'

'Oh you,' said the President, 'You write the pictures?'

'Yes I do,' said Pat.

The President glanced over into Pat's property.

'I suppose—' he said, '—that you get lots of inspiration sitting by the side of that fine pool.'

'Yes,' said Pat, 'Yes, I do.'

... Pat filled his cup at the cooler in the hall. Down the hall there was a group approaching—Jack Berners, Ben Brown and several other executives and with them a girl to whom they were very attentive and deferential. He recognized her face—she was the girl of the year, the It Girl, the Oomph, the Glamour Girl, the girl for whose services every studio was in heavy competition.

Pat lingered over his drink. He had seen many phonies break in and break out again, but this girl was someone to stir every pulse in the nation. His heart beat faster—as the procession drew near, he put down the cup, dabbed at his hair with his hand and took a step into the corridor. The girl looked at him—he looked at the girl. Then she took one arm of Jack Berners' and one of Ben Brown's and, without the suggestion of an introduction, the party walked right through him—so that he had to take a step back against the wall.

An instant later Jack Berners turned around and called back, 'Hello, Pat.' And one of the others glanced around, but no one else spoke, so interested were they in the girl.

In his office Pat looked gloomily at the scene where President McKinley offers a United States commission to Fitzhugh Lee. Berners had written on the margin, 'Have McKinley plug democracy and Cuban-American friendship—but no cracks at Spain as market may improve.' Pat gritted his teeth and bore down on his pencil as he wrote:

LEE:
Mr President, you can take your commission and go straight to Hell.

Then Pat bent down over his desk, his shoulders shaking miserably as he thought of that happy day when he had owned a swimming pool.

TWO OLD-TIMERS

PHIL MACEDON, once the Star of Stars, and Pat Hobby, script writer, had collided out on Sunset near the Beverly Hills Hotel. It was five in the morning and there was liquor in the air as they argued and Sergeant Gaspar took them around to the station house. Pat Hobby, a man of forty-nine, showed fight, apparently because Phil Macedon failed to acknowledge that they were old acquaintances.

He accidentally bumped Sergeant Gaspar, who was so provoked that he put him in a little barred room while they waited for the captain to arrive.

Chronologically Phil Macedon belonged between Eugene O'Brien and Robert Taylor. He was still a handsome man in his early fifties and he had saved enough from his great days for a hacienda in the San Fernando Valley; there he rested as full of honours, as rollicksome and with the same purposes in life as Man o' War.

With Pat Hobby life had dealt otherwise. After twenty-one years in the industry, script and publicity, the accident found him driving a 1935 car which had lately become the property of the Acme Loan Co. And once, back in 1928, he had reached the point of having a private swimming pool.

He glowered from his confinement, still resenting Macedon's failure to acknowledge that they had ever met before.

'I suppose you don't remember Colman,' he said sarcastically. 'Or Connie Talmadge or Bill Corker or Allan Dwan.'

Macedon lit a cigarette with the sort of timing in which the silent screen has never been surpassed, and offered one to Sergeant Gaspar.

'Couldn't I come in to-morrow?' he asked. 'I have a horse to exercise——'

'I'm sorry, Mr Macedon,' said the cop—sincerely, for the actor was an old favourite of his. 'The captain is due here any minute. After that we won't be holding *you*.'

'It's just a formality,' said Pat, from his cell.

'Yeah, it's just a——' Sergeant Gaspar glared at Pat. 'It may not be any formality for *you*. Did you ever hear of the sobriety test?'

Macedon flicked his cigarette out the door and lit another.

'Suppose I come back in a couple of hours,' he suggested.

'No,' regretted Sergeant Gaspar. 'And since I have to detain you, Mr Macedon, I want to take the opportunity to tell you what you meant to me once. It was that picture you made, *The Final Push*, it meant a lot to every man who was in the war.'

'Oh, yes,' said Macedon, smiling.

'I used to try to tell my wife about the war—how it was, with the shells and the machine-guns—I was there seven months with the 26th New England—but she never understood. She'd point her finger at me and say "Boom! you're dead," and so I'd laugh and stop trying to make her understand.'

'Hey, can I get out of here?' demanded Pat.

'You shut up!' said Gaspar fiercely. 'You probably wasn't in the war.'

'I was in the Motion Picture Home Guard,' said Pat. 'I had bad eyes.'

'Listen to him,' said Gaspar disgustedly. 'That's what all them slackers say. Well, the war was *some*thing. And after my wife saw that picture of yours I never had to explain to her. She knew. She always spoke different about it after

that—never just pointed her finger at me and said "Boom"!
I'll never forget the part where you was in that shell-hole.
That was so real it made my hands sweat.'

'Thanks,' said Macedon graciously. He lit another
cigarette. 'You see, I was in the war myself and I knew how
it was. I knew how it felt.'

'Yes, sir,' said Gaspar appreciatively. 'Well, I'm glad of
the opportunity to tell you what you did for me. You—
explained the war to my wife.'

'What are you talking about?' demanded Pat Hobby
suddenly. 'That war picture Bill Corker did in 1925?'

'There he goes again,' said Gaspar. 'Sure—*The Birth
of a Nation*. Now you pipe down till the captain comes.'

'Phil Macedon knew me then all right,' said Pat resentfully. 'I even watched him work on it one day.'

'I just don't happen to remember you, old man,' said
Macedon politely. 'I can't help that.'

'You remember the day Bill Corker shot that shell-hole
sequence, don't you? Your first day on the picture?'

There was a moment's silence.

'When will the captain be here?' Macedon asked.

'Any minute now, Mr. Macedon.'

'Well, I remember,' said Pat, 'because I was there when
he had that shell-hole dug. He was out there on the back
lot at nine o'clock in the morning with a gang of hunkies
to dig the hole and four cameras. He called you up from a
field telephone and told you to go to the costumer and get
into a soldier suit. Now you remember?'

'I don't load my mind with details, old man.'

'You called up that they didn't have one to fit you and
Corker told you to shut up and get into one anyhow.
When you got out to the back lot you were sore as hell
because your suit didn't fit.'

Macedon smiled charmingly.

'You have a most remarkable memory. Are you sure
you have the right picture—and the right actor?' he
asked.

'Am I!' said Pat grimly. 'I can see you right now. Only

you didn't have much time to complain about the uniform because that wasn't Corker's plan. He always thought you were the toughest ham in Hollywood to get anything natural out of—and he had a scheme. He was going to get the heart of the picture shot by noon—before you even knew you were acting. He turned you around and shoved you down into that shell-hole on your fanny, and yelled "Camera".'

'That's a lie,' said Phil Macedon. 'I *got* down.'

'Then why did you start yelling?' demanded Pat. 'I can still hear you: "Hey, what's the idea! Is this some god-damn gag? You get me out of here or I'll walk out on you!"'

'And all the time you were trying to claw your way up the side of that pit, so damn mad you couldn't see. You'd almost get up and then you'd slide back and lie there with your face working—till finally you began to bawl and all this time Bill had four cameras on you. After about twenty minutes you gave up and just lay there, heaving. Bill took a hundred feet of that and then he had a couple of prop men pull you out.'

The police captain had arrived in the squad car. He stood in the doorway against the first grey of dawn.

'What you got here, Sergeant? A drunk?'

Sergeant Gaspar walked over to the cell, unlocked it and beckoned Pat to come out. Pat blinked a moment—then his eyes fell on Phil Macedon and he shook his finger at him.

'So you see I *do* know you,' he said. 'Bill Corker cut that piece of film and titled it so you were supposed to be a doughboy whose pal had just been killed. You wanted to climb out and get at the Germans in revenge, but the shells bursting all around and the concussions kept knocking you back in.'

'What's it about?' demanded the captain.

'I want to prove I know this guy,' said Pat. 'Bill said the best moment in the picture was when Phil was yelling, "I've already broken my first finger-nail!" Bill titled it, "Ten Huns will go to hell to shine your shoes!"'

'You've got here "collision with alcohol",' said the captain, looking at the blotter. 'Let's take these guys down to the hospital and give them the test.'

'Look here now,' said the actor, with his flashing smile, 'my name's Phil Macedon.'

The captain was a political appointee and very young. He remembered the name and the face, but he was not especially impressed because Hollywood was full of has-beens.

They all got into the squad car at the door.

After the test Macedon was held at the station house until friends could arrange bail. Pat Hobby was discharged, but his car would not run, so Sergeant Gaspar offered to drive him home.

'Where do you live?' he asked as they started home.

'I don't live anywhere to-night,' said Pat. 'That's why I was driving around. When a friend of mine wakes up I'll touch him for a couple of bucks and go to a hotel.'

'Well now,' said Sergeant Gaspar, 'I got a couple of bucks that ain't working.'

The great mansions of Beverly Hills slid by and Pat waved his hand at them in salute.

'In the good old days,' he said, 'I used to be able to drop into some of those houses day or night. And Sunday mornings——'

'Is that all true you said in the station,' Gaspar asked. '——about how they put him in the hole?'

'Sure, it is,' said Pat. 'That guy needn't have been so upstage. He's just an old-timer like me.'

THREE HOURS
BETWEEN PLANES
[1941]

IT WAS a wild chance but Donald was in the mood, healthy and bored, with a sense of tiresome duty done. He was now rewarding himself. Maybe.

When the plane landed he stepped out into a midwestern summer night and headed for the isolated pueblo airport, conventionalized as an old red 'railway depot.' He did not know whether she was alive, or living in this town, or what was her present name. With mounting excitement he looked through the phone book for her father who might be dead too, somewhere in these twenty years.

No. Judge Harmon Holmes—Hillside 3194.

A woman's amused voice answered his inquiry for Miss Nancy Holmes.

'Nancy is Mrs Walter Gifford now. Who is this?'

But Donald hung up without answering. He had found out what he wanted to know and had only three hours. He did not remember any Walter Gifford and there was another suspended moment while he scanned the phone book. She might have married out of town.

No. Walter Gifford—Hillside 1191. Blood flowed back into his fingertips.

'Hello?'

'Hello. Is Mrs Gifford there—this is an old friend of hers.'

'This is Mrs Gifford.'

He remembered, or thought he remembered, the funny magic in the voice.

'This is Donald Plant. I haven't seen you since I was twelve years old.'

'Oh-h-h!' The note was utterly surprised, very polite, but he could distinguish in it neither joy nor certain recognition.

'—Donald!' added the voice. This time there was something more in it than struggling memory.

'. . . when did you come back to town?' Then cordially, 'Where *are* you?'

'I'm out at the airport—for just a few hours.'

'Well, come up and see me.'

'Sure you're not just going to bed.'

'Heavens, no!' she exclaimed. 'I was sitting here—having a highball by myself. Just tell your taxi man . . .'

On his way Donald analysed the conversation. His words 'at the airport' established that he had retained his position in the upper bourgeoisie. Nancy's aloneness might indicate that she had matured into an unattractive woman without friends. Her husband might be either away or in bed. And—because she was always ten years old in his dreams—the highball shocked him. But he adjusted himself with a smile—she was very close to thirty.

At the end of a curved drive he saw a dark-haired little beauty standing against the lighted door, a glass in her hand. Startled by her final materialization, Donald got out of the cab, saying:

'Mrs Gifford?'

She turned on the porch light and stared at him, wide-eyed and tentative. A smile broke through the puzzled expression.

'Donald—it is you—we all change so. Oh, this is re*mark*able!'

As they walked inside, their voices jingled the words 'all these years,' and Donald felt a sinking in his stomach. This derived in part from a vision of their last meeting—when she rode past him on a bicycle, cutting him dead—and in part from fear lest they have nothing to say. It was like a college reunion—but there the failure to find the past was disguised by the hurried boisterous occasion. Aghast, he realized that this might be a long and empty hour. He plunged in desperately.

'You always were a lovely person. But I'm a little shocked to find you as beautiful as you are.'

It worked. The immediate recognition of their changed state, the bold compliment, made them interesting strangers instead of fumbling childhood friends.

'Have a highball?' she asked. 'No? Please don't think I've become a secret drinker, but this was a blue night. I expected my husband but he wired he'd be two days longer. He's very nice, Donald, and very attractive. Rather your type and colouring.' She hesitated, '—and I think he's interested in someone in New York—and I don't know.'

'After seeing you it sounds impossible,' he assured her. 'I was married for six years, and there was a time I tortured myself that way. Then one day I just put jealousy out of my life forever. After my wife died I was very glad of that. It left a very rich memory—nothing marred or spoiled or hard to think over.'

She looked at him attentively, then sympathetically as he spoke.

'I'm very sorry,' she said. And after a proper moment, 'You've changed a lot. Turn your head. I remember father saying, "That boy has a brain." '

'You probably argued against it.'

'I was impressed. Up to then I thought everybody had a brain. That's why it sticks in my mind.'

'What else sticks in your mind?' he asked smiling.

Suddenly Nancy got up and walked quickly a little away.

'Ah, now,' she reproached him. 'That isn't fair! I suppose I was a naughty girl.'

'You were not,' he said stoutly. 'And I *will* have a drink now.'

As she poured it, her face still turned from him, he continued:

'Do you think you were the only little girl who was ever kissed?'

'Do you like the subject?' she demanded. Her momentary irritation melted and she said: 'What the hell! We *did* have fun. Like in the song.'

'On the sleigh ride.'

'Yes—and somebody's picnic—Trudy James's. And at Frontenac that—those summers.'

It was the sleigh ride he remembered most and kissing her cool cheeks in the straw in one corner while she laughed up at the cold white stars. The couple next to them had their backs turned and he kissed her little neck and her ears and never her lips.

'And the Macks' party where they played post office and I couldn't go because I had the mumps,' he said.

'I don't remember that.'

'Oh, you were there. And you were kissed and I was crazy with jealousy like I never have been since.'

'Funny I don't remember. Maybe I wanted to forget.'

'But why?' he asked in amusement. 'We were two perfectly innocent kids. Nancy, whenever I talked to my wife about the past, I told her you were the girl I loved *al*most as much as I loved her. But I think I really loved you just as much. When we moved out of town I carried you like a cannon ball in my insides.'

'Were you *that* much—stirred up?'

'My God, yes! I—' He suddenly realized that they were standing just two feet from each other, that he was talking as if he loved her in the present, that she was looking up at him with her lips half-parted and a clouded look in her eyes.

'Go on,' she said, 'I'm ashamed to say—I like it. I didn't know you were so upset *then*. I thought it was *me* who was upset.'

'You!' he exclaimed. 'Don't you remember throwing me over at the drugstore.' He laughed. 'You stuck out your tongue at me.'

'I don't remember at all. It seemed to me *you* did the

throwing over.' Her hand fell lightly, almost consolingly on his arm. 'I've got a photograph book upstairs I haven't looked at for years. I'll dig it out.'

Donald sat for five minutes with two thoughts—first the hopeless impossibility of reconciling what different people remembered about the same event—and secondly that in a frightening way Nancy moved him as a woman as she had moved him as a child. Half an hour had developed an emotion that he had not known since the death of his wife—that he had never hoped to know again.

Side by side on a couch they opened the book between them. Nancy looked at him, smiling and very happy.

'Oh, this is *such* fun,' she said. 'Such fun that you're so nice, that you remember me so—beautifully. Let me tell you—I wish I'd known it then! After you'd gone I hated you.'

'What a pity,' he said gently.

'But not now,' she reassured him, and then impulsively, 'Kiss and make up—

'. . . that isn't being a good wife,' she said after a minute. 'I really don't think I've kissed two men since I was married.'

He was excited—but most of all confused. Had he kissed Nancy? or a memory? or this lovely trembly stranger who looked away from him quickly and turned a page of the book?

'Wait!' he said. 'I don't think I could *see* a picture for a few seconds.'

'We won't do it again. I don't feel so very calm myself.'

Donald said one of those trival things that cover so much ground.

'Wouldn't it be awful if we fell in love again?'

'Stop it!' She laughed, but very breathlessly. 'It's all over. It was a moment. A moment I'll have to forget.'

'Don't tell your husband.'

'Why not? Usually I tell him everything.'

'It'll hurt him. Don't ever tell a man such things.'

'All right I won't.'

'Kiss me once more,' he said inconsistently, but Nancy had turned a page and was pointing eagerly at a picture.

'Here's you,' she cried. 'Right away!'

He looked. It was a little boy in shorts standing on a pier with a sailboat in the background.

'I remember—' she laughed triumphantly, '—the very day it was taken. Kitty took it and I stole it from her.'

For a moment Donald failed to recognize himself in the photo—then, bending closer—he failed utterly to recognize himself.

'That's not me,' he said.

'Oh yes. It was at Frontenac—the summer we—we used to go to the cave.'

'What cave? I was only three days in Frontenac.' Again he strained his eyes at the slightly yellowed picture. 'And that isn't me. That's Donald *Bowers*. We did look rather alike.'

Now she was staring at him—leaning back, seeming to lift away from him.

'But you're Donald Bowers!' she exclaimed; her voice rose a little. 'No, you're not. You're Donald *Plant*.'

'I told you on the phone.'

She was on her feet—her face faintly horrified.

'Plant! Bowers! I must be crazy. Or it was that drink? I was mixed up a little when I first saw you. Look here! What have I told you?'

He tried for a monkish calm as he turned a page of the book.

'Nothing at all,' he said. Pictures that did not include him formed and re-formed before his eyes—Frontenac— a cave—Donald Bowers—'You threw *me* over!'

Nancy spoke from the other side of the room.

'You'll never tell this story,' she said. 'Stories have a way of getting around.'

'There isn't any story,' he hesitated. But he thought: So she *was* a bad little girl.

And now suddenly he was filled with wild raging

THREE HOURS BETWEEN PLANES 377

jealousy of little Donald Bowers—he who had banished jealousy from his life forever. In the five steps he took across the room he crushed out twenty years and the existence of Walter Gifford with his stride.

'Kiss me again, Nancy,' he said, sinking to one knee beside her chair, putting his hand upon her shoulder. But Nancy strained away.

'You said you had to catch a plane.'

'It's nothing. I can miss it. It's of no importance.'

'Please go,' she said in a cool voice. 'And please try to imagine how I feel.'

'But you act as if you don't remember me,' he cried, '—as if you don't remember Donald *Plant!*'

'I do. I remember you too . . . But it was all so long ago.' Her voice grew hard again. 'The taxi number is Crestwood 8484.'

On his way to the airport Donald shook his head from side to side. He was completely himself now but he could not digest the experience. Only as the plane roared up into the dark sky and its passengers became a different entity from the corporate world below did he draw a parallel from the fact of its flight. For five blinding minutes he had lived like a madman in two worlds at once. He had been a boy of twelve and a man of thirty-two, indissolubly and helplessly commingled.

Donald had lost a good deal, too, in those hours between the planes—but since the second half of life is a long process of getting rid of things, that part of the experience probably didn't matter.

THE LOST DECADE

[1939]

ALL sorts of people came into the offices of the news-weekly and Orrison Brown had all sorts of relations with them. Outside of office hours he was 'one of the editors' —during work time he was simply a curly-haired man who a year before had edited the Dartmouth *Jack-O-Lantern* and was now only too glad to take the undesirable assignments around the office, from straightening out illegible copy to playing call boy without the title.

He had seen this visitor go into the editor's office—a pale, tall man of forty with blond statuesque hair and a manner that was neither shy nor timid, nor otherworldly like a monk, but something of all three. The name on his card, Louis Trimble, evoked some vague memory, but having nothing to start on, Orrison did not puzzle over it—until a buzzer sounded on his desk, and previous experience warned him that Mr Trimble was to be his first course at lunch.

'Mr Trimble—Mr Brown,' said the Source of all luncheon money. 'Orrison—Mr Trimble's been away a long time. Or he *feels* it's a long time—almost twelve years. Some people would consider themselves lucky to've missed the last decade.'

'That's so,' said Orrison.

'I can't lunch today,' continued his chief. 'Take him to Voisin or 21 or anywhere he'd like. Mr Trimble feels there're lots of things he hasn't seen.'

Trimble demurrred politely.

'Oh, I can get around.'

'I know it, old boy. Nobody knew this place like you did once—and if Brown tries to explain the horseless

378

carriage just send him back here to me. And you'll be back yourself by four, won't you?'

Orrison got his hat.

'You've been away ten years?' he asked while they went down in the elevator.

'They'd begun the Empire State Building,' said Trimble. 'What does that add up to?'

'About 1928. But as the chief said, you've been lucky to miss a lot.' As a feeler he added, 'Probably had more interesting things to look at.'

'Can't say I have.'

They reached the street and the way Trimble's face tightened at the roar of traffic made Orrison take one more guess.

'You've been out of civilization?'

'In a sense.' The words were spoken in such a measured way that Orrison concluded this man wouldn't talk unless he wanted to—and simultaneously wondered if he could have possibly spent the thirties in a prison or an insane asylum.

'This is the famous 21,' he said. 'Do you think you'd rather eat somewhere else?'

Trimble paused, looking carefully at the brownstone house.

'I can remember when the name 21 got to be famous,' he said, 'about the same year as Moriarity's.' Then he continued almost apologetically, 'I thought we might walk up Fifth Avenue about five minutes and eat wherever we happened to be. Some place with young people to look at.'

Orrison gave him a quick glance and once again thought of bars and grey walls and bars; he wondered if his duties included introducing Mr Trimble to complaisant girls. But Mr Trimble didn't look as if that was in his mind—the dominant expression was of absolute and deep-seated curiosity and Orrison attempted to connect the name with Admiral Byrd's hideout at the South Pole or flyers lost in Brazilian jungles. He was, or he had been, quite a fellow—that was obvious. But the only definite clue to his environment—and to Orrison the clue that led nowhere—was his countryman's obedience to the traffic lights and his predilection for walking on the side next to the shops and not the street. Once he stopped and gazed into a haberdasher's window.

'Crêpe ties,' he said. 'I haven't seen one since I left college.'

'Where'd you go?'

'Massachusetts Tech.'

'Great place.'

'I'm going to take a look at it next week. Let's eat somewhere along here—' They were in the upper Fifties '—you choose.'

There was a good restaurant with a little awning just around the corner.

'What do you want to see most?' Orrison asked, as they sat down.

Trimble considered.

'Well—the back of people's heads,' he suggested. 'Their necks—how their heads are joined to their bodies. I'd like to hear what those two little girls are saying to their father. Not exactly what they're saying but whether the words float or submerge, how their mouths shut when they've finished speaking. Just a matter of rhythm—Cole Porter came back to the States in 1928 because he felt that there were new rhythms around.'

Orrison was sure he had his clue now, and with nice delicacy did not pursue it by a millimetre—even suppressing a sudden desire to say there was a fine concert in Carnegie Hall tonight.

'The weight of spoons,' said Trimble, 'so light. A little bowl with a stick attached. The cast in that waiter's eye. I knew him once but he wouldn't remember me.'

But as they left the restaurant the same waiter looked at Trimble rather puzzled as if he almost knew him. When they were outside Orrison laughed:

'After ten years people will forget.'

'Oh, I had dinner there last May—' He broke off in an abrupt manner.

It was all kind of nutsy, Orrison decided—and changed himself suddenly into a guide.

'From here you get a good candid focus on Rockefeller Centre,' he pointed out with spirit '—and the Chrysler Building and the Armistead Building, the daddy of all the new ones.'

'The Armistead Building,' Trimble rubber-necked obediently. 'Yes—I designed it.'

Orrison shook his head cheerfully—he was used to going out with all kinds of people. But that stuff about having been in the restaurant last May . . .

He paused by the brass entablature in the cornerstone of the building. 'Erected 1928,' it said.

Trimble nodded.

'But I was taken drunk that year—every-which-way drunk. So I never saw it before now.'

'Oh.' Orrison hesitated. 'Like to go in now?'

'I've been in it—lots of times. But I've never seen it. And now it isn't what I want to see. I wouldn't ever be able to see it now. I simple want to see how people walk and what their clothes and shoes and hats are made of. And their eyes and hands. Would you mind shaking hands with me?'

'Not at all, sir.'

'Thanks. Thanks. That's very kind. I suppose it looks strange—but people will think we're saying good-bye. I'm going to walk up the avenue for a while, so we *will* say good-bye. Tell your office I'll be in at four.'

Orrison looked after him when he started out, half expecting him to turn into a bar. But there was nothing about him that suggested or ever had suggested drink.

'Jesus!' he said to himself. 'Drunk for ten years.'

He felt suddenly of the texture of his own coat and then he reached out and pressed his thumb against the granite of the building by his side.